Paranova: Shapers Legacy

By: Joel D. Lundberg

Joel D. Lundberg

Joel D. Lundberg

DEDICATION

Much love and gratitude to my spouse Kassia, whose continuous support has served as my foundation while I've worked toward a dream of becoming a published author. Without her encouragement I don't think I would have rediscovered the joy and passion of writing.

I found the motivation to begin the process of creating this book with Kassia's generous encouragement. Her gentle push helped me gain the confidence to finish a project that I hadn't attempted to get started on for more than a decade. Kassia, you've been an inspiration throughout my creative pursuits, always there to support and stimulate me. Thank you for being a reliable source of support throughout my journey.

Love,

Joely D.

Joel D. Lundberg

INTRODUCTION

Welcome to the world of Paranova! I'm thrilled to embark on this journey alongside you, delving into the wonders of this vast and diverse universe born from my lifelong passion for storytelling and fantasy. The ability of words to take readers to extraordinary places has always interested me.

My own journey as an author started a few years ago, spurred on by my imagination and a desire to develop a vast universe full of stories, history, and wonder at a young age where readers could lose themselves in thrilling tales. With each page I wrote, I discovered a deep passion for crafting narratives that combine elements of magic, world-building, and the complexities of sapient nature.

I had originally created a board game concept prior to writing. When I envisioned Paranova as a board game, I couldn't resist myself in creating a world for the players to immerse themselves in while playing the game. Paranova evolved into a world that had been swirling in my mind since I was just ten years old. Fulfilling my childhood dreams that I once pushed aside, I aim to expand upon the vast stories within the world of Paranova and far-reaching realms, creating celestial stories, sapience and worlds brimming with magic and complexity.

There are many different types of sources that inspire my writing. Not only the world-building and stories that are yet to be shared but also the mysterious Shapers, the celestial beings who shape the very fabric of the universe—the concept that lies in the background within the unknown has always interested me. Their delicate balance of order and chaos serves as a powerful metaphor for the intricacies of life and beyond. The perspective of light and dark has been told a hundred times, but it has always fascinated me with the opportunities to enlighten on that unique perspective.

Within the pages of Paranova, you'll encounter a variety of diverse races being born, each with their own rich history and unique journey. From the different Elven Kingdoms struggling to reclaim their former glory to the resilient Dwarven strongholds etched into the mountains, or with the advancements of Human kingdoms or the primal colonies and various clans' quest for expansion, every race contributes to the vivid picture of an evolving world. The tapestry does not stop there, it has unlimited potential to uncover the mysteries of what will come of the world and the creation of more diverse sapience, there is much to expand on within the universe of Paranova!

My goal as an author is to create immersive stories that take you into fantastic stories while inviting you to follow the civilizations and characters on their own paths, with their own difficulties and victories. Through what I've written so far, I hope to entertain, inspire, and stimulate your imagination, leaving you with a sense of wonder long after you've turned the last page.

With your support, this journey becomes more fulfilling, and I am excited about sharing the fantasy that lies ahead. Thank you for joining me on this wonderful journey. May the stories of Paranova capture your imagination and place you into a realm where anything is possible.

Love,

Joel D. Lundberg

CONTENTS

Joel D. Lundberg

Joel D. Lundberg

Chapter 1: Birth of Paranova

In the beginning, there was a pulsating star known as Luminara that existed deep on the outside of the cosmos and shined brighter than every other star in the universe that was known at the time. Its shifting luminosity cast a shadow across the void of space, filling it with a shimmering radiance. During Luminara's time in space, it would often dim for some time, then shine bright again as if it were signaling something in the distance. Suddenly, it appeared as though a mysterious cosmic force was pulling Luminara on a journey, and the star started to traverse out of its own position in space. As it traveled farther away from its origin, it became closer and closer to a whirling maelstrom of mysterious elements. When Luminara approached the maelstrom, an enormous cosmic collision began, which served as the primary source of energy for the formation of a completely different world.

When Luminara and the storm came into contact with each other, it was a momentous clash of the elements that sent shockwaves through the fabric of existence, causing the previous world deep inside the maelstrom to change. In a breathtaking display of the power in the cosmos and the process of creation, in the distance, the views of both light and darkness were dancing together. The combining of fundamental forces and the varying motions of energy in the cosmic dance gave rise to a physical universe within the space where Luminara once traveled.

The collision attracted mysterious beings, which gave themselves the name of the Shapers. They had watched the formation of the entire cosmos with fascination as the stars spread throughout the universe. These ancient mysterious beings have the power to reshape and alter the very essence of reality. The Shapers focused their attention on the aftermath of the collision and discovered the freshly formed world. They were drawn to it because of the promise it carried and as they stood in awe before its splendor, they were aware of the immense potential that lay inside its vibrant world.

The unusually rich and unique ecosystems of this world compelled the Shapers to investigate them. The rivers carved their ways through the landscape, and the vast wilderness teemed with towering trees and lush vegetation that swayed in rhythm with the river's currents. Calm lakes reflected the stars above, and towering mountains reached towards the sky. Beyond it, all the deserts spread out with their dry sands, keeping ancient mysteries and secrets hidden from the world it once was.

Prior to the formation of this world, its essential origins were unknown and shrouded in mystery. The world before the collision brought immense curiosity amongst the Shapers. The imagination was teased with enticing views into a time period that was unknown because remnants of a long-vanished civilization lingered throughout the world. The mysteries of that ancient civilization, which were buried in the depths of the past, had waited patiently to be unearthed by adventurous explorers and mortals who were interested in history. The pre-world has temporarily managed to avoid the explosion that Luminara caused, which has made it something of a mystery that is still unsolved.

The Provisioner oversaw the Order sector, which prioritized harmony, togetherness, and a careful balancing act. He was the esteemed leader of the sector that was formed of many celestial beings, all of whom had a purpose and strength within the sector. The Provisioner believed that the balance of life, light, and nature on Earth depended on the careful construction of each element of its ecosystems. He also believed that in this new world, there was an opportunity to create an ideal society in which peace and life could flourish without interference from the reaches of the worlds before.

The Order considers its mission to maintain universal peace and order. They believe that for the world and its inhabitants to flourish, a delicate balance between life, nature, and celestial powers must be preserved. The Order considers its mission to be the protection and preservation of ancient knowledge and wisdom. They work to preserve and transmit ancient wisdom to future generations so that they too, may grow in understanding and enlightenment.

The members of the Order sector are selected for their mastery in the delicate art of world-crafting and their persistent pursuit of cosmic balance. While a select few among them are bestowed with the monumental task of leading the charge to breathe life into new worlds, others dedicate their essence to the upkeep of worlds already created into the existence. United in purpose yet scattered across the boundless cosmos, the Shapers operate within a complex, interwoven system with each thought carefully tuned to ensure their grand designs are made in perfect, predestined order.

The Order sector is responsible for protecting and encouraging all forms of life. They do not see any living thing as more or less important. The Order believes everything is tied together. This includes everything from tiny little insects to the largest trees. The main goal of the Order is to make the world better for every living thing that is able to prosper. The Shapers of the Order are familiar with the deep cosmic energies that form a world. They try to bring these energies into balance by directing them through motion in harmony with the world's natural rhythms. By doing this, they hope to stop harmful imbalances and keep the world stable. They believe that's the sole explanation for why they exist.

The Order thinks that living creations ought to strive to reach wisdom and learn about themselves. Their plan is to connect with the mortal races they create to join them on spiritual journeys to find inner knowledge and reach higher states of consciousness. The Order sees awareness as a way to get more connected to the world and help it grow in a way that is more peaceful. They believe in actively shaping the world, not by taking over or controlling it but by making things better and providing for them as well. The Order seeks to shape every part of the world and leave a feeling that everything is connected.

On the other hand, the Chaos sector, which was led by the Anarchist, who loved the wild energy of change and uncertainty. He was the ruler of the Chaos sector and enjoyed the raw power of chaos. He had attempted to upset the established order long ago so he himself could enjoy the surprises it brought upon the worlds that they created. The Anarchist wanted to live in a world without rules and where every moment could bring exciting changes.

When news of the cosmic collision rippled through the tapestry of existence, the Anarchist saw opportunity. Approaching the leaders of his own unpredictable realm, he proposed the unthinkable: an alliance with their long-standing rivals in the Order sector. The Anarchist argued that their goals could converge in a striking symphony of balance. He envisioned mortals imbued with attributes akin to the Shapers yet graced with the gift of free will—a chaotic essence that could dance in harmonious steps with order. In his mind, this daring blend would not merely offer mortals a richer existence; it would also serve as a crucible, enlightening them to accept and revel in their own inherent complexity, as if inviting them to become the very architects of their destinies.

In the grand design of the cosmos, where the Order sector weaves patterns of detailed design, the Chaos sector exists as its counterpart, a brushstroke of unpredictability across the canvas of existence. Like their counterparts in Order, the Chaos Shapers are dispersed throughout the void, guardians of a different but equally vital balance. Yet their touch on worlds is often momentary; their meddling brings violent disruptions, leaving ripples that defy their original intentions. The Anarchist have steered their approach toward a more measured chaos ever since the unsettling disturbance in the Death realm and it was a consequence of their own unpredictable actions. The Chaos sector has scaled back its world-building efforts and is exercising more restraint as they leave their permanent imprints on reality's ever-evolving space. Many of the other Chaos sector leaders denied Anarchist on working with the Order sector and the few that went along with him would instill in them the wisdom of world-crafting.

The Chaos sector believes that accepting change and not adhering to rules and frameworks is the only way to be truly free. They say that being yourself and showing who you are is the most important thing, and that the world should always change and grow. They see themselves as leaders who challenge the established order and defy its constraints. Their sector believes that rules and limits disrupt innovation and personal growth, and they want to live in a world where mortals can do whatever they want while accepting their chaotic nature.

They believe that the world should be a mix of different situations and points of view. According to their argument, innovation and growth can only occur when chaos and uncertainty are accepted. Chaos accepts the unknown and what is not understood about living. They do not believe in a predetermined celestial plan or destiny. Chaos, on the other hand, sees uncertainty and unpredictability as sources of excitement and evolution for mortals. They believe that embracing chaos allows you to wield all of the world's power. The Anarchist believes that if they can gain a firm grip on the world and its living creatures, it will envelop them and liberate them from nonsense.

The Anarchist held a secret meeting with another promising leader named Archon. She was one of the most powerful leaders in the Chaos sector and she had little experience building worlds and creating ideals. The Archon brought along Havoc, one of her devoted followers to the meeting held by the Anarchist. With an enchanting yet powerful voice, the Anarchist told them something that would change their views about the creation process for this newfound world. The Anarchist talked about a plan that would only succeed if the Chaos and Order sectors worked together.

The Anarchist explained to Archon and Havoc that they were picked for their skill and intelligence, and to oversee developing this new world alongside the leaders of the Order sector. This surprising relationship between Chaos and Order was to be the result of a new world where their combined forces would alter the very foundations of the world together. Unifying the two sectors that would otherwise oppose each other. It became a daunting task with plenty of articulation on both sides. The Provisioner was not keen to have inexperienced chaotic players alongside him, but he was welcoming the trust from their superior.

Havoc was an interesting Shaper within the Chaos sector. Everything about him seemed dark and twisted, from his thoughts to his physical appearance. He would smile wickedly, hinting at the mere mystery of what he was thinking, as if he were always plotting. The Archon enlisted Havoc by her side as a skilled right-hand to her. He would always listen to her demands. She wanted to take this opportunity to build a new world to her full attention, but she always felt the urge to do more than what she was capable of. Havoc did not help her thoughts either, as he was always an advocate for her or swayed her to follow her chaotic nature.

After talking to the Anarchist, the Archon felt better knowing she would be taking the lead on this project. The Anarchist taking a step back for once had intrigued her; she did not want to let him down, but she did not want to miss her opportunity again. She insisted Havoc follow the Anarchists' words closely, as Havoc was expressing a wicked smile. He told her that he was pleased to hear about their plans; it was as if he were imagining devious ways to ruin those plans. Knowing that the Shapers have a plan on how to construct this world and how it would help the Archon and Havoc achieve their covertly chaotic goals. For now, they remained silent by listening in on the plans of the other leaders so they could gain insight into how to disrupt those plans.

The Archon and Havoc formed a wicked partnership in secret, away from the Anarchist's attentions over the years, by whispering to one another and creating a twisted perspective on the living. They were both hungry for power, which brought them together initially. Havoc, an example of constant ambition and a thirsty desire to be in command, gave in easily to the Archon's demand. He respected her authority, and he may have developed feelings for her over the years spent together. While the two would talk amongst the shadows, they came up with a plan to control the complex planning of the new world's creation, all while keeping their true intentions hidden from the Anarchist and the Order sector. With their inexperience, they knew that could be used later if they were gaining attention, and the Anarchist would have their backs regardless due to the political and hesitant nature of the new alliance among the Order sector.

The Archon and Havoc drew up their wicked schemes in complete secret. They wanted to take advantage of the world's faults for their own malicious purposes. They planned to spread chaos and disrupt the delicate balance between Chaos and Order. Their desire for power outweighed any ideas of unity or peace, as they looked forward to being the sole individuals to take control of the new world. With the Anarchist being more of a background leader in the project and acting as an advisor, this gave the two twisted Shapers the opportunity to create something spectacular.

•••••••

In the realm of the sectors, which is ruled by the two opposing powers of Order and Chaos, there have been rare times when the sectors of both sides found a delicate balance and lived together peacefully, if only for a short time.

One of these situations happened in the past at the Harmonious Haven, a peaceful area that was on the border between the Order and Chaos sectors. Representatives from both sides saw the value in putting aside their differences and working together for the good of society in this unique area. In the past, the Harmonious Haven was used when multiple sectors had issues with each other about the first worlds created within the Life and Death realms. It was a place of peace, and many issues have been solved in the haven between celestial shapers.

Shortly after the collision of Luminara, the leaders of the Order sector and the rulers of the Chaos sector met in the Harmonious Haven. They talked about how they both want to look into the world that the collision has created. After much arguing and negotiating, the Provisioner and his loyal followers knew that their strict rules and constant dedication to their beliefs had boundaries. They realized that a little bit of chaos could give their carefully planned and closely monitored society fresh energy and ideas. At the same time, the Chaos sector, which was led by the Anarchist knew they needed some form of order to keep their beliefs from transforming into total chaos and despair.

Representatives from both sectors saw the potential for synergy after plenty of discussion and negotiation. They found that by combining their strengths and reducing their extremes, they could make a world that was more stable and balanced. The Order sector brought its knowledge of organization, structure, and long-term planning, and the Chaos sector brought its creativity, skill to adapt, and ability to come up with ideas immediately.

And so, the Shapers of both sectors all agreed at the Harmonious Haven that they would be the ones who would construct the world, which they called Paranova. After observing and learning, they possessed a deep understanding of how the world functions and how challenging it is. It would take various efforts to improve the natural beauty of the world, encourage creativity, and build a sense of belonging. They vowed to work together to restore and protect the world's different ecosystems, making sure that the forests, rivers, deserts, mountains, and lakes all formed well together. But because the celestial Shapers bodies were so massive, they were unable to walk on the surface. The sheer magnitude of the Shapers' contact with the physical world would have caused an immense amount of destruction and catastrophic consequences for the world, a risk that could cause Paranova to shatter.

A celestial shaper's form is a swirling dance of stardust and ethereal light, constantly evolving like a living nebula yet exuding an aura of ageless wisdom. Streams of cosmic energy flow around them as if they were a living conduit between realms, a bridge between the finite and the infinite. Eyes resembling galaxies peer out from their visages, holding within them a depth that seems to capture the very essence of time and space. It's as if they are sculpted from fragments of various realms, a harmonic fusion of both order and chaos, life and death. Veins of luminescent energy course through their translucent skin, making them appear as living constellations. To gaze upon a celestial Shaper is to glimpse the awe-inspiring complexity of the universe itself, momentarily frozen in a form incomprehensible to mortal and immortal eyes alike.

The Shapers' ability to create elements was infinite, but it was hard for them to bring their celestial essence into the real world of Paranova. They were extremely motivated, so they requested the Forger and the Provisioner, who were both highly intelligent, to assist with coming up with a way to connect their ethereal selves to the physical world they wanted to alter. The Avatars were made by the Forger, who was a master crafter and constructor of incredible creations. The essence of the Shapers was captured in these avatars, which were constructed with careful attention to detail. They took the form of majestic trees and strong and sturdy stones, much like the ones found on Paranova.

Each Avatar was a body for the Shapers' minds, which let them live in the physical world and interact with what they had created. These Avatars had a limit on how much influence the Shapers could connect with them, but it was enough for the Shapers to celebrate another creation as a solution to their problem. They could now step onto the world they could see by using the avatars physical forms as vessels.

The Forger was revered as the pinnacle of creative genius in Shaper culture; his celestial shaping abilities transcend mere world-crafting to touch the very essence of reality itself. While most Shapers sketch the outline of worlds, the Forger delves into the detailing. His powers are finely tuned to manipulate the smallest quark and the grandest galaxy with equal grace. It is this extraordinary mastery that compelled the

Order sector to dedicate him to the exalted title of World-Forger, trusting him with the most intricate of cosmic creations.

The Forger gave the avatars life through his skilled hands, giving them intricate details blended with the spirit of the Shapers. However, it was the Provisioner who gave them the spark of life. The Provisioner had a deep understanding of how life force flowed through all living things. He used this knowledge to channel the avatars' energy into them, giving them life and awareness. So, the avatars grew into beautiful beings who stood between the ethereal world of the Shapers and the real world of Paranova. They had the wisdom, knowledge, and essence of their creators inside of them. Through these Avatars, the Shapers could see the wonders of what they had made, communicate with the living and see different parts of the world, and use their endless creativity and resourcefulness to shape the future of Paranova.

The tree and stone avatars helped the Shapers communicate with the creatures of Paranova. Through these animated bodies, the Shapers were able to interact with the world, talk to plants or animals, and see the landscapes from a more relatable perspective. The Avatars had the unique ability to see the world as the creatures did. This helped the Shapers understand what the creatures went through and what they needed. This provided the Shapers with the information they needed to make decisions and shape the world in keeping with the hopes and dreams of all creation.

Avatars of Tree were tall beings with a strong connection to nature. With their huge size and spiritual presence, they became the protectors of the forests, making sure the animals who lived there were safe. These elegant avatars would walk through the woods, and their tender steps would make the earth vibrate with life. Since the tree avatars were able to talk to plants and animals, they understood what they needed and how to help them grow and stay safe.

In the old groves, the Avatars of Tree would care for the young trees, and their touch would give them strength and vitality. They would carefully cut back branches that were getting too big, making sure there was a balance between growth and peace in the forest ecosystem. Because they knew so much about how nature works, the avatars could lead animals to food and water sources that were good for them. This kept animals from going hungry and helped their habitats grow.

But they cared about more than just what the animals needed; they tended to every living thing in their world. The Avatars of Tree knew a lot about how everything in the ecosystem worked together. They would subtly change the way plants grew, change the way rivers flowed, and shape the landscapes to increase biodiversity. With a touch of their hand, they could change the landscape, making safe places and barriers to keep animals from getting hurt. They could do this out of their own will, outside of the Shapers control.

The Order sector constructed the Avatars of Stone. They worked to keep the land stable and safe, which was similar to what their tree counterparts accomplished. These statues, which were carved out of the rock of Paranova, stood as silent reminders of strength and endurance. They would traverse mountains, valleys, and cliffs, and their strong bodies would help shape the world's geological features.

The Avatars of Stone had a deep understanding of geology and the elements that shaped the planet. This helped them stop landslides, prevent erosion, and regulate the flow of rivers. They would dig caverns and underground spaces for creatures that needed a place to stay. They would work with the tree avatars to make delicate ecosystems where plants and animals could live and grow together in harmony.

The Avatars of Stone were able to talk to the rocks and stones that made up Paranova. They could feel changes in the earth, which let them know about potential dangers and let them take actions to avoid them. Their touch could fix cracks in the bedrock, making it stronger and less likely that something terrible would happen. When earthquakes or volcanoes erupted, the Avatars of Stone used their powers to direct the energy away from vulnerable areas. This kept the damage to animals and landscapes to a minimum. Together, the avatars of tree and stone guided Paranova into an ensemble of care and responsibility. The delicate balance of life and nature was kept safe by their cautious involvement.

The Avatars demonstrated exceptional skills in ensuring the safety of the animals inhabiting Paranova. These creatures found peace within sheltered groves and enjoyed bountiful sustenance amidst carefully maintained landscapes, shielded from any natural calamities by vigilant avatars. The relentless devotion these guardians showed to ensuring Paranova's well-being over centuries was visible to the mortal races firsthand. This invaluable experience has instilled in them a deep appreciation for environmental preservation and harmonious coexistence with all living beings that share their domain. Some mortals chose to venerate these avatars as celestial entities deserving worship.

Even so, the Avatars of Tree and Stone were not invincible, regardless of how hard the natural disasters would hit them. As the world kept shifting, Paranova faced its share of problems and dangers. The guardians' resolve was put to the test. They kept a very fragile balance, and the other creatures looked to them for guidance and strength when things got rough.

The Keeper, who was the Provisioner's trusted and loyal friend, was an important part of the big picture for Paranova. The Keeper oversaw maintaining the balance and harmony of the world. He also watched over life and took care of the avatars. As the Provisioner's right-hand man, it was his solemn job to keep an eye on the living things the Shapers created.

He wanted to keep the Avatars of Tree and Stone as his main priority in the world-crafting duties above all else for the Order and that the avatars were safe and happy. As they moved through the different parts of Paranova, he stood as a sentinel, always on the lookout. It was his solemn duty to keep them safe from anything that could hurt them, since they weren't mere objects but instead held the essence and consciousness of the Shapers; to him, they were kin.

The Keeper and the Provisioner had a strong relationship based on trust and a shared goal. The Provisioner knew that the Keeper did an important job and relied on his steadfast commitment to keep Paranova's delicate balance. Together, they worked in harmony, with their minds and hearts in alignment, to care for life, shape the world, and protect the avatars who were a link between the Shapers and the living creations.

While performing the sacred duty of observing the avatars, the Keeper experienced profound delight. Within the living entities of both trees and stones, he gained insight into aspects of the world that lay beyond his massive physical presence. He took pleasure in admiring the intricate beauty of landscapes, the vibrant hues displayed by plants, and the gentle sounds produced by animals. Each instance he witnessed and felt through the avatars' perspective deepened his connection to life's complex network. Consequently, the Keeper developed a true understanding of Paranova's essence, thereby appreciating its fragile balance between existence and progression, disorder and organization. These invaluable moments bestowed upon him a sense of serenity and joy as he recognized, with great significance, how every living being deeply influences this ever-evolving tapestry known as Paranova.

The Provisioner oversaw keeping Paranova's delicate balance in check. He had a close relationship with the Oracle, a wise woman and seer whose visions could see through time. The Oracle's insights gave the Provisioner glimpses into the vast variety of the future and helped him decide what to do next. As the Oracle's visions showed them the way forward, they worked together with mutual respect and understanding.

The Oracle watched the world change with awe and respect from her observatory in the cosmos. She saw how the different ecosystems fit together perfectly, how mighty rivers carved their way through lush forests, how majestic tall mountains were, and how peaceful clear lakes were. From where she stood, she could see the delicate movement of life, in which animals roamed free and the natural order thrived. The Oracle's heart swelled with pride and awe as she looked at Paranova's thriving ecosystems, which were a sign of the Shapers' compassion and of how all living things are connected. The Oracle found comfort in these times of quiet observation because she knew that the world she and the Provisioner had made together was thriving in perfect harmony.

The Oracle stood at the threshold of reality, her eyes beholding the majestic tapestry that was Paranova—a realm born from her whispers and crystallized by the Provisioner's skill. Her celestial gaze swept across this vibrant world, and she felt a thrill of exhilaration surge through her ethereal form. It was as though her visions, intricate tapestries of foresight, had sprung to life in an expanse far surpassing even the grandest tableau she had ever conjured in her mind's eye. Her heart, if one could call it the core of her celestial essence, thus swelled with an emotion akin to love—not just for Paranova but also for the Provisioner. As she marveled at the intricate symphony of life and landscape before her, her faith in their next monumental milestone solidified. If they could birth Paranova from the whispers and vision of possibility, then surely their upcoming venture would be equally grand and ambitious as the realms of life and death they had once forged. It would be another resounding ode to the everlasting story of existence.

Between the Provisioner and the Oracle, there was a deep trust and connection. With their previous creations and situations in the past that had brought fruition to their goals and plans, The Provisioner, who was always trying to shape and care for life, sought advice from the Oracle, whose knowledge was not limited by time or space. The Oracle's ethereal presence and ability to see into the future helped the Provisioner in his work by giving him insights and visions that showed him the way forward. He delighted himself in seeing that he would bring the Oracle's visions into existence, and she was overjoyed when she witnessed them.

In the vast expanse of existence, long before Paranova was even a tiny particle from a cosmic perspective, the Oracle and the Provisioner shared a deep and unbreakable connection. These two celestial beings, bound together in love and harmony, set out on a journey that would take them across the cosmos, where they would shape worlds and nourish the forces of creation. The Oracle and the Provisioner, as a dynamic duo in the Order sector, bonded deeply over their appreciation for life's intricate dance.

The world of life that resulted from their joint imagination was full of lush vegetation and exotic wildlife. The Provisioner, who had a thorough understanding of the energies that animated all living things, gave the world new life and harmony. While all this was happening, the Oracle looked on with their ageless wisdom and foresight, taking note of life's wonders and documenting their ever-evolving stories.

The harmony between evolution and longevity that the miracle of creation had produced pleased both the Oracle and the Provisioner. Through the culmination of these occurrences, they obtained a deep comprehension of existence and its correlation with the universe. Their shared passion for nurturing life led them to find peace in the realms of the Order sector, where they could entirely dedicate themselves to engaging in their beloved pursuits.

They both kept their creative wheels turning within the Order sector, each bringing their own special talents and insights to the table. The Provisioner infused the infant worlds with life by maintaining ecological balance and promoting the development of new forms of life. Through their all-knowing eyes, the Oracle directed the course of events, illuminating the threads of fate that ran through the universe. Their union, formed in the earliest moments of creation, is now fundamental to peace throughout the universe. For the Oracle and the Provisioner, working together to create and sustain life was a source of great joy. Through their combined efforts, they were able to create worlds rich in beauty, diversity, and opportunity.

The Provisioner had a lofty objective in mind because of his altruistic desire to enhance life and consciousness on Paranova. He had hoped to one day help bring intelligent races of sentient mortal beings into existence. He explored the complexities of life methodically, learning about the elements of life and the symphony of nature. He wanted his creations to share this profound quality, so he gave them intelligence, compassion, and free will. The Provisioner focused efficiently, carefully piecing together the puzzle of existence and experimenting with various blends of energies in an attempt to craft his magnum opus. He visualized a species that would safeguard the tranquility and concord of Paranova by embodying these principles.

In the cosmic theater where Shapers play their roles, the Provisioner emerges as a visionary yearning for more than the mere semblance of life. Though his creations were awe-inspiring, they lacked the spark of sapience, the nuanced tapestry of consciousness that gives depth to existence. Tired of birthing only celestial entities akin to the Shapers themselves, he hungered for the realization of diverse mortals who could navigate the labyrinth of life and death, thought, and emotion. It was in the Life realm—the cradle of Shaper origins—that he found an ally in the Oracle. Together, they envisioned a realm teeming with mortal life, sculpted not merely in flesh and bone but woven with the intangible threads of awareness. For the Oracle and the Provisioner, this was no mere dream; it was a quest of unparalleled magnitude, a symphony they were destined to compose in the harmonious key of existence.

Together, they represented the essence and design of the universe, having a hand in the creation of countless worlds. The realms of Life and Death, from which the entire cycle of existence would eventually emerge, were among their numerous creations. They became close because they respected each other and wanted to work together to make another world. They both felt the urge and pull to fulfill their destiny together.

To the Provisioner, mortal's capacity to coexist harmoniously with the natural world and make significant contributions to its abundant tapestry was paramount to any other pursuit in life. As time passed, his excitement swelled, for he stood on the precipice of witnessing the dawning of a new era—the genesis of a sentient entity. These individuals would eventually blossom into Paranova's thriving mortal civilizations.

Of all relations, the connection between the Anarchist and the Provisioner was fascinating and unusual due to the fundamental differences in their worldviews. To the Provisioner, the patchwork of creation is an atmosphere of harmony, while the Anarchist sees beauty in controlled chaos and finds inspiration in the unknown. Despite their philosophical differences, the two celestial beings respected one another and understood the value they brought to the universe.

In their dealings with one another, the Anarchist frequently confused the Provisioner with his erratic behavior. The Provisioner, who valued order and thorough preparation, couldn't understand the Anarchist's preference for acting on the impulse of the moment. Underneath their noticeable dissimilarities, however, was common knowledge and an appreciation for the importance of harmony in the cosmos. The patience the Provisioner would give to the Anarchist and the respect given from the Anarchist are what each other desired in outcomes of quarrels between the two and also between each of the sectors.

The Anarchist's prescience allowed him to anticipate the roles played by Archon and Havoc in the development of Paranova. Since the Anarchist knew the Archon was lacking experience in the creative space, he warned the Provisioner to be on the lookout. The Anarchist advised the Provisioner, whom he saw as more of a bystander than a participant in his goals, to pay close attention to his surroundings and be flexible. Both the Anarchist and the Provisioner understood the value of harmony and acknowledged the worth of everyone's contributions to the cosmos, despite their fundamental differences in outlook. They knew that the inclusion of Archon and Havoc would bring about unexpected dynamics and difficulties in the creative process. Each sector was committed to maintaining a delicate balance, so they cautiously approached the unfolding events, expecting the unexpected.

While the Provisioner labored on to develop a conscious race that exemplified the values of order and harmony, the Archon, who had a different vision for Paranova, secretly plotted to undermine his efforts. The Archon beheld the opportunity to exploit the finely balanced system of power of the shaper culture with a malicious glint in her eye. She feared that the emergence of an intelligent race would throw the natural world out of balance and threaten her control of the realm of chaos. In her quest to seize the Provisioner's creation through his web of fascination, the cunning and manipulative Archon used her skills in the arts of deception and manipulation. She set out to sow the seeds of discord, selfishness, and chaos within the developing intelligent beings' very essence.

The Archon planned to destroy the structure that the Provisioner had painstakingly built by sowing the seeds of unrest and conflict. Instead of destruction, her plan called for subversion, with the goal of reshaping Paranova's future in opposition to the good intentions of the Provisioner. As she patiently waited for the right time to deal a fatal blow to the Provisioner's grand vision, the Archon's dark machinations remained shrouded in secrecy, hidden from the prying eyes of the Shapers. She sought out her sinister partner to execute her plans.

Within the shadows, the Archon had a loyal and cunning confidant in Havoc, a formidable agent of chaos whose allegiance to the Archon was unflinching. The Archon counted on Havoc as a loyal and clever confidant while operating within the realms of chaos. Havoc, an accomplished master of deception and manipulation, took great pleasure in the anarchy and disorder that echoed through the passageways of her shadowy domain. The Archon was aware of Havoc's unquenchable desire for power and chaos, and she recognized in Havoc a valuable instrument that could be used to advance the Archon's own goals. Their shared belief that anarchy should rule supreme and their desire to thwart the Order's plans led them to come together and form a potentially harmful alliance.

The relationship between the Archon and Havoc was one of strategic manipulation and mutually beneficial ambitions and objectives. The Archon, with her keen intellect and strategic mind, exploited Havoc's insidious desires to further her own objectives. She played Havoc like a puppet on a string, playing to her sharp intelligence and strategic mind. The Archon, acting under the disguise of a guide, honed Havoc's skills of chaos and shaped her into a formidable weapon for their ongoing secret conflict with the Order. This was all done while Havoc was unaware that the Archon was actually steering him.

Havoc's insatiable desire for power and the possibility of untamed anarchy, in return, kept him steadfast in his allegiance to the Archon. Havoc received recognition for his loyalty from the Archon with calculated favors and promises of dominion. The Archon knew that she could utilize Havoc's destructive tendencies to further their common goal, so she bestowed these gifts upon Havoc. Together, they concocted devious plans and conspiracies, their sinister schemes intertwining like tendrils of shadow as they worked toward their common objective of upsetting the fragile balance of Paranova and reshaping the world in accordance with their twisted goals.

Havoc was a vile being that embodied both chaos and deception, and he possessed an innate dark talent for manipulating the very foundation of existence. Through the use of his nefarious abilities, he conjured the spectral Avatars, which are ethereal beings with haunting beauty and a sinister allure. These avatars, which emerged from the warped energies of chaos, were given the mission of infiltrating the world of Paranova and spreading discord among its inhabitants.

Archon and Havoc were the trusted architects, sketching out the blueprints for spreading world resources, structures, and the very creatures that would populate the crafted world. Their roles provided them with a cover of respectability, a curtain behind which their secret activities could unfold. While they excelled in their official duties, laying out plans that even the most discerning of Shapers would approve, their true mastery lay in the realm of subterfuge. Havoc devised an intricate scheme involving the spectral avatars that shapers could commune with to perceive worlds at an even finer level of detail, much like the other avatars present on Paranova.

This innovation fooled everyone, serving its public-facing purpose remarkably yet holding deeper implications known only to him. Archon, ever the observant counterpart, was the sole figure who saw through the gambit. Nevertheless, the spectral avatars proved effective, serving as both a groundbreaking tool for the Shapers and a mask concealing the duo's deeper, more sinister designs.

These spectral Avatars were born from the twisted energies of chaos. They wailed and whispered as their spectral forms captivated the creatures of the land, who were unaware of their presence. They were shrouded in darkness and mystery. Because of their eerie presence, Havoc was able to gain insight into the lives of his foes. The spectral avatars would calm their victims into a false sense of security before binding them and draining them of their life essence, memories, and emotions.

The process of extracting life essence was more than just a means to an end for Havoc; rather, it was a source of twisted pleasure for him. He took pleasure in the torment and suffering that the spectral avatars inflicted on their victims while they wailed and drank the life force from their bodies. The stolen recollections and feelings served as playthings for him, feeding his urgent appetite for power and control.

Havoc was like someone who was addicted to a drug; the essence of life, with all its unfiltered energy and vitality, fed his nefarious desires and gave him a perverted sense of fulfillment. He felt that his influence over Paranova was growing deeper with each extraction, and his appetite for chaos was increasing as a result. The Archon, who was always conscious of his nefarious pleasure, actively supported Havoc in his wicked activities, taking pleasure in the anarchy and destruction that slowly occurred as a direct result of his orders. Together, they worked to turn the life essence that had been stolen into a weapon that could be used against the Provisioner. They hoped to use such a weapon to disrupt the Order's plans and sow additional discord among the mortal races of Paranova.

When compared to the stone and tree avatars, the creation of the spectral avatars added a new dimension to the creative efforts of the Shapers. These spectral avatars presented a different point of view and served a different purpose. These ethereal beings were intended to personify the essence of secrecy and observation. They were created to act as spectral spies and to become revered as ghosts in the eyes of the mortal races that were yet to come into existence. At least that is how Havoc explained their design and purpose.

The stone and tree avatars had solid and distinct forms, but the spectral avatars existed in a realm that was somewhere between the physical and the ethereal. They were able to traverse realms and pass through barriers, which enabled them to move among the living creatures without being seen or noticed. They had the exceptional ability to observe and gather information without interference from or detection by life because of their ethereal nature.

The Shapers had a vision of the spectral avatars acting as conduits for knowledge and secrets, and they charged these avatars with the responsibility of watching how events unfold around the world. Because of their spectral appearance and their ability to pass through solid objects without being detected, they were perfect for slipping into constrained areas of Paranova and obtaining knowledge there. The spectral avatars, in their capacity as keepers of hidden knowledge, would be extremely important in the formation of Paranova's foreseeable future.

Their observations and reports would provide the Shapers with invaluable insights, assisting in the understanding of the triumphs, struggles, and aspirations of the mortal races. They would become mysterious figures in Paranova's folklore and mythology as a result of their ethereal presence, which would be connected to the foundation of Paranova's history.

Within the depths of Havoc's ambitious imagination, a sweeping plan started to take shape, one that traveled beyond the realms of significance and into the ethereal. The creation of spectral avatars sparked Havoc's concept of the construction of an ethereal realm, a domain that would connect with the mortal world of Paranova.

This ethereal world would serve as a conduit, an unseen avenue via which Havoc might spread chaos and discord while staying hidden from the Shapers' inquisitive eyes. Furthermore, Havoc would be able to achieve all of this while staying undetected. It would be a world of shadows and illusions, where his influence would spread like a whispered rumor, gradually compromising the delicate balance that the Order and Chaos sectors had diligently formed thus far. With this ambitious scheme in mind, Havoc put into action the initial steps towards the realization of his big plan, twisting a complicated web of intrigue and malice that would test every aspect of Paranova itself.

The Provisioner was busy formulating the first sentient mortal race, but the Archon and Havoc remained engaged, devising plans in the background. Their plans had been kept under wraps from the Provisioner. Due to their own pride and thirst for power, they plotted to force their way into the Oracle's inner sanctum. The Provisioner and the Oracle passionately sketched out the routes of Paranova's initial mortal sapience in the Oracle's sanctuary.

After succumbing to Havoc's ideal of his plans, the once-respected Archon in the Chaos sector plotted to poison the very essence of the Provisioner's creation. The Archon and Havoc, prowling in the shadows, examined the Oracle's shelter with caution as they arranged to strike. They were on watch for weaknesses in the Order sector defense, which they could use to prevent their plans. Havoc, who is renowned for his ability to influence others, plotted cleverly for entry into the creation chamber and to disrupt the Provisioner's plan.

The Provisioner, who was unaware of the impending betrayal that was taking place in the shadows, poured the essence he and the Oracle had curated and placed his creative energy into the process of development in the hopes of giving birth to beings that possessed profound wisdom and beauty. He had no idea that he would soon be the victim of a treachery that would test the strength of his convictions and put the delicate balance of Paranova at risk.

The Archon and Havoc were getting ever closer to their sinister goals, which posed a threat that cast a deep shadow over the future of the mortal race. They were also poised to reshape the conflict between order and chaos, which would put the Provisioner's resilience to the test like never before.

A foreboding feeling of betrayal took over the Oracle just prior to the fateful infiltration of her sanctuary. Because of her deep connection to the shifting patterns of celestial energies, the Oracle had an innate intuition that something threatening was on the horizon. This gave her the ability to foresee the future. Even though she was unsure of the specifics, she felt a sense of impending danger that was overwhelming.

As she walked cautiously to the creation chamber, she told the Provisioner with a heavy heart about her uncertainties, knowing that their collaboration and shared objectives were essential to the success of Paranova. She also knew that their partnership was essential. Fearing the consequences of him ignoring the warning signs, she pleaded with him to give serious consideration to investigating the situation before moving forward with the final stages of creation. However, the Provisioner, who was solid in his faith in the naturally noble nature of their effort, soothed her fears and assured her that they must carry on with their work as he could not stop in the middle of his creation or there would be consequences. He placed his faith in him to shed light on the mysteries that haunted the Oracle's mind, and he entrusted the Oracle's protection to the sacredness of their sanctuary.

Reluctantly, the Oracle understood. With their shared vision, which persisted amidst uncertainty, combining determination and remorse, she resolved to complete the arrangements for the mortal race. She hoped that before her vision came to pass, her worries would turn out to be unfounded and that Paranova's fate would follow its intended course. She feared for the Provisioner's life more than her own. She saw him with everything they wanted to achieve—a family, mortal worlds spread across the cosmos—but then a vision of her alone. Her lover is being murdered over and over, trying to reach her looming darkness. Another vision of blood spilled underneath the worlds they created. She could not rest, knowing something dark was near, but she continued to wonder.

She had no idea that her visions may have contained some element of truth, and that the impending infiltration of her sanctuary would set in motion a series of events that would put the Provisioner and Oracle's unity and the delicate balance that they had worked so hard to establish to the test. She thought that her visions were simply her sense of wonder and fear.

She did her best to keep all the horror that was going on inside of her quiet so they could keep focused while she struggled to maintain her composure. She knew it was her duty to guard the delicate seeds of their creation. Although there lingered a hidden question in the very depths of her consciousness, in spite of herself, she was picturing an inescapable answer that loomed ahead.

The sanctuary of the Oracle was sacred; she used the sanctuary space for peace and meditation as she communicated through her celestial powers of sight, seeking glimpses into the future. Under the cover of night, the Archon infiltrated her sanctuary and gained unauthorized entry to it. The Oracle was rendered immobile from perceiving or intervening in the unfolding events as a result of the Archon's use of a combination of enchantments and clever traps, which rendered her incapacitated.

Even though the Oracle's foresight was dark and her visions were shattered, she had a mind's-eye intuition that something threatening was on the verge of happening. A strange intuition warned her of an impending threat—a wicked force that was attempting to upset the delicate balance that the Shapers had created.

However, the specifics of the Archon's schemes remained elusive, shrouded in shadows that concealed the length and depth of her deceit. It was difficult to determine the precise nature of the Archon's arrival and when it would occur based on the Oracle's insights because they were clouded in ambiguity. However, it was happening mere seconds after the Oracle made sense of the vision. The Oracle was able to set off an alarm, but shortly after she was helpless.

The Archon, utilizing her own formidable powers of manipulation, ensnared the Oracle in a tapestry of clouded illusions and shattered visions by surrounding her with a web of shadows that she had cast around her, tethering the Oracle to the ethereal realm. Her connection to the celestial realm beyond was severed, which caused a clouding in the Oracle's once clear and prophetic sight. The realm of dreams and prophecies, which had previously served as her source of insight and wisdom, morphed into a confusing and disorganized labyrinth.

The Oracle's influence started diminishing as a result of this state of disempowerment, and her sight, which had previously been reaching, became blind. The Archon took great pleasure in her victory, for she understood the mortal races would be helpless and defenseless in the absence of The Oracle's direction, making them susceptible to her manipulations and the untamed anarchy that she planned to unleash upon Paranova.

The Oracle found herself bound in a confusing labyrinth of shattered visions and concealed truths as the wicked plot continued to develop and the Archon's machinations tightened their hold within the celestial realm. She was overcome with a strange sense of unease and confusion, which caused her once perceptive mind to become shrouded in a cloud of uncertainty.

The Oracle, who was normally a shining example of wisdom and insight, was beginning to sense a growing dissonance within her own unique being. She could feel the shadows growing larger around her—the threads of deception that were being woven, crossing into the threads of her fate. Despite her best efforts, she was unable to see through the haze that covered the specifics of the Archon's plan. She tried everything she knew to do. It was as if someone had purposefully blocked her vision, replacing her typical reliable vision with distorted fragments and fractured glimpses of the world around her. She was unaware of who was doing this to her, but she also lost her sense of reality.

The Oracle experienced a growing combination of feelings that made her experience helplessness and frustration. The unexpected loss of her ability to sense the paths destiny laid out for the upcoming mortals and guide them towards unity created immense hardship within her. She began to wonder how she could have fallen victim to the assassin's cunning trap without being aware of it. Her self-assurance and clear judgment were deeply impacted as a result of these occurrences.

Despite the turmoil going on inside her, the Oracle kept her resolve. She firmly refused to give in to hopelessness or give up her role as a guiding light for the upcoming mortals. She clung to the belief that there was still a glimmer of hope, a path that had not yet been revealed, despite the fact that her visions were clouded and her foresight was diminishing.

The Oracle knew in her very core that even in the most trying of circumstances, the seeds of recovery and determination would find a way to emerge and develop into something beautiful. She clung passionately to the unshakeable conviction that the mortal races possessed the strength and resilience to navigate the dangerous journey ahead, even if she did not provide direct guidance to them. The gloom and uncertainty that had descended upon her served only to strengthen her resolve to vanquish the darkness and reclaim her sight for the sake of Paranova and the mortals who would live there in the future.

A wave of anguish and guilt washed over the Oracle as she struggled with the realization that her own foresight had failed and that the Provisioner was left vulnerable without her guiding vision. During this time, the Oracle was overcome with both of these emotions. She was burdened with the responsibility of ensuring the safety and wellbeing of Paranova, and the weight of the momentary compromise in her abilities weighed heavily on her core. She carried the weight of responsibility.

In an instant, the Oracle was overcome with deep regret. It had always been her source of pride to be the guardian of peace and serenity, utilizing her unique gift of clairvoyance to guide the Provisioner and shield him from imminent dangers. However, her visions were now muddled, and her connection with the cosmic forces was severed. Consequently, she found herself incapable of fulfilling the sacred responsibility that had been bestowed upon her.

With each passing moment, a sense of unease gripped the Oracle's soul. This anxiety became entangled with a profound fear that she had failed both the Provisioner and the delicate equilibrium they had tirelessly strived for. At this juncture, it seemed as though the weight of an uncertain future burdened her shoulders while she yearned passionately to reclaim her sight. The darkness that surrounded her abilities would only then allow her to once more break through it.

After successfully disabling the Oracle and shrouding her sight in darkness, the Archon withdrew into the depths of her secluded chamber. There, she remained hidden from prying eyes and immersed in the twisting corridors of her own thoughts as she retreated into seclusion. Her vengeful satisfaction at upsetting the unstable balance of power was manifested in the form of a triumphant smile that played across her lips. She placed the blame on a Chaos sector apprentice, whom she had previously prepared as another hidden piece in her arsenal to keep in the shadows.

In the peace and quiet of her haven, the Archon took pleasure in the disorder that she was responsible for sowing. She was aware that the peaceful order that had once prevailed over Paranova would tremble on the brink of uncertainty now that the Oracle was unable to perform her duties. It was a moment she had been eagerly awaiting, relishing the opportunity to carry out her grand design and push the world further into the embrace of untamed chaos.

She allowed herself to become engaged in an act of ominous meditation, her thoughts a whirlwind of carefully plotted maneuvers and complicated processes. The Provisioner's grand plan to create a sentient race was disrupted, but this was just the beginning of her devious game; it was just a taste of the chaos she intended to wreak upon Paranova. Since the Archon's ambitions had no limits and since the Oracle had been rendered blind, the Archon's path was filled with perverse opportunities.

As she wove her webs of darkness, the thoughts of the Archon cascaded through the intricate pattern of her strategic mind like threads in a tapestry. She sat there imagining the shattered dreams of the Provisioner and the world thrown into disarray, with each piece fitting perfectly into place according to her vile orchestration of the situation. She took great pleasure in anticipating this event because she could not wait to witness the struggles of the mortals and their feeble attempts to reestablish order in a world that was becoming more and more chaotic.

The Archon understood the time had come to put her master plan into action because all of her plans were thoroughly laid out before her. She would take advantage of every possible source of discord and dissent, working to her advantage the fractured beliefs that were common within the shaper culture. She would pull the strings that would cause the very foundations of Paranova to fall apart, delighting in the upheaval and destruction that would follow as she played the role of the chaos's puppet master.

Archon surveyed the stolen plans and cosmic seeds with a calculating gaze. These were no ordinary artifacts; they were the distilled essence of the Oracle's visions and the Provisioner's labors, blueprints for worlds still gestating in the womb of possibility. By infiltrating the Oracle's sanctum and absconding with these celestial treasures, Archon had achieved something audacious. As she meticulously studied each sketch and seed, she gained an intimate understanding of the Provisioner's every intended step, arming herself with the knowledge to either facilitate or foil his grand designs. In this stolen moment, Archon found herself perched at a precipice, holding in her hands the delicate threads that could unravel or reweave the very fabric of future realms.

As she pondered the upcoming segments of her dark symphony, a sinister sparkle flickered amidst her fervent eyes. The Archon, driven by an insatiable hunger for control and superiority, was filled with excitement as she prepared to unleash the complete chaos upon an unprepared world. Her path had already been set, and she remained determined that no obstacle would deflect her from carrying out her malicious mission to reshape Paranova's history in accordance with the disturbed vision she had conceived.

As the moment of triumph drew near, the Provisioner remained steadfast in his resolve as he took his place above Paranova, where he became enveloped in a feeling of profound energy. He accumulated all the necessary elements and energies with extreme care and attention to detail, drawing from the fundamental understanding of harmony and order that influenced the entire world. As he carefully organized and crafted this intricate spell that would give birth to a new sentient race—a race destined to embody the principles of the Order and bring further harmony to Paranova—the air crackled with anticipation. He was focusing on the spell's creation at precisely the same time as the atmosphere around him. Every action, every incantation, and every intention were infused with love and hope for a world in which peace would prevail over all other conflicts.

The alarm set off in the Oracle's sanctuary while the final steps for the creation began. The Provisioner kept focus as this was the moment they had worked tirelessly for. However, the Provisioner was unaware that Havoc, the agent of chaos, had made his way through the cracks in reality and entered the sacred chamber before the final steps were taken, where the inception ceremony was intended to take place. As he hunkered down in the shadows, his eyes sparkled with satanic glee as he clutched a foul vessel that contained harvested souls that would suffer for all of eternity in his ethereal realm. The vessel was packed to the brim with tormented souls, the anguish of which fueled his malicious plotting.

Havoc approached undetected above the location where the Provisioner's spellcasting energies converged while remaining stealthy and malevolent. His fingers were trembling with anticipation as he did so. In a single deft action, he poured the contents of the vessel into the swirling vortex of creation, hence contaminating the very essence that the Provisioner had intended to infuse into the newly developing gifted race. As the tormented souls mingled with the delicate energies, agonized cries echoed throughout the chamber.

The cries tainted the very substance of the soon-to-be-created phenomenon with anguish and discord. The intrusion caught the Provisioner off guard, and he experienced a ripple of unease throughout his being. His concentration faltered for a brief moment as he sensed the presence of chaos interwoven with the carefully constructed spell that he had been casting, but he needed to finish the spell or monstrosities would form.

At that significant moment, the tension between order and chaos was barely poised on the precipice, and the future of the developing sentient race was hanging in the air. Would it be possible for the Provisioner to reclaim his creation and direct it toward a path that leads to harmony despite the disturbing influence that Havoc has brought into play? Or would disorder win out, resulting in unanticipated repercussions that would determine the course of events for Paranova? The scene was prepared, and an intricate movement of powers and intentions began to play out in a realm where the fate of an entire world hung by a thread so thin that it could snap at any moment.

Chapter 2: Ripples of Creation

The aftermath of Havoc's disruptive act weighed heavily on the Provisioner's heart. Guilt washed over him as he mourned the unintended consequences of his creation. Remorse over the tortured souls that had surrounded the very core of his celestial energy plagued him. He had felt the agony from all the mortal souls howling and pleading for torment. For a moment, he felt each soul's pain and suffering, all while channeling his own essence into the energy that formed sapience. The Provisioner's sorrow had fueled his determination to put an end to the disorder that had descended on this newborn race and the consequences that would come for Paranova.

As he stood in the midst of the chamber filled with tormented souls, screams echoed through the air, and eerie pleas for help filled the Provisioner's mind. His normally composed and confident demeanor sank in the face of this unexpected chaos. He had carefully designed the creation process, making certain that every detail matched his vision, but he had not anticipated this wicked intrusion. His mind was foggy as he searched the chamber for evidence of interference or tampering. He came across no issues. What could have initiated this? His thoughts raced as he attempted to make sense of the unknown torment that had infiltrated the once harmonious sanctuary.

The Provisioner's heart sank when he realized how bad the situation was. Something terrible had gone wrong, putting every aspect of his creation in danger. He could feel the weight of his responsibilities—the weight of the lives he was supposed to take care of and manage. He was shocked at first, believing the infiltration was caused by his own accord, but a rush of determination pushed the shock away. He knew he had to find a way to restore things back to balance and protect the delicate mortal race from this terrifying disorder.

The Provisioner braced himself for the difficult task that lay ahead of him, despite the lingering sense of unpredictability in the air. He committed every bit of energy of his being to the task, as he was passionate about his mission to guide the mortal races towards the fulfillment of the Oracle's prophecies. He was steadfast in his commitment, even knowing that he was well aware that the path ahead would be difficult with struggles and challenges.

The Provisioner developed a plan of guidance after gathering his wisdom and channeling his boundless energy. He recognized the delicate inner workings that had to be impacted between order and chaos, knowing that the mortal races had to navigate the intricate web of existence with purpose and clarity. His advice would act as a compass, guiding them through a web of choices and consequences that awaited them.

Within the fundamental fibers of his being, the Provisioner bore the weight of responsibility. He understood that the fate of Paranova rested on his shoulders, and he accepted the pressure of this heavy responsibility. He considered how his actions might affect the world and the races of mortals, always working to promote peace, progress, and the pursuit of knowledge. With each decision he always had others on his mind while committing to a direction.

Despite the uncertainty, the Provisioner drew strength from the belief that the Oracle's visions held the key to a brighter future. He embraced the task of shepherding the mortal races, understanding that their individual journeys would weave together a tapestry of a collective destiny. His dedication to their guidance was consistent, and he embarked on this momentous undertaking with both uncertainty and passion. He was ready to continue the grand plan for the fate of the new race and the living world.

As the Provisioner prepared to focus his efforts, he took comfort in knowing he was not alone in this journey. The Tree and Stone Avatars, strong companions and representations of Shaper essence, their wisdom and connection to nature counseling him. Together, they established a partnership, a harmonious power united in their determination to nurture the mortal cultures and direct the progression of life in Paranova.

In spite of the unpredictability of the wicked circumstances, the Provisioner found that their unity gave them strength. He recognized that the shapers, avatars, and mortal races would need to work together to overcome the challenges ahead. With hope as his guiding light and determination as his compass, he knew that the journey to fulfill the Oracle's prophecies would be full of both victories and failures.

The Provisioner's heart brimmed with purpose, for he understood that creating a sapient race was more than just a task to be completed but a profound opportunity to shape the very essence of Paranova. Knowing that his creations were boundless to the Shapers will and had unlimited potential to live freely in the world that the Shapers provided. As the Provisioner shifted his focus forward, he promised to accept all uncertainty, grow from the upcoming challenges, and guide the races of mortals to a better future that was full of harmony with life.

The diverse ecosystem inspired him to create many diverse intelligent species where all could live and roam together in harmony. The Provisioner's fleeting thought held him together in his mental space; he had clung to it to keep him steady as the ominous memories from the creation chamber would serve as reminders.

As the Provisioner thought about the tormented souls and the unexpected chaos that had occurred in the creation chamber, his thoughts drifted to the visions that the Oracle had seen in the past. He couldn't shake the feeling that her foresight had predicted these disturbing events and that she had seen the disruption that was now afflicting their sanctuary unknown to the Provisioner.

What would have happened if he had stopped and listened to the Oracle? Would stopping the creation cause even worse outcomes than this? Or why did she not see the corruption? These thoughts quickly overshadowed his positivity. He knew he must seek out the Oracle and inform her of the events that had unfolded inside the creation chamber.

Filled with queries and uncertainty, the Provisioner hastened to seek peace from the Oracle in her sacred dwelling. Upon entering, he was instantly overwhelmed by an overpowering sight that pierced him deeply. Witnessing her anguish struck a chord within him, leaving a lasting mark. Aware of the consistent urgency enveloping their surroundings, he knew vigilance dictated discretion when discussing his own predicaments within those walls. Deep sorrow encased within the Oracle's eyes, which replaced any trace of hope that might have dwelled there previously. No longer radiating luminance as before, she seemed entangled in a mesh of utter despair.

The Provisioner approached the Oracle slowly and carefully. He was not sure how to convey the events that unfolded, but with a deep breath and his voice filling with compassion and determination. He relayed to her the events that had unfolded in the creation chamber, the tormenting souls, and the inexplicable screams that filled the air. He sought her guidance, hoping that her wisdom and insight could shed light on the nature of this disturbance and offer a glimmer of hope in their darkest hour. However, as he spoke, the Oracle's eyes which were usually filled with deep understanding, only seemed clouded with a sad defeat and quivering lips. He felt sad that he was listing off more problems for her to bear. A sense of guilt gathered around him.

She listened intently, her gaze fixed on a distant point, as if trapped within her own visions. It was clear that she too was struggling with the weight of the unfolding chaos, unable to find peace or answers within her own foresight. She gave the Provisioner a faint smile and would nod to let him know that she could hear him; however, she could not speak as it was too hard for her to process everything between what she witnessed and what the Provisioner had explained to her. Everything seemed to be pieces of a grand puzzle and she could not gain a foothold within her mind to piece them back together.

The Provisioner felt a hard feeling of sorrow and empathy, realizing that both their destinies had become entwined in this moment of uncertainty and despair. He longed to alleviate the Oracle's burden, to restore her hope and faith in their shared purpose, but as he gazed at her, he also recognized the immense strength within her, even in the face of apparent hopelessness. He had worked alongside his partner for what they would call a "celestenial time." He knew that she would bounce back, but she needed his comfort and optimism to overcome this darkness.

Amidst all the sadness and chaos, the Provisioner turned his attention to consoling the Oracle; she had lost her sight in the disruptive aftermath of the corruption. With words of comfort and reassurance, he sought to lift her spirits, reminding her that the power was not only from her visions, but she also saw more than the future and the importance of her role in shaping the future of Paranova.

Optimism became their guiding light amidst the darkness that had befallen them. He reminded her that she is brilliant; without her real vision, she could see things that other Shapers could not imagine. He called it the "Graph" that only the two had shared together in an intimate setting before. The Provisioner and the Oracle shared laughter upon him brining the graph up, but the Oracle knew he was right. She had a vision for the world and so did he.

As the Provisioner spoke with the Oracle, his words of reassurance and steadfast belief in their shared vision began to mend the wounds of her lost sight. The Oracle, once plagued by doubts and uncertainty, felt a renewed sense of confidence stirring within her. The Provisioner's optimism and determination ignited a spark of hope, reminding her of the immense potential that lay within the mortal races and their capacity to shape the destiny of Paranova.

The Oracle's doubts vanished with each word the Provisioner spoke, replacing them with a strong sense of purpose. She realized that her role, though changed by her loss of sight, was far from diminished. She was able to see the fateful threads tying together the mortal races and the tapestry of Paranova thanks to intuition and ancient wisdom that sharpened her inner vision. The Provisioner had a knack for consoling her worries and gave her confidence in all of her decisions.

Embracing her new role as a guide and advisor, the Oracle resolved to use her intelligent insights and connection to the cosmic energies to empower the mortal races on their journey. She understood that her lack of physical sight did not hinder her ability to see the potential within each individual and to seek out the hidden paths that led to harmony and enlightenment. The Oracle's confidence soared as she fully embraced her role as a beacon of wisdom and guidance, ready to offer her unwavering support to the mortal races as they ventured forth into the uncharted world of Paranova.

The Oracle frequently meditates while in her sanctuary, away from the Order sector and the other shapers. This had always given her clarity and serenity. She thanked the Provisioner for his support and had asked the Provisioner to leave. She kneeled in her meditation area and cried for the first time. She had a fear of losing her sight and did not think it would ever happen.

As the Oracle attempted to glimpse into the future, she felt a deep loss. Her once keen sight, capable of traversing the vast expanse of possibilities, had faltered and failed her. No matter how hard she tried, the threads of destiny remained shrouded in darkness, elusive, and unattainable. Yet, amidst her frustration and despair, the words of the Provisioner resonated within her. His unwavering support and belief in her abilities touched a chord deep within her heart. In his presence, she found peace and a glimmer of hope. She realized that, while her sight may have abandoned her, her insight and wisdom still held great power.

The end of her meditation gave her a feeling of a new sense of purpose, and the Oracle embraced her role as the Provisioner's guide. She would offer him the depths of her knowledge and the wealth of her perception, drawing upon her past encounters and the wisdom that lay within her core. Though blind to the future, she would become a shining light of guidance, relying on her intuition and the bond she shared with the Provisioner to navigate the challenging journey that lay ahead. As she stood up, looking out to the horizon and seeing Paranova and its beauty, she thought to herself that together they could build anything.

While he was in his own quarters, the Provisioner reflected on when he met with the Oracle. Seeing that his words and his attempt at consolation influenced her made him feel better. Their journey to this point together prompted him to reflect on their past actions. These thoughts encouraged him because they made him feel confident in his passion.

While in this clarity state of mind, he focused his attention on his first sapient creation, and they would be known as the Elves. The Provisioner found security in their magic and their relentless pursuit of order and knowledge. The elves originated as inquisitive beings with innate grace and a strong connection to the elements. They took on the responsibility of deciding the fate of Paranova and thus became keepers of knowledge and keepers of harmony. The Provisioner took great pride in his creation; he wanted these elves to be an image of himself, the Oracle, and the Order sector.

As the Elves set out on their journey, their first encounters with the world reflected their desire to bring about peace and harmony. They supported the growth of the mountains, rivers, and woods, all the while recognizing the mystical potential within themselves. The tree and stone avatars, animated representations of the Shapers' essence, became their strong allies, guiding their actions while providing them with a fresh perspective on the world they wished to preserve.

In all aspects of creation, the Forger used his skilled hands and infinite imagination to give life to the landscapes of Paranova. With each stroke of his celestial world-crafting, cities appeared from the depths of his imagination. Majestic spires reached for the heavens, intricately carved and glittering with the essence of magic. Bustling markets, lively festivals, and majestic gatherings filled the streets with an exhilarating spirit. The Forger's cities were architectural marvels meant to serve as evidence of mortal creativity and the everlasting flame of inspiration.

The Forger's touch resulted in the emergence of lush woodlands that murmured long-forgotten information within the beautiful tapestry that was Paranova. There was a hallowed canopy of trees that towered overhead, protecting the forest's inhabitants from the elements. The sunlight penetrating the lush greenery caused the shaded light to pour onto the forest floor, where a symphony of life had been flourishing. Rivers and streams wound their way across the lush landscape, their clean waters satisfying the needs of every living thing. Magical animals and creatures found refuge among the ancient trees. Their presence added an enchanting aura to the natural beauty of the Forger's creation.

The Forger's skilled hands formed stunning lakes all over the world, their peaceful surfaces reflecting the vibrant colors of the surrounding landscape. These calm bodies of water became safe havens for animals of all sizes, providing peace and quiet in an otherwise unpredictable world. There were islands in the oceans and lakes, their sandy shores beckoning to weary travelers and offering an opportunity for discovery and adventure. Each island had its own special allure and mysteries for those who were brave enough to explore them. These unknown territories brought myth and legend to the mortals of Paranova, stories to be told to their youth, which inspired many to explore.

Perhaps the most awe-inspiring were the gigantic trees and structures that rose like titans from the earth, their roots reaching deep into the heart of Paranova. These colossal beings stood as guardians of ancient wisdom, their immense presence a living proof of the power of nature and the wonders that magic could shape. Within their towering trunks, magical essences flowed, infusing the surrounding lands with mystical energies. These structures, whether towering castles or ethereal sanctuaries, held the essence of the divine, serving as beacons of hope, knowledge, and spiritual enlightenment.

Through the Forger's careful craftsmanship, cities grew, forests breathed, rivers flowed, and islands called out to be explored. Under his skilled hand, the world of Paranova blossomed into existence, serving as a testament to the endless imagination and infinite possibilities that lay within the realm of creation. The forger was proud of his wonderful creations; he was not ideal for maintaining them, however. He enlisted a longtime friend and co-worker within the Order sector to help keep the avatars in check with their duties and tend the landscapes of Paranova.

The Keeper, who was entrusted with keeping a close watch on the avatars, understood the delicate balance between guidance and independence. While the avatars encouraged communication between the shapers and the mortal races, the Keeper desired to empower the races to forge their own paths and gain wisdom through their own experiences. He knew plenty about how individuals grow and learn, so he thought that true understanding and self-realization could only come from personal exploration and the lessons learned along the way. He recognized that the mortal races had an innate curiosity and thirst for knowledge that, if properly nurtured, could lead to extensive revelations and growth.

Instead of imposing rigid rules, the Keeper encouraged the races to seek their own explorations. He thought that the avatars, who could see the world from different points of view, would give subtle nudges and hints that would help the races find hidden truths and make their own decisions. The Keeper saw the process of self-discovery as valuable, knowing that the wisdom gained through personal triumphs and struggles would be far more extreme than any dictated knowledge.

In his interactions with the mortal races, the Keeper found a delicate balance. He was patient and kind as he led them to discover their own answers. He shared glimpses of the world's wonders via the avatars, encouraging the races to explore, experiment, and embrace their innate potential.

The Keeper's noble path was deeply intertwined with the ancient wisdom that the races were blessed with an innate potential for boundless growth and the ability to shape their own path in life. He viewed himself as a mediator, a protector of possibilities, who would enable the races to negotiate the complexities of Paranova and determine their own fates.

The Keeper aspired to instill a deeper appreciation for personal strengths and individual contributions in mortals through fostering independence and self-reliance. Recognizing that the true allure of their voyage lay not only in reaching their ultimate goal but also in the immense potential for transformation given off within each unique encounter.

The Keeper's advice had been subtle, but it had a big impact. It enabled mortal cultures to establish their own courses, make their own discoveries, and unearth the vast wisdom that had laid dormant within themselves. His firm belief in their potential served as a compass, inspiring the races to navigate the intricate tapestry of Paranova and uncover the truths that would shape their paths in life.

Beholding the wondrous transformations brought forth by the mystical Forger and the wise Keeper, the Oracle's heart swelled with elation. In the depths of her mind, she reawakened the remains of distant memories, tapping into her old sketches of visions and dreams.

She would often view the desire of the mortal races, searching for strong foundations and places of refuge they could proudly claim as their own. In her boundless wisdom, she ventured forth to seek the aid of the Forger, a legendary Shaper whose name echoed through the celestial realms, celebrated for his unparalleled mastery in the art of construction and world-crafting.

The Forger emerged as the ideal comrade in the grand work of crafting her visions; he did so with detailed sketches of kingdoms throughout the sprawling world of Paranova. The Forger set out on his mission to build magnificent kingdoms in prominent geographic positions, and he did so with the utmost attention and fierce adoration. The first one was constructed in the eastern part of the continents, directly in the heart among some verdant surroundings and some fertile plains. It was envisioned as a shining example of wealth and abundance, a place where mortals of all races could seek refuge and create a thriving community for themselves.

He envisioned this kingdom teeming with vibrant energy and industrious creativity. His vision enveloped a kingdom built upon innovation, where towering factories and workshops would hum with the rhythmic symphony of machinery and skilled artisans. The kingdom would be renowned for its mastery of craftsmanship and technological advancements, with the Forger's touch evident in every intricate detail.

As the first rays of sunlight peeked over the horizon in the east and painted the kingdom's busy streets and thriving marketplaces with their ethereal golden glow, the Forger envisioned a society fueled by vitality and intensity for advancement. The land to the east was destined to become an embodiment of mortal imagination, with its innovations serving as a source of immense joy for its mortals and a wellspring of motivation for all the other Paranova inhabitants.

In the heart of the continent, amidst grand mountains and rapid rivers, arose an empire—the second kingdom. Determined to create a stronghold that would withstand the ages, the Forger centered their efforts on constructing a fortress for the inhabitants to feel secure and united within its walls. The Oracle had a vision of an essential kingdom located in the center of Paranova that would function as an economic center for the mortal races in terms of unity, knowledge, and collaboration.

This kingdom would stand out for having a vast cityscape that was filled with beautiful libraries, ornate monuments, and bustling markets. It would be a place where mortals of different races would come together to discuss various topics, give one another advice, and engage in other intellectual pursuits. The Oracle saw this central kingdom as a beacon of enlightenment, where scholars, philosophers, and artisans from every region of Paranova would come together, fostering a spirit of discovery and innovation. The Forger believed that the architectural marvels of the kingdom and the harmonious blend of different cultures would demonstrate the variety and connection of mortal groups of sapience, thereby representing the Oracle's belief in the power of unity and shared knowledge.

Lastly, the Forger constructed a kingdom in Paranova's south, overlooking the mighty and fiery volcano. The kingdom's foundations were laid in volcanic plains and rocky terrain, creating an interesting contrast between the volcano's raw power and the elegant structures that emerged from its surroundings.

The Forger's exceptional skill and artistic vision were on full display in each kingdom. The diverse characteristics of the mortal races and their aspirations were reflected in the kingdom's elaborate decorations, which included towering citadels, intricate architecture, and harmonious landscapes. The Forger put his whole being into every one of his buildings, infusing each of them with a sense of splendor and significance as he worked.

This kingdom, according to the Oracle, would be a place of opportunity and difficulty where the mortal races could use the volcano's elemental energies to their advantage. This was a test in the eyes of the Oracle, as she knew living in the territory would bring upon a harsh living standard, but she recalled in her old visions of a resilient race that was resourceful. The blazingly hot environment and geothermal resources offered a singular setting for the evolution of the mortals living in this kingdom, encouraging a spirit of inventiveness and determination. The land had its own uniqueness around it, though to the eyes of a mortal it may not seem as much; it was a secret yet to be discovered.

The kingdom's proximity to the fiery volcano was a constant reminder of the dangerously beautiful and ever-shifting nature of their kingdom. It whispered tales of lost magic and whispered secrets about the need to embrace transformation and rebirth. From the vantage point of the kingdom, perched high above the swirling mists and glowing lava, the mortal races would witness the raw power of the volcano and gain a deeper appreciation for the forces that shaped their world. The Oracle believed that this awe-inspiring spectacle would inspire the races to tap into their inner strength and ignite the flames of their own creativity and ambition.

The Oracle's passionate hope was for the mortal races, under the watchful guidance of the cosmic avatars and stimulated by their passionate thirst for knowledge, to go forth on daring quests and the opportunity towards captivating places of beauty. In her heart, she held a firm belief that discovering these ancient kingdoms would create an intense wonder and a deep feeling of similarity among the races. It would draw them to embrace these mysterious places as their rightful homes, where they could shape their paths and weave their lives together within the impenetrable fortresses of security.

Through the collaboration of the Oracle and the Forger, the foundations were laid for the mortal races to uncover the hidden vast kingdoms and foundations for cities that lay scattered across the lands. It was proof of their shared vision and steadfast commitment to provide the races with a sense of place and belonging. As the kingdoms stood in all their magnificence, their allure beckoned the mortal races, promising a future filled with promise, growth, and the realization of their deepest aspirations. It was a sense of connection to the world and its sapience.

Meanwhile, within the realm of chaos, the Chaos sector responded to the creation of the elven kind by guiding their own distinct race known as the Dark Ones. They were the outcome of a creation that Archon and her fanatical partner Havoc had ruined through the agony and suffering of countless souls.

The Dark Ones had possessed traits like those of elves; however, the race was contaminated by the creation that the Provisioner intended and emerged as mutated shadows of the elven kind. They also had a knack for causing disruption and chaos. The dark ones appeared with pale skin and an aura of mystery. They took immense pleasure in their chaotic nature, sowing discord and actively challenging the existing order. Their eyes were gloomy, and they possessed angled ears along with razor-sharp teeth. They referred to their counterparts as the Light Ones or Light Elves because they gave off an aura of energy and life. The elves considered the dark ones as horrific creatures, contrasting them strongly as their opposition to what they represented.

With the dark ones, when they journeyed on their own personal voyage, they unknowingly provoked the disorder within themselves by engaging with the external world. This interaction heightened the chaos that was already deeply ingrained in their beings. They created a disturbance in the darkness, moved with a sense of unpredictability, and left in their wake the aftermath of affected lives as they sought to alter and manipulate others. Their very existence acted as a check and balance on the elven efforts to create harmony, thereby influencing the path between the two races distancing themselves from one another.

As the dark ones roamed the lands of Paranova, a mysterious and powerful force beckoned to them from the heart of the volcano. They were pulled to it as if it were a force of divinity that they could not resist. They marched forward, their pale faces glowing with the mystical light that came from the inferno. The forces stirring within the volcano were calling out to the Dark Ones, which they were not yet aware of. The signaling of it did not come as words but as a feeling—a burning desire they had never known.

As the dark ones made it up the steep slopes to the top, their eyes showed them an empty kingdom. The large structures nestled on the top of the mountain look just as if they have been lit by fire from the volcano, seemingly carved from the very essence of lava and molten rock. The dark ones, filled with a sense of destiny, believed that this was the dwelling place of their god, a sacred haven crafted specifically for them. In the presence of the towering structures and the fiery glow of the volcano, they felt a deep connection and a deep understanding that they had arrived at their true home.

As the Dark Ones established their newfound kingdom atop the volcano, a belief system began to form among them that centered around the worship of Pyrothos, the Eternal Ember, who was a powerful and ancient god. In the Dark One newfound culture, Pyrothos represented the unstoppable and all-consuming power of chaos and destruction who would accumulate and shape chaotic energies until the world was consumed in inferno, creating a clean slate for rebirth. They believed that Pyrothos could change the reality around them and reshape matter according to its will. These representations became the core of the dark one's belief system.

The dark ones gave Pyrothos passionate prayers and praises as they immersed themselves in rituals and ceremonies driven by their devotion. They communed with the spectral avatars, emissaries of chaos, who whispered secrets of ancient knowledge and whispered of the chaotic power that lay dormant within their souls. The dark ones believed that by harnessing the chaotic energies and embracing the fiery wrath of Pyrothos, they could align themselves with the divine will and become agents of transformation.

Their communion with the spectral avatars deepened their connection to the chaos sector unknowingly, as Havoc and the Archon manipulated the mortal's desires, exploiting their passion for their own twisted purposes. The dark ones, drawn in by the chaos' allure, turned into willing conduits, and Pyrothos, their revered Fire God, served as the inspiration for their deeds. Pyrothos' faith promised both destruction and rebirth.

In their consistent devotion to Pyrothos, the dark ones embraced a practice of sacrificial rituals. They believed that through the offering of lives and the release of blood, they could appease the fiery deity and strengthen their bond with the chaotic forces of the world. In twisted ceremonies conducted within the shadowy depths of their volcanic kingdom, they would select individuals from their own ranks or from captive creatures, viewing them as vessels of sacrifice to feed the insatiable hunger of Pyrothos. During the rituals, dark ones would gather atop the volcano to join in celebration.

Chants and incantations that reverberated through the volcano's chambers accompanied these sacrificial rituals, turning them into a sinister spectacle of maniacal passion. As the flames danced and the smoke swirled, the dark ones believed that their offerings fueled the inevitable awakening of Pyrothos by stoking the fires of chaos and destruction. The sacrificed lives were seen as sacred conduits, their essence merging with the volatile energies of the volcano, amplifying the power of the fire god they revered.

The Dark Ones, driven by their twisted faith and the manipulations of the spectral avatars, willingly partook in these gruesome rites, convinced that their sacrifices played a vital role in the grand design of Pyrothos. They perceived themselves as instruments of chaos, carrying out their unholy duty to fan the flames that would bring about the cataclysmic renewal that their fiery deity had in mind. It was in these wicked rituals that the dark ones sought both communion with Pyrothos and the fulfillment of their own desires for chaos and destruction. Not all of the dark one kind celebrated these rituals; however, they would continue their daily lives knowing that their God may have provided them everything, but their God would come on its own time and did not need fuel as the deity is the Eternal Ember itself.

....

While discussing with the Provisioner, the Archon wanted to bring about some form of chaos in the stance of the creatures of Paranova. She had informed the Provisioner that there were too many passive creatures that could not defend themselves from the newly created mortals. She had ideas in mind for designs of creatures in the world that would stand against mortals and prey on other creatures. The Provisioner was hesitant at first, but he did want to blend the Order and Chaos sectors together in the world-building process. The Archon pressed about the creatures and mortals to ensure that balance was the goal.

With the Provisioner's blessing, the Archon unleashed her creative powers to bring forth a host of predatory creatures upon the vast expanse of Paranova. The creatures rose from the depths of the ocean and down from the towering mountains, conquering their surroundings to find food necessary for sustenance. These apex creatures fiercely emerged, with each beast embodying the primal instincts of hunting and survival. Teeth and claws, sleek bodies, and ferocious gazes became the defining features of these living predators. Some creatures that slipped past the Order sectors watchful nature were gigantic but were only of a few in remote areas. The Archon found pleasure in the potential of these massive beasts causing chaos—a natural balance to the once peaceful world.

As the creatures roamed the diverse landscapes of Paranova, a delicate dance of life and death unfolded. The newly created predators became the apex hunters, their predatory nature driving them to seek out and capture their prey. A harmonious, albeit ruthless, balance was established as they became the crucial components of the intricate food chain that spanned across the world.

From swift and cunning predators stalking their prey in the thick jungles to mighty winged creatures swooping down from the skies, the Archon's creations brought both awe and fear to the other living creatures of Paranova. Survival became an art, and the prey species developed their own strategies to avoid detection and escape the jaws of their relentless pursuers. Adaptation became the key to survival as evolution played out in a never-ending cycle of predator and prey.

The presence of these living creatures, with their predatory traits, transformed Paranova into a world pulsating with the rhythm of life. As the balance of nature found its balance, the interdependence of all creatures became apparent. One can see that while the predators were fierce and terrifying they played an important role in the health and vibrancy of the ecosystems they inhabited. It was no wonder why many mortals feared these dreadful creatures and beasts that lurked in their domains. The predatory creatures also became a thrill for the brave mortals of Paranova and provided them with a sport of hunting.

Through the Archon's collaboration with the Provisioner, the cycle of life and death took on a vivid intensity across Paranova. From the smallest of insects to the largest of beasts, each played their part in the intricate circle of life. Amidst it all, the Archon's predatory creations stood as a tribute to the raw power and adamant force of nature, shaping the destiny of Paranova with every heartbeat and every hunt. The Provisioner was proud that together, Order and Chaos could become in tune with each other to create and maintain balance. The Archon realized that even with her insidious thoughts and desires, she could imagine them working together in harmony. She smiled for the first time since working with the Provisioner, without remorse for what she had secretly done to his partner.

After a fleeting moment of positivity between the Provisioner and the Archon, the serene atmosphere was abruptly shattered as the Shaper guards stormed through the winding corridors, their urgency noticeable. In their custody, they held another shaper from the chaos sector, who was accused of the attempted assassination responsible for the attack on the Oracle, leaving her suppressed of her unique gift of sight.

The Provisioner's smile widened as he glimpsed undeniable evidence: stolen sketches from the Oracle's sacred sanctuary, now in the hands of the accused shaper. Anguish and rage boiled within the Archon, seemingly driven by a seething need for her plan to work, and she lunged at the alleged assassin. It took the swift intervention of the Provisioner to quell the rising tempest, pulling them apart and preventing an impulsive act of violence.

The Archon claimed that it was her sector, she was acting leader, and it was her responsibility to take care of the prisoner, but the Provisioner interrupted her and told the Archon that he would be taking the shaper to be interrogated by himself. The Archon had faith that her planted assassin wouldn't expose her secrets, but she couldn't take any chances, so she came up with a plan for Havoc to sneak into the holding cell and kill the shaper before they could reveal their purpose.

. . . .

As the Spectral avatars roamed the mortal realm, they enacted Havoc's secret devious plan with sinister precision. These ethereal beings, shrouded in the essence of the transition realm, became harbingers of doom for unsuspecting mortals. With their allure and deceptive charms, they lured countless souls into their grasp, drawing them into the depths of the transitional ethereal realm.

Once captured, these unfortunate individuals discovered that the spectral was consuming and siphoning their souls, imprisoning them in an endless torment. Their cries of suffering and sounds of hopelessness reverberated throughout the ghostly dimension, creating a chilling symphony that harmonized with darkness and caused uneasiness for everyone it reached.

Those caught by the lure of the spectral avatar would suffer an excruciating fate as their soul was violently torn from their mortal body, causing intense agony. Casting their soul into the ethereal realm, a faint space between the mortal world and the ethereal plane, their haunting soul is left in unending torment, yearning for belonging and purpose. Stripped of peace in the afterlife or the possibility of reincarnation, the soul exists in eternal unrest, their identity shattered.

The tales of these lost souls and their gruesome fate spread among the elves who recounted the chilling legends as cautionary bedtime stories. Parents would hush their children with whispered tales of the insidious spectral whispers and the dire consequences of falling prey to their enchantment. It became a tale of caution, a reminder of the uncertainty that awaited those who strayed too close to the harbingers of the ethereal realm.

Little did the mortals know that their suffering served a greater purpose within Havoc's grand plan. The energy harnessed from their tormented souls fueled the ethereal realm, strengthening its connection to the mortal realm and feeding Havoc's insatiable hunger for power. The screams and moans of the lost mortals became the ethereal chorus that echoed through the transition realm, a siren's call drawing more unsuspecting victims into its grasp. The mortals would hear beautiful songs or see tempting visions when in proximity to a spectral avatar. As Havoc didn't want the Order sector or the other avatars to notice these events, he took care to keep them hidden. Not all spectral avatars accepted Havoc as their keeper, as he was arrogant, demanding, and insufferable to communicate with.

Amidst these wicked unfolding events, the Keeper, ever watchful and vigilant, began to harbor concerns as he sensed the presence of the spectral avatars created by Havoc. He felt an unease at the thought of their manipulative ways and the potential threat they posed to the delicate balance woven by the Shapers. His duty to protect the avatars and the world they inhabited weighed heavily on his shoulders. The purpose that the spectral avatars served to the Chaos sector was for observation and information in areas unreachable to the other avatars; however, the insidious intentions behind Havoc have shown suspicions within them and their actions to the Keeper.

Recognizing the need for vigilance and information, the Keeper devised a unique strategy to gather intelligence on the activities of the dark ones and the spectral avatars in the volcanic region. Using his ancient knowledge of shaper magic, he imbued small plants with a fraction of his essence, shaping them into delicate and resilient seedlings. These seedlings, adorned with vibrant petals and glowing tendrils, served as messengers and scouts within the treacherous landscape of the volcano.

The Keeper released these seedling avatars into the volcanic region, entrusting them with the vital task of observing and gathering information. They would stealthily navigate the rugged terrain, their small forms allowing them to go unnoticed by the dark ones and the spectral avatars. These botanical messengers possessed a strange ability to absorb and interpret the energies and vibrations appearing in their surroundings, enabling them to perceive the subtle fluctuations of chaos and the sinister deceptions at play.

Through this creative method of communication, the seedling avatars would relay their findings back to the Keeper, sharing glimpses of the dark ones' rituals, the accused manipulations of the spectral avatars, and the growing influence of Pyrothos. The messages encoded within the plants vibrant petals and glowing tendrils contained vital information, a witness to the Keeper's resourcefulness and unwavering dedication to maintaining balance and protecting the mortal races from the threatening forces of chaos.

With each seedling's return and the transmission of its message, the Keeper would gain valuable insights into the unfolding events in the volcanic region. Armed with this knowledge, he could strategize, coordinate with the tree and stone avatars, and guide the mortal races towards countering the wicked plans of the dark ones and the mysterious benefactors behind the manipulations. The seedling avatars became the silent sentinels of the Keeper's watchful eye, enabling him to stay one step ahead in the intricate dance of order and chaos that unfolded across Paranova.

The Keeper became overwhelmed with a sense of dread and horror as he saw what the spectral avatars would do to the unsuspecting mortals. He'd strive to maintain balance through his avatars and to keep peace and harmony within the lands of the mortal races. The revelations of the spectral avatar's sinister intentions struck the Keeper to his core. He had dedicated himself to safeguarding the mortals, guiding them towards enlightenment and growth. The notion that these ethereal beings, under the influence of Havoc's wicked schemes, sought to manipulate and consume the souls of innocent mortals filled the Keeper with an overwhelming sense of outrage and despair.

As the Keeper kept watch over the mysteries surrounding the spectral avatars, he understood that patience was needed in order for him to uncover their devious intentions. The intricacies of their plans and movements were evasive, and their motivations were difficult to comprehend; they were veiled in shadows and deception. The Keeper understood that rushing into action without a thorough understanding would only lead to his watchful eye being detected and would result in an elusive uncertainty. With a calm and measured demeanor, the Keeper observed and analyzed the movements of the spectral avatars. He studied their patterns, their interactions with mortals, and the effects of their ethereal influence. Every piece of information, no matter how small, was carefully cataloged and examined, forming a network of understanding.

As the Keeper continued to explore the deception behind the spectral avatars, he began to ponder what plan he could come up with to prove who was a true avatar and who was deceiving the Shapers. And what did it mean to him? He recognized that these ethereal entities held an aversion to the other avatars crafted by the Shapers. They seemed to fear or avoid direct encounters, fleeing whenever other avatars approached them.

With this realization, the Keeper saw an opportunity. He summoned the Tree and Stone Avatars, sharing his observations and formulating a strategy to keep the spectral avatars occupied and away from mortals. The tree avatars, with their deep connection to nature, would spread their branches and roots across the land, creating a protective barrier that the spectral avatars would instinctively shy away from. Meanwhile, the stone avatars would patrol the borders, their imposing presence deterring any aggression from the spectral avatars.

The Keeper's plan relied on keeping the spectral avatars busy and contained away from civilization, allowing him to focus on unraveling the mystery behind their intentions. He tasked the avatars with vigilance, sending them to areas where the spectral figures were known to appear. Whenever a spectral avatar attempted to cross borders, get close to mortals, or lure unsuspecting souls into their clutches, the other avatars would intercept them, driving them back with their formidable presence.

Despite the initial shock and confusion caused by the spectral avatars' unexpected behavior, the Keeper's keen observation and insightful intuition allowed him to perceive a pattern. While some spectral avatars sought to consume the souls of mortals, there were many who chose a different path. These spectral avatars, rather than feasting on mortal essence, sought to establish a connection and commune with the inhabitants of Paranova.

This revelation presented a new challenge for the Keeper. While he remained steadfast in his mission to protect the mortal realms from the sinister intentions of the spectrals, he also recognized the delicate balance between Order and Chaos. The Provisioner's earlier words echoed in his mind, reminding him of the Chaos sector's role in the creation process. The Keeper understood that not all actions stemming from chaos were inherently nefarious and that some interactions between the spectrals and mortals could serve a purpose beyond immediate comprehension.

With this understanding, the Keeper made a calculated decision. He allowed the spectral avatars that sought communion to establish contact with mortals, albeit under his watchful eye. He closely monitored these interactions, ensuring that they did not result in harm or manipulation. The Keeper's perceptive judgment and ability to determine intentions allowed him to distinguish between genuine connections and deceitful schemes.

Recognizing the urgency of the situation, the Keeper sought counsel from the Provisioner. He relayed his findings, expressing his concerns about the spectral avatars' dual nature and the potential threats to Paranova. The Provisioner listened attentively, acknowledging the Keeper's vigilance and determination in handling the situation. He affirmed his trust in the Keeper's judgment, emphasizing the importance of maintaining the delicate balance between Order and Chaos.

With the Keeper's intense resolve and the Provisioner's support, a unified front was established to address the complexities posed by the spectrals. The Keeper continued his detailed observations, studying the behavior of both consuming and communicating spectral avatars. He sought to unravel the deeper motivations and intentions behind these ethereal entities, driven by a relentless pursuit of understanding and the preservation of Paranova. The Keeper concocted plants that when consumed, brought great health benefits to the living creatures of Paranova. He had infused a dye that was tied to the soul of a mortal and was only shown when a spectral avatar would consume a living being. They would become more visible and change hues in their ethereal forms. This gave the Keeper more control to understand which spectrals were evil and which were carrying out the Chaos sectors duties.

As the Keeper navigated the intricate dwellings of the spectral avatars' actions, he remained steadfast in his commitment to protecting the life on Paranova. He recognized the significance of his role as a guardian and mediator between the realms of Order and Chaos. The Keeper's vigilance ensured that the delicate balance between creation and destruction was upheld, even amidst the mysterious nature of the spectral presence.

....

Undeterred by the disruption that has been caused by mysterious circumstances secretly curated by the Archon and Havoc, the Provisioner remained steadfast in his pursuit of the Oracle's vision. He held onto the belief that, despite the challenges and setbacks, his grand plan to create a sapient race aligned with the harmony and order the Oracle had foreseen. The Provisioner's optimism became a beacon of hope, driving him forward in his quest to manifest the Oracle's vision.

In his stubborn pursuit of unity, the Provisioner devised a daring plan to forge two more races that would embody the delicate balance between order and chaos, seeking to find common ground with the Archon so she would agree with his creation. With careful planning, he crafted a blueprint for the next race, imbuing them with the essence of innovation, curiosity, and intellectual prowess. These life forms would crave information while wholeheartedly embracing the principle behind order because of their insatiable curiosity and determination to push the boundaries of what is possible and probable.

Simultaneously, he breathed his celestial essence into another race, focusing his energy to gift them with a vibrant spirit, boundless energy, and a deep connection to the primal forces of nature. They would be the symbol of controlled chaos, embracing spontaneity and freedom, and finding comfort in the ever-changing flows of existence. With these two races, the Provisioner hoped to present the Archon with proof of the harmonious coexistence of order and chaos, offering her a vision of unity where innovation and spirit intertwined, fostering a shared destiny for Paranova.

When the Provisioner unveiled his intricate blueprints for two potential new races, he couldn't help but notice an underlying tension in the room, even with his limited perception. The Archon appeared conflicted. Her initial response was marked with intrigue and happiness, but a faint frown on her face revealed her unease as she looked over the sketching. Despite a sense of appreciation for the Provisioner's inclusion in his plans, she departed hastily, leaving behind a cloud of mixed emotions. It was as though a gust of uncertainty had swept through the room, leaving many questions yet to be answered.

In the hidden depths of her chambers, the Archon scoured over the stolen sketches from the Oracle's sacred sanctuary. Her eyes fell upon the design for a colossal race intended for another world. In the dimly lit chamber, a sinister smile played upon her lips. She fully grasped her own limitations compared to the Provisioner's immense shaping talents, but his gesture did not quench her ambition. Rather, it stoked the fires of a devious plan taking root within her mind. She was ready to venture into the uncertain, not bound by the Order sector. She wanted to bring her own vision to life, whatever the cost.

Despite momentarily reveling in the Provisioner's act of kindness and the creation of the balanced races, the Archon's thirst for power and desire to assert her own mastery as a shaper overwhelmed her. Fueled by ambition and envy, she went into the creation chamber and retaliated by birthing the Gantum race—gigantic, disfigured beings with immense physical strength who lacked intellect and harmony. They became rash of emotion and had an impulse for destruction, pawns in the Archon's bid to disrupt the carefully woven tapestry of order and chaos, intended to sow chaos and undermine the Provisioner's vision.

The Archon's actions were a test of her stubborn determination to assert her own dominance and challenge the delicate balance that the Provisioner sought to achieve. With this twisted act of creation, she designed them as instruments of destruction, bent on wreaking havoc upon the world she perceived as an obstacle to her chaotic reign.

The Gantum race fell short of the ideal envisioned in the original sketches, much to the Archon's chagrin. Her ambitions, driven by a dark determination, had led her down a path far removed from the Provisioner and the Oracle's intentions for these colossal beings. Her interference and lack of skill during their creation had resulted in a disfigured, monstrous race that bore little resemblance to the grand vision that had inspired it.

In her moment of triumph, however, the Archon seemed oblivious to the consequences of her actions. Her pride swelled, blinding her to the potential repercussions that might soon threaten the world of Paranova. The celebration of her achievement echoed through her chambers, while the true extent of her deviation from the original design remained shrouded in shadow, a foreboding omen of things to come.

Tensions simmered between the two powerful beings entrusted with the responsibility of shaping the world of Paranova. While they were supposed to work in harmony, collaborating to bring forth a balanced creation, their differing perspectives and desires threatened to strain their relationship. She was constantly jealous of the creativity that the Provisioner had in his alignment. Chaos represents creativity, and she did not like that the Provisioner himself seemed to be the most creative of all the shapers.

As the Provisioner witnessed the Archon's independent creative ventures, he felt a growing sense of frustration. He believed that the act of creation should be solely entrusted to his hands, for he held the conviction that his vision alone would bring about the desired balance that all sectors seek to achieve. In his eyes, the Archon's involvement threatened his domain and diluted the purity of his creative intentions. He was appalled that she would go out to create something that had so much consequence and posed a threat to all of what they had worked hard to create. Even more so, she did not follow her orders from the Anarchist and did not come to either of them for guidance or wisdom.

The Provisioner confronted the Archon and expressed his concerns and frustrations because of his conviction. He voiced his belief in the importance of unity and faithfulness to their shared purpose. However, the Archon, weary of being overshadowed and desiring recognition for her own contributions, grew defiant. She expressed her yearning for a share of the limelight, insisting that her creative struggles held their own brilliance and significance.

During their confrontation, the Provisioner recognized the validity of the Archon's perspective. He understood her desire for recognition and her belief in the value of her own creative limitations. Yet he remained resolute in his belief that the balance of creation could only be achieved through a singular guiding force. He acknowledged her contributions but firmly stated that he would be the sole creator, entrusted with the responsibility of bringing Paranova to life. He reminded her that together they created the creatures of the world and that she does not need to be forming new sapient races without the proper knowledge and training to fully develop mortals, as they are very complex.

This clash of ideologies, while causing a strain between the Archon and the Provisioner, also served as a catalyst for introspection and growth. They both realized the importance of their individual roles within the grand design of creation. The Provisioner saw the need to acknowledge and respect the Archon's creative contributions, even if they differed from his own. And the Archon, in turn, understood the significance of unity and collaboration in achieving a harmonious outcome.

In a solemn conversation, the Provisioner addressed the Archon, emphasizing the irreversible nature of her actions. The disfigured Gantum race, born from her hasty interference, would take time to evolve or dilute, its fate uncertain and shrouded in unpredictability. With a sense of responsibility, he offered a solution and a chance for the Archon to gain a deeper understanding of the intricate art of creating sapient beings.

He proposed a unique opportunity for her to receive training during the development of the next races he had planned. Through this collaborative effort, the Archon could grasp the complexities and nuances of shaping sapience with care and caution. The Provisioner stressed the significance of allowing the Order to lead the way in sapient creation, highlighting the importance of maintaining order and balance in the universe. Remarkably, even the Anarchist agreed with this approach, signifying the severity of the situation and the need for a unified vision in the wake of the Archon's daring experiment.

The Provisioner, his tone laced with suspicion, probed the Archon's motivations, questioning the reckless path she had chosen. Her response was a veiled deflection, as she hoped to find acceptance in his eyes. She claimed her actions stemmed from a passionate desire to become a creator of sapient beings, a motive that, though sincere, had led to unintended consequences.

As the conversation deepened, the Provisioner's perceptive observation struck a chord. He couldn't help but notice striking similarities between the gantums and the sketches he and the Oracle had crafted together. This led to a pointed question: How had the Archon managed to bring this race to life without any prior knowledge or a blueprint to guide her?

Caught off guard, she faltered, sensing an accusation within his inquiry. Her words grew increasingly flustered as she struggled to explain her actions, eventually placing blame on the Provisioner, asserting that her own visions and abilities were equally valid and that he had no right to question them. Tensions between these powerful shapers simmered, casting a shadow of uncertainty over their collaboration.

The Archon stormed away from the Provisioner as her mind raced with ideas and reflections as she struggled with the realization that the Provisioner's ever-vigilant eyes had picked up on her plans, which she had developed in collaboration with Havoc. Every move they made, every step towards their grand design, had been meticulously observed, leaving them vulnerable and exposed. She wanted the Gantum race to be more evolved from a prototype beast she had created so that they could cause chaos on Paranova.

Hidden deep within her being, a flicker of resolute determination burned. She comprehended the complex road that lay ahead, recognizing that maintaining secrecy and employing cleverness were crucial to achieving their goals. The Archon fully grasped the necessity of shielding her true intentions and skillfully veiling the intricate web she was weaving from her partners. With great consequences at stake, failure simply could not be entertained.

As time elapsed, the burden of accountability continued to bear down on the Archon. She realized that her plans required accuracy, precision, and strategic maneuvers. She could no longer afford to operate in the open, for every action taken would be scrutinized, analyzed, and potentially ineffective. She had to become a master of stealth as she navigated the intricate dance between her aspirations and the prying eyes of the Order sector.

Silently, the Archon resolved to be more discreet, to keep her intentions hidden even from those within her own faction. She knew that to accomplish her grand design, she would need to embrace the art of deception and cunning. She would orchestrate her moves in the shadows, carefully manipulating events and alliances, ensuring that her true objectives remained shrouded in mystery.

•••••••

Observing the emergence of the Giants, the Keeper recognized the imminent threat they posed to the delicate balance of Paranova. With urgency in his voice, he warned the Provisioner of the need for swift action. Realizing the urgency of the situation, the Provisioner responded by creating the Ranuk, smaller versions of the gantum crafted whole and imbued with more alluring and positive traits. The ranuk became a counterbalance, embodying resilience, humility, and a desire for harmony amidst the potential chaos that threatened to engulf the mortal races of Paranova.

In a haste uncharacteristic of his normally deliberate demeanor, the Provisioner spread out his own drafted blueprints of life forms he and the Oracle had envisioned for nascent worlds. His eyes quickly settled on the designs for the Gantum and Ranuk races, originally intended for separate worlds—one for the colossal, non-sapient gantums and another where ranuks would thrive in an untamed wilderness along with their gigantic counterparts.

Yet, the reckless intervention of Archon had disrupted these plans, prematurely bringing forth a flawed version of the Gantum race. Realizing the urgent need to restore balance, the Provisioner swiftly activated the design for the Ranuk race. Given that the gantums and ranuks shared certain unique qualities meant to bond them in the natural order, he hoped the timely emergence of the ranuk would counterbalance the botched creation of the Gantum race, preserving the delicate harmony that both he and the Oracle had so meticulously dreamed into existence.

Amidst the pressing urgency of forging the Ranuk race, the Provisioner's mind was burdened with unsettling thoughts. He pondered the possibility that the Archon had somehow gained unauthorized access to his past designs of races. These designs, he believed, were securely protected, and the idea that someone had breached that sanctity sent shivers down his spine. The Archon's origins were described as being of the Shaper lineage by the Anarchist, but doubt gnawed at the corners of his mind.

With the Ranuk project at the forefront of his priorities, the Provisioner resolved to remain vigilant. He acknowledged that, after the completion of the ranuk race, he would need to scrutinize the Archon's actions more closely, seeking answers to the unsettling questions that had taken root in his consciousness. There was now a cloud of uncertainty obscuring the harmony between the two Shapers.

As the need to create the Ranuk race pressed upon the Provisioner, his reservations about the Archon's intentions weighed heavily on his mind. Originally, he had considered bringing her into the creation chamber to collaborate, but now, with doubt casting a shadow over their partnership, he felt compelled to act swiftly and proceed on his own. The urgency of the task at hand left no room for uncertainty, and he was determined to ensure the ranuk creation with a single-minded resolve, even if it meant forsaking the collaboration he had once envisioned with the Archon.

•••••••

In the vast world of Paranova, the mortal races embarked on their individual journeys, unaware of the cosmic dance unfolding behind the scenes of the Shapers. The elves, blessed with a natural connection to magic, flourished in their pursuit of knowledge and order. They sought to define the world with their harmonious touch, nurturing the lands and creatures they encountered. They found comfort in the Kingdom of Unity; a beacon located in the central lands.

Simultaneously, the dark ones, guided by the mysterious forces of chaos, felt an irresistible pull towards the southern heart of the world. They believed it to be the calling of a fire god, an entity of immense power that resonated with their chaotic nature. Devoting themselves to this unknown deity, they engaged in rituals and practices that aligned them with the unpredictable energies swirling around them.

With towering height and a certain sense of power, the Gantum emerged as a force to be reckoned with, a confirmation of the Archon's retaliatory might. Their colossal forms traversed the vast landscapes, leaving a mark that the ground itself struggled to bear. Born from primal instincts and shaped by the Archon's essence, the gantum embodied a blend of fear and awe in their disfigured features. Though their intellect may have been limited, their raw strength and presence commanded respect and instilled a sense of fear in all who crossed their path.

And yet, the Ranuk, the humble counterparts to the Gantum, new and infused with a glimmer of intellect and compassion, emerged as a force of balance. They sought to counter the destructive tendencies unleashed by the gantum, bringing harmony and stability to the land they traversed. They would pose a threat to the colossal race with their equally matched aggression and outsmart them in every confrontation. The ranuk felt it was their purpose to push these beasts further away from civilization.

In the tapestry of existence, woven with threads of ancient wisdom and divine inspiration, the Provisioner's vision took shape like a radiant star in the night sky. The Provisioner worked tirelessly in his domain, planning the intricate and complex nature of a destiny, under the profound influence of the Oracle's prophecies and driven by a sincere belief in the potential of mortal beings.

In the Archon's absence from his initial designs for the next two sapient races, the Provisioner turned to the Oracle for her counsel. He sought her wisdom on how to navigate the inevitable anger and disappointment that would arise when the Archon discovered he had chosen to proceed on his own. The Oracle, with her serene demeanor, offered a comforting response, soothing his concerns. She assured him that, given the doubts and uncertainties surrounding the Archon's intentions, it was essential to prioritize what was best for the world of Paranova.

With a sense of purpose and renewed determination, the Provisioner and the Oracle embarked on a series of passionate conversations and vivid dreams. Together in the creation chamber, they delved into the intricacies of their vision for the new races and how these creations would intertwine and flourish across the vast expanse of the continent. It was a promising beginning to something magnificent in the making—a collaborative effort that held the potential to shape the destiny of Paranova in absolute and unforeseen ways.

With extreme care and passionate dedication, he orchestrated the preparations of two more sapient races—a variety of souls poised to bring about a thorough transformation in the world. Yet, shrouded in secrecy and concealed from the prying eyes of the mortal races, the Provisioner's work remained a covert journey, a silent symphony of creation guided by hope. The emergence of each of these sapient races held the promise of a new era—a world where understanding, unity, and the pursuit of higher truths would flourish like the blossoms of a celestial garden.

Within the expansive tapestry of Paranova, the mortal races launched on their own individual voyages, their footfalls resonating throughout the land as they traversed through enchanting landscapes. Little did they know that each encounter, decision, and triumph intricately intertwined to mold a narrative surrounding far-reaching relevance and ultimately shaping this thriving world's destiny.

While journeying through enchanted forests, treacherous mountains, and sprawling cities, they bore witness to concealed marvels and mysteries interwoven within existence itself. Unaware of epic battles between order and chaos unfolding in unseen realms, they embraced their lives wholeheartedly, propelled by dreams, aspirations, and an unwavering quest to forge their unique stories.

Unaware of the lasting impact they would have on Paranova's destiny, their combined actions, along with the harmonious and conflicting aspects of Shaper's actions, served as a crucial catalyst that ultimately shifted the course of events. Suspended in anticipation, the world teetered on the edge of transformation while life's intricate tapestry continued, eagerly awaiting the unfolding melody and narrative to follow suit.

Chapter 3: Conflict of Consequence

Amidst the growing troubles in Paranova, the mysterious Anarchist could not resist his curiosity. He set up a meeting with the Archon and Havoc to get updates on what they were up to. The meeting was meant to help everyone understand the changing situation in their world.

As the meeting began, it was a crucial time to share information and ideas about the challenges facing Paranova. The Anarchist had his own reasons for wanting to know more, and he wanted to make sure he stayed in the loop in this complex and ever-changing world. He had thoughts that the two were giving in to their chaotic tendencies and wanted to instill in them the primary goal, which is to work with the Order sector.

The Archon, determined to represent both herself and Havoc, provided a broad overview of the current situation. She revealed that the Provisioner had plans for two additional races and shared her role in diversifying the world's creatures. She also mentioned the use of avatars to facilitate communication with the Shapers. However, she deliberately omitted any mention of the Gantum race and the menacing spectral avatars that had been devouring mortals. These dark aspects of recent events were kept concealed, their unsettling truths hidden from the discussion.

The Anarchist, deeply disheartened and feeling betrayed by the Archon and Havoc's omissions, was well aware of the existence of the Gantum race and the menacing spectral avatars. Observing the Archon's deliberate omission of these troubling truths, he could not help but feel a profound sense of disappointment. He made a conscious decision not to bring up these crucial details in the hope that the Archon or Havoc would eventually share the concealed information with him. The veil of secrecy, however, cast a shadow over their meeting, leaving the Anarchist with lingering concerns about the true state of affairs in Paranova.

The choices made by the Archon and Havoc cast a looming shadow over the sector's domain. The Anarchist who is the guiding force of chaos, looked upon the Archon and Havoc with a mixture of disappointment and growing concern. They did not listen to commands initially set when they decided to join the Order sector on the task of creating a new world. Their actions had not aligned with the vision of balance and collaboration that the Anarchist had hoped for in them.

The Anarchist, clearly dissatisfied with the Archon and Havoc, scolded them for withholding crucial information about the disorder unfolding in Paranova. He had received reports of the ominous spectral avatars consuming mortals and the growing threat posed by the uncontrollable giants on the continent. He gave them a moment to confess their involvement in these issues, harboring hope that they were not to blame.

In addition, the Anarchist disclosed that the Oracle had been targeted by a member of the Chaos sector, who was eliminated before any interrogation could occur. He was dissatisfied that the elves were disrupted, but he also believed it was the Provisioners fault; therefore, no blame could be pushed onto his comrades, but he could not help but wonder if they were involved. He emphasized that many of the conflicts revolved around the forces of chaos, warning that such a path could lead to consequences beyond their control. These consequences, he cautioned, might include conflicts between the sectors or even the catastrophic destruction of their newly formed world.

In a moment of silence, the Archon and Havoc shared a look but could not provide a clear answer to the Anarchist's questions. The Archon felt guilty, while Havoc essentially said that life is unpredictable and chaos is beyond their control, echoing the Provisioner's stance. It seemed like they were trying to deflect blame. The unresolved issues and the secrecy surrounding recent events left the Anarchist with more questions and a sense of unease.

Once a partner in the act of creation, the Archon now seemed to be going in the opposite direction. Mostly since she was so ambitious and wanted to be recognized, she made choices without consulting the Order sector. The Anarchist, a firm advocate of controlled chaos, was at odds with the Archon's independent decisions. But it was Havoc, the Archon's cryptic follower, who drew the Anarchist's fury the most. Havoc's insatiable desire for power and impulse for chaos had become a source of concern and mistrust. As far as the Anarchist seemed concerned, he was a dangerous wild card who could upset the peace they had worked so hard to establish.

The Anarchist spoke harshly to the Archon and Havoc, bringing up previous failures and the disastrous results of the choices the sector had made in the Death realm. Their mistakes had resulted in the permanent installation of most of the Chaos sector within that realm. It served as a humbling reminder that the world they were entrusted with molding would be significantly affected by the decisions they made; it affected not only an individual but also the Chaos sector.

The Anarchist composedly warned the Archon and Havoc that they would be held accountable for their part in undermining the collective efforts of the Chaos and Order sectors. The Anarchist made it clear that they would not stand for any more negative interference with the world they were crafting by threatening to withdraw their participation in the developing process. The Anarchist forbade the Archon and Havoc from the creation chambers for the remainder of their time surrounding Paranova.

The Archon, feeling the weight of the Anarchist's disapproval, contemplated the consequences of her actions. She had once believed that her innovative ideas and fearless approach would be welcomed by the Chaos sector. However, the Anarchist's stern words made her think and reconsider her methods.

Deep down, the Archon knew that she had strayed from the original vision of collaboration between chaos and order. The allure of power and recognition had clouded her judgment, leading her to make decisions without consulting the Provisioner or the Anarchist. She realized the severity of her mistake and the potential harm it could cause to Paranova.

The Archon stood at a crossroads torn between the path of conformity and the allure of her chaotic nature. Her mind was a mixture of conflicting desires and responsibilities. On one road, she longed to regain the trust and approval of the Anarchist as a respected leader, to restore the fragile balance between chaos and order. She understood the importance of collaboration with others and the need for accountability for her actions.

Yet there was a part of her that she held deep within her core; she desired the raw power and freedom that chaos offered. The temptation to unleash her own untamed celestial energy and revel in the unpredictable and transformative nature of her being tugged at her inner choices. The Archon wrestled with the weight of her decision, knowing that her choice would shape not only her own leadership status but also the fate of Paranova itself.

She pondered the repercussions of each choice in her moments of solitude. Submission would bring peace and harmony, allowing her to collaborate with the Provisioner to achieve a shared vision for the mortal species. Discipline, sacrifice, and a willingness to surrender control over her chaotic impulses would be required. She understood the assignment thoroughly, and her inner struggle would be the hurdle that she needed to overcome.

If she chose to embrace her chaotic nature, she would have immense power to reshape reality and challenge the established order within the cosmos. It would be a path of rebellion and unpredictability, one that could lead to both triumph and devastation. The Archon knew that such a choice would come at a great cost, potentially fracturing the delicate balance the Shapers sought to achieve. During these times of reflection alone in solitude, she found comfort in navigating her own chaotic thoughts, but this time she started to feel a sense of rage within her and could not control it. The words of the Anarchist forbidding her from entering the creation chamber repeated in her mind over and over.

At the end of her reflection, the Archon's decision remained uncertain. The internal battle continued, with each option pulling at her with equal force. She understood that her choice would define her legacy and impact the world she had helped shape. The ultimate question lingered in her mind: Would she choose to conform to the expectations of the Anarchist and the Provisioner, or would she embrace her inherent chaotic nature, for better or for worse?

In contrast, Havoc embraced and found satisfaction in the disorder and upheaval he had scattered. He perceived himself as a catalyst for transformation, liberated from any regulations or limitations. The Anarchist's disdain for his unpredictable nature only fueled his desire to defy expectations. Havoc was determined to forge his own path, even if it meant defying the guidance of the Anarchist and his beloved Archon.

Havoc had completely given himself over to the chaotic forces that were coursing through his veins because of his insatiable desire for power. He no longer saw chaos as a challenge to overcome but rather as a test, a trial set forth by the Anarchist himself. In his twisted perception, chaos became his ally and his guide in this grand scheme of creation. With every word the Anarchist said, he thought there was a riddle to uncover.

With each step he took, Havoc reveled in the unpredictable nature of chaos, finding pleasure in the disruption it caused. He saw himself as an instrument of the Anarchist's will, a vessel through which chaos could manifest and reshape the world. He believed that by pushing the boundaries of chaos, evaluating its limits, and embracing its most destructive aspects, he would prove himself worthy of the Anarchist's favor. Though Havoc did not tell the Anarchist how he constructed the Transition realm or how he managed to create the Dark Ones, he felt the Anarchist was proud of what he was capable of accomplishing.

While the Archon wrestled with her own internal conflicts, Havoc saw her as a kindred spirit, someone who understood the true power and potential of chaos. He saw their collaboration as a means to unlock greater heights of chaos, to defy the constraints imposed by the Order sector, and to forge their own path in the creation of Paranova.

However, in his reckless pursuit of chaos, Havoc became blind to the consequences of his actions. He failed to recognize the true intentions and concerns of the Anarchist, who saw chaos as a force that should be harnessed and balanced rather than unleashed without restraint. The Anarchist grew increasingly disappointed and wary of Havoc's fanaticism, fearing the irreversible damage he might cause. Havoc henceforth started scheming and working in the shadows of the Chaos sector, only revealing himself when needed.

As Havoc delved deeper into his chaotic plans, he began to lose sight of the initial purpose behind the creation of Paranova. His hunger for power overshadowed the original vision of unity and harmony that the Provisioner and Order sectors had sought to achieve. The actions of Havoc posed a relentless threat to disrupt the intricately maintained equilibrium, relentlessly testing the limits of disorder to an alarming extent.

Havoc remained oblivious to the fact that the ultimate challenge was not simply accepting disorder but rather being able to navigate amidst it in a harmonious manner. It was a test of wisdom, restraint, and understanding qualities that Havoc, in his twisted passion, had neglected. Whether he would realize this test and rectify his path or succumb to the overwhelming allure of chaos would ultimately determine his role in the destiny of Paranova.

In the midst of this disorder, the Anarchist's words about the Death realm lingered in their minds. The vision of the Provisioner, which had been tarnished by the Chaos sector's interference, served as a reminder of the consequences of their actions. The Anarchist's threat to withdraw their involvement in the world-building process resonated deeply, for they knew that the absence of chaos would leave Paranova imbalanced and that no one would embrace unpredictability.

With mounting concern for the Archon and Havoc, whom he had entrusted with the Chaos sector, the Anarchist sought comfort and guidance from the Provisioner. Interrupting a private moment between the Provisioner and the Oracle in the creation chamber, he apologized for the intrusion and emphasized the urgency of the matter. The Anarchist were determined to address the growing tensions and conflicts between the two sectors that had been plaguing Paranova.

He openly admitted that he could not be entirely sure if the Archon and Havoc were responsible for all the troubles but acknowledged their inherent connection to the forces of chaos. To prevent further upheaval, he stressed the need to limit their involvement from this point onward. It was a pivotal moment in their quest to maintain balance in their world, and the Anarchist's resolve was resolute.

The Anarchist, weighed down by remorse, confessed that he had pressured the Archon and Havoc to meet the standards of the Order sector, acknowledging his own culpability in the world's chaos. He went on to lament the ways he could have done better and the opportunities he had missed, reflecting on his role in the unfolding crisis. His self-critique seemed endless, with him contemplating various paths he could have taken. The Oracle, however, interjected, reminding the Anarchist that it had been his conscious choice to involve the Archon and Havoc for his own reasons, implying that there were valid motivations behind his decisions. The Provisioner listened patiently, awaiting the Anarchist's ultimate revelation.

With a hesitant tone, the Anarchist revealed his perceived failure in the Death realm and how the majority of his sector had been permanently stationed there due to his leadership. He felt that he needed to return and carry out his sentence, but not before finding a worthy successor to lead the reformed Chaos sector. That successor, he believed, was the Archon.

With guidance, he was confident that she could replace him once she had learned his teachings and received support from the Order sector. The Provisioner, understanding the magnitude of the Anarchist's vision, recalled the chaos of the Death realm and the Anarchist's pivotal role in it. It became clear that the Anarchist's insistence on involving the Archon was not merely about undermining his own creations, as the Provisioner had previously suspected. Instead, it was a deeply rooted plan, carrying a profound sense of purpose.

The Provisioner and the Oracle unveiled their ambitious plans for the forthcoming races, eagerly sharing their diagrams and blueprints with the Anarchist. They expressed their desire for the Archon to join them and observe the intricate details. However, the Anarchist, perhaps still harboring some reservations, suggested that the Archon could watch the creative process from outside the chamber alongside him.

United in their understanding of the Anarchist's hesitancy, the trio began to coordinate and organize the preparations for the upcoming endeavor to shape the next races in Paranova. Their collaboration, guided by mutual respect and a shared vision for the future, promised to set the stage for remarkable and harmonious creations.

The Provisioner's plan to bridge the gap between order and chaos manifested in the creation of the Dwarves, a race crafted with the traits of the Chaos sector. With skilled hands, he endowed the dwarves with a blend of chaos-inspired qualities, such as resourcefulness, adaptability, and a fiery spirit that burned within them. They emerged as a small but sturdy race, capable of enduring hardships and embracing the unexpected twists of fate. They were a race that represented resilience in all aspects of life.

Alongside the Dwarves, the Provisioner set out to bring humans to life, meticulously shaping them according to the Oracle's vision. Drawing upon the virtues described by the Oracle—endurance, balance, vitality, and vigor—he breathed life into the humans, granting them a versatile nature and a deep connection with the world around them. They became a race of resilient individuals, capable of adapting to various circumstances while maintaining a sense of harmony and vitality. The humans helped represent the unpredictability that the Chaos sector cherished; the creation of humans brought a smile across the Archons face.

As the Provisioner breathed life into his creations, the Oracle stood beside him, her heart brimming with joy. Her gaze was often drawn to him, and she was unable to look away as he poured his passion into the act of creation. The mortal lives blossoming across the continent before her were proof of his tireless dedication and love for his craft. In that moment, she found herself torn, for she could not quite decide what stirred her soul more deeply: the love and constant dedication of the Provisioner or the beautiful world unfolding before her, a living embodiment of her visions. It was a magnificent moment of artistic passion and prophetic insight when the two danced within the creation chamber to celebrate life on Paranova.

As the Anarchist and the Archon observed the creation process from outside the chamber, he could not help but notice a genuine smile on her face, a rare departure from her usual sly demeanor. This moment encapsulated what he hoped to convey: a harmony between the Chaos sector and the Order sector. He wanted the Archon to see that there was a place for balance, and he desperately wished for her not to tread the path he had taken with the Death realm. Wrapping his arms around her, he spoke of the significance of this moment—the coexistence of creation and guidance—reminding her that they had forged these races and now held the responsibility of guiding them.

The Archon comprehended the Anarchist's intentions, but she remained torn between his desires and her own instincts, a conflict that raged within her. As she watched the Provisioner and the Oracle inside the chamber, their joyful chaos danced and laughed around boundless energy, all the while holding one another as they watched the creation unfold.

In that moment of watching them in the chamber, she could not help but daydream, and the Archon found herself at a crossroads. She could not help but feel jealous of the Oracle, imagining herself as the Provisioner's partner and confidant. She envisioned a harmonious life as the leaders of the Shapers, blending chaos and order seamlessly as King and Queen. Conflicting emotions swirled within her, leaving her with a weighty decision that would define her path in life.

The creation of the Dwarves and Humans brought The Oracle immense pleasure, as she had recalled that she had seen new civilizations after the elves, each reflecting the ideals and influences of their respective sectors. The Oracle found the development of the dwarven civilization to be fascinating because of their organized behavior and tenacious quest for knowledge. She had envisioned a race deep within their magnificent underground cities who mined precious ores, created magnificent weaponry, crafted intricate machinery, and developed advanced technologies. She had seen the human civilization spread all throughout the land, unifying with rich diversity among all the other mortal races. She would hum tunes that the humans and dwarves would sing and dance to, and she would often laugh at their joys in storytelling.

The Oracle, steadfast in her vigilance, watched with hope as the Provisioner readied to steer the path of Paranova back toward the course envisioned in her prophecies. With each creation, the Oracle's admiration grew, for the dwarves and the humans were the final pieces of the intricate puzzle she had foreseen. She eagerly anticipated the innovative ideas and harmonious possibilities that the Provisioner would unveil, longing for the day when her visions would be fully realized. In the face of mounting challenges and the ever-present conflict between order and chaos, the Oracle's unwavering faith in the Provisioner's guidance remained unshakable, a beacon of hope that illuminated the path toward a harmonious and balanced future.

The Archon's curiosity drove her to seek more information about the ongoing creation. She abruptly entered the chamber, disrupting the connection between the Provisioner and the Oracle. With determination in her voice, she requested a private conversation with the Provisioner. The Oracle, initially skeptical but recognizing the importance of their partnership in overseeing the two sectors of Paranova, obliged. She left the chamber and stood alongside the Anarchist, waiting patiently for the forthcoming discussion.

Intrigued and deeply thoughtful, the Archon began to pose intricate questions as she observed the Provisioner at work, skillfully shaping the mortal beings. She frequently showered him with compliments, capturing his attention with her genuine appreciation. As he walked her through the intricate diagrams and offered insights into his energy usage, he revealed that he drew energy from her and others to infuse the mortal beings with traces of each Shaper's personality, passions, and intellect.

The Archon, captivated by the concept of energy convergence, expressed her desire to contribute her energy to combine with his in the future, subtly planting the idea of becoming an ultimate duo of order and chaos. After their prolonged interaction, a magnetic connection seemed to draw the Archon closer to the Provisioner, and in a passionate embrace, she radiated her pleasurable energy to him. Their eyes met with an unspoken understanding, and the Archon turned to a genuine smile. The Provisioner, acknowledging her embrace as a sign of apology, reciprocated with forgiveness, creating a profound and intricate moment that held the promise of unity and balance between the forces of order and chaos.

While locked in their embrace, the Archon's demeanor shifted. Her genuine smile gave way to a devious smirk and a suspicious expression as her eyes fell upon the Oracle. She expressed her gratitude to the Provisioner, wished him luck with the task at hand, and instructed him to seek her out in her quarters when he had completed his work. Her mention of discussing the magic of Paranova hinted at a hidden agenda, leaving an air of intrigue and uncertainty in the chamber.

Outside the chamber, the Anarchist and the Oracle engaged in a heartfelt conversation about their past. The Anarchist expressed his belief that the Provisioner had truly outdone himself with the creation of mortals this time around. The Oracle concurred, sharing that they had engaged in passionate discussions and ideas for a celestial span of time. The Life and Death realms played a pivotal role in their vision for bringing mortals to life in the cosmic tapestry.

The Anarchist was astounded by the Oracle's words, as it seemed as though they had shared this vision since the emergence of the Life and Death realms. Overwhelmed by guilt from the past, he offered a sincere apology. The Oracle, however, gracefully waved off his apology, urging him to let go of the weight of the past and focus on the present. She assured him that his actions, which had caused chaos to grow, had paved the way for the Provisioner to make the decision to depart the Life realm, creating perfect harmony as the two realms were separated. The

Provisioner was deeply involved in the daily dealings of the Life realm; it was his destiny to do what he has done here.

The Oracle went on to reveal that the Provisioner was grateful for the Anarchist and proud of the choices he had made, even if he could not openly admit it. Before their conversation could continue, the Archon interjected, seeking a discussion with the Oracle to gain insight into how she worked alongside the Provisioner and how best to prepare him for the creation. Frustrated by the Archon's continual interruptions, the Oracle responded by humming a soothing tune. Her melodic notes carried a hint of impatience, perhaps signaling her desire for a more harmonious and undisturbed conversation.

While humming the victory tunes of the humans she heard in visions, the Oracle allowed the Archon to approach and begin her inquiry. Patiently, the Oracle responded to each of the Archon's questions regarding the two new races, offering intricate details about her visions and the role she played in preparing the Provisioner for their creation. She emphasized that this responsibility was hers alone, aligned with the Provisioner's preferences, and respectfully made it clear that her role in this regard was exclusive to her. The exchange was steeped in a sense of duty and professionalism, defining their respective roles in the world of Paranova.

Realizing that the Oracle was not willing to relinquish her duties, the Archon attempted to manipulate the situation, playing on her own feelings of guilt. She held onto the thought that she was the one responsible for rendering the Oracle's visions blind. During their conversation, the Archon could not help but notice that the Oracle was smiling, her attention fixed on the Provisioner as he continued to shape the new mortals.

Sensing the Archon's guilt, the Oracle unexpectedly extended heartfelt forgiveness toward her, which left the Archon somewhat frustrated. In a hasty manner, she retreated to her own quarters, her emotions and intentions remaining shrouded in mystery. The exchange had left behind a web of intrigue and unresolved tensions.

With a smile, the Anarchist acknowledged the Oracle's unique ability to guide the Archon toward the right path, expressing his confidence in her capacity to do so. The Oracle concurred, recognizing that the Archon, as a relatively new Shaper born in the Life realm, had much to learn. She assured the Anarchist that she would keep a watchful eye on the Archon, offering her guidance and insights to aid in her development. Their shared commitment to helping the Archon find her way reflected the harmonious balance of guidance and wisdom within Paranova.

As the final stages of creation unfolded within the chamber, many of the Shapers stood in awe, their eyes fixed on the radiant beauty of Paranova. Meanwhile, Havoc, lurking in the shadows, began to communicate with his spectral followers, issuing orders for them to migrate to the areas where new life was emerging. His sinister plan was to harness some of these fresh souls, hoping to tap into their celestial energy for a creation of his own.

Havoc possessed a unique ability to sense entities native to the world of Paranova, predating the cosmic collision with the Luminara star and the subsequent evolution by the Shapers. Much of this history remained a mystery, but Havoc was determined to uncover the secrets before others could unravel the enigma. With a vigilant eye and a thirst for knowledge, he began a shadowy quest that held the potential to shape the future of Paranova.

Inspired by the unique qualities of the dwarven people, the Forger's imagination was tickled as he envisioned a grand kingdom befitting their resourcefulness and resilience. With meticulous precision, he set his sights on the northwest mountains, a vast expanse of rugged terrain that would serve as the foundation for this magnificent realm.

The Forger's stone avatars, with their skilled hands, had carved intricate pathways into the mountains, etching a network of trails that wound their way along the contour lines and through the rocky slopes. These pathways served as a tribute to the resilience and determination of the dwarven race that would come to inhabit this land as they navigated the treacherous terrain in search of their destiny.

Deep within the heart of the mountains, the Forger crafted magnificent chambers and halls where the dwarves would find refuge and build their thriving civilization. The underground kingdom and all its interconnecting tunnels, along with its hidden chambers below, show how adaptable the dwarven people were and how much they admired the intricacies of the crafted kingdom. The Forger could not wait to see how the dwarves would delve into the depths below and uncover the kingdom's secrets he had stored within.

As the Forger shaped the landscape, he ensured that the land was abundant with resources, he strategically placed rich deposits of minerals, gems, and ores throughout the continent, mostly within the northern regions. The mountains themselves held the promise of wealth and prosperity, providing the resources necessary for mortals to thrive and flourish.

While the Forger was deeply engrossed in the act of world-crafting, the Provisioner stood nearby, his face beaming with joy. With a sense of pride, he revealed that the dwarven race had been shaped in his image, bestowing upon them attributes and passions aligned with the Forger's love for construction and tinkering. This revelation filled the Forger with a passionate sense of honor and pleasure, igniting his enthusiasm to be even more detailed and creative in the forging of the dwarves' lands. The exchange between these two creators was a harmonious celebration of their shared vision for Paranova.

The Forger's vision for this kingdom was a testament to his creative prowess and deep understanding of the race he was crafting it for. Every element of the land was carefully designed to cater to the needs and aspirations of its future inhabitants, providing them with a fertile canvas on which they could forge their own destiny.

As the final additions were made, the Forger beheld his creation with a sense of pride and anticipation. The stage was set for the arrival of this remarkable race, and the kingdom eagerly awaited the footsteps of its first inhabitants. Unfortunately, this had caught the attention of the gantums, massive, misconfigured beasts. They started to flock toward the northern continent in search of this magical witness.

As the grand creation was complete, the Provisioner was in high demand, receiving congratulations from fellow Shapers. However, his path led him to the Archon's quarters. There, he found her gazing at the flourishing Paranova and invited him to join her. The Provisioner appeared eager to celebrate with the others, but the Archon recognized his desire to discuss business and plans.

She encouraged the Provisioner to take a break, to embrace the uncertainty, and to take pleasure in the beauty of their own creation. She pulled him into a warm, comforting side of herself that was nearly completely concealed but yet radiated moments of vulnerability. The provisioner braced himself for a few moments, having not let these intimate emotions travel through him in quite some time with another Shaper, other than the Oracle.

The Archon, attuned to his celestial energies, began to ease his stress and tension. She acknowledged that the world's magic had become immensely orderly, a sentiment the Provisioner shared. As she continued to tend to his energies and soothe him, he found himself thoroughly enjoying every embrace, letting out a few laughs in the process. The Archon inquired if this were something he would like on a regular basis—a moment to rest and discuss plans as leaders. The peaceful interlude and the Archon's newly discovered role as a source of comfort captivated the

Provisioner, who could only keep his attention on his task throughout their conversation.

Laughter filled the room as the Archon continued to soothe the Provisioner's celestial energies that he had overworked throughout the creation procedure. The sheer pleasure was almost overwhelming for the both of them. The Provisioner, sensing that things might progress in an uncomfortable direction and seeing the Archon mirroring the duties that the Oracle fulfilled, gently urged the Archon to get to her point.

With a sly smile, the Archon complied, sharing her vision of restoring balance to the magic system on Paranova. She emphasized the need for a touch of chaos, although not to the point of causing instability among the mortals. As she spoke, she used her powers to demonstrate the concept of passion and intensity, pleasuring the Provisioner's celestial being to a point where he could feel the depth of what she meant. Overcome by the experience, he sprang up, and their eyes met with a mixture of understanding and passion.

In the midst of their charged connection, the Archon retrieved her plans, presenting the Provisioner with a map of Paranova. The map was marked with points indicating each kingdom and unique locations where they could establish magical balances, serving as conduits to harmonize the magical energies across the world. Together, they contemplated the intricate path they would take to bring balance to the magical forces that flowed throughout the world.

The level of detail on the Archon's map genuinely shocked the Provisioner. He was thrilled to see how attentive and observant she had been throughout the existence of their shaped world. Their shared passion and enjoyment of each other's company made the moment all the more special.

As the Archon pointed to the various locations on the map, she explained how these places could serve as perfect points of magical balance. Her vision included the eastern kingdom with the citadel crafted by the Forger, and she showcased how all these locations would connect seamlessly. The Provisioner was pleased with her plan and entrusted her to proceed with its execution. He emphasized the importance of finding a solution for the gantum race, as their future depended on it. Despite the gantums' apparent displeasure, the Archon received his assurance with a passionate smile that he looked forward to discussing plans with her going forward.

Once the Provisioner left to join the other Shapers, the Archon swiftly retrieved her notes and made secret changes. Her aim was to add more chaos to the magic than she had originally revealed. This hinted at a hidden plan full of mystery and uncertainty. She referred to this hidden source of chaos as the "Arcane," a vast abundance of magic that could be controlled and shaped as chaos into a resemblance of order. She believed it would be enough to deceive the Provisioner when he inevitably asked questions later.

•••••••

The Dwarves, a race gifted with unparalleled innovation and renowned for their industrious nature, carved their place within the intricate tapestry of Paranova. Drawn to the mountains and the depths of caverns, their affinity for these elevated and subterranean realms was not merely a matter of preference but a tactical advantage rooted in their short stature and inherent resourcefulness.

In the towering peaks and labyrinthine tunnels, the dwarves found peace and inspiration. They constructed magnificent underground cities, masterpieces of engineering that harmonized with the natural contours of the earth. With precision, they harnessed the power of the mountains, delving deep into the rich veins of ore to extract precious minerals that fueled their ingenuity.

Every dwarf pulsated with innovation. They had an inherent talent for fabricating complex machinery, unraveling revolutionary technologies, and refining their abilities as artists and craftsmen. Their inventions, ranging from clockwork wonders to intricate constructions fueled by steam, exhibited their never-ending quest for advancement and dedication to acquiring wisdom.

However, beneath their hardworking exterior, the dwarves harbored a deep disdain for the gantums. The disorderly nature and destructive tendencies of their gigantic neighbors were opposite to the organized world that the dwarves had laboriously constructed for themselves. With an increase in gantums lurking in the northern mountains, the dwarves retreated into their underground cities.

They eventually had to hide at all times because the gantum was pursuing them relentlessly. They felt trapped within their own cities, but they found comfort knowing they could not be found. This led many dwarves to find a solution to their massive problem. They were aware of their own insignificance when compared to these tenacious hunters; they knew that combat could not be the answer, but they were determined to devise plans to outwit them in battle and train any dwarf willing to go to war.

The oppressive weight of their survival and struggles had weakened many dwarven spirits, leaving them feeling exhausted as they sought refuge in the safety of concealment in their kingdom and underground cities. The dwarves found a way to brew a drink that helped them through these tough times and forget the constant fear of being mauled by a gantum. Many claimed that the brew lifted spirits and made them feel wonderful.

When Dwarven culture wasn't preoccupied with the continual threat above ground, they focused on order, hierarchy, and craftsmanship. Every aspect of their existence was predetermined and carefully planned forward. They placed a high priority on discipline, hard work, and pushing for achievement. Their kingdom became hubs of activity, bursting with forges, laboratories, and workshops where ideas flowed freely and innovation thrived.

In times of conflict, the dwarves found tactical prowess. Their intimate knowledge of the mountains and caves gave them a distinct advantage. They employed guerilla tactics, utilizing their understanding of the terrain to their benefit. They staged strategic strikes against their foes while scaling the heights of the mountains or maneuvering through the intricate network of tunnels, taking advantage of their small stature and knowledge with the environment to outmaneuver their opponents.

Due to their shared ancestry and tenacity, the dwarves were a formidable force. They stood as guardians of order and progress, and their settlements reflected examples of creativity and resilience amid the chaos that threatened to consume Paranova. Their disdain for the gantum, born out of the clash between order and chaos, fueled their determination to protect their way of life and uphold the principles they held dear.

After triumphing over a colossal Gantum, the dwarves would revel in a glorious celebration, their joyous spirits elevated to new heights. The halls of their mighty strongholds would come alive with the sounds of glory as feasts of abundant food and drink were laid out on grand display. The dwarves, renowned for their expertise in brewing, would showcase their mastery by crafting potent and flavorful concoctions that could rival the stars themselves. These libations, known for their strength and potency, were intended to drown their troubles and allow them to drift into blissful slumber with smiles on their faces.

In the intricate wonders of Paranova, the dwarves carved a unique niche. Their industrious spirit, steadfast dedication to innovation, and strategic mindset shaped their destiny. With each invention, each innovation, and each executed plan, they propelled their civilization forward, resolute in their quest for progress and driven by the desire to leave a legacy amidst the hard conflicts that defined their existence. No longer were the dwarves known for hiding amongst the rocks and rubbish;

they were fierce people who took challenges straight forward and succeeded.

·······

The Humans, who are a multifaceted and adaptable race, embarked on diverse journeys that led them to multiple locations all over Paranova. As they ventured further, they fragmented into distinct groups, each following its own path and embracing its unique aspirations and ideals.

Some humans, drawn to the allure of the Eastern Kingdom that the Forger created and settled in its fertile lands, established bustling communities and sought to harness the resources and potential of the region. These people, driven by their inventiveness and work ethic, embraced progress and development by creating cities in the eastern lands and cultivating a society that valued intellectual and technological pursuits.

In contrast, there were those who felt a deep connection with the primal forces of nature. These humans, attuned to the mysteries of the forests, chose to dwell among the ancient trees. They revered the natural world and lived in harmony with its rhythms, valuing simplicity, wisdom, and the untamed beauty of their surroundings. Away from the complexities of other civilizations, they sought to preserve their primal way of life, nurturing a deep bond with the wilderness.

However, not all humans were inclined to follow the paths of progress or harmony. Some people found themselves drawn to the volcanic realm, where the dark ones held sway, by the allure of power and chaos. These humans, enthralled by the promise of untamed energies and the destructive might of the fire god they revered, became friendly with the dark ones. The humans immersed themselves in the volatile currents of chaos, embracing the darker aspects of their nature and adopting a life of passionate devotion to their fiery deity.

Furthermore, among the populous were individuals who opted for a more obscure trajectory. Delving into the spheres of gloom and crypticness, they established secluded enclaves in concealed nooks and crannies within Paranova. Leading lives as predators and pilferers, they traversed through the underbelly of society, depending on their wit and versatility to persevere. These people who lived in the shadows took pleasure in the uncertainty it brought about as well as their own pursuit of self-benefits, consciously excluding themselves from social interactions facilitated by light and polite behavior.

As the humans began their individual journeys, they encountered both opportunities and challenges, shaping their destinies in diverse ways. Their lack of unity and guidance at the outset led to the increase of distinct human civilizations, each with its own customs, beliefs, and aspirations. Humanity progressed in diverse ways and set a divide amongst the people and cultures. This was not all bad, though, as the Shapers would agree. Humans had much potential to shape their own path within Paranova.

Gazing upon the expansive domain of human societies, the Provisioner experienced a blend of curiosity and satisfaction. While he had no intentions of intervening in their proceedings presently, he possessed unwavering faith in their potential for growth and unity. The Provisioner passionately believed in the notion that personal progress held great power, believing wholeheartedly in the inherent capability of different races to shape their own futures. Hence, he understood and sympathized with the diverse approaches' humans had opted for when navigating through life.

As he witnessed the humans spreading across Paranova, the Provisioner was delighted to see the dwarves united as a cohesive force within their mountainous domains. Their innate affinity for innovation and industriousness had led them to establish thriving societies, drawing upon the resources of the land and delving deep into the intricate craftsmanship that defined their culture. The dwarves' strong bond with their environment and their strategic choice of high ground or lower ground appealed to the Provisioner's own understanding of tactical wisdom.

While the humans and dwarves pursued their own paths, the Provisioner maintained his belief that their journeys would eventually converge and unfold into a greater connection of unity. He recognized the importance of allowing them the freedom to explore and develop their civilizations, for it was through their individual growth and experiences that true progress could emerge.

With an optimistic perspective, the Provisioner remained a silent observer, confident in the capacity of humans and dwarves to evolve, learn, and ultimately find common ground. He reveled in the diversity of Paranova's inhabitants, understanding that it was through the interplay of their distinct cultures and aspirations that the world would be shaped into something extraordinary. The Provisioner's trust in the potential of the mortal races fueled his determination to guide them indirectly, allowing their collective journey to unfold and eventually intertwine in a harmonious unity that would fulfill the Oracle's vision.

In contrast, the Chaos sector observed the emergence of the Gantum, a race born from the chaotic essence of the Archon. These massive beings, disfigured and unpredictable, embodied the untamed and primal aspects of chaos. With their towering presence and little intellect, the gantum roamed the untamed lands, driven by their chaotic impulses and a primal desire for destruction.

The Archon was tasked with enlightening the race of gantums by the Provisioner, but it was proven too hard to do without destroying them. She had to wait and be patient while observing the race thoroughly to seek a vulnerability to manipulation. She urged the Provisioner to give her more time to evolve the gantum race so that they become less of a threat to existence among the mortals.

As the Dwarves and Gantum flourished in their own ways after many years of living alongside one another, tensions between them began to escalate. The influences of their respective sectors shaped their interactions and, often times, ignited conflicts rooted in their fundamental differences. The dwarves, driven by their structured nature, sought stability and progress through knowledge and innovation. On the other hand, the gantum, guided by their chaotic tendencies, reveled in mayhem and destruction, finding pleasure in disrupting the dwarven civilization.

The Gantums, with their gigantic stature and disfigured features, harbored a deep-seated pleasure in hunting and killing the dwarves. The stark contrast in their sizes only fueled their sadistic enjoyment, as the gantum reveled in the act of devouring the dwarven people whole, relishing the taste of their conquests. The mere thought of feasting on the flesh and bones of the dwarves sent shivers of pleasure and excitement down the spines of the gantums, who saw themselves as superior beings capable of dominating their smaller enemies.

The Ranuk, who had proven their valor by defeating numerous gantums in battle, stood as a testament to their indomitable spirit. Despite their relatively small stature compared to the gantum, the ranuk possessed unparalleled agility and cunning that enabled them to outmaneuver their colossal foes with remarkable precision. Through their strategic prowess and unwavering determination, they emerged victorious time and again, their victories becoming the stuff of legends in the records of Paranova's history. The Ranuk emerged as a formidable power, earning the esteem and admiration of their peers through their exceptional combat skills.

With an indomitable spirit and honorable obligation, the Ranuk assumed the significant task of expelling colossal creatures destroying their realm. Possessing fearless valor and unparalleled prowess as hunters, they traveled on treacherous journeys to seek out and face the towering Gantums. Armed with their ingenuity, resourcefulness, and faithful unity, the ranuk ventured into the heart of danger, facing formidable challenges head-on.

Through their relentless pursuit, they became the hunters instead of the hunted, seeking to restore balance and safeguard the lands they cherished. The Ranuk's valorous exploits in taking down these colossal beasts became the stuff of legend, inspiring awe and respect among their kin and earning them a rightful place as revered guardians of their realm. Over time, the ranuk seemed to be a terror in the eyes of all the other races. The unique and diverse combat styles the ranuk developed were admired by many mortals throughout Paranova.

The Gantums retreated on a relentless march toward the northern mountains, with the Ranuk perching on their backs. With their predatory instincts honed and their hunger for dwarf flesh, they sought to track down the hidden domains of the dwarves, eager to lay waste to their mountain strongholds. The gantums, driven by a primal desire for dominance and the pleasure derived from the slaughter, moved with fierce determination, leaving a trail of destruction in their wake. The gantums realized that they were more dominant in groups, so they met in the northern regions to gather.

As rumors of the Gantums' relentless pursuit reached the dwarven communities nestled within the northern mountains, a sense of unease and fear filtered their temporarily peaceful existence. The dwarves built their walls, relying on their cunning and mastery of the rugged terrain to repel the impending invasion. The gantums' ominous presence caused the dwarves to be constantly attentive, ready to defend their homes and lives against the persistent marauders.

In this intense time, the delicate balance of power between the dwarves and the gantum stood on a knife's edge. The Gantum, driven by their insatiable hunger and savagery, sought to overpower and consume the dwarven race, while the dwarves, fueled by their determination and resourcefulness, fought tooth and nail to protect their existence. The clash between these primal forces would shape the destiny of the north, leaving behind a legacy of bloodshed and bitter rivalry. The ranuk were resorting to different tactics with the mountains and often coming at clashes with the dwarves simultaneously.

The Provisioner, despite being intrigued by the unfolding drama, remained solid in his position of non-intervention while the world around him descended into disorder and conflict. With complete trust in the dwarves' resilience and ingenuity, he predicted they would outmaneuver and repel the gantums' advances. The Provisioner had complete faith in the dwarves' ability to adapt and overcome, and he awaited the final result of their struggle with anticipation, knowing that their victory would pave the way for a future where order and balance could prevail.

The news of the Gantums' pursuit and their constant appetite for dwarven flesh spread throughout the various races of Paranova. This had inspired deep feelings of fear and concern for everyone. The very existence of these enormous, deformed beings posed a threat to the delicate balance of the world, which prompted unease among the various races who feared becoming the next victims of these monsters. One particular race, the Elves, who are well-known for their grace and affinity with nature, decided to take action against this imminent threat and eliminate the gantums once and for all from Paranova.

The Elves, known for their keen intellect and undeniable curiosity, took a keen interest in the unfolding conflict with the gantums and the newer races. When hearing the dire news, the elven society was quick to prepare for battle. They were in the middle of observing the societies of the primal civilizations around them and thought that to preserve that innocence, they needed to rid themselves of the beasts that could wipe them out completely.

They noticed the delicate balance was beginning to tilt recklessly, so in their quest for knowledge and comprehension, they decided to study the developing societies in an effort to gain insight into the effects of the grand dance between order and chaos. Observing the primal civilizations and the clash between structured order and untamed chaos, the elves recognized the potential consequences of such a struggle as a civilization that was building itself up. The elves thought their role in the grand design of life was to protect the unorganized societies and to help nurture them; this raised their spirits when preparing for battle.

Driven by their firm belief in a sense of duty and their commitment to preserving the harmony of the world, the elves set out on a quest to seek out and confront the marauding gantum. Armed with their formidable archery skills, mastery of the elemental magic, and the newfound arcane, they embarked on a lengthy journey, traversing treacherous landscapes and venturing into the heart of darkness in the northern reaches of the land, where the gantum were said to dwell.

The elves, guided by their innate connection to the natural world and their deep understanding of the delicate balance of life, moved stealthily through the shadows, accurately tracking the path of destruction left in the wake of the gantum. Their determination to protect the sanctity of Paranova and ensure the survival of all its inhabitants fueled their resolve as they drew closer to their formidable enemies. The plan was to attack them while they were weak inside their caves or lying dormant on the grounds around them.

As the elves closed in on the lairs where the gantums resided, a fierce and epic battle occurred. The elven archers' precise aim guided the arrows as they whistled through the air, finding their targets with deadly accuracy. Spells of elemental fury erupted as the arcane energies of the elves collided with the brute strength of the gantum. It was a clash of grace and savagery, of precision and raw power, as the elves fought to rid the world of this menacing threat. Paranova shook as many gantums rose, seemingly unaffected by the ambush.

The confrontation that occurred between the four different races—the dwarves, gantum, ranuki, and elves—led to a violent and devastating conflict. Working with the dwarves and ranuk, the elves managed to defeat a few gantum, but the constant attack from the giants ended in defeat. The elves started to retreat to their kingdom, but the gantums, driven by their chaotic desire for revenge and destruction, pursued the defeated elves back to the central kingdom.

There, the gantum were met with the remaining Elven army, with the ranuk at their side. The dwarves were on the gantum's back, trying to pick apart the back of the horde. Despite the heroic efforts of the Elven and Ranuk armies defending their lands and kingdoms, they were unable to withstand the overpowering might of the Gantums united. The gantum banded together in a massive horde and were successful in destroying almost the whole region. The once-majestic central kingdom that represented unity had fallen into ruins, and its once-great cities had been reduced to rubble.

In the face of this defeat, the surviving elven and ranuk races made the difficult decision to retreat to the sanctuary of the lush western islands, seeking peace and safety away from the relentless pursuit of the gantums. Meanwhile, the gantum, emboldened by their victory, turned their attention to the dwarves, their hatred for the industrious race driving them to hunt down every last dwarf they could find.

The Gantum desire for vengeance and domination drove them to relentlessly search for the dwarves, who sought refuge in the mountains, utilizing their tactical advantage and resilience to fend off their relentless pursuers. The fate of the dwarves hung in the balance as they fought to preserve their existence in the face of the gantum's relentless onslaught. Once more, the dwarven people had to hunker down deep within their cities until the pursuit from the gantum would dwindle away with time.

As the primal human civilizations observed the devastating defeat and the rise of the victorious gigantic beings, some tribes were filled with awe and reverence for these mighty creatures. They saw the gantum as symbols of power and strength, believing them to be all-powerful beings capable of shaping the destiny of Paranova. These tribes, swayed by the chaotic nature of the gantums, turned away from their own plans and aspirations, instead choosing to worship and follow these colossal beings. They saw in the gantum a force that could bring about a new order, one defined by raw strength and dominance.

The particular human tribe embraced the chaotic energy and destructive tendencies of the gantum, viewing them as a path to power and survival in the ever-changing world. In their eyes, the colossal gantum became deities to be revered; their actions and whims were believed to hold the key to unlocking hidden truths and granting blessings to their devoted followers. Thus, the primal human civilizations fragmented further, some becoming passionate worshippers of the gantum, while others clung to their own primal instincts, seeking to survive and thrive during the chaotic aftermath of a war.

Other human tribes fled to remote areas all over Paranova in fear that the gigantic beings would come back to destroy them. Particular tribes would claim regions of land like forests, mountains, caves, deserts, and islands. If anyone were to travel in their region, they were usually met with hostility.

•••••••

Witnessing the devastating consequences of the mortal conflicts, the Keepers Avatars intervened against the Provisioners wishes; their purpose was to restore balance and prevent further destruction. Collaborating with the other Stone and Tree avatars, they crafted a formidable border stretching across the continent, characterized by towering mountains to the north. This natural barrier, with its majestic peaks and treacherous terrain, acted as a physical and metaphysical divide, separating the northern territories of the other races.

The creation of the border had far-reaching consequences. For the dwarves, it made them secluded from the other races, and they had to defend themselves as they remained in the safety of their underground sanctuaries and mountain strongholds. There, they thrived against the circumstances by building on their fortified underground kingdom and cities, delving deep into the earth for precious resources, and establishing an intricate network of tunnels and passages. They found ways to go beyond the border; however, they flourished in isolation, their industrious nature unbothered by the chaotic forces that roamed within their border.

The irrational gantum were unable to overcome the formidable border that the avatars had erected. They made numerous attempts to locate them and breach the mountainous border using their ferocious strength and unwavering determination, driven by their insatiable thirst for dwarven blood and destruction. However, the dwarves, renowned for their cunning and mastery of underground fortifications, proved to be formidable foes. They had honed their skills in hiding and constructing intricate tunnels and underground cities, effectively eluding the relentless pursuit of the gantums.

As time went on, the gantum fascination for the dwarves began to waver. The gantums gradually changed their focus as a result of their repeated failures and the dwarven civilization's cunning tactics. Their basic impulses and the lure of the wild drew them to the untamed territories across the border. They found peace in embracing their primal nature, living off the terrain, and indulging in their most primitive urges, despite their brutal power and towering stature.

The Gantum settled into their own primal ways, carving out a savage existence in the wilderness. They became nomadic, roaming the untamed lands, hunting fearsome creatures, and reveling in the untamed chaos of the wild. They built crude encampments and wicked spires acting as fortifications, relying on their physical might and innate ferocity to protect their territories. Some spires were built so that the gantums would attempt to go over the border, but after many failed attempts, they gave up.

With the dwarves eluding their grasp and their bloodlust subsiding, the gantums forged their own path, far removed from the ordered realms and the conflicts that once consumed them. In the wild, they found a freedom that they had longed for, embracing their primal instincts and playing with their savage desires. However, food was becoming a lingering issue for their kind, and with their gigantic stature, they needed to feed constantly. This worried their kind as they started to learn about themselves and work together as a community for the first time since birth.

·······

The Elves, under the leadership of their queen, decided to part ways with the Ranuk following the Gantum assault. They retreated to the lush western islands and turned their focus toward the study and preservation of the primal civilizations that coexisted in their vicinity. The elves observed and learned from these cultures, appreciating the wisdom and simplicity they offered, driven by their curiosity and thirst for knowledge. They found inspiration in the unspoiled beauty and untamed energy of the world's primal forces.

The Ranuki, who lived in Paranova's western regions were one of the various civilizations that the Elves found particularly fascinating. The Ranuk way of life was simple, and they believed they could glean valuable insights from this primal civilization without direct involvement. Over time, the Ranuk society began to splinter into distinct clans, and the elves noticed that disputes often revolved around the color of their skin.

In the midst of heated debates among the elven regarding leadership and their tolerance of the ranuk, a momentous decision was reached. An emerging leader determined that the island and kingdom should be reserved exclusively for elves to preserve their own kin and ensure their safety. The bitter memories of the gantum's destruction had left the elven kind wary, and they pledged to stay out of the troubles of other races. Their doors were open for trade and sharing wisdom, but from a distance, as they observed the world's races without direct involvement.

The Elves, driven by their resilience and determination, embarked on a new chapter of rebuilding and renewal. On the lush western islands, they began constructing a new kingdom on top of foundations that had seemingly been started, a tribute to their indomitable spirit and their desire to reclaim what was lost. With their inherent affinity for craftsmanship and architectural mastery, the elves weaved their intricate designs across the islands, connecting them with bridges and pathways that spanned the shimmering waters. They chose a large island that was not far from the coast of the mainland.

With every stone laid and every structure erected, the elven kingdom grew, mirroring the grandeur and magnificence of the once-prosperous Central Kingdom. They worked tirelessly to recreate the beauty and harmony they once knew and loved, infusing their new kingdom with echoes of the past while embracing the opportunities for growth and transformation.

Recognizing the need for security and isolation, the elves built massive walls around their kingdom, creating a barrier between the outer world and their emerging society. Within the gates of their kingdom, the elves worked hard to become the best at everything they did. They utilized their skills in art, magic, and studies. They created educational academies where knowledge was treasured and passed down through generations, ensuring the preservation of their remarkable past.

As the emerging Elven kingdom began to take shape, the islands prospered with a renewed sense of life and purpose. The steadfast elves, undaunted by the scars of the past, looked to the future with optimism and focus, eager to construct a legacy that remembered their lost family while celebrating their limitless potential. The elves have built a new home for themselves, demonstrating their determination and steadfast spirit.

The elves are carving out a new home, living proof of their resilience and unwavering spirit. As they worked diligently to rebuild what they had lost, the walls of their kingdom stood as a symbol of their unity, protecting and nurturing the flame of elven heritage. The stage was set for a new era of prosperity, where the echoes of the past mingled with the promise of a brighter future and the western islands shimmered with the hope of a resurgent elven civilization.

The world shifted and evolved, while the races of Paranova adapted to their newfound realities. Primal civilizations thrived, embracing the rhythms of nature and the delicate balance of chaos and order. The scars of war remained, a testament to the consequences of unchecked conflict but also a reminder of the resilience and enduring spirit of the mortal races.

As the Gantum threat subsided in the western and central regions, the Ranuk saw an opportunity to break off into distinct clans and venture in separate directions. They dispersed across the western and central continents, with each clan identifying themselves by the color of their skin. In their belief system, they considered themselves chosen by a deity to belong to a specific clan based on their skin color. This division marked a new chapter in Ranuki history as they embraced their own paths and destinies on Paranova.

• • • • • • • •

Perched upon her dark throne, the Archon observed the newly erected mountainous border with a mixture of satisfaction and intrigue. She understood the significance of this barrier and the challenges it posed to her chaotic ambitions. Torn by the circumstances that seemed to find her, with her leader tracking her movements and her emotions growing closer to the Provisioner, she knew she had to devise new methods to sow disorder.

A subtle smile curled upon her lips as she contemplated her next move. She realized that a direct assault would only lead to more setbacks and the potential unity of forces against her, drawing unwanted attention. Although tasked with guiding these colossal beings, she began to formulate a plan to aid them while also advancing her own chaotic agenda.

She cast an unnoticed glance at Havoc, her loyal companion and co-conspirator. Within the depths of her eyes, there was a flicker of focus, and radiance appeared brightly. Setbacks did not deter the Archon; instead, she saw them as opportunities to fine-tune her methods and sow disruption in more subtle ways.

Whispering words of darkness and mischief to Havoc, she outlined her new plan. It would be a subtle manipulation, a twisting of the threads of fate, which would sow discord and chaos among the races. The Archon understood that her power lay not in brute force alone but in the insidious nature of her influence.

Together, the Archon and Havoc delved into forbidden knowledge, seeking hidden secrets and ancient texts that would allow them to infiltrate the hearts and minds of mortals. They hatched a scheme to exploit the desires, fears, and vulnerabilities of the races, weaving a web of intrigue and deception that would slowly erode the stability and unity established by the Provisioner.

With their newfound knowledge, the Archon and Havoc began their subtle campaign, manipulating events and planting seeds of doubt and conflict. They would carry out their plans in the shadows, where they would go unnoticed by the mortals they hoped to influence. The Archon reveled in the art of manipulation, relishing in the chaos that would arise.

As Havoc vanished into the shadows, the Archon felt a sense of regret for her Gantum creations. In her desire to help them, she provided trees in the northern regions that produced a sweet nectar containing enough sustenance to feed a giant. This plan was driven not by malice but by the deep affection she held for her first solo creation. It was maternal love—a mother's care for her child.

The Archon engineered the nectar to subtly alter the Gantum DNA. Over generations, it would cause their offspring to become smaller and smaller. Additionally, the nectar had different effects depending on the race of the consumer, a peculiar and unexpected outcome. The Archon could not bear to witness the extinction or destruction of her gigantic children, and she believed that this approach was the best means for them to continue their existence in the world of Paranova.

Havoc, the cunning architect of chaos, devised a devious plan to exploit the Spectral Avatars and their connection to the dark ones. He saw an opportunity to stoke the flames of animosity and division, planting seeds of hatred and discord within the hearts of the dark ones towards their elven counterparts.

With a wicked gleam in his eyes, Havoc called upon the Spectral Avatars, whispering dark whispers into their ethereal forms. He commanded them to weave their spectral threads into the very fabric of the dark ones' consciousness, implanting thoughts of resentment, envy, and a thirst for vengeance. The Avatars, under Havoc's insidious guidance, became agents of chaos, sowing the seeds of hatred with their spectral touch.

Invisible to mortal eyes, the Spectral Avatars glided among the dark ones, whispering twisted tales of elven superiority and perceived injustices and slights. They stoked the flames of rivalry, exploiting the darkest corners of the dark ones' minds, making them see the elves as enemies and oppressors.

As the whispers of chaos seeped into the hearts of the dark ones, a noticeable shift began to take hold. Hatred brewed, fueled by the spectral influence and the lingering wounds of past conflicts. The dark ones, once distant from the disturbance within the elven realms, now felt a burning desire for retribution and dominance.

With great delight, Havoc celebrated the triumph of his scheme, fully aware that he had instilled a severity of discord within the dark ones. He took pleasure in anticipating the forthcoming mayhem and unrest—a colossal clash between two races teetering on the brink of warfare. Havoc saw a rare opportunity for chaos to rule supreme and for unrelenting conflict to stoke the flames that would consume the entire world.

Havoc's subtle plan took root, setting in motion a chain of events that would test the resilience of the dark ones and the delicate balance of Paranova. The Spectral Avatars, guided by Havoc's wickedness, continued their whispered manipulation, sowing the seeds of hatred and fueling the flames of chaos that would shape the destiny of the world.

Havoc successfully planted the seeds and then turned his attention to the spectral followers sent to feed on the fresh human and dwarven races. These spectrals drained the energy from the souls created by the Provisioner, gathering what Havoc needed for his own creation—an entity of darkness. Sneaking into the creation chamber, he gathered the necessary materials and the remaining energy to birth this new entity.

He then directed this energy down into the atmosphere of Paranova, initiating the cycle for the creation to manifest on its own. Havoc took immense pleasure in conducting his own plans, separate from the influence of the Archon or other shapers. He acknowledged the crucial role of the Archon's arcane energy in the preparation of his creation. Insights gathered about the entities present in the world before Paranova existed gave Havoc the knowledge needed to craft this new entity of darkness, intending to bring true balance to the world in a way that had never been seen before.

Unbeknownst to Havoc and the Archon, the ever-watchful Keeper had devised a clever means of tracking their secret machinations. The plants that he had scattered across the realms served as his silent witnesses, attuned to the whispers of chaos and the dark dealings that unfolded. They absorbed the secrets carried in the wind, transmitting their knowledge to the Keeper's vigilant mind. While chaos brewed and schemes took shape, the Keeper remained vigilant, gathering the pieces of the puzzle that would soon reveal the true extent of Havoc's treachery.

The Keeper informed the Provisioner of the worrying news through the whispers of his watchful plants, exposing the depths of Havoc's deceit. Despite the urgency of the situation, the Provisioner's unwavering faith in the mortal races held firm. He recognized the delicate balance that must be maintained and understood that creating more borders would only maintain the cycle of conflict.

Instead, he chose a path of trust and patience, allowing the mortal races to navigate their own destinies and learn from their triumphs and mistakes. He believed that, through their experiences and growth, they would forge their own paths towards unity and harmony. Thus, the Provisioner refrained from intervening directly, placing his hope in the innate resilience and potential of the mortal races to rise above the whispers of chaos and steer their own course towards a brighter future.

The Provisioner, understanding the delicate balance between the races and their respective territories, made it clear to the Keeper that he preferred not to intervene in the conflicts between the races. Recognizing that the mountains served as a natural barrier, secluding a portion of the world, the Provisioner believed that it was necessary for each race to find their own path and coexist in their own domains.

The Keeper, realizing the potential destruction and disruption caused by the behemoth creatures, expressed his regret and apologized for his intervention. He shared the Provisioner's desire to witness the flourishing of the other races, free from the looming threat of the colossal beasts. Grateful for the Keeper's understanding, the Provisioner thanked him for his efforts while also urging him to refrain from taking such drastic measures again, emphasizing the importance of allowing the races to navigate their own destinies.

The Provisioner found himself standing outside the Oracle's sanctuary, ready to seek advice on the newfound evidence of Havoc's influence. However, something inside him compelled him to change his course and head directly to the Archon for a discussion. He found her more alluring than ever when he entered her quarters because of her transformed celestial energies. The Archon descended from her throne, where she oversaw the world below, and she warmly embraced the Provisioner, curious about the reason for his visit.

While the Provisioner had important matters to discuss, he decided to savor the moment and share his thoughts with the Archon. She encouraged him to lay his burdens on her and speak in a relaxed manner. He informed her about reports of spectral avatars sowing discord among mortals, causing hatred, and undermining unity. The Archon, initially upset with Havoc's actions, could not help but feel sympathy for the Provisioner's passionate dedication to Paranova.

She contemplated ending these meetings because they were drawing her and the Provisioner into an intimate connection, something she knew was her own doing. However, instead of cutting it short, she assured him that she would investigate the situation. She mentioned that Havoc had been out of sight for some time, following the scolding from the Anarchist, and assured the Provisioner that Havoc's influence was nothing to worry about. The Archon emphasized that the beauty and excellence of the Provisioner's creations had mirrored those of himself, leaving him flattered and content as he allowed the Archon to embrace and relax him further into her quarters, where he would rest.

As the Provisioner chose to place his faith in the mortal races and abstain from direct intervention, little did he know that Havoc, fueled by a sinister determination, had yet another cunning plan hidden in the depths of his twisted mind. With the seeds of chaos sown and the specter of hatred growing within the hearts of the dark ones, Havoc's ultimate intentions remained shrouded in mystery, hinting at a looming threat that would challenge the very foundations of Paranova's fragile equilibrium. The stage was set for a new chapter of turmoil and confrontation as Havoc's sinister deceptions continued to unfold, threatening to plunge the realm into an abyss of darkness and chaos.

Chapter 4: Realms Unveiled

Paranova saw the growth and expansion of numerous civilizations that had formed as an outcome of the onslaught of Gantum as the very motions of the Order and Chaos suspense drew near. The traits and objectives that were distinctive to each racial group ultimately determined their own trajectories.

The Dwarves, who were persistent in their pursuit of technological advancement and commercialization, kept themselves busy within their fortified underground cities. They were prepared for any danger that might come their way because of the superior quality of the weapons and armor they had crafted.

The passage through the years after the Gantum War had brought about a natural division among the dwarven kind, which gave rise to three distinct clans within the growing dwarven civilization. Each of these clans had their own separate priorities and characteristics, and each had their own special place in society.

The Underground Clan, led by the first king, passionately cultivated their hidden kingdom buried beneath the foundations of the earth, where darkness ruled and mysteries rested. This was done under the wise direction of King Loden, who was constant in his commitment to the cause. Their efforts centered on the extraction of resources and the mastery of craftsmanship, and what they did was proof of their constant devotion to quality. Their operations centered on the mastery of craftsmanship.

The Underground Dwarves had uncovered the mysteries of mining and excavation deep within the earth's embrace. They did this by tirelessly exploring the labyrinthine network of tunnels that connected their underground region. They searched for the earth's hidden splendor, uncovering valuable minerals, shimmering gemstones, and abundant veins of priceless ores with skillful hands and tenacious spirits. The kingdom they had carved out of the darkness glistened with the results of their labor.

Their vast underground cities resounded to the music of roaring forges and the steady tinkling of hammers on anvils. Expert craftspeople, their fingers calloused and steady, toiled tirelessly, channeling the energy of flame and molten metal. The flickering glow of their forges gave birth to magnificent works of art, which were the result of a combination of innate ability and generations' worth of accumulated wisdom and knowledge. From intricate jewelry to elaborate weapons, the underground dwarves' work showed that they were experts in both metalworking and craftsmanship.

The cities themselves were feats of engineering, serving as a demonstration of the underground clan's inventiveness and resourcefulness. Massive chambers that were linked together by a convoluted system of tunnels housed bustling workshops. These workshops were where skilled craftspeople honed their abilities and crafted items of exquisite beauty. The architecture, which had been hewed from the very bones of the earth, blended in perfectly with the organic contours of the underworld it was a part of. Magnificent halls that were decorated with stalactites and stalagmites served as witnesses to the elegance of the kingdom.

The Underground clan had abundant resources that promoted their expansion and economic growth. The metals and minerals that they mined from the earth served as society's lifeblood, allowing them to produce not only magnificent works of art but also highly sophisticated tools and machinery. These materials were extracted from the earth. As they pushed the limits of innovation and engineering, their forges became full, overflowing with the flames of progress.

It goes without saying that the underground dwarves thrived below, far away from their enemies, predators, and the political nonsense that afflicted the surface. The clan was often made fun of for living in isolation, but nobody could match their skill when compared to their craftsmanship. Other clans that departed the underground kingdom as a result of various differences made the decision to do so in order to look for their own lands in which to live their lives in a different manner after departure.

Perched atop the craggy summits of the majestic mountains, the Mountaintop Clan had claimed their rightful place, forging a realm of strength and security amidst the lofty heights. The land they inhabited was proof of their faithful commitment to fortitude and defense. From their rocky strongholds, expertly chiseled into the rugged terrain, they stood as sentinels, guardians of the heavens. They had used their expertise from building within the underground cities to construct strong foundations within the mountains.

Strategic in their choices, the Mountaintop Dwarves had built their dwellings in locations that offered both natural advantages and impenetrable barriers. With a keen understanding of the land's topography, they harnessed its formidable features to create fortresses that seemed to blend seamlessly with the very stone from which they were carved. These architectural marvels stood as symbols of their resilience, impenetrable bastions that withstood the test of time.

The mountaintop clan had honed the art of fortification to perfection. Their structures were not mere monuments; they were living, breathing entities designed to repel any threat that dared approach their sacred peaks. Elaborate defensive mechanisms, cunningly crafted traps, and intricate mazes wove together to create an intricate web of protection. Within the heart of these fortresses, the mountaintop dwarves trained in the arts of war, their skills in military strategy unmatched.

From their lofty vantage points, the mountaintop clan gazed down upon the world below, their watchful eyes scanning the land with unwavering vigilance. They were the vigilant guardians of their clan and its treasures, entrusted with the responsibility of preserving their ancient legacy. The mountains whispered secrets to them, and their winds carried messages of approaching danger. With stubborn dedication, they stood ready to defend their domain, their resolve as unshakable as the peaks they called home. They had used the peaks to traverse over the northern border or for trade amongst the other dwarven clans.

Within the walls of their mountain strongholds, life thrived in a harmonious blend of functionality and beauty. Halls adorned with intricate carvings and grand tapestries spoke of the clan's rich heritage. Laboratories and workshops hummed with activity, as the mountaintop dwarves were similar to the underground clan within the realm of craftsmanship and innovation. Their creations, crafted with detailed precision, were renowned far and wide, showcasing their mastery over both art and science.

As the sun cast its golden glow upon the jagged peaks, the mountaintop clan remained steadfast, united in their commitment to protect their mountain domain. Their dedication to security and defense infused every aspect of their existence. Within the rugged contours of the mountains, the clan had built strongholds of resilience and watchfulness, a testament to their unbreakable spirit and the strength that lay within their fortified realm.

A resilient clan developed amidst the raw beauty and rugged terrain found in the wilderness, where fresh snow covered the territory in a shimmering white blanket. These dwarves, known as the Wilderness Clan, embraced a way of life that was significantly built on nature's vital core. Their spirits melded with the wild as they honed their survival instincts and forged a connection with the bountiful yet unforgiving landscape.

The Wilderness Dwarves displayed the full essence of hardship and adaptability, dwelling the center of dense woods and steep slopes. They were the masters of the hunt, navigating the woods with grace and skill that appeared essentially exceptional. They roamed across the snow-covered pathways, tracing the footprints of their land and exploiting the resources that the environment provided, with keen senses and tracking expertise.

Often, these dwarves would find themselves in conflict with other wilderness dwarves or gantums. The various settlements declared which tribe a wilderness dwarf belonged to, as the wilderness dwarves had small tribes among the wilderness clan, which were often dedicated to a territory among the harsh lands sprawled throughout the northern reaches of Paranova.

Their settlements blended in with the natural beauty. Their buildings and homes melded into the surrounding environment, made of strong materials taken from the old trees and large stones. These homes served as both sanctuaries and castles, providing shelter from the freezing cold and defense against the dangers that lurked in the wilderness. The dwarves used the environment as camouflage wherever they chose to settle.

The woodland dwarves were known for their self-sufficiency and ferocious independence. Each member of the clan was raised to be a warrior, understanding that survival in the harsh wilderness required both strength and ability. These warriors were masters of their particular combat practices, using their weapons with a ravaging elegance reminiscent of snowflakes falling in the wind.

Despite their tough exteriors, they had a genuine respect for the region they called home. They were more than just conquerors of the wilderness; they were its defenders. They recognized nature's fragile balance and worked to maintain it by using its resources with the greatest care and respect. Their way of life had an unbreakable connection to the seasonal cycles, and they celebrated the shifting tides of the wild with rituals and traditions that revered the spirits of the land.

The Wilderness clan remained faithful in their loyalty to their ancestral lands as the breezes moaned through the towering trees and the snowflakes gracefully grasped the earth. They stood as the pioneers of the woodland, defending their territory from any threat that dared trespass on their reign with unrelenting endurance. Their strength, ingenuity, and deep connection with nature distinguished them as an unstoppable force in Paranova's untamed wilderness.

Though these three clans had their own distinct focuses and priorities, they shared a common heritage and remained connected through a deep-rooted kinship. Together, they formed a formidable force, each contributing their unique strengths and expertise to the collective strength of the dwarven civilization. Despite their differences, a shared pride in their ancestry and faithful dedication to their people bound them together, ensuring their continued prosperity in the face of the ever-unfolding challenges that lay ahead.

....

After the fall of the Central Kingdom, certain factions of mortals from other races went to the eastern lands for safety instead of going west with the rest of the refugees. Many of the refugees dispersed throughout the eastern lands after hearing stories about the city of the sands. The city had developed a reputation for sanctuary and entertainment. Many mortals were drawn to the city in search of new opportunities and refuge.

The growing settlement proclaimed itself to be a vibrant city capable of competing with those found in any kingdom. Baldreth became the name of the city. The resourceful and inventive mortals who lived in this eastern landscape achieved great success as a result of their dedication to creative ideals and self-sufficiency. They harnessed the desert's power and took advantage of its abundant resources. They had used their creativity to build a thriving community in what seemed like a barren environment.

Their excellent engineering and infrastructure were clear evidence of the challenging efforts of the eastern humans. The Baldreth humans were the first of their kind to demonstrate advancement through their evolution as humans. They created complicated water channel and reservoir systems, cleverly gathering and storing scarce water resources to sustain agriculture and meet the requirements of their increasing population. Their skilled artisans and workers created stunning designs and artwork that reflected both their rich cultural background and the majestic beauty of their barren surroundings.

As the easterners sought imaginative solutions to the obstacles provided by their surroundings, creativity blossomed in Baldreth. They devised effective desert farming practices, applying specialized techniques and drought-resistant crops to generate sustainable food sources. Their architects designed one-of-a-kind structures that fit into the desert terrain by using locally accessible materials in unconventional ways.

Baldreth's diligent inhabitants were also well-known for their trade and commerce. They created booming marketplaces that attracted traders from all over the world and fostered a lively flow of products, ideas, and cultural influences. Their creative minds encouraged them to seek new opportunities, making them an essential component in global trade networks and contributing to the city's financial prosperity.

Among their many efforts, the residents of Baldreth recognized the value of maintaining their cultural history and traditions. They honored their heritage through diverse types of art, storytelling, and lively festivals that drew the community together. Craftspeople, scholars, and thinkers from many origins gathered in the city to contribute to the collective development and growth of eastern culture among humans.

Baldreth's industrious and innovative individuals continued to shape their purpose through this expanding hub of invention and creativity, finding inspiration in their environment's difficulties and using their resourcefulness to construct a prosperous future for themselves and future generations.

Baldreth, which became the new city of unity and resilience, stood as a testament to the resilient nature of all mortal races. Within its bustling streets, diverse inhabitants from every corner of Paranova put aside their differences, united by the common goal of survival in the face of the harshest conditions. With refugees coming from the Gantum onslaught, it brought an opportunity for Humans, Elves, Ranuk, and Dwarves to live together in a city that was far away from civilizations. Each of them found common ground here, fostering a spirit of cooperation, respect, and mutual understanding.

Traditions intertwined, wisdom was shared, and alliances were formed in this vibrant variety of cultures, resulting in a harmonious community that thrived against all odds. Baldreth became a shining example of what could be accomplished when unity triumphed over division, reminding all who entered its gates that they could overcome any challenge that the world threw at them.

Yet, beyond the borders of this thriving metropolis, a primal civilization appeared, drawn by curiosity and a desire to claim Baldreth's riches for their own. This civilization, made up of two distinct tribes known as the Gorn and Rook, had made their home on the outskirts of the deserts, seeking to own territory in the oases created by Baldreth ingenuity. These small oases held lush vegetation and water pools scattered all around the desert that helped support and navigate wandering travelers.

The wonders of the city of Baldreth enthralled the Gorn and Rook tribes, who had initially been nothing more than scavengers. They kept a watchful eye on the shadows, their animal instincts stimulated by the allure of what could be found within the walls of the city. Their desire to acquire the wealth of understanding and precious items that the city held excited their passion for their growing desire to learn more about the advancing humanity. The two groups had absolutely no intention of making peace with the people of Baldreth. The people of Baldreth were resources for the tribesmen.

As the tribes made their way closer to Baldreth City, they became aware of the oasis' that was scattered throughout the region. These natural sanctuaries provided comfort and rest from the harshness of the desert and ended up playing an essential role in the survival of these primitive tribes. These oases provided the Gorn and Rook tribes with a place of refuge, allowing them to regain their strength and satisfy their thirst while navigating the harsh desert.

The arrival of these primitive tribes, however, caused the landscape outside of Baldreth to change. Their presence turned what were once peaceful areas into hostile territories, making the journey hazardous for those who wanted to explore beyond the confines of the city. Both the Gorn and the Rook tribes had insatiable curiosity and fierce territorial instincts, which led them to fiercely defend their newly acquired shelters because they saw them as their own territory.

It was inevitable that hostilities would break out between Baldreth city and the Gorn and Rook tribes. The scavengers had developed into fearsome warriors who were skilled at surviving in hostile environments and driven by a strong desire to take possession of the city's treasures. Baldreth's advanced technologies clashed with the primal forces of the tribes, resulting in skirmishes and battles that echoed across the desert sands.

Baldreth's history is characterized by the struggle between modernism and animal instinct. It was a constant reminder of the precarious balance that exists between mortal progress and the forces of nature. While the city thrived within its walls, with innovation and enlightenment lighting the lives of its people, the primitive tribes that lived outside the city walls sought to reclaim what they believed to be rightfully theirs, as they had seen the desert as their territory.

The struggle between the city and the tribes grew throughout time, resulting in regular conflicts and tensions. The tribes, strongly anchored in their traditional traditions, saw the city's development as a threat to their way of life and a violation of their ancestral territory. This collision of philosophies and territorial claims generated a volatile situation that established the complex history of Baldreth.

In the ongoing struggle for dominance, Baldreth city stood as living proof of the determination of civilization, whereas the Gorn and

Rook tribes embodied the wild spirit of the desert. Their conflict would determine the course of events in the region, giving rise to tales of heroism and resilience, as well as the age-old struggle between the primal and the civilized.

The clash between Baldreth City and the tribes was not just a battle for land but also a clash of ideologies. The tribes believed in the freedom of the desert, while the city dwellers valued order and progress. This clash would shape the future of the region, forcing both sides to question their own beliefs and ultimately leading to unforeseen consequences.

········

During this time, the Dark Ones, who were deeply rooted in their passionate devotion to the Fire God, began to investigate destructive forms of magic. They established their own castes, channeling their chaotic energies with the goal of molding the world in accordance with their passionate beliefs. The fierce fires of their religion burned brightly, casting a sinister gloom over the realms they ruled.

They had discovered the arcane source that the Archon had placed within their volcano, and due to their natural connection with elemental magic, they swiftly devised methods to tap into and utilize the arcane energy. This connection drew them nearer to chaos, unlike the Light Ones, who kept the arcane under more control.

The Dark Ones' impact grew to the south of Paranova, and their presence of chaos and disorder spread throughout the area like a menacing shadow. As they delved further into forbidden magics and embraced the darker sides of their nature, their castes expanded in strength and influence. An unexpected friendship among the dark ones and the infamous human raiders from the south-west began to take shape within this region of the world. All the while the friendship began to take shape, the seedlings that the Keeper planted observed that these two groups were interacting with one another more frequently and immediately recognized the presence of a vicious plot.

The Keeper overheard rumors of sinister ceremonies and illegal pacts, which filled him with fear and apprehension. The fact that the chaotic nature of the dark ones and the ruthlessness of the human raiders were able to combine gave the impression that they were working together in some evil scheme. The Keeper had a sneaking suspicion that their union would result in the release of a formidable force, a catalyst for destruction, and an upset of the delicate balance that existed in Paranova.

As the signs of their collaboration grew more apparent, the Keeper remained vigilant, his gaze fixed upon the unfolding events. He knew that the harmony of Paranova hung in the balance, and he would not rest until he uncovered the true extent of their chaotic planning and devised a countermeasure to protect the mortal races from the impending storm.

Deep in the rugged southwestern region, the human raiders found an unlikely refuge within the decaying carcass of a massive Gantum defeated during the war. The colossal creature, once feared for its destructive power, now served as a formidable fortress for the resourceful raiders. Its towering skeletal remains provided a natural shield against intruders and a grim reminder of the gantums' former reign of terror.

Within the hollowed-out body of the fallen behemoth, the raiders established their home, utilizing the sturdy bones as a framework for their defenses. The twisted remains of the creature's innards were repurposed into chambers, armories, and lookout points, creating a labyrinthine network within the organic fortress. The raiders transformed the grim surroundings into a base of operations, where they plotted their next raids and fortified their position against potential enemies.

The eerie atmosphere of the Gantum corpse served as a constant reminder of the primal forces that once dominated the land. The raiders, drawn to its dark allure, saw in this gruesome shelter both protection and a symbol of their defiance against the established society. With each passing day, their unity with the decaying gantum grew stronger, fueling their ambitions and driving them to unleash chaos upon Paranova.

Unbeknownst to the raiders, the ancient bones whispered ancient secrets and carried remnants of the gantums' primordial power. As they made their home within the confines of the colossal corpse, the raiders unwittingly tapped into an ancient energy, intertwining their fate with the remnants of a fallen titan. Little did they realize the true consequences of their chosen abode, as the dormant forces within the gantum's bones began to stir, imbuing the raiders with a strange resilience and a hunger for destruction.

The gigantic corpse that they inhabited exuded unknown energy, not only nourished their spirits but also affected their physical forms. Over generations, the raiders transformed into larger physical forms, displaying a blend of Human and Gantum characteristics. They would later name their dwelling Gloomrot, a place known for its eerie ambiance and intimidating physicality. Their alliance with the Dark Ones aided the humans in acquiring knowledge of magic, a skill the Elven kind disapproved of primal civilizations acquiring.

·······

Amidst the grand tapestry of Paranova, the primal human tribes thrived in their respective domains. Divided into many tribes, however, there were six of them with a vast population of humans during that time: forest, mountain, snowdrop, desolate, rocky, and desert areas. They fiercely guarded their ancestral territories, remaining hostile to outsiders who dared to trespass. Each tribe held its own unique customs and traditions, forging their own path through the wilderness.

A strong connection with nature and the rhythms of the forest was recognized by the Human Forest Tribe, who lived within the expansive verdant forests of Paranova. Their traditions and culture revolved around their harmonious coexistence with the extensive nature and fauna that surrounded them.

The forest tribe worshiped the spirits of ancient trees and believed in the intricate web of life that spanned their sacred groves. To make peace with the forest spirits and gain their blessing and protection, they engaged in ceremonial and spiritual practices. Their culture respected nature's balance, and they were aware of the delicate balance between living things and the forest's alluring world.

Forest tribal elders preserved traditional wisdom. They taught the younger members about herbalism, tracking, and survival techniques, assuring the continuation of their rich heritage. The tribe's members had an instinctive grasp of the forest's mysteries, allowing them to forage for medicinal plants, hunt sustainably, and navigate the curved routes with a remarkable accuracy.

Community and cooperation were at the core of the forest tribe's values. They celebrated unity and shared responsibilities, with each member contributing to the tribe's well-being. Together, they constructed dwellings nestled among the trees, woven with branches and adorned with vibrant foliage. They would gather around communal fires, their laughter and songs echoing through the forest canopy, forging deep bonds of kinship.

The Forest tribe adopted a simpler way of life, attuned to the whispers of woodland creatures and the murmurs of ancient trees. They found peace and meaning in their strong relationship with nature, deriving inspiration from its beauty and wisdom. Their culture was immersed in an appreciation for the beauties of the forest, cultivating a sense of belonging and a strong affection for the area they called home.

Amidst the extensive branches of an elegant tree, brought to life by the expert hands of the Forger, the tribe discovered serenity and harmony at the heart of the ancient forest. They were unaware that Vigoroth, an elemental entity that Havoc had discovered, lay asleep underneath a complex underground system of elements below the surface.

In their primal wisdom, they had discovered a deep connection to this towering creation. They gathered around the massive tree, their spirits entwined with the essence of nature that pulsed through its bark and leaves. They spoke to the tree, seeking guidance, protection, and a deeper understanding of the world around them. They believed they were communicating with a god, an entity they called Vigoroth, unaware of its true nature.

Vigoroth, ancient and bound to the very essence of the forest, remained a silent observer, listening to the pleas and prayers of the human tribe. It drew sustenance from their reverence and devotion; its presence amplified the natural energies that flowed through the surrounding lands. The tribe looked to Vigoroth as their guardian and guide; their faith was unshakeable.

Underneath the forest canopy, the human tribe held ceremonies, their chants and rituals echoing through the ancient trees. They offered gifts of flowers, fruits, and delicate trinkets, believing that their offerings would please Vigoroth and grant them favor. Little did they realize that their rituals stirred the slumbering entity, awakening a connection between their world and the elemental forces that lived within it.

Through this communion with Vigoroth, the Forest tribe found harmony and wisdom. They learned the secrets of the terrain, understanding its ebb and flow and its cycles of life and decay. Vigoroth, in its silent presence, bestowed upon them a deeper understanding of the natural world, granting them the ability to harness the raw energy that surged through the roots and branches of the colossal tree.

Unbeknownst to the Forest tribe, their communion with Vigoroth was a testament to their innate connection with the primal forces of the world. The tree, an embodiment of the Forger's artistry, had become a conduit through which they could tap into the elemental energies that coursed through Paranova. They unwittingly shared their hopes, dreams, and fears with an entity that transcended their mortal comprehension.

In the depths of the forest, the tribe thrived under the watchful presence of Vigoroth, their lives intertwined with the mystical energies that pulsed through the gigantic tree. They celebrated their unity with nature, guided by the entity they believed to be a divine presence. Little did they know that their communion with Vigoroth would shape their destiny and reveal the true extent of their primal connection to the world around them.

The forest tribe, with their connection to Vigoroth, once made a collective request for rain to nurture their crops beneath the forest canopy. Their plea was answered, and a blessed rainfall rejuvenated their crops and allowed sunlight to filter through the trees. This place, where the miraculous event occurred through their God's assistance, became known as the Dew. In time, it evolved into the central hub around which the tribe built their community.

The Human Mountain Tribe, who were deeply connected to their mountainous environment, had a great affection and regard for the varied diversity of creatures who called the rough peaks home. They had a special relationship with the animals, regarding them as divine friends and protectors of their ancestral territories.

Within the mountain tribe's customs and culture, animals played an important role in the traditions and culture. They thought that every animal possessed a spiritual soul and possessed certain characteristics that mirrored the features valued by their civilization. Members of the tribe would frequently embrace animal totems, embracing the attributes and strengths connected with their chosen creature.

Rituals and ceremonies were held to honor and speak with the animal spirits. The mountain tribe sought direction, protection, and harmony with the natural world through their sacred activities. They believed that by developing a close relationship with the animals, they would obtain wisdom and learn essential lessons about survival, adaptation, and strength.

The tribe's affection for animals went beyond the spiritual realm. They had a strong preference for domesticating and training animals to help them in their daily lives. The mountain tribe possessed a great awareness of animal instincts and behavior, allowing them to form unique connections with species such as mountain goats, rams, falcons, and wolves.

Mountain goats and rams were respected for their agility and surefootedness, acting as trusted guides and companions on risky travels through the steep terrain. Falcons, with their keen eyesight and aerial prowess, were regarded as messengers and guardians, offering protection and providing insights into the mysteries of the mountains, while wolves, renowned for their loyalty and pack mentality, were regarded as scavenging companions and guardians of the tribe's camps and settlements.

The mountain tribe's regard for animals was mirrored in their environmentally friendly habits. They hunted responsibly, taking care not to disrupt the delicate natural balance of the landscape. They saw themselves as land stewards, carefully controlling their interactions with animal life to ensure harmony and abundance for future generations.

Through their intimate connection with animals, they embraced a culture that valued the diversity and interconnection of all living species. Their traditions honored the wisdom and teachings provided by animals, directing their daily activities and instilling admiration for the natural environment that surrounded them.

High amidst the towering peaks, where the air was crisp and the rugged terrain unforgiving, the human mountain tribe ventured forth on their daring expeditions. It was during one such journey that they unexpectedly crossed paths with the dwarven mountaintop clan; their encounter initially shrouded in tension and conflict. The primal humans, driven by their primal instincts, saw the dwarves as rivals, while the dwarves, wary of intruders, stood their ground.

Both groups of mountain-dwelling people faced numerous frigid nights and howling winds as a recurring challenge over the years. The conflicts between humans and dwarves, though frequent, didn't prolong themselves. Their battles typically reached a standstill atop the lofty peaks. Each victory for one side meant descending into a downhill struggle for both groups.

However, as the years passed and the clashes gave way to conversations, a surprising relationship began to emerge. The human tribe, known for its strength and endurance, discovered a kindred spirit in the mountain-dwelling dwarves. They recognized in each other the will to withstand the treacherous heights and challenging conditions that surrounded them.

Curiosity won out over rivalry as the two groups exchanged stories and experiences, discovering common ground in their struggle for survival and prosperity. Renowned for their mastery of ale brewing, the dwarves taught their knowledge to the humble humans. They taught them the technique of extracting the essence of grains, fruits, and herbs, altering them into powerfully potent beverages that could warm even the coldest of nights and bring joy to hearts that were heavy with exhaustion.

The human mountain tribe, for their part, revealed their intimate knowledge of the peaks, guiding the dwarves over risky roads and hidden pathways. They showed the natural treasures that littered the mountainsides, ranging from rare medicinal herbs to mineral-rich caves. The dwarves used their mastery of crafting to make tools and trinkets that improved the lives of the primitive humans. In exchange for the dwarven friendship, the humans were willing to share the patient nature and compassion necessary to domesticate the mountain creatures.

As trust grew between the human mountain tribe and the dwarven mountaintop clan, so did friendship. They learned to value the distinct abilities and characteristics that each group possessed. The primal humans respected the dwarves' inventiveness and pristine craftsmanship, while the dwarves adored the humans' tenacity and resourcefulness in navigating the harsh, rocky environment.

As the mountain tribe and the dwarves gathered around crackling fires, trading stories and raising their cups loaded with the finest drinks, laughter and happiness resonated through the peaks. The dwarves introduced the primitive humans to a world of flavors and thrilling concoctions, filling their lives with the joys of good company and lively celebration. The mountain tribe, who had previously suffered from their solitary existence, found comfort and delight in the companionship of their newfound acquaintances.

From that point forward, the human mountain tribe and the dwarven Mountaintop clan became steadfast allies, their paths intertwined as they explored the majestic peaks together. The primal humans learned the art of brewing, infusing their lives with newfound warmth and camaraderie. In return, they guided the dwarves to untapped resources, expanding their knowledge and fortifying their creations.

In the vast expanse of the mountains, the friendship between the two unique groups flourished, their shared adventures leaving an indelible mark on both societies. They proved that amidst initial conflict, understanding and friendship could grow, bridging the gap between two distinct races and enriching their lives with the bonds of unity and shared experiences.

Both groups recognized the mutual challenges of living high in the mountains and found common ground. They decided to permit passage through the rugged terrain and even considered cohabitation, forging a pact of understanding and unity.

The Rocky and Desert Tribes had temporarily combined for many years to seek out Baldreth City for the majority of their time in the timeline. Nomads to the outskirts of the desert and rocky paths in the eastern lands. The tribes together worked harmoniously but were ruled by two leaders who were battle-hardened. The first leaders were called Gorn and Rook, and the traditions were passed down to whomever was the leader for generations as the two tribes moved on after many years of attempting to take over Baldreth city. They were the only two tribes that were welcoming of outsiders within their tribes as long as they were children or babies.

The Gorn tribe developed a growing interest in trade. They transitioned from raiding to engaging in commerce, conducting operations on villages and travelers journeying to and from Baldreth to acquire valuable items. Originally, when the Gorn tribe wanted inventory, they resorted to old habits with raids or stolen goods. The trading tradition of the Gorn tribe became a legacy passed from one leader to the next. Their alliance with the Rook clan proved beneficial, as they exchanged knowledge: the Rook clan taught the Gorn how to fight, while the Rook learned from the Gorn how to adapt, survive, and communicate effectively with outsiders.

The rocky tribe, under the leadership of Rook, had predominantly resided along the rugged path connecting the central-eastern lands to the desert, living in caves near the shores or close to the main route. Unlike the Gorn tribe, they maintained their role as raiders, continuing this tradition. They were known for their minimal interaction with the outside world, limiting communication to only the Gorn tribe, whom they accepted as allies. The Rook tribe harbored aspirations of claiming Baldreth as their own haven away from civilization, yet they recognized the need for the Gorn tribe's support to pursue this goal.

The Human Desolate Tribe, situated in the western region that bore the fresh scars of the Gantum devastation, had developed a tenacious culture that blended the art of scavenging with a warrior spirit. The ongoing battles they had with the Ranuk as well as their constant struggles against the harsh environment shaped their traditions and way of life.

Scavenging was not just a means of survival for the desolate tribe; it was a deeply ingrained part of their identity. They possessed an innate ability to uncover hidden resources amidst the wreckage left in the wake of the gantum. Their scavenging expertise extended beyond mere sustenance, as they sought to find valuable relics, salvaged weapons, and pieces of technology that could give them an edge in their battles against their enemies.

The tribe's culture was marked by a strong warrior, Ethanar. Each member of the desolate tribe was trained from a young age in the arts of combat and survival, preparing them for the constant skirmishes with the ranuk. They embraced a spirit of resilience, tenacity, and adaptability, understanding that their very survival depended on their ability to defend their territories and secure vital resources.

Ethanar played a crucial role in training the fighters of the desolate tribe. He demonstrated his skill by taking on multiple fierce ranuk opponents, earning the tribe's utmost respect. Despite his efforts, the tribe realized they needed to seek help beyond their own ranks due to the harsh conditions they faced after the Gantum destruction. Fortunately, they found allies in the form of the human forest tribe. However, to their surprise, these allies chose not to engage in battle but instead offered sanctuary and seeds to aid in the restoration of the lands ravaged by colossal beasts.

Despite finding sanctuary, a significant portion of the tribe held firm to their honor-bound goal: establishing their presence in the desolate region. Meanwhile, the women in the tribe took on the vital role of nurturing the lands, striving to restore them for the benefit of future generations.

In battles against the Ranuk, the desolate tribe showcased their formidable skills as guerrilla fighters. They utilized their knowledge of the harsh terrain and their scavenged weaponry to launch ambushes, hit-and-run tactics, and stealthy raids on their enemies. Their ability to blend into their desolate surroundings, coupled with their resourcefulness in utilizing makeshift traps and concealed hideouts, made them a force to be reckoned with.

Traditions within the desolate tribe revolved around the honor and glory of battle. They celebrated acts of bravery, valor, and strategic prowess, with stories of heroic deeds passed down through generations. Warriors adorned themselves with symbols of their victories, donning armor crafted from repurposed gantum bones and displaying intricate tattoos that told tales of their triumphs and allegiances.

Despite their fierce nature and ongoing conflicts, the desolate tribe held a deep respect for the balance of nature and the land they inhabited. They recognized the importance of conserving resources and preserving the fragile ecosystems of their territory. They practiced sustainable hunting and gathering, ensuring that they did not deplete the already-scarred and ravaged environment further.

The love for scavenging in the desolate tribe was not only driven by necessity but also by a desire to reclaim and repurpose the remnants of a broken world. It was a testament to their resolute spirit as they sought to find hope, meaning, and a sense of purpose in the midst of desolation.

Through their traditions, warrior culture, and skill in scavenging, the human desolate tribe embraced a way of life that blended survival with honor and resourcefulness with valor. Their battles with the ranuk shaped their identity and forged a resilient spirit within them as they continued to thrive amidst the ruins, determined to carve out their place in a harsh and unforgiving world undeterred by the constant threats around them.

The Snowdrop Tribe, once devoted to the Gantum giants, soon realized the destructive nature of these colossal beings. Even during their ceremonies honoring them, they constantly feared succumbing to the gantum. Feeling trapped in the north with these giants, they had to adapt to their dire circumstances. The snowdrop tribe eventually discovered comfort in the valleys of the southeast of the northern part of the continent.

As they sought a way out, they found abandoned passageways and expanded them to create an escape route through the northern border wall. This became their lifeline, a means of fleeing if the gantum giants ever closed in on them. In their harsh environment, the Snowdrop tribe grew ruthless, resorting to cannibalism and raiding the settlements of wilderness dwarven clans to survive.

The ongoing raids in the north sparked substantial conflicts between the dwarves and humans, lasting for generations. The dwarves viewed human survival as a form of threat, seeing them as not quick to adapt to the environment as effectively as the dwarves had. While the dwarves employed different methods to thrive in the challenging environment, the humans resorted to taking what they needed to survive.

········

The Ranuk, finding comfort in the western woodlands and southern marshlands, sought to distance themselves from the Elven culture that once clashed with their own. They created fortified arenas within their territories, serving as battlegrounds to settle disputes and conflicts. Through a democratic process, warlords and chieftains were elected to rule their clans. Notable among them were the Mirefang Clan, the Thornshade Clan, the Tranquil Tide Clan, and the Ironspine Clan, each embodying distinct values and forging their own destinies.

A well-known woodland ranuk clan known for their tenacious defense of their territory is the Thornshade clan, under the command of their formidable Warlord Grusk Ironbark. Deeply connected to the dense forests and ancient trees, the clan holds a strong bond with nature, considering themselves guardians of the forests. They have developed unique traditions and a distinct culture that sets them apart from other ranuk clans. Thornshade are often found with green-tinted skin; this is how they are identified within one another. They believe their spirit chose a certain clan and believe that their spirit is connected to their traditions and bound to the clan.

The Thornshade clan lives under a code of honor and respect for nature, believing that their survival and growth are inseparably linked to the balance of nature. They adore woodland spirits and perform rituals to request blessings before hunting or battle. Their expertise of stealth and camouflage allow them to blend in with their surroundings and strike with lightning speed and lethal accuracy.

The clan's society is organized around a tribal structure, which is led by a warlord, Grusk Ironbark. Grusk is a fearsome leader known for his tactical brilliance and constant commitment to the preservation of their woodlands. His clan members admire him favorably and look up to him as a symbol of power and wisdom. The Thornshade clan has remained fiercely self-sufficient under his leadership, valuing their freedom and fighting any attempts by outsiders, particularly the human desolate tribe, to move in on their territory. The warlord poses difficulties for the chieftain, especially when clashes with the desolate tribe threaten their sanctified woodlands. During times of peace, however, the chieftain is praised for his or her role in spiritual leadership and clan growth.

The Thornshade clan has extensive experience in tracking, hunting, and surviving in the harsh woodland environment. They use their woodland talents to gather medical herbs, lay traps, and search for supplies. They have a strong awareness of animals and use animalistic tactics in battle, frequently adopting hit-and-run tactics and guerrilla warfare to exploit their opponents' weaknesses. They are frequently territorial towards their territories, which leads to frequent clashes with outsiders.

The clan's culture emphasizes unity, with each member offering their particular skills for the clan's improvement. They honor their ancestors and take pride in their history, handing down stories and traditions from generation to generation. Despite their aggressive and solitary character, the Thornshade clan acknowledges the value of alliances and will occasionally create temporary agreements with other races or clans when their objectives are aligned.

While they may share similarities with the human desolate tribe, the Thornshade clan guards their woodlands vigilantly, not allowing the humans access to their territory. They perceive the desolate tribe as a potential threat to their way of life and the delicate balance of their woodland ecosystem. The Thornshade Ranuk are prepared to defend their domain with loyalty, using their intimate knowledge of the woods and their formidable skills in battle to repel any intruders.

The Mirefang are a formidable Ranuk clan known for their aggressive temperament and persistent protection of their territory. Under the leadership of their esteemed Chieftain Dragaar Bloodthorn and the ruthless Warlord Gorrok Shroudfang, the Mirefang clan established distinct traditions and unique customs that reflect their harsh environment and ongoing conflicts with the dark ones and Gloomrot raiders in the south. Brown-skinned individuals, who represent the vast bulk of the Ranuk population, serve as the clan's primary members. They consider their clan to be the spiritual leader of all clans.

The Mirefang clan values strength and battle ability. They think that power is acquired through physical might and bravery on the battlefield. Their rites revolve around warrior rituals in which young ranuk establish their worth through duels and feats of strength. These rituals are used not just as tests of talent but also to strengthen relationships within the clan and foster a sense of cooperation and loyalty among the members.

Chief Dragaar Bloodthorn, a seasoned and experienced leader, commands the respect and allegiance of the Mirefang clan. Chief Dragaar, known for his strategic intellect and tenacity, commands his clan with a strong aim of safeguarding their ancestral marshlands from external threats. Under his guidance, the Mirefang clan has grown into an overwhelming presence in the region, fiercely protecting their territory against the lurking threat of the dark ones and raiders.

The military mind of the Mirefang clan is Warlord Gorrok Shroudfang, a tough and battle-hardened warrior. Warlord Gorrok, renowned for his ferocity and tactical insight, rallies the clan's warriors into combat, leveraging their in-depth understanding of the swamps to gain an advantage over their enemies. His sheer presence on the battlefield inspires bravery and commitment in his clanmates, making him an admired individual throughout all ranuk clans.

The Mirefang utilize their violent nature as a direct response to the fatal threats in the south. They see these other groups as enemies; therefore they fight back in skirmishes and battles to keep their marshlands under their control. While they prioritize protection of their land, the Mirefang clan is not afraid to take the fight to their enemies, initiating raids and preemptive strikes when they detect a threat to their boundaries.

The clan's survival in the harsh and hostile swampy regions has shaped their way of life. They have a strong awareness of the environment, using its resources to sustain themselves and using stealth and ambush tactics in warfare. The Mirefang are expert hunters, adept at navigating rough terrain and exploiting its risks.

Loyalty, strength, and martial prowess are highly respected within the Mirefang clan. They value their ancestral traditions, handing down stories of epic achievements and gallant warriors from generation to generation. The Mirefang ranuk forge a strong sense of identity through their shared experiences and their unwavering belief in preserving their way of life in the face of threats from the southern region.

A terrifying sight occasionally affects all those who dare venture too close to the wetlands. Imagine the Mirefang warriors mounted on powerful crocodiles or accompanied by domesticated swamp beasts for added combat force. These incredible warriors, known for their mastery of the marsh environment, strike terror into the hearts of all who witness them.

The Mirefang warriors, descended from a primitive society strongly bonded to the marshes, have formed an unrivaled alliance with the vicious swamp crocodiles. These gigantic reptiles, sleek and powerful, become their trusted companions and steeds. Having been trained from birth to cohabit with these dangerous beasts, the Mirefang warriors have honed their talents in riding and controlling the unpredictable nature of the crocodiles and other species that live inside the swamplands.

The Tranquil Tide Clan, a peaceful clan on a western island, is renowned for their boatsmithing and trading skills. The attractive environment and abundance of natural resources on the island produced the clan's culture and way of life. The peaceful Tranquil Tide clan has embraced an orderly existence and a great appreciation for the world and its waterways by living in harmony with the sea and their surroundings. These ranuk had blue skin and were frequently spotted mixing with the Thornshade clan. These clans frequently adopted one another as members of their clan, apparently because their skin tones were similar and they shared the same values as communities.

Boatbuilding is central to their culture, and the Tranquil Tide clan possesses exceptional abilities in the construction of numerous forms of vessels. From durable fishing boats to magnificent merchant ships, their creations are an example of their attention to detail and deep understanding of the sea. The clan's boatsmiths, recognized for their skill with wood and other materials, create vessels that are not only useful but also charming.

For the members of the Tranquil Tide clan, trade is a crucial component of their day-to-day lives. They engage in a variety of transactions as knowledgeable traders, including fishing, marine trade, and the exchange of goods with adjacent communities. Their reputation as fair and dependable traders has made them sought after by merchants from faraway territories who value their honest dealings and high-quality items.

The serenity that binds the Tranquil Tide clan goes beyond their trade and boatbuilding. They care deeply about the environment and work hard to keep it in a state of balance with themselves. Farmers from the clan have diligently maintained the lush gardens and bright vegetation that adorn their island home. They apply sustainable practices and protect their delicate surroundings.

Leadership within the Tranquil Tide clan is a very different matter and is derived from the Council of Elders, which are normally the more wise and respected members of the clan; therefore, decisions made are on a majority rule basis rather than relying on a sole leader to lead their collective efforts. The Chieftain of the Tranquil Tide is chosen from the Council of Elders, which is different as it serves as a symbol to exhibit their gentle nature and that of the whole clan.

Despite their serene demeanor, the Tranquil Tide clan is not without defense. For the purpose of ensuring that their island and their people are secure, they operate a trained guard unit called the Tideguard. These capable warriors are skilled in both martial warfare and maritime tactics, and they are prepared to protect their island home from any threats that may emerge.

The Tranquil Tide clan is a great example of harmonious cohabitation attained through handicraft, trade, and commitment to the environment. A symbol of tranquility in the vast land of Paranova, their constant commitment to unity and skill have won them the respect and confidence of other communities. The clan is known to appear all around Paranova, crossing the oceans or rivers to initiate peace and trade.

The Ironspine Clan, known for their fierce and warlike nature, is a formidable ranuk clan hailing from the northeastern parts of Paranova. Their traditions and culture revolve around combat and the relentless pursuit of hunting down their archenemies, the Gantum. The clan takes its name from the prominent iron spikes and armor adornments they wear, symbolizing their strength and resilience in battle.

After the Gantum War concluded, several ranuk chose to go their separate ways by creating division among clans, each with their own pursuits and goals. However, the ranuk who remained steadfast in their original purpose, which was to drive the colossal giants out of the land, became known as the Ironspine.

At the helm of the Ironspine clan stands their esteemed chief, a battle-hardened and respected leader known as Chief Ragnof Ironspine. Chief Ragnof is revered for his strategic prowess, unmatched combat skills, and faithfulness to the clan's cause. Under his guidance, the Ironspine clan has gained a fearsome reputation for their relentless pursuit of gantums and their unyielding battle cry that strikes fear into the hearts of their enemies.

The Ironspine clan is led on the frontlines by their ruthless warlord, a fierce warrior named Skarr Ironblood. Skarr is known for his exceptional strength, unmatched ferocity in combat, and unwavering loyalty to the clan. As the Warlord, he leads the Ironspine warriors into battle, coordinating their tactics and inspiring them with his stubborn determination.

The Ironspine were pale in comparison to most other Ranuk; they did not believe in the spiritual ways of the other clans. They believed that all ranuk were born of different tints. They saw that half of the population were brown, and that was their natural color, and that the color of their skin or imprints on their bodies was that of a unique identifier within their birth. The Ironspine had all sorts of colorful ranuk inside their clan, but they were all pale in comparison to the other clans.

One of the most distinctive aspects of the Ironspine clan culture is their unique approach to battle injuries. When a warrior is wounded or loses a limb in combat, it is seen as a mark of honor rather than a setback. The clan had skilled blacksmiths, known as the Ironforgers; they would craft sturdy iron prosthetics to replace lost limbs. In the most revered cases, when a warrior displays exceptional valor, they may choose to sever their own hand in combat to receive an iron hand as a symbol of their bravery and dedication to the clan.

The Ironspine clan's relentless pursuit of the colossal giants had instilled fear in the hearts of these formidable creatures. The Gantum have come to dread encountering the Ironspine warriors, knowing the ferocity and unwavering determination with which they hunt them down. The Ironspine clan has become a constant thorn in the side of the gantums, with each encounter serving as a reminder of the clan's unbreakable spirit and never-ending resolve.

Within the Ironspine clan, the value of strength, courage, and honor in battle is deeply ingrained. They engage in rigorous training and rituals to hone their skills, constantly striving to become better warriors. The clan's warriors are taught to embody the spirit of the Ironspine, standing tall and unyielding in the face of death.

As they continue their relentless pursuit, the Ironspine clan remains a formidable force in the northeastern regions of Paranova. Their stubborn determination, iron resolve, and distinctive iron adornments serve as a reminder of their unbreakable spirit. The only ranuk clan to keep their heritage from the beginning of their creation stood as their commitment to protect their kin and rid the world of the gantum menace.

The Ironspine clan, fueled by their unwavering determination to expel the colossal giants, took great pride in their prowess. Their conquests extended beyond battles, as they often captured prisoners from the wilderness dwarves or the Snowdrop humans, forcing them into servitude to build the grand Ironspine Kingdom. Whispers in the southern realms spread rumors of the clan capturing a colossal giant tamed to aid in the construction of their iron empire. This message echoed across Paranova, a proclamation that the Ironspine clan was not only formidable in battle but also possessed the strength to command even the mightiest beings, solidifying their reputation as a force to be feared.

The Ranuk leaders, stewards of a proud lineage, have diligently passed down the torch of their strength through the ages, upholding the esteemed Bloodthorn, Shroudfang, Ironbark, and Ragnof bloodlines for countless generations. The echoes of their ancestry resonate in the very core of Ranuk society, forging a legacy that withstands the tests of time.

········

The Gantums, burdened by their dwindling food supply and the challenges of procreation, find themselves grappling with a pressing struggle for their survival. Despite their imposing size and strength, they faced a complicated dilemma as their youth continued to emerge smaller and weaker than their predecessors. In an attempt to address this issue, the gantums are forced to make a difficult choice.

The scarcity of resources leaves them with no alternative but to resort to cannibalistic tendencies, where the stronger gantums prey upon their weaker kin to sustain the growth of their youth. The gantums continued this depressing cycle as they fought valiantly to maintain their dwindling population and secure food out of an instinctual need to survive.

The harsh reality that their very existence and nature are now in danger due to their own struggle for survival hits the gantums as they wonder why their kind is declining. It was the Archon who planted this plan, unknowingly, in the nectar of their favorite food. The nectars allowed the gantums to live another hundred more years while they recreated smaller versions of themselves, where mortals would be more accepting of the gantum people than the sheer giant versions of themselves currently.

As the smaller Gantums grappled with their diminishing size and the challenges it posed, they began to form their own distinct tribes, separate from the massive Gantums. Although their numbers were small, these tribes sought refuge in the massive structures and caverns left behind by their larger counterparts.

The smaller gantums found comfort and safety within the vast, towering architecture that once belonged to their ancestral gantums. They repurposed these structures, adapting them to their own needs, and began creating miniature societies within the confines of these cavernous dwellings.

In these newfound tribes, the smaller gantums established their own set of customs, traditions, and social hierarchies. They relied on their resourcefulness to make the most of their diminished stature. The smaller gantums developed a keen sense of unity and cooperation, recognizing that their survival depended on their collective strength. Through close-knit bonds and collaborative efforts, they thrived in their modest numbers, utilizing the shelter of the massive structures to protect themselves from external threats and the harsh realities of their environment.

Although the smaller Gantums may have been physically smaller than their predecessors, they compensated for their size with remarkable adaptability and resilience. In the shadow of the towering remnants of the past, these new tribes of gantums carved out their own existence, embracing their unique identity and finding a sense of purpose amidst the challenges they faced. They forged their own path, guided by the tenacity of their spirit and the determination to preserve their heritage, even as the world around them underwent changes.

As they attempted to establish themselves in a world where their enormous elders held sway, the smaller, evolved race had to overcome a particularly difficult obstacle. They found themselves caught between the formidable Ironspine and the long-standing enmity with the wilderness-dwelling dwarves. Surrendering to the ranuk would likely lead to their annihilation, and the deep-seated animosity between the gantum and the dwarves made peace a distant possibility, given the centuries of hatred between the two races.

As Paranova's tapestry continued to spread, the intricate threads of destiny weaved a complex tale where civilizations thrived, clashed, and adapted in their pursuit of survival and purpose. Within this ever-shifting landscape, the seeds of ambition, conflict, and hidden truths took root, foretelling challenges yet to come and the profound impact they would have on the future of the world. In time, the Dwarves, Gantum, Ranuk, and Humans all had much evolution to experience, each with its own unique path of development. However, for now, our story turns to the Elves, who had transcended primal existence, forging a future filled with mysteries, wisdom, and enchantment.

Chapter 5: From Ashes to Glory

As the story unfolded and the other civilizations were beginning to evolve, the focus shifted to the magnificent civilization of the elves, under the leadership of Queen Alora. She has stood alone since her husband was killed in the devastation during the Gantum War, and she has not accepted a partner as her king since his passing. The elven society thrived on the development of magic and knowledge; their intellectual pursuits and mastery of the arcane and elemental arts became the pillars of their culture. The re-building of their sprawling kingdom, a testament to their resilience and determination, the architecture was a sight that even the Forger would be proud of.

In the construction of the new kingdom that would eventually be named after the queen, the kingdom of Alora, the elven architects and spellcasters achieved a remarkable feat, blending their craftsmanship with the power of arcane magic. Every stone in the city was carefully imbued with arcane energy, a process that required the skilled touch of elven enchanters. Through intricate rituals and incantations, they channeled the essence of magic into the very core of the stones, infusing them with an otherworldly glow. The result was a city adorned with ethereal architecture, where every structure radiated with the pulsating energy of the arcane.

At the heart of the kingdom of Alora stood a magnificent center pool, a shimmering body of water that held profound significance for the elves. It was not merely a decorative feature but a source of immense power. The elven mages, harnessing their deep connection with the arcane, wove spells and enchantments around the pool, imbuing it with potent magical energies. The water itself became a conduit of arcane power, flowing with ethereal currents that seemed to dance and swirl with every movement.

The pool became a focal point of the city, a place of tranquility and magical resonance where the elves would gather to draw inspiration and seek comfort in their connection to the arcane forces that shaped their civilization. It was rumored that when elves would swim in this pool, they would slow their aging process. This let the elves live for a very long time, even though they already lived longer than all of the other races on Paranova. When the elven hierarchy was established, it was only granted to the upper tier of society to gain access to swim in these waters uninterruptedly, and the pool would be monitored day and night.

The infusion of arcane magic into the stones and the central pool of Alora represented the harmonious fusion of elven craftsmanship and their deep understanding of the arcane arts. Their admiration for arcane magic tested their self-control as well as their commitment to creating a kingdom that embodied the very essence of their culture. The kingdom of Alora stood as a living inspiration to the elven civilization's extraordinary achievements, a symbol of their mastery over the arcane and their dedication to creating a kingdom of enchantment and wonder.

In the mystical realm of arcane magic, a unique convergence of energies unfolds, intertwining the elemental, divine, and chaotic essences into a harmonious tapestry of power. This intense branch of magic involves a vast spectrum of spells and incantations, drawing upon the raw forces that govern the very fabric of existence. Arcane is as spectacular as it is beautiful, and the strange mysteries surrounding its origins sparked many curious scholars. The energies that the arcane and elemental emit were unfathomable and beyond comprehension; this brought scholars and intellectual magic users to discover the secrets and uses the energies could behold.

The elven race within the community of Alora possesses a distinctive connection to the complex and connected realm of elemental and divine magic. Over multiple generations, these individuals have diligently refined their abilities, harnessed the fundamental powers of nature while accessing celestial forces bestowed upon them by unknown heavenly entities. Through unwavering dedication to their craft, the elves have achieved mastery in both branches of magic, navigating through channels that connect with earth, air, fire, and water, as well as embracing grace and strength acquired from celestial energies.

Recognizing the unpredictable and potentially destructive nature of chaotic magic, the elves have deemed it too volatile to be wielded freely. The chaotic energies associated with the unruly forces of chaos and disorder are seen as a potential threat to the delicate balance of the world. Therefore, the use of chaotic magic is strictly forbidden and comes with severe consequences. The elves knew order and balance when it came to the use of arcane magic; they knew the immense powers that could be unleashed if the arcane were left unchecked, so rules were established amongst the race to ensure elves were not abusing arcane magic. Cases of elves attempting to go against the laws established were met with execution or exile from the kingdom.

While the Elves of Alora predominantly focus on the mastery of elemental and divine magic, their understanding of other forms of magic is not entirely dismissed. They acknowledge the existence of destructive magic, but its usage is heavily regulated and restricted. Such magic, capable of unleashing devastating powers, is only permitted in dire circumstances or under strict supervision, ensuring that its potential for harm is minimized and controlled.

The sophisticated blend of elemental and divine magic wielded by the elves of Alora gave them an unusual perspective and a deep connection to the natural and spiritual realms. Their spellcasters use elemental energies to modify the environment, calling wind gusts, conjuring fires, manipulating the ground, and shaping the waters to their satisfaction. Additionally, they summon heavenly powers, requesting the blessings and direction of their beloved divinities and channeling healing energy, divine protection, and holy wrath.

In their pursuit of mystical knowledge, the elves of Alora have found a delicate balance between the elemental and divine, forging a path that respects the harmonious order of the world. They remain steadfast in their commitment to wielding magic responsibly and mindful of the potential consequences of unrestrained power.

As the guardians of the natural and divine realms, the elves of Alora serve as both custodians and practitioners of this blended arcane magic, upholding their traditions and preserving the balance that sustains their realm.

Queen Alora established a hierarchy that made the most sense to her at the time. With their civilization being wounded and on the rise of re-building, she thought that having districts, guilds, and a hierarchy among society would best keep elves in order.

Within Alora society, the queen's strict hierarchy was established. The Archers, skilled marksmen, and the Paladins who were skilled combatants, both served as defenders of the realm, and they stood together as one group called the vanguards for the elven military. The arcane artisans, practitioners of magic, and keepers of ancient wisdom had played a crucial role in preserving their mystical heritage; they formed a group called the Arcanists, and the noble Highborn, esteemed for their grace, beauty, and leadership qualities, held positions of power and influence in the kingdom.

Since the elves' creation, they had faced a particular challenge: Havoc's disruption had resulted in a very low fertility rate among the elven kind, which led to the decision to include the Highborn as a tier among society early on. Mystified by this unfortunate trait, the elves identified certain individuals with higher fertility among them as Highborn elves.

Highborn women mainly became a valuable resource, chosen to act as surrogates for couples with higher-grade genetics, ensuring the continuation of the elven bloodline and ensuring their heritage as prosperous elves as generations would pass on. There were few highborn men that held the gift of the highest fertility, but they would either join the vanguard, become arcanists or help the leadership of the kingdom instead of solely focusing on fertility.

Queen Alora believed there should be a clear hierarchical structure that determined one's role and privileges based on their genetic traits and accomplishments. Each tier had its own distinct characteristics and responsibilities. The tiered structure of Elven society fostered a sense of unity and purpose, as each tier played a crucial role in the overall functioning and well-being of the kingdom. Despite the distinctions between tiers, there has been an underlying understanding of the interconnectedness and interdependence of all individuals for a long time.

At the lowest tier were the Lowborn, individuals with undesirable lower genetic traits. They were entrusted with tasks such as manual labor, domestic work, gathering essential resources, and serving on the front lines of defense when needed. They played a vital role in the functioning of the kingdom, often working tirelessly to support the needs of the higher tiers and their own. The lowborn, although occupying the lowest tier, were valued for their hard work, resilience, and dedication. They were the backbone of the kingdom, responsible for the essential tasks that sustained daily life. Their contributions, though often overlooked, were fundamental to the smooth operation of Alora.

The next tier was the Working Class, comprising individuals with average genetic traits and skills in various trades and crafts. Often called the tradeborn amongst the other tiers, they were the artisans, crafters, and professionals who contributed to the development and maintenance of the kingdom's infrastructure. Most of the kingdom would reside in this tier, creating districts of their own throughout Alora.

Through long-term dedication and service, those in the working class had the opportunity to prove themselves and earn the privilege of starting a family, an honor granted to those who demonstrated their commitment and skills. The tradeborn possessed a range of skills and craftsmanship that brought beauty and functionality to the kingdom. They excelled in various trades and crafts, such as blacksmithing, woodworking, weaving, teaching, and construction. Through their expertise, they contributed to the efficiency of Alora's architecture and infrastructure.

Above the Tradeborn was the Military Class, which is often referred to as the Vanguard, comprised of brave warriors who pledged their lives to serve and protect their queen and the kingdom. The military class welcomed anyone who was willing to fight, regardless of their genetic traits. The elves that pledged their lives to the vanguard would live in a utopia compared to the other tiers, which would encourage many to join the military. However, the lives spent in the military district were often spent training and not having as much free time to enjoy the luxuries that would lure elves to live in the military class. If a person left their military duties, they would be thrown to the lowborn district regardless of where they came from previously, as it was a disservice to the queen and the kingdom to abandon their duty.

Only a select few high-ranking officers and champions of the military class were deemed worthy of starting a family. It was a long and challenging path that required exceptional skills, intense loyalty, and proven worthiness. This ensured that the strongest and most capable traits were passed down through the generations, bolstering the kingdom's defenses and maintaining a formidable military force. If an elf had the gift of good genetics, they would be given titles within the military class to honor such significance.

The Vanguard had their own unique hierarchy within their own ranks. To determine the most deserving warriors, the military held tournaments where combatants of average traits or lower could showcase their prowess and earn the privilege to consummate with a highborn, ensuring the continuation of their lineage and the preservation of their exceptional genetic traits during rigorous training. This tournament brought entertainment for the highborn elves in particular, as they would favor their own combatants and place bets on certain fighters.

One of the highest tiers equal to the Highborn was the Arcanist class, distinguished by their insightful intellect and mastery of arcane arts and other magics. These individuals were highly respected within elven society for their deep understanding of magical forces and their ability to manipulate them. Possessing a range of desirable genetic traits, arcanists were regarded as scholars, advisors, and guardians of elven knowledge. Their ability to infuse arcane magic into objects and structures was instrumental in the construction of Alora. By imbuing the stones with magical energy, they enhanced the durability, enchantment, and even defensive properties of the kingdom's buildings.

The kingdom's center pool, a sacred and focal point of Alora, was a reservoir of potent arcane energy, carefully channeled and controlled by the arcanists. Its radiant glow and mystical properties were a tribute to the mastery of the arcanists and their ability to harness the forces of magic. However, even among the arcanists, not all were automatically granted the right to start a family. They too had to prove themselves worthy through their contributions, discoveries, and advancements in the field of magic.

In the Elven Kingdom, the Highborn Class held a position of utmost respect and responsibility. The women of this esteemed class not only served as surrogates for other elves but also engaged in charitable favors throughout the kingdom. Their male counterparts were equally dedicated, helping wherever needed and distributing resources such as food, supplies, and books to those in lower tiers of the hierarchy. Within the highborn class, relationships often resulted in starting families amongst themselves. However, a unique practice emerged where highborn women couldn't raise their biological children and were sometimes adopted by families in lower tiers.

While adoption with children or infants coming from two highborn parents weren't a frequent occurrence, highborn women learned to suppress emotional attachments to their own offspring. This practice led most highborn children to grow within the broader community of the highborn class rather than in traditional, intimate family households. The queen determined that this arrangement was necessary to ensure the survival of the elven race, despite being tragic for first-time mothers in the highborn class. The Highborn, understanding their pivotal role in society, acknowledged the rarity of their gift of fertility and embraced the queen's directive for the greater good of their elven kin.

Through this tiered system, elven society sought to balance the contributions of individuals with varying genetic traits and ensure the preservation of desirable qualities within their population. It emphasized both merit and genetic potential, providing opportunities for advancement and recognition to those who proved themselves worthy in their respective roles. The tiered system that the queen established worked well in harmony throughout the re-building process and blended in harmony for a couple decades.

In Alora, the tiered structure of elven society was not a source of division but rather a means to allocate resources, honor achievements, and preserve the genetic legacy of the race. It promoted a sense of collective purpose as each tier recognized its unique contributions to the flourishing of the kingdom. Through this system, the elves strove to create a harmonious society that valued both individual merit and collective well-being, ensuring the continued growth and resilience of the kingdom of Alora in the face of challenges and threats.

The queen held a steadfast belief that the loss of their first kingdom, coupled with the widespread dispersal of elves across Paranova and the significant casualties during the Gantum onslaught, had led to a deep divide within elven society. She firmly believed that her choices were necessary for the benefit of her subjects, guided by her tiered hierarchy system and structured approach to fertility. In her vision, the new kingdom would rise from the ashes of the old, reminiscent of the once-great realm her husband had built, known as the Kingdom of Unity.

The Elves possessed a remarkable trait that set them apart from other mortal races—the gift of natural longevity. With lifespans far exceeding those of other mortals, they became witnesses to the ever-shifting tides of history. This extended lifespan not only fueled their passion for knowledge but also anchored their commitment to preserving the ancient traditions that defined their existence. While their struggle with fertility remained a challenge, the elves found balance through the harmonious combination of their prolonged lifespans and the mystical properties of the vast pool located at the heart of Alora. This unique synergy gave them the potential to experience thousands of years of existence on the world. When the Archon placed arcane energies on the western islands, she bestowed a gift that the elves were unaware of.

The Elves of Alora are a proud kin and hold grand cultural festivals and traditions that are eagerly anticipated throughout the year. These events serve as important milestones in elven society, fostering a sense of community, pride, and shared heritage. They celebrate the elven unique talents, history, and values while also promoting harmony and unity among the different tiers of society.

The Festival of Enchantments is a stunning annual gathering in which Alora's arcanists exhibit their mastery of the arcane arts. The festival is going to happen in a magnificent outdoor amphitheater that has lights and shimmering crystal decorations. Spellcasters from all around the kingdom gather to cast complex spells, illusions, and elemental manipulations. It's a fascinating display of skill, creativity, and the wonderful powers of magic. The festival also includes exhibitions, workshops, and discussions on various magical disciplines, encouraging knowledge-sharing and innovation. The elven youth look forward to the Arcane Academy when they make an appearance to showcase their school and pick young novices eager to learn and join the academy within the Arcanist district.

The Day of Unity is a festive occasion, primarily hosted in the center of Alora. It acts as a reminder to acknowledge and appreciate the power that lies in embracing diversity and fostering collaboration between various tiers within elven society. During this day, individuals from diverse backgrounds unite to partake in numerous activities like communal banquets, musical and dance showcases, as well as civil contests. The Day of Unity highlights the interdependence and shared responsibility within the kingdom, promoting understanding, respect, and collaboration among the Lowborn, Tradeborn, Arcanists, Military and Highborn. While the Day of Unity is underway, the elves take weeks in preparation by putting on art and displays of past events that have led them to where they are in the present, educating the youth on their history.

Elven soldiers' fighting skills are shown off in the Vanguard Tournament, which is a much-anticipated event. Every year, each time before each seasonal change, the competition takes place in a large stadium. Skilled warriors from various sections of the military engage in a series of combat challenges, showcasing their agility, strategic thinking, and weapon skills. The tournament develops a healthy competitive spirit, allowing soldiers to prove their worth and advance in rank. Spectators applaud for their favorite champions, generating an environment of excitement, unity, and shared pride in elven combat traditions.

The Rite of the Elders is a reflective rite that respects the elves and their elders' wisdom, experience, and contributions. During this event, the younger generations meet to pay respect to their respected elders, requesting their advice and blessings. The elders tell stories from their past, passing on important lessons and acquired wisdom to future generations. It is a time for reflection, honor, and the transfer of cultural history from generation to generation, strengthening the elven community's relationships.

During these festivals, the elves participate in a variety of rituals and traditions that strengthen their bond with their cultural heritage. Ceremonial dances, recitations of ancient poems, the lighting of enchanted bonfires, and the sharing of traditional meals and drinks are all attainable. The celebrations also allow elven youth to learn about their history, values, and ancestral traditions through storytelling and educational sessions.

These cultural events and rituals not only serve as enjoyable festivities but also enhance the elves of Alora's perception of identity, belonging, and kinship. They embody the spirit of their civilization, encouraging a pursuit of greatness, the acknowledgment of diverse skills, and the peaceful coexistence of the kingdom's various tiers.

While the elves of Alora generally kept their celebrations exclusive to their own kind, there was one exception to this rule: the village of Pallas. Nestled on the mainland, Pallas stood as a beacon of openness and acceptance, embracing the diversity of races that inhabited the land. In this village, the elven inhabitants extended a warm invitation to other races, allowing them to immerse themselves in the splendor of elven festivals.

The elven festivals held in Pallas were grand spectacles, enchanting the senses with their vibrant displays of music, dance, art, and culinary delights. Intricate parades with shimmering costumes, dexterous masks, and mesmerizing choreography would wind through the streets to melodic tunes that rang with the very essence of magic. The air would be filled with the tantalizing aromas of exquisite elven cuisine, crafted with precision and infused with enchanting flavors.

For the residents of Pallas, the elven festivals were an opportunity to share in the cultural riches of the enchanted kingdom inside Alora and to revel in the splendor and elegance that defined elven traditions. It was a time when barriers were momentarily dissolved and friendships were formed amidst the laughter and relationships that formed within the festivities.

Even though while mortals of all kinds were welcome to attend elven festivals in Pallas, the village's permanent residents were exclusively elves. Pallas became a place where the unique elven way of life flourished, as well as a place where the cultural practices and customs of the elves were treasured and preserved. The elves of Pallas took pleasure in representing the kingdom and the elven way of life, and they were happy to welcome the festivities each year, they never lost sight of the importance of preserving the core values of their elven queen in everyday affairs. Pallas would go on to become the trading hub for elven society for generations.

As the enchanting melodies echoed through the streets of Pallas and the laughter of elves and non-elves mingled in harmonious celebration, the elven festivals became a symbol of unity and the power of cultural exchange. It was a reminder that, for a brief moment in time, all who gathered in Pallas could partake in the elven world of enchantment and immerse themselves in the wonders of the elven kingdom.

The wise and stern Queen Alora made the strategic decision to keep a distance between her elves and the other races that lived on Paranova. Recognizing the natural distinctions and different natures of the various races, she held the opinion that it was of the highest priority to keep the integrity of the Elven Islands unaffected from the outside world.

Even though Queen Alora placed importance on maintaining open lines of communication and trade with the neighboring races, she ultimately decided to build walls around the islands to protect her kingdom, with enforced protection on bridges to the mainland. She did this to preserve the cultural heritage and the unique customs and traditions that were essential to the Elven society. She believed it was necessary for the elves to live in isolation, with a singular focus on progressing the Elven kind. She allowed the festivals in Pallas to commence to give the elves something to look forward to and build world wealth in the process.

Situated on a distant island, the kingdom of Alora served as a strategic location for the queen to maintain distance between her elven society and other races. Expanding upon this island was the queen's goal to prevent any possible confrontations or misinterpretations stemming from cultural disparities. It is crucial to note that the rationale behind her decision did not stem from feelings of superiority or exclusion but rather from the queen's aspiration to secure a harmonious coexistence for her elven kin while safeguarding their long-standing traditions.

Within the walls of the kingdom, a wide range of educational structures flourish. This framework serves as a firm foundation for elven society, intentionally designed to cultivate the skills, knowledge, and ethical principles of the younger generation. Recognizing that social classification in youth was initially determined by genetic heritage, both the Queen and Elven Council firmly believed in providing equal opportunities for personal growth and development. Throughout the entire kingdom, numerous academies and training establishments were established with faithful dedication to refining the potential abilities and talents naturally possessed by young elves.

The Arcane Academy serves as a bastion for imparting mystical wisdom, offering a haven of education where aspiring magicians are nurtured to master the intricacies of the arcane arts. Inside these walls, they unravel how best to harness their natural magical capabilities while fully unleashing their potential under the guidance of experienced mentors and intellectual scholars.

The Military Academy, on the other hand, serves as a training ground for aspiring warriors or archers. The youth who show a passion for combat and a desire to defend their kingdom are given the opportunity to develop their martial skills and strategic thinking. They undergo rigorous physical training, combat simulations, and tactical studies while preparing them for challenges they may face in the future.

There are various academies and institutions that focus on other fields such as craftsmanship, diplomacy, natural sciences, and more. These institutions aimed to provide a full education, instilling in the elven youth not only practical skills but also a deep understanding of ethics, compassion, and the importance of community.

Education in Alora is not simply a journey to acquire knowledge and skills; it is intentionally designed to shape the minds, hearts, and values of the elven youth. The council takes pride in the way education works for Alora, where everyone is allowed to access the same level of knowledge and the same benefits regardless of class or genetic path. The council deeply believes in caring for each individual and nurturing their talent. The council is generous enough to provide scholarship packages and mentorship programs, especially to the youth who have demonstrated exceptional talent. With the comprehensive nature of the education systems coupled with the commitment of the council to provide ample room for personal growth and exploration, the youth of Alora have been sufficiently equipped and empowered to unearth their potential and effectively contribute to its growth.

The Elven civilization of Alora stood as a testament to their deep understanding of arcane arts, ancient wisdom, and the relentless pursuit of knowledge. Among their many achievements, their mastery of magic held a prominent place. The elven arcanists, admired as scholars and practitioners of the arcane, honed their skills to unparalleled levels. They delved into the intricate mysteries of spellcasting, unraveling the complexities of incantations and enchantments. Through their understanding of magical theory and rigorous training, they could manipulate the very fabric of reality, conjuring flames, shaping elements, and calling upon the forces of nature with precision and finesse.

In addition to their mastery of traditional arcane arts, the Elves of Alora found a deep connection to the celestial realms. Their understanding of astronomy was unparalleled with the ability to navigate the stars and decipher the secrets written in the cosmos. Through careful observation and mathematical calculation, they mapped the movements of celestial bodies while forecasting celestial events and harnessing the energies of the cosmos. These astronomers created their own cosmic guild eventually in the future; however, they focused on the use of their divinity magic, as it was a practical and unique branch of elven magic that allowed them to tap into the ethereal radiance of celestial beings, channeling the pure essence of light for healing, protection, and spiritual enlightenment.

Among the scholars of Paranova, there existed a captivating and intriguing topic of discussion: the sightings and tales of celestial beings traversing the expanse of the starlit sky. Whispers would circulate among the scholarly circles, speculating whether these ethereal figures could possibly be the unknown shapers, the legendary beings said to have shaped the very fabric of existence.

Although no concrete evidence could verify the authenticity of these accounts, the tales served as a source of fascination and wonder, inspiring vivid imaginations and spirited debates. Scholars would gather in hallowed halls or around crackling hearths, sharing tales and theories, each weaving their own narrative of what these celestial beings might represent.

Some speculated that these ethereal figures were gods, guardians of cosmic balance, who moved among the stars to oversee the harmonious order of the universe. The elves who speculated on this line of thought felt a deep connection between the celestial realm and the mortal world.

Others proposed that the sightings could be attributed to celestial spirits, mysterious entities that dwelled within the cosmic realms and occasionally manifested themselves as shimmering lights or radiant figures in the night sky. These ethereal apparitions were believed to possess great wisdom and could potentially impart celestial knowledge to those with a keen eye and an open heart. These elves would be referred to as Mystics, Wiccans or Prophets as spiritual guides amongst the mortals of Paranova, as they had a deep understanding of the ethereal.

Many mortals have believed or told the stories of these sightings and experiences throughout the world as bedtime stories for children or tales over the campfire after long travels. Whatever tales of celestial beings moving amongst the stars were exaggerated in myth, legend, and speculation. They were thoughts and stories of the unknown, where imagination intertwined with the desire to uncover the secrets of the universe above. Scholars reveled in the allure of these stories, not as facts but as sparks that ignited their passion for knowledge and exploration.

Whether these celestial sightings were truly glimpses of the shapers, manifestations of celestial spirits, or simply the wistful imaginings of curious minds remained a subject of endless fascination and debate. Regardless of the truth of these tales, they served a purpose in the scholarly realm, fostering a sense of wonder and igniting the flame of intellectual curiosity.

In the enlightened realm of higher learning, celestial beings traversing the expansive heavens were a subject matter that sparked infinite intrigue. These ethereal tales spurred discussions, incited intellectual curiosity, and propelled the frontier of knowledge further into uncharted territory. Thus, within the confines of academia and among inquisitive scholars, these chronicles held an esteemed place as both a topic of cherished discourse and a constant wellspring of inspiration. Never-ending cosmic possibilities beckoned those yearning to uncover mystical truths while instilling enduring fascination among avid seekers of wisdom amongst the stars. It would serve as a guiding light for young elves who sought answers amidst boundless constellations in their quest for understanding. Thus bringing a guild into formation over time, dedicated to the understanding of the stars and the celestial realm.

Elemental manipulation was yet another practice where the elves succeeded; they had a natural talent for bending the elements. The understanding of elemental energies was deeply ingrained in elven culture from a young age. Through the mastery of elemental manipulation, the elves could shape and command the primal forces of fire, water, earth, and air. These elves that became one with the elements were able to achieve a harmonious balance of control and respect for the natural world. They were able to harness these elemental powers to protect their kingdom, create breathtaking displays of elemental artistry, and eliminate external threats.

Masterful elemental manipulators became known as Elementalists, and each spellcaster had to go through rigorous training to become one with the elements, as it was a hard balance to maintain with such a force of energy to withstand flowing through oneself as a mortal. These elementalism spellcasters belonged in the Arcanist class but were often used amongst the vanguard and would hold a high rank within the military as protectors over units.

The Elves of Alora excelled in achievements of magic and knowledge that were not limited to the arcane and celestial arts alone. Their pursuit of wisdom extended to various fields, including philosophy, history, and the natural sciences. Their scholars and mystics delved into ancient tomes and scrolls, preserving the collective wisdom of their ancestors and contributing their own discoveries to the vast pool of knowledge. Their respect for nature and the interconnectedness of all living things drove them to study herbalism and botanical sciences, unlocking the healing properties of plants and harnessing their innate magical essences.

In the kingdom of Alora, the advancements and achievements in elven magic and knowledge were proof of their deep connection to the arcane, their admiration for the celestial realms, and their desire for wisdom. Elven knowledge of the arcane arts, mastery of divinity light magic, elemental manipulation abilities, and contributions to various academic disciplines strengthened their position as keepers of ancient wisdom and seekers of truth. The elves of Alora continued to push the boundaries of understanding, unraveling the mysteries of the universe and bringing their civilization into a haven of magical expertise and intellectual brilliance.

The enchanting realm of the kingdom did not only confine itself within its own magnificence. Instead, it actively fostered relationships with various races and civilizations through the means of trade and diplomacy. Earning themselves a renowned reputation for their unique craftsmanship, mystical artifacts, and rare exotic knowledge, they became coveted partners in trade.

Employing their attention to detail combined with an extensive grasp of magical arts, the elves from Alora had devised marvelous creations that possessed both compelling visual appeal and infused enchantments of immense power into objects. Collectors, scholars, and daring adventurers from all over the vast world sought after these enchanted objects as highly prized possessions.

In their pursuit of peaceful relations and mutual respect, the Elves of Alora employed diplomacy as a powerful tool. They recognized the importance of fostering alliances and maintaining harmonious interactions with other races. Through diplomatic efforts, they sought to bridge cultural differences, establish trade routes, and facilitate mutual understanding. One notable trade alliance was formed with the Tranquil Tide Clan, a renowned group of boatsmiths and traders. The elves of Alora had recognized the value of the Tranquil Tide clan's expertise in naval craftsmanship and maritime trade. In exchange, they offered their enchanted artifacts, rare magical tomes, and other exquisite goods.

The trading relationship with the Tranquil Tide clan proved mutually beneficial, allowing the elves of Alora to expand their influence and access new markets while also offering the Tranquil Tide clan with the opportunity to purchase rare and enchanting items to strengthen their trade businesses. The relationship strengthened the two cultures' relationships, developing a sense of kinship and mutual respect. Through this and other diplomatic efforts, the elves of Alora displayed their dedication to establishing bridges of understanding and collaboration with other races, solidifying their reputation as fair and honorable trading partners.

The engagement of the kingdom with other races and civilizations through trade and diplomacy showcased their desire for peaceful coexistence and the recognition of the benefits that come with shared understanding. Their valuable exports of enchanted artifacts, rare magical tomes, and fine craftsmanship not only brought them economic success but also served as a testament to their unparalleled mastery of arcane infusion and art. By forging alliances and fostering diplomatic relations, such as the one with the Tranquil Tide clan, the elves of Alora extended their influence beyond their borders, creating a network of connections and friendships that helped to strengthen the bonds of unity among different races and civilizations.

On the western island of Tide Cove, where the elves had formed a steadfast alliance with the newly formed, neighboring Ranuk tribe, an intriguing mystery captured the imaginations of the seafaring inhabitants. As they embarked on their boats and sailed across the shimmering waters, whispers circulated among the sailors about a fabled sunken island lurking beneath the surface.

According to the tales passed down through generations, the elves claimed to catch glimpses of this mysterious sunken island as they sailed over its hidden depths. The surface waters would shift and shimmer, revealing a haunting silhouette that hinted at a long-lost city nestled beneath the waves. Stories grew wild and fantastical, woven with the threads of legends and elaborated with each retelling.

The elves, guided by their vivid imaginations and the lure of untold treasures, believed that this sunken island was home to a wondrous underwater city. They spun tales of sprawling metropolises adorned with shimmering pearls, where water-people, endowed with ethereal beauty, thrived in harmony with the aquatic realm. They spoke in the soft voices of an ancient god or goddess of the sea who reigned supreme over this mysterious territory with an astonishing level of power and benevolence.

Unfortunately, it was difficult to tell what the was and what fiction in these stories were. Each time the tales were recounted, they gained new details and eventually took on a life of their own. Some skeptics dismissed them as mere fantasies, born from the depths of imagination and the desire for adventure. Still, others clung to the belief that there might be a kernel of truth hidden within the extravagant narratives.

The elves of Tide Cove were eager to explore the submerged island and learn its secrets because they were curious and had a thirst for knowledge. They embarked on daring expeditions, diving into the depths with hopes of reaching the fabled underwater city. However, the treacherous depths proved to be difficult for them to navigate because of the harsh currents and ominous darkness that guarded the hidden realm below.

Regardless of the authenticity of these stories, the allure of the sunken island and its mystical undersea city persisted. It became a source of inspiration, fueling the imaginations of storytellers and artists who sought to capture its essence. The tales wove themselves into the cultural fabric of Tide Cove, becoming part of the identity of its mortals and the unforgettable thread in their shared folklore.

So, as the sails of their boats billowed in the wind and the waves whispered tales of the sunken island, the elves within Tide Cove continued to set their sights on the horizon, forever in search of the truth that lay beneath the surface. Whether the sunken island existed as a tangible reality or a figment of their collective imagination, the stories they spun remained about the boundless wonders that awaited those who dared to venture into the uncharted depths of the seas.

The Elves of Tide Cove, in collaboration with the Ranuk tribe that distanced itself from the Tranquil Tide clan, forged a harmonious partnership. They worked together peacefully, establishing Tide Cove as a flourishing trading hub and harbor, a precursor to the grand harbor of Alora that would soon be built.

Following the guidance of the elven council, an alliance with Tide Cove was solidified, and they were tasked with venturing along the southwestern shores of Paranova. Their mission was to claim small villages and towns for the queen, expanding her territorial influence. Many of these elven settlements willingly submitted to her rule, finding benefit and protection in return for resources and labor. However, a handful of resistant villages, inhabited by Dark Ones, faced the force of the vanguard to comply or vacate the southwestern territory.

The respected Elven Council, which works closely with Queen Alora, is at the core of the kingdom's governance. Bringing their experience and insight to the table, the council's members, who are a varied group of reputable individuals, make sure the kingdom operates successfully. Distinguished scholars, elders, military commanders, renowned Arcanists or Highborn, and important leaders from various social groups establish the members of the Elven Council. Each council member has specialized expertise and experience in their respective industries, which allows for a thorough awareness of the kingdom's requirements and issues.

In the council's contemplation of significant matters, a methodical and broad approach is employed, allowing members to voice their perspectives, ideas, and suggestions during deliberations. Civilized debates are held to discuss the most promising course of action for promoting the welfare and interests of the elven community, with the ultimate objective being agreement. Queen Alora assumes a pivotal role as the focal figure and guide in these discussions, offering her insight as the ultimate judge.

The council promotes harmony and well-being in society; its objective is to resolve any differences and disputes among its members; it arrives at a neutral selection that allows all parties an equal chance of resolving a disagreement or argument and to gain greater understanding and clarity. When disagreements emerge between socioeconomic classes or tiers, the council works hard to bridge the gaps, fostering harmony and mutual respect among themselves and their citizens. The Elven Council also advises Queen Alora on matters ranging from diplomacy and trade to magical developments and societal growth. Their collective skills and expertise are crucial in shaping the kingdom's policies and direction, allowing for a well-balanced governance framework that meets the elves' many needs and goals.

The kingdom flourishes as a realm of thoughtful decision-making, polite dispute resolution, and respect for the voices of the elves due to collaborative efforts between Queen Alora and the Elven Council. This esteemed council willfully embraces inclusive governance, harmony, and the relentless pursuit of collective wellbeing. Consequently, the kingdom stands as an enduring symbol of insight, balance, and sympathy that will endure throughout future generations.

Queen Alora, a symbol of wisdom and elegance, is summarized as an extraordinary leader whose qualities have lasting influence on the destiny of the elven kind. Her leadership approach is characterized by a blend of strategic wit, empathy, and comprehension of elven society. Being one of the brave spellcasters who valiantly fought against the gantum, she possesses both the fortitude of a warrior and the keen intellect of a mage. Innately perceiving the necessity for a fresh start, she steered her followers towards the western islands, where they sought sanctuary and commenced their restoration efforts.

Through countless trials, Queen Alora has demonstrated her resolute determination and visionary outlook, always prioritizing the well-being of her subjects. Her expertise at bridging societal divides and cultivating a sense of togetherness has played a pivotal role in nurturing harmony and fostering growth within her kingdom. Under the guidance of this remarkable ruler, the elven civilization thrives magnificently, as she remains stubborn in preserving their heritage and ensuring the ongoing success of her subjects.

....

Long ago, while the Ranuk and Elves fled from the colossal Gantum together, Queen Alora told the Ranuk leaders to find their own lands. The dispute between the Ranuk leaders and Queen Alora remains shrouded in mystery for the elven kind. While the exact reasons behind the conflict may be unclear, the queen remains steadfast in her decision to exclude other races from their sacred islands.

Believing that these outsiders pose a potential threat to the existence and harmony of the elven civilization, she fiercely protects her domain. Queen Alora's determination to preserve the elven way of life and ensure the safety of her followers drove her resolve to keep the islands exclusive to the elves.

She firmly believes that protecting their existence necessitates keeping their lands free of outside influences, despite the fact that some may find her position to be controversial. The true nature of the dispute and the depths of Queen Alora's concerns are known only to her, but her commitment to the Elven race and their homeland remains solid.

Respecting Queen Alora's wishes to maintain a certain level of seclusion and separation between the elven kind and other races, the Tranquil Tide clan, known for their harmonious ways and affinity for the tranquil shores, gracefully agreed to the queen's decree. With a heavy heart, they bid farewell to their potential homeland and traveled the shores towards the northern reaches of the realm, where a serene island awaited them.

Establishing themselves on this new island, the Tranquil Tide clan embraced their newfound solitude, dedicating themselves to the preservation of their traditions and the serenity of their surroundings. The island, blessed with beautiful beaches, gentle waves, and lush foliage, provided an ideal haven for the ranuk to dwell in harmony with nature.

However, not all Ranuk clans took the news of the Queen of the elves' desire for separation kindly. Anger served as fuel for the emergence of an independent spirit and a desire to shape their own futures. They started off on their own journeys, seeking territories where they could thrive on their own terms and establish their own clans without the help of the queen, who directed everyone to safety after the onslaught from the Gantum destruction in the central lands.

These Ranuk clans, known as Thornshade and Mirefang, dispersed across the vast lands and journeyed on diverse paths. Some sought comfort amidst the dense forests, becoming one with the primal wilderness and harnessing their innate connection with nature. Others ventured into the rugged marshlands, embracing the challenges of the swamps and drawing strength from the elemental forces that resonated in the marsh.

. . . .

Queen Alora, while initially maintaining the kingdom exclusively for elves, faced a significant arrival of Dark Ones migrating from the south to the kingdom. Despite her insistence on the kingdom being primarily for the elven kind, the cultural blend and coexistence gradually led to a shift in perception. Over time, about half of the elven population came to consider the dark ones as part of the elven community. This harmonious integration reflected the evolving and inclusive nature of the kingdom, fostering unity and understanding among the diverse inhabitants.

Although Queen Alora allowed the inclusion of Dark Ones within elven society, they were automatically classified as lowborn due to their origins. Recognizing them as elven beings, Queen Alora believed in offering them a place within the community. However, these Dark Elves were not afforded the same opportunities as the rest of the elven population when it came to starting a family with a highborn child. The distinction in their lineage led to certain restrictions and limitations. Instead, they were permitted to form families among their own kind, primarily with other lowborn individuals. This unique dynamic gave rise to a blending of elven culture with the customs and traditions of the dark ones, interbreeding resulting in a subgroup of elves known as Gray Elves over a length of time.

The structure of the existing hierarchy in the kingdom of Alora had long been a source of admiration and inspiration for many, but it also contributed to the challenges and demands of the elves. Recognizing the need for adaptability and inclusivity, Queen Alora took a bold step, opening her kingdom's doors to the dark ones who sought refuge and acceptance within its borders. They would call them Dark Elves to make them feel comfortable and equal to them instead of the old ways of origination long ago.

Word spread swiftly among the Dark One communities, carried by the whispers of hope and the promise of a new beginning. Drawn by the prospect of finding a place where their unique gifts and talents could be recognized, many dark ones would journey to the kingdom of Alora, their hearts filled with anticipation and longing for a fresh start. The thought of being accepted as an elven person gave them hope to live a life outside of the lifestyle the dark ones had built around.

Queen Alora, renowned for her wisdom and foresight, understood that integrating the dark elves into the existing hierarchy would require time, patience, and a delicate balance of understanding and acceptance. She saw the potential for mutual growth and enrichment, envisioning a future where the highborn women of the kingdom could find common ground with the dark elves or bridge the gaps between their respective cultures and traditions. As well as finding dark elves with pristine genetic traits to serve as Dark-Highborn to avoid birthing more of the newcoming mix of elves.

Despite Queen Alora's tireless efforts to foster unity and harmony within the different tiers of society, it is inevitable that pockets of discontent and unrest may arise within the walls of Alora. Particularly among the lowborn district, there might be individuals or groups who question the existing hierarchy and yearn for greater opportunities and recognition. These sentiments can give rise to tensions and divisions within the kingdom as aspirations clash with the established order. Queen Alora must navigate these challenges with wisdom and fairness, striving to address the concerns of the disenchanted while upholding the overall stability and well-being of her beloved realm.

Inside the kingdom, the lowborn district area presents a striking contrast to the lavishness and magnificence observed in the upper echelons of society. This locality is marked by deteriorating residences, narrow meandering lanes, and an overall lack of upkeep. Tattered walls and broken windows are evidence of the district's once magnificent architecture succumbing to neglect. Trash and scrap clutter the streets, while an unmistakable sense of abandonment hangs heavily in the air.

Within this impoverished area, tensions run high between the light-elven and dark-elven inhabitants. The two groups' significant divides have created a hostile environment defined by constant squabbling, quarrels, and sometimes clashes. Each group blames the other for its challenges, with both sides accusing the other of unfairness and discrimination. The lowborn have become fragmented, forming their own sub-hierarchy within, further worsening the divisions and power struggles within their own ranks.

The sense of unity and communal support that Queen Alora strives to foster in her society seems absent within the lowborn area. Instead, it has deteriorated into a place where every person is out for themselves, clinging to whatever advantages they can find in the difficult conditions. Self-interest has replaced cooperation and teamwork as elves worked to provide for themselves and their families. The competition for limited opportunities has fueled an atmosphere of mistrust, where alliances are fragile and allegiances can shift in an instant.

As Queen Alora contemplates the state of the Lowborn district, she is faced with the challenge of bridging the deep divides that have formed within her kingdom. She recognizes that true unity cannot be achieved if a significant portion of the elves remain marginalized and embroiled in conflict. Addressing the disparities and grievances within the lowborn area becomes a pressing task, requiring not only practical solutions such as infrastructure improvements and resource allocation but also a concerted effort to mend the social fabric and foster a sense of belonging and collective purpose.

In addition to the challenges of neglect and social division, the lowborn district of Alora also grapples with the issue of overpopulation. The limited resources and infrastructure strain to accommodate the growing number of residents within the cramped confines of the district. The overcrowded living conditions increased the already difficult circumstances, leading to heightened tensions and a sense of desperation among the lowborn population. The lack of space, coupled with inadequate access to basic amenities, further fuels the discontent and unrest that simmer within the district, leaving many elves to sleep on the streets, presenting an additional hurdle for Queen Alora to address in her pursuit of unity and progress.

Queen Alora understands that the well-being of her entire kingdom hinges on the inclusion and empowerment of all its citizens, regardless of their birth or social standing. She seeks to implement initiatives that provide opportunities for education, skill development, and economic upliftment in the lowborn area, aiming to break the cycle of discord and poverty. Queen Alora seeks to bring the lowborn into the deliberations of the kingdom in order to bind the wounds that have torn the community apart over the years. If she can bring them into the decision-making process, they will become more united, which in turn will lead to a more harmonious society.

During the reconstruction of the elven kingdom, Queen Alora learned that the beautiful elven homeland she so much sought had possessed many wonderful amenities but also came at the cost of her own well-being. With numerous refugees, particularly dark elves, seeking shelter and her authority extending across claimed territories, the queen began to feel the strain on her sanity. Faced with the overwhelming challenges, she devised plans for the establishment of towns and villages on other islands, foreseeing them as essential for future growth. However, the rapid pace of expansion surpassed her initial expectations, leaving her to rely on the patience of her subjects as the islands continued to develop.

Within the lowborn district of Alora, a complex issue arises when a dark elf and a light elf come together to conceive a child. The result of this union is a Gray Elf, a unique individual caught between two worlds. However, in the intricate web of elven society, this peculiar existence creates a dilemma of identity and belonging.

The unexpected consequences of interbreeding between the dark elves and the light lowborn elves stirred confusion within the elven council. Contrary to expectations, the fertility rates of the offspring from these unions were on par with those of the light elves of Alora. This unforeseen development prompted the council to initiate a thorough study and observation of the phenomenon, seeking to unravel the complexities of the interactions between the two elven races and their impact on the overall fertility of the elven kind.

To the surprise of the elves, the lowborn district witnessed an unprecedented increase in fertility rates among the lowborn elves. Joyous cries filled the air as news spread of newborn babies arriving in abundance from mixed-elven parents, their arrival heralding a new era of hope and possibilities. This phenomenon intrigued the elven council enough that they reinstated the Genetic Pathway Organization, a group dedicated to understanding and mapping the intricate pathways of heritage and lineage of the elven kind.

Recognizing the significance of this unexpected development, the Genetic Pathway Organization quickly began planning stages that would build a thorough structure for the dark elves and the newborn gray elves within the kingdom of Alora. Their objective was to navigate the intricate structure of genetic variation and establish a system that would respect the distinct background and lineage of these classifications.

The method entailed rigorous study, comprehensive consultations, and cooperation with specialists from several disciplines. Academics, genetic experts, historians, and representatives from the Elven Council came together, pooling their combined expertise and perspectives. Their goal was to create an organizational hierarchy that would recognize the unique characteristics and capabilities of each grouping while promoting harmony and collaboration, guided by the principles of equality, diversity, and appreciation for cultural differences.

When a gray elf is born, there is often a sense of doubt surrounding their place within the hierarchy. The Genetic Pathway Organization, responsible for assessing the genetic traits and potential of each child, takes custody of these infants. Subjected to rigorous tests and evaluations, the fate of the gray elven child hangs in the balance until an evaluation is complete.

Should an infant fail to meet the standards set by the organization, they are deemed unfit for the higher tiers of society and are cast aside into the lowborn community to be claimed by their parents or as an orphan. Some of these children grow up without the support or acknowledgment of their elven lineage, left to navigate the harsh realities of the lowborn district on their own. It is a fate that continues the cycle of disadvantage and maintains the division between the classes.

On the other hand, if a gray elf passes the tests administered by the Genetic Pathway Organization, they are deemed worthy of integration into a higher tier of society. This success story becomes a glimmer of hope for parents who seek a better future for their bloodline. The possibility of their gray elven child securing a place among the higher classes fuels aspirations and dreams of upward mobility as families strive to provide their offspring with opportunities denied to them.

This system of evaluation and classification preserves the desire for social advancement, creating a subtle competition among lowborn elven parents. The birth of a gray elf becomes not only a question of lineage but also a reflection of parental aspirations and hopes for a brighter future for themselves.

Yet, amidst the passion for upward mobility, the underlying question remains: What is the true cost of forsaking those who do not meet society's predetermined standards? The plight of the gray elves served as a steady reminder of the complexities and challenges faced by those caught between the cracks of the kingdom's rigid social structure.

The Gray Elves, born from the intricate blend of light and dark elven characteristics, exhibit a fascinating convergence of features. Their eyes, a mesmerizing light array of grays, whites, and purples, hint at the dual nature coursing through their veins. Angular ears, reminiscent of their dark elven ancestry, coexist with a variation in tooth structure, ranging from sharp fangs akin to the supernatural tales of bloodlusters created by the Archon ages ago to the more refined dental patterns reminiscent of the light elves.

The texture of skin among the gray elves shows a delicate balance between the smoothness of the light elves and the ruggedness of the dark elves, further emphasizing the harmonious fusion of their dual heritage. In this intricate dance between light and dark, order and chaos, the gray elves embody a neutral essence, their evolution remaining a captivating mystery waiting to unfold.

The distinction among the three varieties of elven kin lies in their physical attributes. Light elves are characterized by lighter eye colors, light-colored hair, pointy ears, and smooth skin, all while giving off a slight glow of radiance. On the contrary, dark elves present a stark contrast, featuring darker eye and hair hues, rugged skin adapted for fire tolerance, and angular ears. Despite their paleness, the dark elves boast a unique blend of dark skin tones with colors that are almost identical to those of the Ranuk.

However, the sands of time whisper tales of change, as newfound knowledge shows the potential that Light and Dark Elves share better fertility rates with each other than within their own kin. The Genetic Pathway Organization foresees a future in a thousand years where the distinctions between the elves' blur and the meshing of their traits render them indistinguishable. Yet, looming over this potential convergence is Queen Alora's steadfast determination for preservation, hinting at the possibility of a divergent path in the elven evolution in appearance.

Collaborating with the Genetic Pathway Organization, the queen implemented measures to address the temporary population strain. Dark elves were assigned to the working class and military ranks; their ascent to higher tiers as Arcanist or Highborn was dependent not only on genetics but also on strict societal standards. This approach, though effective in mitigating overpopulation, had fueled bitterness among the dark elves as the process was too slow at dispersing the overwhelming population. Many felt disillusioned while having hoped for a kingdom better than the one they fled, finding themselves grappling with societal expectations and barriers inside the kingdom of Alora.

....

Within the shadows of the lowborn district, a secretive cult thrives in secrecy, delving into forbidden realms of magic. Unbeknownst to the elven hierarchy, this group practices dark arts such as dark arcane known as shadowmancy, necromancy, blood magic, and mind-flaying. At the cult leader stands a dark elven known as Morvain, a master of these forbidden arts. His true identity concealed from the prying eyes of the elves of Alora, he carefully selects a troubled youth orphan named Fumar, who was a gray elf as his successor, recognizing the young elven potential and his thirst for power.

Fumar was born to parents who carried the shame of not having a child with genetic traits deemed deserving of a higher class, leaving them without anyone to claim him as their own. The weight of disappointment and embarrassment clouded the hearts of his birthing parents, leading them to turn their backs on the innocent child.

Over the course of many years, under the tutelage of Morvain, Fumar is initiated into the arcane mysteries of forbidden magic. The cult's hidden sanctum becomes a haven for their dark practices, where ancient tomes and forbidden artifacts adorn the chamber walls. In the depths of their studies, they delve into the manipulation of life and death, the harnessing of blood as a source of power, and the insidious art of mind control.

Morvain's secret sanctum beneath the lowborn district provided him with access to an ancient tunnel network, allowing him to move through the kingdom unnoticed. Collaborating with local vandals, the cult engaged in covert activities, stealing food and supplies from the higher classes. Morvain, adopting the role of a hidden hero, distributed these resources among the elves, offering them a means of survival while awaiting the queen's decision on their migration, which he suspected would be the removal of dark elves. Morvain harbored a deep disdain for the light elves, fueled by their reluctance towards the dark elves. His belief in embracing the chaotic nature had driven his actions and fueled his opposition to the established order.

As a young Fumar progresses in his training, the power of the forbidden magic courses through his veins, corrupting his mind and soul. He becomes deeply entangled in the cult's evil deceptions due to loyalty and the promise of ultimate power. The cult members, shrouded in secrecy, carry out their sinister deeds under the cover of darkness, ever mindful of the consequences should their actions be exposed to elven society.

On a dark night, Morvain orchestrated a sinister plan involving Fumar's biological parents. Capturing them, he woke Fumar to the unsettling reunion. Fumar's mother, a dark elven laborer, and his father, a light elven drunk, stood before him. Disgust filled Fumar as he gazed upon them, the seething hatred intensifying. When his father attempted to strike him, Morvain commanded obedience from the father while also silencing the mother. Fumar, intrigued by the power Morvain wielded, expressed him as his true father.

As his parents kneeled on their knees with blank expressions and fear in their eyes, Fumar began yelling at his parents for abandoning him. Morvain presented a choice in his anger: if Fumar killed his parents, he would be free of the torment that haunted his mind throughout his existence. Without hesitation, Fumar coldly ended his mother's life, a wicked smile playing on his lips. Remorse had briefly crossed his face, but as he turned to his father, an unfathomable rage consumed him. The blade struck mercilessly until he became calm. In the aftermath, Morvain held Fumar through the night, a twisted bond forged in darkness.

Unknown to Queen Alora and the Elven Council, this hidden cult poses a threat not only to the delicate balance of power within the lowborn district but also to the unity of the kingdom. The forbidden magic that they wield holds the potential to unleash chaos and destruction if left unchecked, and it is only a matter of time before their presence is unveiled, testing the limits of Queen Alora's leadership and the stability of the elven kingdom, amongst the multiple layers of troubles that the kingdom has yet to overcome.

Chapter 6: Flames and Shadows

As the shadows deepened inside Alora and tensions between the Dark Ones escalated throughout the years with Alora being rebuilt, Havoc, the insidious Shaper orchestrating the chaos through spectral entities, reveled in the unfolding discord. With a cunning intellect and a deep-rooted hatred for the Elven Kingdom, he devised a master plan to unravel Alora and sow seeds of resentment within the hearts of the dark ones. Havoc recognized that by stoking the flames of animosity, he could turn the dark ones against Alora, transforming them into a formidable force driven by vengeance.

Havoc's plot was intricately woven and calculated to exploit the historical grievances between the dark ones and Alora. He skillfully manipulated events and whispers to incite anger and resentment among the dark ones, convincing them that Alora had grand plans to build their empire, enslave their kind, and suppress their true potential. Every move Havoc made was a strategic step towards shattering the fragile peace that had existed between the two races, fueling their desire for hatred and destruction.

Through subtle manipulation and covert alliances, Havoc infiltrated the darkest corners of Dark One society. He preyed on the discontent and frustration that had simmered beneath the surface for centuries, exploiting their longing for peace and equality. With whispers in the ears of influential dark one leaders, as he sowed doubt and mistrust, portraying Queen Alora as the oppressor and the catalyst behind their suffering. The carefully crafted web of deception cast a shadow of doubt over the kingdom of Alora's intentions and cast them as enemies in the eyes of the dark ones.

Havoc's manipulation extended beyond mere words. He delved into the depths of dark one culture, exploiting their customs, rituals, and beliefs to further his cause. He harnessed their honor for the fire god, stoking their faith and convincing them that the flames of destruction were the means to achieve their salvation. Through twisted interpretations of their own heritage, he forged a bond with the dark ones, uniting them in a shared purpose: the downfall of Alora.

His objective was to spark a sense of uprising among the Dark Ones harnessing their fury as a power that would unleash wrath upon Alora. He understood that by stoking the fires of animosity, he could rally the dark ones to rebel against those they perceived as oppressors, aiming to obliterate their enemies and regain their dominance in society. The mounting tensions between Havoc and the dark ones were but a prelude to the storm that would soon descend upon Alora, leaving the fate of the kingdom hanging by a thread.

All the Dark Ones had to do was listen to the insidious whispers that Havoc had carefully orchestrated and dispatched to the Spectral Avatars who resided within their society. For years, he had meticulously laid the groundwork, subtly planting seeds of doubt and stoking the embers of resentment. His ultimate goal was to ignite an inextinguishable fire within the hearts of the dark ones and make them fuel their every action with a burning desire for vengeance and liberation. Havoc sought to harness their collective rage and redirect it towards Alora, ensuring that their actions would unleash a storm of chaos and destruction, shaking the foundations of the elven kingdom to their core.

As rumors spread about the Queen's territorial expansion in the southwest of Paranova, those attuned to Havoc's whispers began to believe. Gathering like-minded individuals, they rallied others to join their cause, viewing the elves of Alora as a looming threat encroaching upon their lands. Refugees from the affected villages reported that the Vanguard, the Queen's enforcers, left them with stark choices: abandon their homes or face enslavement as their villages were claimed. Tensions simmered as the whispers of dissent echoed through the hidden corners of Paranova.

Havoc marveled at the seamless execution of his sinister plots, recognizing the intricate ripples they created in the tapestry of Paranova. The subtlety of his manipulations allowed chaos to unfold naturally, like a well-played symphony. Yet a lingering desire gnawed at him—an aspiration to manifest his physical presence in the world he had masterfully influenced from the shadows. In the depths of his thoughts, Havoc yearns for a way to step from the realm of whispers into the tangible realm of Paranova.

As Havoc delved into the secrets of Paranova's ancient past, he discovered the dormant elemental entities that slumbered within the world's crust. Recognizing the potential for their power to cause chaos, Havoc couldn't resist the temptation to unleash their wrath. However, his newfound love for the dark ones, which were his own creation, tempered his sinister intentions. With devious schemes in mind, Havoc plotted ways for the dark ones to tap into the natural elemental power, setting the stage for an awakening that would ripple throughout Paranova.

········

The Dark Ones hold steadfast to ancestral traditions that have been passed down through generations, each one steeped in faith for their esteemed deity, the fire god. Flames hold profound significance within their rituals and ceremonies, symbolizing the transformative power and destructive force that reside within them. The dark ones believe that fire is a divine manifestation, representing both creation and destruction, and they pay homage to its potent energy.

Their rituals often involve the skillful manipulation of fire, with dances, incantations, and offerings performed in its flickering glow. Through these sacred practices, the dark ones seek to commune with their deity, to draw upon its fiery essence, and to unleash its power in their lives.

Fire holds significance not as a source of light and warmth but as a way to connect spiritually tapping into our inner strength and unlocking untapped potential. In traditions those who follow the dark ones perceive fire as a symbol of rebirth and transformation, symbolizing the cycle of life and death. They perceive the flames as a cleansing force, dispelling negativity and ushering in change. Through their rituals, they aim to harness this transformative energy to manifest their desires in the realm.

These age-old customs play a role in uniting the dark ones and fostering a sense of unity and common purpose among them. They gather around the sacred hearths, where flames dance and crackle, and offer their prayers and devotion to Pyrothos, the fire god.

The Dark Ones believe that through their connection to fire, they inherit its resilience, passion, and determination. It is through the guidance of their deity that they navigate the challenges and trials of life, finding peace in the flickering embers and drawing inspiration from the eternal flame.

At the core of the dark one belief system stands the mighty deity known as Pyrothos, the Fire God. Seen as the embodiment of fire and its transformative power, Pyrothos holds a central place in the dark one ancestral traditions. Their rituals and ceremonies are intertwined with the worship of this divine entity, seeking blessings and guidance from the fiery deity. Pyrothos is said to have created the very first flame, which ignited the universe and brought light to the darkness.

The Dark Ones hold the conviction that fire embodies not only devastation and disorder but also creation and renewal. They view it as a representation of life's recurring cycle, where demise paves the path for fresh beginnings while alteration remains ever-present. This belief system filters their way of existence as they willingly embrace the tribulations and ordeals presented to them, striving to emerge from such encounters fortified with wisdom and resilience. The dark ones likewise perceive fire as an influential means of transformation on both internal and external planes.

Utilizing fire within their rituals and ceremonies, they employ this elemental force to symbolize shedding old patterns to conform to new ones instead. Moreover, in their practices pertaining to healing, honoring fire with the potential to cleanse both the body and mind from toxins along with negative energies is central. However, despite acknowledging its formidable destructive prowess, the dark ones do not disregard the crucial significance of responsibly wielding this element with utmost regard.

The Dark Ones uphold the belief that with great power comes great responsibility, thereby leading lives intertwined with the natural realm. In addition to their admiration for fire, they possess a strong regard for the intricate patterns of nature. They view themselves as guardians of the earth, much like their counterpart elves and strive towards an existence harmonized with the environment. This entails respecting the ebb and flow of seasons and their connections to the rhythms dictated by mother nature and adjusting their customs and traditions accordingly.

They are convinced that aligning their lives with nature enables them to access its inherent potency and wisdom, consequently fostering a sustainable and enriching way of life. Therefore, they change their practices and traditions according to the changing seasons and the natural changes of the land throughout the year. They think that by living close to and paying attention to nature, they can borrow and gain its power and wisdom to create a more sustainable and prosperous life.

The Dark Ones, born from the essence of chaos and darkness, possess a unique resilience to fire that baffles the other mortal races. They can touch or manipulate flames without succumbing to their burning embrace. The dark ones themselves believe in a deep connection with fire, claiming that they were forged from its very essence. To them, as long as the flames remain pure, they can withstand the fiery trials that would consume others. This exceptional trait sets them apart, shrouded in a mystical aura that leaves other races marveling at their mysterious affinity with the element of fire.

Below the Dark Ones' kingdom lies a vast and ancient volcano, known as the Inarus Inferno. It is believed to be the sacred dwelling place of Pyrothos, where the Fire God's essence resides. The volcano, with its constant flow of molten lava and billowing plumes of smoke and fire, serves as a tangible connection between the mortal realm and the divine presence of Pyrothos.

In Dark One culture, the Inarus Inferno is viewed as a sacred site and the physical manifestation of their deity's power. The dark ones gather near the volcano to conduct their rituals, offering sacrifices and prayers to Pyrothos. The intense heat and fiery glow of the volcano serve as reminders of their devotion and the divine energy that flows through their existence.

The volcanic activity within the Inarus Inferno is seen as a direct expression of Pyrothos' will. Eruptions are interpreted as messages from the Fire God, guiding the dark ones and shaping their destiny. The flowing lava is believed to carry the essence of Pyrothos, representing the purifying and transformative qualities of fire. By immersing themselves in the molten fire, the dark ones seek spiritual renewal and a deeper connection with their deity. However, most dark ones would be consumed by the mystical fires from the inferno, but there were instances where certain individuals would come out from the molten fire unharmed and claim to be reborn by Pyrothos.

Pyrothos and the Inarus Inferno are revered symbols of their faith, representing the power, passion, and ever-burning flame that reside within their culture. The presence of Pyrothos and the volcanic landscape serve as a constant reminder of their ancestral ties and the eternal strength they receive from the divine fire. In addition to its religious significance, fire plays a crucial role in the daily lives of the dark ones. They use it for cooking, warmth, and even as a tool for crafting their weapons and tools. The dark ones greatly admire the skill of fire manipulation and hold those who possess it in high regard.

In the inhospitable volcanic landscape that is their home, the dark ones have thrived primarily due to their utilization of fire. The flames have endowed them with not only sustenance through cultivating crops but also an interconnectedness with the divine. For them, fire symbolizes an eternal flame present within all living creatures, forging a spiritual bond between mankind and the gods. Consequently, it frequently finds itself at the heart of their religious ceremonies and rituals as a method for communication. Furthermore, in embracing its purifying capabilities, they employ fire to cleanse one's spirit as well. Therefore, fire has become integral to their culture and daily lives—an essential practical tool blending naturally with symbolic significance.

At the brim of the towering Inarus Inferno, the dark ones gather to partake in sacred rituals that demonstrate their devotion and seek favor from Pyrothos, the Fire God. The air is thick with anticipation as flames dance upon the rugged rocks surrounding the volcano, casting an eerie glow upon the worshippers.

Perched atop this majestic volcanic formation is an exquisite ceremonial altar fashioned out of immense stone bearing elaborate carvings resembling mighty flames and adorned with ancient symbols that constitute its centerpiece during these rituals.

The offerings, carefully chosen and imbued with meaning, are placed on the altar. These may include bundles of aromatic herbs and sacred woods, precious gemstones that gleam with inner fire, and even small animals symbolizing vitality and sacrifice.

The rituals would begin with an elegant sequence led by the high priest, who is adorned in intricate robes with symbols of fire and embers. The dark ones, wearing ceremonial garments woven with fiery hues, follow in respectful silence. They carry offerings in their hands, symbols of their gratitude and desire for the blessings of Pyrothos.

The air would resonate with the rhythmic pulse of drums while the ritual proceeded towards the mouth of the volcano. The flickering flames illuminate the worshippers' faces, and their expressions are a mix of respect and fear for the Fire God. As they come closer to the climax, the high priest extends his hands in appeal, his voice resounding across the rugged expanse. The dark ones mimic his actions, harmonizing their voices as they prepare their offerings to Pyrothos.

The atmosphere vibrates with tension, as if even the slightest misstep could cause immediate displeasure from this formidable deity and unleash upon them his wrath. The high priest stealthily moves forward, elevating his arms upward, signaling Pyrothos's presence while conjuring the divine fire dwelling within the volcano's depths. The dark ones watch as the flames of the volcano hungrily consume the offerings, transforming them into smoke and embers that ascend towards the heavens.

Amidst the crackling of the volcanic activity, the high priest leads the worshippers in chants and prayers, their voices rising in harmonious devotion. They plea to Pyrothos for protection, strength, and guidance while seeking his favor in both personal and communal matters. The heat emanating from the volcano had matched the intensity of their prayers, creating an atmosphere charged with spiritual energy.

On certain occasions, the dark ones may engage in acts of self-sacrifice as a profound demonstration of their dedication to Pyrothos. This may involve individuals voluntarily stepping into the brim of the volcano and offering themselves to the divine fire as a testament to their loyalty and willingness to undergo transformation.

These sacrificial rituals serve as a deep connection between the dark ones and Pyrothos, reinforcing their bond and seeking divine intervention in their lives. It is believed that through these acts of devotion, the Fire God will bestow his blessings upon the worshippers, granting them strength, success, and the power to shape their own destiny within the eternal flame.

In the society of the Dark Ones, when individuals commit grave wrongdoings or disobey the laws of their community, it is viewed as a deliberate act of embracing chaos and defying the order set forth by Pyrothos. As such, the punishment system for the crimes is severe and symbolic. Those deemed guilty of wicked acts are cast into the fiery depths of the volcano, an act believed to be an honorable passage to be united with Pyrothos.

The conviction regarding the potency of fire and its capacity to cleanse one's spirit is embedded profoundly within the culture of those known as the dark ones. Serving as a fundamental principle of their religious beliefs, it acts as a compelling motivation for their journey.

The eternal fire embodies not only their divine nature but also represents the strength and righteousness of Pyrothos in a tangible manner. Believers agree that those who align with the never-ending flame will gain immortality in the afterlife, while those who resist it will forever endure damnation. The dark ones tend to be extremely particular about following religious rules and traditions because they want to keep their society sacred. This has often caused problems with non-believers and those from other faiths. Although these problems have occurred, they continue to keep progressing toward their final goal of achieving eternal enlightenment.

This form of punishment carries significance among the dark ones. It is not seen as a mere act of retribution but rather as a spiritual reconciliation and a means for the guilty to meet their maker in a sacred union. The act of being thrown into the inferno is considered a transformative journey, where the convicted individual becomes one with the essence of the Fire God and is consumed by the eternal flame.

While this punishment may seem extreme to outsiders, the dark ones perceive it as an ultimate act of atonement and purification. They believe that by facing the flames and offering themselves to Pyrothos, the guilty souls find redemption and become part of the eternal cycle of creation and destruction symbolized by the Inarus Inferno. It is an act believed to restore balance and order within society, ensuring that the dark forces of chaos are purged and harmony is preserved.

The sight of someone being thrown into the volcano serves as a powerful reminder to the dark ones of the consequences of embracing chaos and deviating from the path set forth by Pyrothos. It reinforces the importance of loyalty to their cultural values and upholding the sacred flame that burns within them.

The punishment system, deeply embedded in their belief system, serves as evidence of the intense spiritual bond between the dark ones and the Fire God. It demonstrates their unyielding dedication to upholding societal order. For example, if a dark one is convicted of committing an obvious offense like murder, they face being cast into the volcano for retribution. This not only serves as a preventative action against potential offenders but also represents their wholehearted devotion to Pyrothos and the sacrifices that they are willing to undertake in service of shared prosperity. Individuals see the volcano erupting as a sign from the divine that they can trust them, which makes their faith even stronger.

The cultural practices of the dark ones are firmly established in their conventions and act as foundations of their shared identity. They have elaborate rites of passage that signify a person's integration into the dark one society and mark important life events. These rituals are intricate and frequently entail demanding examinations and trials intended to evaluate the physical and mental capability of the participants. Accomplishing these rituals successfully indicates the development, strength, and preparedness to take on the obligations of becoming an adult.

Sacred events hold a special position in dark one culture, bringing the community together in celebration. These gatherings provide occasions to pay tribute to Pyrothos, strengthen their spiritual bond, and request the divine favor of the fire God. During these ceremonies, the dark ones perform an elaborate dance, recite arcane spells, and present sacrifices to Pyrothos, frequently in the shape of consecrated flames or valuable gemstones representing the intense essence. These gatherings cultivate a feeling of oneness, cohesion, and mutual dedication to their god, reinforcing the communal connection that supports their culture.

Aside from their religious significance, these gatherings also function as crucial social occasions for the evil entities. Individuals from diverse castes and lineages gather, engaging in the exchange of narratives, indulging in lavish meals, and commemorating their collective cultural legacy. The elders transmit the customs and ideals that have supported their elven kin for thousands of years to the younger generations, providing wisdom and direction. During these gatherings, the dark ones not only enhance their bond with Pyrothos but also with one another, establishing an effective and enduring group capable of overcoming any obstacle.

Among the Dark Ones, communal feasts hold deep significance as they embody joyous festivities that involve storytelling and generous food sharing. These feasts are beloved traditional gatherings, often organized in honor of notable milestones like seasonal transitions or momentous triumphs. Summoned around a magnificent blazing fire, the dark ones savor scrumptious dishes prepared with affection while engaging in narratives recounting the awe-inspiring feats of their ancestors and legends whispered through multiple generations.

Ultimately, these lively banquets cultivate a spirit of unity, granting opportunities for connection and cross-cultural exchange while fortifying their shared heritage and cherished values among the dark one community.

In conjunction with these communal festivals, food occupies an important role in the everyday existence of the dark ones. The cornerstone of their society is agriculture, as every family is charged with cultivating crops and rearing livestock. An air of pride envelops the dark ones due to their self-sufficiency and the high caliber of their produce, which is frequently exchanged or sold within nearby communities. Over time, traditional recipes and methods for cooking have been mastered and fine-tuned, resulting in a luscious culinary heritage that warrants both celebration and preservation. From hefty stews to dainty pastries, dark one cuisine outlines resourcefulness and creativity amidst the hardship that they endure daily.

Despite the immense difficulties their demanding environment presents, the dark ones have developed a strong sense of community and a deep attachment to their land and traditions. Their unwavering dedication towards self-reliance and sustainability serves as a beacon of inspiration for others while simultaneously showcasing the influence resilience possesses through their delightful dishes.

Within the realm of various customs and traditions, the dark ones actively embrace their shared identity while emphasizing the significance of their beliefs, values, and association with Pyrothos. By engaging in ceremonies that mark important life transitions, gatherings that are considered sacred, and celebratory meals aimed at unifying the community, they deepen their comprehension of their place within the world and fortify the bonds that unite them as a collective. These long-standing practices not only stimulate cultural pride but also play an essential role in upholding social unity, fostering peaceful coexistence, and cultivating a deep sense of belonging among members of the dark ones.

The Dark Ones exhibit an extraordinary artistic heritage that mirrors their deep spiritual connection with the elemental energies, specifically fire. Their art forms are fascinating and breathtaking, demonstrating their expertise in manipulating fire and harnessing its strength. One of their distinctive artistic practices involves crafting elaborate flame sculptures, in which highly experienced artisans precisely control and mold flames with exceptional accuracy. From massive, intimidating constructions that pulsate with life to smaller, more delicate components, these sculptures cover a wide range of designs. The captivating combination of illumination and darkness within these sculptures produces an intense feeling of wonder and respect for the potency of fire.

Flame performances occupy a significant position within dark one culture, alongside flame sculptures. These captivating and spellbinding displays merge elegant motions with authority over fire, resulting in a captivating spectacle for audiences. Dancers dressed in vivid costumes decorated with whirling flames move in sync with the music and rhythms, their bodies becoming extensions of the fire itself. Through their attentive actions, they infuse vitality into the flames, resulting in a harmonious interaction of radiance and movement. Since fire performances represent the close bond that exists between elves and the elemental forces they honor, they serve as both a medium for creative expression and a means of spiritual development.

The dark ones express their admiration for fire and its importance in their lives through these distinctive art forms. The elaborate flame sculptures and captivating fire performances are sincere manifestations of their devotion, showcasing their comprehension of the fundamental force and transformative potential of fire. These art forms not only demonstrate their artistic skill but also generate a feeling of wonder and admiration among both individuals with dark characteristics and audience members from various cultures. The complex intricacies, graceful motions, and otherworldly elegance of their artistic expressions fascinate the senses, compelling spectators to ponder the deep bond between the mysterious figures and the elemental forces that influence their existence.

Moreover, the intangible essence of the dark ones extends beyond their creative attempts. It spread throughout all aspects of their everyday existence, influencing not only their connection with nature but also their interactions with fellow individuals. They wholeheartedly embrace the notion of interconnectivity among all aspects of the universe, comprehending that even the smallest actions hold deep implications for the surrounding world. This perspective on spirituality has steered them towards maintaining a balance with their environment, enabling them to flourish amidst even the most formidable situations.

In the embrace of isolation, the dark ones flourished, reveling in the freedom that set them apart from the other mortal races, including the elves. Guided by their faithful devotion to their Fire God, the dark ones built a vibrant and chaotic society. Thriving amidst the shadows, they embraced their uniqueness and found strength in their connection to the element of fire. As the world around them unfolded with the arrival of new races and the chaos of the Gantum War, the dark ones remained steadfast in their independent and lively way of life, a testament to their resilience and the fiery spirit that fueled their existence.

The foundation of the kingdom belonging to the dark ones indicates their strong affiliation with the subterranean volcanic domain below them. The structures harmoniously blend with the rugged landscape, embodying the raw power and mystique of the volcano. The buildings are crafted from dark volcanic stone and adorned with intricate carvings and symbols that pay homage to their fiery deity, Pyrothos.

The architecture reflects a courageous and geometric design, giving the impression of lava suspended in eternal stillness. Majestic towers ascend towards the heavens, reminiscent of volcanic summits, while descending terraces and balconies mirror the flow of molten streams. These structures have been intricately crafted to optimize the interaction between light and darkness, resulting in an ambience that shows both magnificence and mystical allure.

A highly remarkable characteristic of the architecture is the widespread utilization of glass infused with volcanic lava. Dark one artisans have mastered the art of shaping molten lava into translucent panels, which are integrated into the structures, allowing the play of light to create an ethereal glow. These glass elements capture the essence of the volcano, mimicking the fiery hues and lending a sense of constant movement and vitality to the buildings. Some of the buildings allow lava to flow in and out of them, making for magnificent views throughout the kingdom.

Within the kingdom, there are sprawling complexes dedicated to various purposes. The central citadel, known as Inarus Keep, houses the ruling elite and serves as the seat of power. It displays a powerful presence due to its large fortifications, which stare out over the region nearby. Other structures include the Ember Cathedral, where religious rituals and ceremonies take place, and the Forge of Embers, an immense complex where trained crafters form weapons and objects infused with fire magic, glass, and metal.

Perched on the highest peak of the volcanic kingdom, the Lava Veil Observatory is a structure that combines both functionality and aesthetics. Dark one astronomers and scholars gather here to observe the patterns of the lava flows and the celestial bodies above. The observatory's architecture integrates lava-resistant crystals that refract the molten glow, creating a mesmerizing display visible from miles away. It serves as a place of both scientific inquiry and artistic inspiration, fostering a deep connection between the dark ones and the elemental forces that shape their realm.

Beyond its practical purpose, the design of the Dark One architecture contains significant symbolic meaning. It represents their love for the volcano, their faith in the transformational power of fire, and their commitment to the elemental forces. The structures act as enduring symbols for their affiliation with Pyrothos and serve as a compelling tribute to the resilience and determination of the dark ones in a state of danger.

The kingdom's architecture harmoniously integrates with the volcanic terrain while also embodying the values and core principles of its culture and beliefs. The Grand Temple of Pyrothos is a significant structure that serves as both a place of worship and a symbol of their devotion to the fire deity. The temple's elaborate sculptures and carvings, which portray scenarios from Dark One mythology, demonstrate how deeply ingrained their beliefs are. Not all dark ones worshipped Pyrothos; others worshipped a different deity. These individuals and their communities have cultivated unique architectural styles that exhibit significant divergence from those observed in the Grand Temple.

Their temples and shrines are often simpler in design, with a focus on functionality rather than ornate decoration. Some even choose to worship their deity in nature, building altars and leaving offerings in secluded small groves or near bodies of water. Despite these differences, the dark ones, who worship different deities, still share a deep bond with the power of magic and the supernatural. It is this shared belief that binds their communities together, even as they practice different rituals and honor different gods.

The Dark One society is structured around a strict hierarchy, with power and lineage playing significant roles in determining one's status and influence. At the pinnacle of their social structure is the Shadow Council, comprised of five master spellcasters who are considered the most powerful and esteemed individuals in dark one society. These council members hold immense authority and are responsible for making important decisions that shape the destiny of their kin. Each council member has survived the mystical fires by diving into the Inarus Inferno and being reborn by Pyrothos, a tradition that they intend to keep.

Each member of the Shadow Council represents a different aspect of dark one culture and magic, bringing unique expertise and perspectives to the council's deliberations. Their roles may cover areas such as elemental manipulation, necromancy, blood magic, shadowmancy, mindflaying, wiccanry, and arcane divination. Together, they ensure the smooth functioning of a dark one society, preserve their traditions, and safeguard their interests.

Under the Shadow Council, the dark one society is further divided into noble families, each tracing their lineage back to esteemed ancestors and respected figures in their history. These noble families hold significant influence and wield power within their respective domains. They are responsible for upholding the traditions and values of their lineage and serve as important pillars of a dark one society.

Beyond the noble families, the general dark one population consists of commoners and practitioners of various magical disciplines. While they may not hold the same level of authority as the nobility or the Shadow Council, they play essential roles in maintaining the functioning of their society. Skilled artisans, craftsmen, warriors, and scholars contribute to the cultural, economic, and defense aspects of this society. The Warlocks are a notable group among the dark one population; they specialize in dark magic, and the nobility frequently hires them for their services.

Warlocks, with their wide range of skills including curses, hexes, summoning horrors, and shadow manipulation, are both admired and dreaded for their extraordinary abilities. Nevertheless, the employment of dark magic frequently imposes a toll on their overall well-being, both physically and mentally. Despite these consequences, numerous warlocks persist in their dedication to the profession, as they view it as a means to acquire power and establish themselves prominently among members of a dark one society.

The Warlocks, weaving their mysterious arts, ushered in a new era in Paranova with the array of arcane disciplines such as Necromancy, Wiccanry, Siphonism, and Shadowmancy. These exotic dark classes became the foundation upon which future generations of Paranova would build their magical prowess. The ancient knowledge and secrets unlocked by the warlocks would echo through the corridors of time, leaving a memorable mark on the magical landscape of the world. As the students of these mystical arts delved into the complexities of each discipline, the world of Paranova witnessed the emergence of skilled spellcasters, each harnessing the unique powers bestowed upon them by these dark and mystical teachings.

The Dark One society places great emphasis on lineage and bloodlines, as they believe it is through their ancestry that they inherit their magical prowess and connection to Pyrothos. Those born into prestigious families or with powerful magical heritage are often given greater opportunities for education and advancement within society. However, exceptional individuals from humble origins can also rise through the ranks if they demonstrate remarkable skill and dedication.

Overall, a dark one society is characterized by its hierarchical structure, devotion to magical power, and the central role of the Shadow Council in guiding its subjects. Despite society's apparent rigidity in its divisions, it is bound together by a common belief in the fire god's supremacy and a shared desire to advance their own interests and defend their way of life.

Within a dark one society, there exist distinct castes that represent different roles and specialties, each contributing to the overall functioning and strength of their community. Each caste has roles within the dark one culture to better the community and master the skills needed to provide for their kingdom and their fire god.

The first caste is that of the Bloodfire, highly revered individuals who have undergone rigorous training and honed their mastery over fire magic. These master spellcasters are the living embodiment of the connection between the dark ones and their fire god, Pyrothos. They possess the ability to manipulate flames with exceptional skill and channel the raw power of fire to devastating effect.

The Bloodfire collect high regard and are actively sought out for their wisdom as well as their exceptional abilities in the realm of magic. Typically, they assume roles such as advisors, mentors, and guardians of dark one customs and ceremonies; they exhibit mastery over fire-based spells that render them formidable threats in conflicts. With the proficiency to conjure blazing strikes and erect protective barriers made of flames, they safeguard themselves alongside their comrades on the battlefield. However, these powers entail an immense responsibility to employ them judiciously while resisting the allure of their destructive influence. Often opting for lives of seclusion, many fire spellcasters dedicate themselves wholeheartedly to refining their skills and contemplating the intricate balance between destruction and creation, which is essentially the essence of fire.

Despite their withdrawn affection, the bloodfire continue to be an inseparable component of dark one society, upholding the age-old customs and convictions that have been transmitted through generations. A single illustration showcasing the fire mage's responsibilities in a dark one society is exercising their role as a safeguard during periods of conflict with the use of their potent enchantment to shield comrades from foe assaults. Another instance entails utilizing their capabilities for medicinal intent, employing the rejuvenating attributes essential as fire to mend wounds and ailments.

Another important caste within dark one society is the Emberblades, skilled warriors who have dedicated their lives to mastering the art of combat. Equipped with formidable weapons and clad in armor crafted from the unique materials found in the depths of the volcano, emberblades are the protectors of their kingdom. They undergo rigorous physical and martial training, becoming agile, swift, and lethal fighters. Their expertise lies in both offensive and defensive techniques, making them invaluable assets in times of conflict or defending dark one territories.

During periods of conflict, emberblades take the forefront in battle, employing their expertise in combat to instill terror in those opposing them. They have earned renown for constructing an impenetrable barrier of protection where each warrior cohesively operates to shield their community from any potential harm.

The Sinister Shadow caste comprises a secretive and mystical caste within a dark one society. They are practitioners of dark magic, harnessing the powers of shadows, illusions, and manipulation. With a strange ability to weave deception and control unseen forces, sinister shadows are skilled infiltrators, spies, and seekers of hidden knowledge. Their understanding of the subtle arts of manipulation and illusion makes them subtly dangerous and invaluable assets in espionage and intelligence-gathering operations. The caste's motives and loyalties often remain shrouded in mystery, adding an aura of intrigue to their presence.

For example, a Sinister Shadow member could use their powers to infiltrate a high-security facility undetected by creating illusions of themselves and manipulating the shadows to hide their true form. They could then gather valuable intelligence and secrets before disappearing into the shadows once again, leaving no trace behind. The mystery surrounding their motives and loyalties would make them a difficult target to track down or predict, making them a dangerous opponent in any situation.

Yet, the Sinister Shadow caste stood apart as a distinct entity born from the ambitions of a master warlock. This visionary sorcerer sought to carve out a niche dedicated to the mysteries of shadow magic, a realm distinct from the broader umbrella of warlocks within dark one society. While the warlocks wield influence and insight across various aspects of the kingdom, the caste was more widely accepted publicly amongst the dark one society.

Due to their wisdom and magical prowess, warlock practitioners frequently found themselves on the perimeter of society and were not well-liked by either the general public or the mysterious Shadow Council. In this intricate dance of power and secrecy, the warlocks were not recognized as a caste publicly and kept to themselves while helping where they could, with distinct roles given by the council wherever they were needed to contribute to the kingdom of dark ones.

Among the diverse castes of dark one society, the rippers hold a secretive and formidable position. These highly proficient specialists excel in the practice of hidden operations, unauthorized entry, and the precise elimination of assigned targets. Rippers, who were raised in the shadow sanctuaries, have incredible agility, dexterity, and deadly accuracy with their special weapons, such as poisoned daggers and camouflaged swords. They possess exceptional skills in stealth and trickery, enabling them to effortlessly blend with their surroundings and execute deadly attacks with extreme precision. The rippers, stealthily maneuvering through the depths of secrecy, perfectly serve essential functions as eliminators, disruptors of plans, and enforcers of power. Their sole purpose lies in safeguarding the security and welfare of the dark ones across their realm and beyond.

The Rippers, a group of highly skilled individuals, undergo rigorous and unforgiving training before being considered eligible to be part of their elite ranks. All members are required to uphold the utmost secrecy; they have sworn never to divulge any information about their organization or how it operates. Although notorious for their menacing reputation, the rippers abide by a set of ethical beliefs and principles. They often align themselves with causes and individuals whom they deem just and deserving of their support.

During times of war or political instability, their exceptional services are in great demand, extending beyond the confines of their home country's borders. Nonetheless, there exist critics who view the methods employed by these assassins as morally questionable while identifying their secretive nature as jeopardizing societal stability. Regardless of personal viewpoints about them, it cannot be denied that the influence wielded by the rippers renders them a formidable force especially when paired together.

Diverging paths weave between the Rippers and the Sinister Shadows, two closely related yet distinct castes within the society of the dark ones. The rippers are highly skilled in the disciplines of stealth, assassination, melee fighting, and accurate archery. They excel in swiftly eliminating prey, gracefully slipping into the shadows to strike with deadly precision.

On the other hand, the sinister shadows adopt a more arcane approach to self-preservation. Preferring to avoid direct confrontation, they rely on their mastery of magic when pressed into combat. Should the sinister shadows find themselves exposed or under threat, their training is the weaving of spells and the manipulation of the mystical forces to defend themselves.

These distinct castes represent different aspects of a dark one society. They each contribute their unique talents and abilities, serving vital roles in the overall functioning and protection of their kingdom. While their paths and specialties may differ, they are bound together by a shared allegiance to Pyrothos, their fire god, and a collective commitment to safeguarding dark one traditions, cultures, and interests.

Each caste within a dark one society plays a distinct role with specific responsibilities, contributing to the overall functioning and power of the kingdom. The Bloodfire, honored as the highest caste, are entrusted with the mastery of fire magic and serve as the primary conduits of the Fire God's divine flames. Their responsibilities include conducting sacred rituals, communing with Pyrothos, and preserving the spiritual connection between the dark ones and their deity. The Emberblades, skilled warriors and defenders of the realm, possess exceptional combat prowess and are tasked with protecting the kingdom from external threats. They undergo rigorous training in weapon mastery and battle tactics, forming the backbone of the dark one military might.

Furthermore, the other two comparable castes: the unseen Sinister Shadows, who master the shadowy disciplines of illusion and shadow-manipulation. They are invaluable resources in cases involving mystery and intelligence because of their proficiency in covert operations, information collection, and mystery solving. Moreover, the Rippers, who possess expertise in stealth and assassination, operate in secret, executing undercover missions and eliminating targets with merciless effectiveness. Although each caste possesses specific roles and responsibilities, their interactions frequently overlap, requiring collaboration and synchronization to uphold the stability and supremacy of a society.

The High Lords are the masters of each caste. They are in charge of all operations by working together and reporting to the Shadow Council. Within each caste, they have their own hierarchy system they follow. The High Lords are at the top, overseeing all operations and ensuring the stability and power of their society. Overall, the dark ones created a complex and organized system with a clear hierarchy and division of labor. Each caste has its own specific duties, and they often work together, requiring cooperation and coordination. The hierarchy within each caste further emphasizes the importance of order and structure in a dark one society.

Central to the core of their faith rests a deep comprehension of the everlasting cycle of birth and death. They perceive reality as a fragile balance, delicately poised between illuminated brilliance and shadowy darkness, structured order and swift disorder. Their conviction lies in the notion that authentic harmony can only be attained through the intricate intermingling of these contrasting forces.

The Dark Ones embrace the inherent duality of existence, recognizing that growth and transformation often emerge from moments of destruction and upheaval. They view themselves as agents of this cosmic balance, tasked with maintaining balance and ensuring that neither light nor darkness dominate unchecked.

Through their devotion to the Fire God Pyrothos, they seek to align their actions and intentions with the natural flow of the universe. They believe in the necessity of sacrifice, both literal and symbolic, to uphold this balance and honor the eternal flames that symbolize the essence of creation. Through their rituals, meditations, and loyalty to the core of their belief system, the dark ones strive to embody the balance they hold sacred.

The Dark Ones maintain a deep and profound connection to their beloved deity, the fire god Pyrothos. They believe that Pyrothos is not only the source of all fire but also the embodiment of strength, wisdom, and the power to shape their destinies. They view the flames as a divine manifestation of Pyrothos' presence, symbolizing both the destructive and transformative aspects of existence. The dark ones believe that by communicating with the fire god, they can tap into his divine essence and channel his fiery energy into their own being. They engage in sacred rituals and ceremonies, offering prayers and sacrifices to Pyrothos at the brim of the volcano, seeking his blessings and guidance.

They hold the belief that by displaying faithful dedication and establishing a strong bond with the deity of fire, they acquire the resilience to withstand challenges, the wit to make well-founded choices, and the capacity to forge their own destinies in accordance with the eternal flames that blaze deep within their beings. The fire god represents not only a source of spiritual motivation but also exemplifies their shared sense of self, embodying the ardor, strength, and unstoppable essence that courses through each member of the community.

The belief in rebirth and the continuity of the soul's journey beyond death is deeply ingrained among the dark ones. In their perception, existence entails an eternal pattern of creating, destroying, and reviving. As per their belief system, the soul surpasses mere materiality and continually sets forth on a quest for enlightenment through diverse dimensions. They hold that when a dark one departs from the mortal plane, their soul blends with Pyrothos, the fire god's essence, initiating a spiritual transformative process. During this transformation, the soul discards its former self and emerges anew, armed with accumulated wisdom and experiences from previous lives.

According to the Dark Ones, with every rebirth, the soul undergoes a refining process and progresses towards achieving its fullest potential. Mortal life is regarded by them as merely a temporary vessel for intellectual and spiritual development; death is perceived as more of a transition to another form of existence rather than an ultimate conclusion. This particular belief fosters in the dark ones a strong sense of purpose and compels them to constantly strive for self-improvement on their ongoing spiritual journey, aiming to reach elevated levels of comprehension and enlightenment through each successive lifetime.

The idea of reincarnation, in addition to highlighting the inherent connectedness between all living creatures, emphasizes the repetitive pattern of life. The followers of the dark ones hold the belief that one's experiences and choices are not confined to oneself alone but rather have a profound impact on the collective awareness of their community and even beyond. This conviction instills within them a deep sense of obligation and answerability for their deeds, as they comprehend that each action in every lifetime plays a role in maintaining balance and peaceful coexistence within the cosmos.

The Dark Ones assume comfort from their faith in the concept of rebirth, which assures them that their existence extends beyond a single lifetime and is part of an expansive cosmic expedition. This conviction grants them hope, resilience, and an unceasing dedication to spiritual advancement while maneuvering through life's intricate fabric woven with cycles of life, death, and rebirth. Additionally, the dark ones perceive death not as a conclusion but as a transition into another phase of their voyage.

They firmly hold that the circumstances surrounding their demise and the state of mind they possess during that moment significantly influence their subsequent embodiment. Therefore, diligently nurturing positive attributes such as compassion, wisdom, and detachment becomes crucial to securing a favorable reincarnation. This emphasis on individual accountability and spiritual evolution constitutes a fundamental pillar in the belief system cherished by the dark ones, thus shaping how they approach existence.

The Dark Ones have established a well-structured educational program that commences at an early stage and molds aspiring practitioners into proficient masters of the mysterious arts. This training primarily emphasizes refining their intuitive magical skills and harnessing the potent forces of fire and darkness that flow within them. With the mentorship of skilled teachers, young dark ones gain knowledge of the complex techniques of casting spells, performing ritualistic magic, and manipulating flames as well as shadows.

Their magical education involves numerous disciplines, with each discipline emphasizing unique teachings and specialized areas of focus. These include elemental manipulation, where they learn to command and control fire in all its forms, ranging from destructive infernos to delicate flames of illumination. They also delve into shadow manipulation, mastering the art of concealing themselves within the darkness, creating illusions, and harnessing the secrets of shadows for offensive and defensive purposes.

In addition to elemental and shadow magic, the dark ones also explore the esoteric arts of necromancy and blood magic, which are considered forbidden by the Light Ones in Alora. Necromancy involves communicating with the spirits of the deceased and manipulating the forces of death, while blood magic taps into the vital life force contained within blood to fuel powerful spells. These darker forms of magic are viewed with fear and apprehension by the Light Ones, who believe they carry inherent risks and can lead to moral corruption and uncontrolled power.

The Dark Ones, on the other hand, regard necromancy and blood magic as fundamental aspects of their magical lineage and spiritual rituals. From their perspective, these arcane practices serve as gateways to other realms and instruments for comprehending the intricate interplay between mortality and eternity. While the use of these forbidden magics is strictly regulated within a dark one society, they are not considered inherently evil but rather powerful forces that demand respect and careful control.

The contrast between acceptance of necromancy and blood magic and the other elves prohibition reflects the divergent perspectives on magic and the differing cultural values between the two races. It is through these differing views on magic that tensions and conflicts arise, as the elves in Alora perceive dark practices as a threat to the delicate balance they seek to maintain throughout the world.

Necromancy, shadow magic, and blood magic carry inherent limitations and risks that affect the individuals who wield them. Mastery of these ominous disciplines requires a deep comprehension of their complexities and places immense weight on the practitioner's heart and mind.

When it comes to necromancy, achieving mastery over death requires maintaining a risky equilibrium between the realms of life and death. Those who dare venture too far into this forbidden practice put themselves at risk of severing their ties to the living world, ultimately becoming detached and utterly engulfed by the domain of the deceased. The wielder of necromantic powers must skillfully navigate through the borderlands that lie between existence and mortality, as prolonged exposure to death's powerful energies can gradually corrode their own life force and undermine their connection with the living.

The mystique surrounding the use of necromancy casts an eerie feeling upon Paranova, with its practitioners drawing upon the mysterious energies from the Ethereal Realm. Unbeknownst to mortals, this transition realm, the creation of Havoc, had served as a wellspring for lost souls from the spectral entities he created.

Necromancers, seeking to bridge the gap between life and death, tap into this spectral reserve, allowing them to commune with the departed or even resurrect the deceased. However, the process is fraught with unnerving complications. When a lost soul is summoned, it may or may not be the intended individual, shrouding the act of resurrection in an unsettling uncertainty. Furthermore, the anchoring of the undead to the physical realm proves a delicate balance, as the temporary nature of the ethereal realm restricts the longevity of such manifestations. As scholars delve into the mysteries of necromancy, the pursuit of immortality intertwines with the ethereal dance between realms.

In the unseen realms of Paranova, the celestial Shapers crafted the intricate tapestry of existence, weaving together the threads of life and death. When a mortal draws their final breath, their spirit embarks on a journey to the celestial realms known as Life and Death. These celestial creations, hidden from the awareness of the mortal populace, cradle the departed souls in a cosmic dance between existence and transition for their spirit.

In contrast, the art of shadow magic requires a deep understanding and control over the dark aspects residing within one's own self. The shadows hold great power, but they can also be alluring and corrupting. Those who wield shadow magic must guard against succumbing to its seductive whispers and darker impulses. The further one delves into the depths of darkness, the higher the chances of losing their own sense of self and becoming engulfed by darkness. The shadows possess a capacity to blur thoughts and twist perceptions, resulting in feelings of suspicion, fragility, and ultimately an inability to maintain dominion over one's own abilities and the possibility of one's own mind.

In the genesis of the Paranova universe, the Archon, perched upon her dark throne, wove the threads of arcane energy with intentions veiled in mystery. The Arcane, born of her creativity, unraveled its potential in ways beyond her initial comprehension. Little did she anticipate the boundless chaotic energies that mortals would later harness from this mystical force.

Among the countless applications of arcane energy, shadow magic emerged as a dark manifestation drawing upon the potent depths of the arcane. The alluring yet destructive nature of shadow magic beckoned mortals to explore its depths. However, the Archon had not foreseen the dangerous path that wielders of shadow magic might tread.

For those who delved too deeply, the unrestrained use of shadow magic had the capacity to plunge mortals into the abyss of madness, tearing at the fabric of their souls. Discipline and restraint became the paramount virtues for those who sought to harness the power of shadow, a warning echoing through the arcane corridors of Paranova.

The practice known as blood magic harnesses the essential life force present within blood. This form of magic demands sacrifices and carries the risk of tainting the user's own soul. The practitioner must carefully manage the balance between giving and taking life, as excessive use of blood magic can lead to a gradual corruption of the individual's spirit. It requires an intimate understanding of the delicate balance between life and death and the acceptance of responsibility for the consequences of manipulating such a primal force. Blood magic is frequently linked to sinister and risky activities, as it entails the control of one of life's utmost essential components. Nonetheless, when employed by skillful individuals, it can become a potent instrument for both mending and safeguarding. Certain societies even perceive it as an esteemed ritualistic act, considering blood as a representation of the vital energy that unites all creatures.

Blood magic, though possessing the potential for both positive and negative impact, continues to be a disputable and often misunderstood magical practice. Many sorcerers who favor more conventional forms of magic regard blood magic with suspicion and wariness due to its perceived capacity for causing damage. Nevertheless, spellcasters of blood magic argue that it is no more naturally hazardous than other forms of magic; what truly matters is one's knowledge of how to responsibly wield it.

Younger conjurers have recently developed a growing interest in blood magic due to its raw power and connection to the primal forces that govern life itself. Whether this mystical art will persist as an object of skepticism or attain broader acceptance remains uncertain; however, one certainty endures as blood magic serves a complex and chaotic subject matter bound to provoke ongoing debate and discourse within the enchanting community.

Just like any kind of enchantment, it is vital to approach it with vigilance and respect, considering the potential aftermaths of mortal deeds. In the end, the decision whether or not to delve into the realm of blood magic lies with each practitioner individually. However, it should be done with an accepting perspective and a comprehension of its origins, customs, and possible hazards.

The constraints act as measures to prevent the improper and excessive utilization of these mysterious arts. They serve as a reminder to practitioners that they must preserve a delicate balance and uphold ethical considerations. Deeply connected with the elemental forces, curators of darkness fully comprehend the limitations attached to these magical practices.

They strive to maintain internal and societal harmony through their belief in maintaining equilibrium. However, even individuals renowned for discipline can succumb to the irresistible allure of forbidden power. The consequences resulting from surpassing these boundaries are grave; one's very soul is at stake, paving a treacherous path into realms shrouded in darkness. The dark ones have established strict guidelines and regulations governing dark magic to address this reality.

They encourage to the belief that employing the darker, more complicated magic ought to only be considered as a final course of action when all controlled alternative avenues have been depleted. Moreover, they inspire their members to partake in rigorous training and examination procedures before granting them permission to engage in the use of dark magic, with the aim of ensuring their mental and emotional readiness for shouldering the associated responsibilities. The dark ones also establish a mechanism for regulating this domain, whereby a council comprised of seasoned individuals supervises the employment of dark magic and possesses authority for intervention when deemed necessary.

In general, although dark magic may provide individuals with immense abilities, it must never be disregarded and should solely be employed with carefulness and accountability. The dark ones have implemented regulations and systems to guarantee the safe and moral utilization of this arcane power; hence, it is critical for those contemplating its application to comprehensively grasp both the potential hazards involved as well as their corresponding responsibilities.

With the rules in place for dark magic in the arcane, the dark ones believed that allowing anyone interested in the dark arts to join the available castes would encourage the use of dark magic in a controlled manner, rather than everyone doing it at free will ignoring the repercussions that come from using dark magic with ignorance.

In contrast, the Light Ones approach magic with a carefully measured and regulated perspective. They firmly believe in the notion that employing magic should strictly serve noble causes, never succumbing to its exploitation for personal gain or power. Their foremost focus lies in ensuring the security and welfare of all individuals, both within their own community and reaching beyond.

Moreover, observing strict ethical standards is fundamental to their practice of magic; they carefully ensure that their actions align with moral values and prevent harm inflicted upon others. While some may perceive this as restrictive, the Light Ones acknowledge its necessity as a means of averting the misuse of magic while upholding societal integrity. Additionally, they possess an instinctive reverence for nature and the world at large.

The elves, who the dark ones believe to be in the light's embrace, see themselves as the protectors of the natural world and work to live in harmony with it. To honor this responsibility, they actively practice sustainable agricultural methods that seek to minimize any harmful impacts on the environment. Moreover, meditation and sacred rituals form an essential component of their way of life, fostering not only a personal connection with the divine but also a shared bond among members of their community. Ultimately, kindness, honesty, and balance represent core principles held in great esteem by this distinct collective.

In the eyes of the Dark Ones, Pyrothos and the boundless energies of the arcane became their divine beacon, guiding their spiritual journey in contrast to the beliefs of the Light Ones. The mystical forces that resonated within the shadows and the chaotic essence of the arcane were praised as the source of their sacred connection, shaping their understanding of divinity and providing a foundation for their unique spiritual practices. The dark ones found solace and purpose in the mysterious realms of Pyrothos and the Arcane, forging a distinct path in their pursuit of divine enlightenment.

....

In the depths of his dark domain, Havoc the master manipulator, sensed a disturbance in the balance. One of the esteemed members of the Shadow Council, by the name of Aleron, had begun to delve into forbidden territory, harnessing the dangerous powers of dark shadow magic. This discovery intrigued Havoc, who recognized an opportunity to exploit the council member's newfound abilities for his own sinister plans.

Aleron, the first dark one to emerge from the mystical fires of Pyrothos, stood as the founder of the Shadow Council. His identity was the sole revelation to the dark one public, a figure shrouded in both honor and mystery. Aleron's descent into madness paralleled his mastery of shadow magic, becoming a vessel for the haunting whispers emerging from dark realms beyond mortal comprehension. As the symbolic head of the Shadow Council, Aleron navigated the delicate balance between divine insight and the sinister allure of chaotic forces.

With his mastery over whispers and manipulation, Havoc subtly reached out to Aleron's mind, planting seeds of doubt and urgency. He whispered of an imminent threat—a war looming on the horizon that threatened the very existence of their society. Stirring Aleron's paranoia, Havoc directed his focus away from his personal pursuits and towards gathering allies to fortify their defenses.

As Aleron delved deeper into his dark arcane powers, his thoughts became consumed with visions of darkness and conflict. The whispers from Havoc fueled his growing obsession, convincing him that his mastery over dark shadowmancy held the key to their salvation. Aleron, formerly a calm and reserved council member, developed a fierce desire to bring the dark ones together and use their combined strength.

Aleron started to build support among the castes under the guidance of Havoc, using his newly acquired powers to show off their strength and potential. He advocated for unity, emphasizing the importance of setting aside personal grievances and rivalries to face the imminent threat. Many dark ones, sensing the urgency in Aleron's words and witnessing the power he wielded, began to rally behind him; they were drawn to his charisma and conviction.

Unbeknownst to Aleron, Havoc reveled in the unfolding chaos and division he had sown. He knew that the dark ones, driven by fear and the promise of power, would be ripe for manipulation. By redirecting their attention towards external conflicts and the gathering of allies, Havoc ensured their focus was diverted from the true intentions lurking beneath his whispers.

Havoc, feeling bored with observing his creation flourishing in a structured and balanced society, yearned for chaos to disrupt the perceived order. An insidious desire festered within him, compelling Havoc to gather the dark ones and orchestrate a conflict that would ignite the flames of war between the forces of light and dark. The thought of discord and hardship for mortals excited him, envisioning the unfolding conflict as a masterpiece of his chaotic design.

As Aleron's disciples multiplied, the passion behind their quest escalated in order. They dedicated themselves tirelessly to refining their abilities and getting ready for the upcoming confrontations. Yet, absorbed in their purpose, they remained completely unaware of the mysterious silhouette of a spectral lurking behind them, biding its time for a well-timed attack. Havoc observed with contentment as his intricate scheme commenced unfolding, fully aware that the ultimate clash approached steadily day by day.

As the Dark Ones started a long preparation for a war, fueled by Aleron's newfound power and Havoc's manipulations, the stage was set for a clash between Alora and the forces gathering in the shadows. The fate of both societies hung in the balance, their destinies intertwined in a web of intrigue and deception orchestrated by Havoc, the puppeteer behind the scenes.

Aleron, fueled by the whispers of the shadows and the allure of chaos, embarked on a journey to seek allies for the looming conflict between light and dark. His path led him to the Gloomrot Raider clan, a formidable group of human warriors dwelling in the remnants of a fallen Gantum. The raiders, known for their cunning tactics and fearlessness, had once shared bonds with the dark ones but had distanced themselves as the dark ones had focused on building their kingdom atop of the volcano severing ties with the primal clan.

In the depths of his scheming mind, Aleron saw the Gloomrot clan as more than just allies; they were a formidable force that could serve as the vanguard in the impending war. With their cunning tactics and fearlessness, the raiders could be the frontline warriors, absorbing the initial impact and creating chaos on the battlefield. The dark whispers echoed in Aleron's thoughts, pushing him to exploit the strength of the Gloomrot clan for maximum impact in the conflict that loomed on the horizon. As he continued his negotiations, Aleron envisioned a strategic alliance that would not only shape the fate of Paranova but also secure his position as a harbinger of darkness.

When Aleron presented his case to the raider clan, he knew that their allegiance would not come without certain conditions. The fierce warriors of the clan were known for their territorial nature, and they saw the alliance with the dark ones as an opportunity to expand their influence closer to the volcano—the very heart of their domain.

Understanding the importance of Gloomrot raider support, Aleron deliberated with the Shadow Council. After careful consideration, they agreed to the clan's request, recognizing that the proximity to the volcano would serve as a strategic advantage in the battles to come. It was a compromise they were willing to make, knowing that the clan's ferocity and intimate knowledge of the surrounding lands would be invaluable assets in the looming conflict.

With the agreement reached, the alliance solidified, and the clan pledged their loyalty not only to the cause but also to the expansion of their territory. They received permission to enter territories closer to the potent forces surrounding the volcano than their clan had previously explored. The dark ones saw the clan's desire for expansion as a testament to their commitment to the alliance and their shared goal of restoring balance.

As the raider clan settled into their new territory, they quickly established their presence and began fortifying their position. They used their creative ways to adapt to the volatile environment, constructing sturdy structures that blended seamlessly with the rugged landscape. They embraced the raw power and energy emanating from the volcano, incorporating its fiery essence into their way of life. For the humans, it was more difficult to withstand the heat compared to the dark ones, but they were able to find ways to keep cool by using the terrain within their new territory.

Day by day, the alliance between the Dark Ones and the Raider Clan grew stronger. The dark ones took comfort in their newfound allies' unflinching loyalty and relentless determination, while Gloomrot figured that the dark ones were a potent force capable of safeguarding their position and keeping the Alora Elven Empire away from their southern territories.

The raider clan had long been an annoying thorn plaguing the Queen's territories. Their nomadic way of life, coupled with their defiance towards Alora's rigid laws and regulations, rendered them prime targets for persecution and subjugation. Nevertheless, rather than succumbing to Alora's pressures, they adamantly defended their way of existence with stubborn resolve. Such dogged resistance garnered deep respect and admiration from none other than the valiant-minded dark ones themselves.

The Dark Ones swiftly showcased their worth as they integrated themselves into the Gloomrot ranks. Their familiarity with the environment and mastery of maneuvering through hazardous terrain bestowed upon the clan a noteworthy edge over enemies. Additionally, these individuals possessed an extraordinary talent for stealth, allowing them to effortlessly glide under the radar and launch unequivocally precise attacks. As a unified entity, this combined force stood ruthless before any opposition that dared challenge them.

The Dark Ones brought with them access to resources that the Gloomrot clan had never had before. They knew where to find fresh water sources, hidden caches of food, and rare medicinal herbs. This knowledge allowed the clan to sustain themselves for longer periods of time and to heal the injured more effectively. The dark ones introduced the clan to new trade opportunities with neighboring tribes, expanding their economic reach and increasing their access to valuable goods. With the dark ones by their side, the clan was becoming a force to be reckoned with in the region.

Amongst all the positive benefits of combining the two forces, they had no idea that Havoc was assembling a more intricate web of deceit that would ultimately decide the future for both societies.

In Havoc's grand scheme, the alliance between the dark ones and the raider clan was a first step, a way to sow unrest and chaos that aimed to cause Alora to fall apart.

Havoc's goal was to take control of the chaos he had created and command it to wither into the life that has flourished on Paranova for his own sick pleasures. He used the Dark Ones and the Raider Clan as mere pawns in his own wicked game.

Chapter 7: Wicked Unrest

Within the Lowborn district of Alora, the atmosphere was heavy with growing tensions and deep-seated discontent after years of harmony with the queen's hierarchy and attempts at keeping peace. The district, home to the marginalized and impoverished, suffered from neglect and a lack of resources. Its once vibrant streets were now falling apart, and the air was thick with despair.

The Dark Elves bore the brunt of this neglect with most of the district predominately Light Elves sharing that same neglect. Their frustrations simmered beneath the surface, fueled by a sense of injustice and inequality. Many felt trapped in a cycle of poverty, their pleas for assistance falling on deaf ears. The lowborn lower district became a breeding ground for resentment, as its inhabitants watched the higher classes flourish while their own lives spiraled further into hardship.

To make matters worse, crime rates in the lower district soared as desperation pushed some to resort to illegal means to survive. Gangs formed, preying on the vulnerable residents and exploiting their dire circumstances. Due to the scarcity of resources and neglect from the authorities, law enforcement was spread thin, hampering their ability to efficiently battle the escalating wave of unlawful actions. The streets morphed into unsafe paths, leaving individuals feeling forsaken by those entrusted with authority. It appeared as if the lowborn district was destined to endure unending sorrow and despair.

The social fabric of the lowborn district grew increasingly frayed. Disputes and conflicts became a daily occurrence as tensions reached their breaking point. Arguments erupted over limited resources, overcrowded living conditions, and the perceived indifference of the ruling elite. The lines between the light and dark elven residents blurred, and the once-diverse community became divided by resentment and distrust.

Amidst this growing unrest, whispers of rebellion and calls for change circulated through the district's narrow alleys and cramped dwellings. The lower district had become a powder keg, with a sense of collective frustration fueling a desire for upheaval. Dissatisfied with their lot in life, many sought to challenge the established order and demand better treatment from those in power.

As the queen's attention was drawn to the mounting troubles, she attempted to address the issues facing the lowest district. However, her efforts often fell short, unable to fully comprehend the depths of despair and systemic issues plaguing the district. The actions she took, driven by good intentions but were misguided nonetheless, like the enforcement of curfews and the imposition of stricter regulations, only succeeded in amplifying the existing resentment and dissatisfaction among the lowborn elves.

As the construction projects on other islands lagged behind, frustration simmered among the denizens of the lowborn district. Many were hesitant to contribute their labor to the seemingly endless tasks. Although some islands had sufficient buildings, the rush of light elven inhabitants from the lowest district swiftly filled the available spaces. The dark elves perceived this as a clear indication that the queen prioritized her own kind, intensifying their resentment. The growing discontent cast a shadow over the once hopeful vision of expanding territories, and the queen found herself facing a precarious situation as unrest brewed among her subjects.

The lowborn district swiftly transformed into a breeding ground for pent-up emotions, hosting a pool of simmering anger, frustration, and an overwhelming sense of injustice among its inhabitants. The once-cohesive community divided into factions that fiercely pursued their self-interests while desperate for change. It was against this backdrop of discontent that the seeds of rebellion took root.

As tensions mounted continuously, fear began to take place within the ruling elite in response to the active unrest, leading them to implement measures aimed at weakening any form of opposition. The lowborn district found itself subjected to intense scrutiny as armed guards conducted patrols and checkpoints expanding throughout the area. Residents fell victim to unforgiving searches, interrogations, and arrests, fueling further fire to an already heated rebellion. Despite facing such oppressive tactics employed by those in power, the elves inhabiting the lowest district remained resolute; they were stubborn in their determination to fight for both their rights and freedom.

Sitting upon her golden throne, Queen Alora wrestled with the intricate dilemma that unfolded before her. On one hand, she clung to the vision of a structured hierarchy system designed to preserve the purity of elven genetics. On the other hand, the pressing reality of the lower district's needs tugged at her conscience, urging her to reconsider the exclusivity of her kingdom. Queen Alora yearned for unity among all elves, a collective strength that transcended societal divisions. The expansion efforts, aimed at integrating the dark elves into Alora, became a monumental challenge, testing the very foundations of her convictions. As she contemplated the path forward, the weight of responsibility settled heavily on her shoulders, and the fate of elven civilization rested on her shoulders.

In a bid to address the growing discontent in the lower district, Queen Alora devised a desperate plan to quell the unrest and offer comfort to the displaced elves. She decided to hold a drawing, selecting a hundred families from the lowborn district to inhabit the island currently under construction. While these islands that were being created were seen as paradises separate from the kingdom, the urgent need to relieve overcrowding pushed the queen to expedite her plans.

The queen's plan was to strategically station trusted leaders and diplomats to govern these smaller islands, hoping to establish a sense of order and provide autonomy under her rule. In her earnest attempt to alleviate the growing unrest, the queen sought a delicate balance between unity and hierarchy, aware that the choices she would make could resonate across the vast territories under her reign.

Despite the increasing tensions and hardships in the lowest district of Alora, the queen remained determined to instill a sense of unity and happiness among her subjects. To achieve this, she made the decision to organize an extravagant festival. The purpose of this grand event was to offer temporary relief from hardship with a chance to start over and serve as a moment for collective celebration. Detailed preparations were executed, with vibrant banners adorning the streets, stages erected for captivating performances, and food stalls offering special treats all at no cost to attendees.

As soon as the festivities commenced, an air of both fear and anticipation engulfed the district. Going deep inside the district while under this much tension was a courageous act for the queen. With a glimmer of optimism gleaming in her eyes, the queen held on to hope that these celebrations could bridge divisions and alleviate some growing discontent. However, what was meant to be an occasion filled with happiness quickly transformed into an overwhelming nightmare.

A group that was angry and resentful emerged from this lively festival and launched a coordinated assault on festival attendees. Chaos erupted as innocent revelers were caught off guard, fleeing in panic to find safety. The joyful atmosphere dissolved into a scene of fear and confusion.

The performers, who had prepared tirelessly to entertain the crowds, found themselves the targets of ridicule and aggression. Their acts were disrupted, their costumes torn, and their efforts belittled. The festival, originally intended to ignite happiness and unity among its attendees, found itself overshadowed by a blend of frustration and hopelessness. Those in charge of organizing the event as well as the security personnel were forced into an urgent scramble to regain control, yet their efforts fell short.

Thus, what was supposed to be vibrant and lively festivity grounds now lay torn apart, with debris scattered all around and decorations purposefully trampled upon. The sudden sight served as a jarring contrast to the joyous atmosphere that had filled the air mere moments ago. As time passed and excitement faded away, many pondered how such a joyous celebration could abruptly transform into an unforgettable scene conveying nothing but chaos and devastation.

In the wake of unforeseen circumstances, the queen found herself overcome with distress. She came to the realization that her efforts to provide a moment of relief had accidentally magnified the profound divisions and resentments prevailing in her kingdom. The festivities transformed into a striking mirror image of the unrest plaguing the lowborn district, unveiling long-standing wounds concealed beneath a deceptive facade.

The queen was shaken to her very core by these unexpected events, prompting her to face the harsh reality of the situation head-on. The festival attack served as a turning point, compelling her to reevaluate her approach and delve deeper into the root causes of the issues afflicting her kingdom. Its aftermath became a vital catalyst for the queen's unwavering determination to seek a lasting solution and restore harmony in her troubled realm.

Aware that she was entrusted with finding ways to heal the wounds inflicted upon their land, she secluded herself in her chambers, contemplating how best to proceed. Furthermore, it dawned on her that she could no longer turn away from those whose voices had long been disregarded or unfairly silenced—she now recognized the importance of listening, comprehending their struggles wholeheartedly and ultimately taking action accordingly.

Motivated by a newfound determination, the queen launched a mission to acquire knowledge and form alliances with potential supporters who could aid her in achieving fairness and equality. She engaged in discussions with representatives from diverse communities, particularly those previously silenced or overlooked. Exhausting herself tirelessly, she strived to put into effect policies that would uplift these communities and foster an equitable society.

The lowborn district, stretching around the inner kingdom and snug against the outer walls of Alora, the kingdom design had featured towering walls and gates that were guarded by the vanguard, marking clear distinctions between societal classes within the kingdom. Though divided, some parts of the lower district hosted trusted businesses that the queen could entrust to be the eyes and ears on the happenings within the district.

Within the intricate lower structure of Alora, an intense dissatisfaction brewed within the dark elves. Despite not being outright slaves, they felt the weight of oppression and limitations imposed upon them. The knowledge that they could never rise to high-ranking positions or pursue certain trades gnawed at their souls. The dark elves, proud and fiercely independent, yearned for opportunities that seemed forever out of reach. As they nurtured their growing resentment, the smoldering embers sparked a flame of frustration that compelled them to doubt where they belonged amidst the intricacies of the kingdom's destiny and fate.

Over time, an increasing population of dark elves began to search for opportunities to liberate themselves from their imposed limitations. A few opted for the underground market, pursuing forbidden wisdom and abilities that could grant them an advantage. Meanwhile, others united in covert organizations, devising strategies to overthrow their suppressors and assert their rightful position within society. However diverse their approaches may have been, one undeniable truth became apparent: the dark elves had grown dissatisfied with a life veiled in secrecy. They were prepared to combat for both their autonomy and the prospects awaiting them.

On the contrary, the less privileged elves who were assigned to the lowborn district or had traveled to Alora with the hope of finding better lives were instead ensnared in a neighborhood overflowing with dark elves. They, too, harbored their own resentments. Firmly convinced that they deserved more than to be confined to the lower district, they felt their potential was hampered by their environment.

The harsh realities of their current situation now overshadowed the aspirations that initially drew travelers to Alora. The elves originating in the lowborn district before the welcoming of outsiders, felt that they should be the first to inhabit the islands offered by the queen because of the longevity they have endured within the district. Yearning for liberation from the limitations imposed on them, they desired to carve out a path towards a more promising future.

Amidst the complex choreography of dissatisfaction, both dark elves and lowborn light elves faced their individual frustrations and aspirations. Though their situations differed, their yearnings combined around a collective desire for an improved life that liberated them from the confines imposed upon them. The collision of these ambitions and the simmering tension between the two factions played a pivotal role in molding their intertwined destinies within Alora, shaping the trajectory of events within this kingdom.

Although distinct, the dark elves and lowborn elves eventually realized that their similarities outweighed their differences. Neither type of elf wanted to be bound together but both longed for meaning and a place to fit in, facing constraints imposed by societal conventions that dictated their existence. Through increased interaction, they unveiled mutual opportunities for growth by absorbing one another's encounters and viewpoints. As a result of their shared determination to create a better tomorrow for themselves and those they hold dear, an alliance between these groups gradually but undoubtedly developed.

Before the festival attack, the guards and upper classes in Alora treated the lowborn with a mix of indifference and contempt. The guards, tasked with maintaining order, often regarded the lowborn with aggression, viewing them as a lower class unworthy of their attention or protection. Instances of mistreatment and discrimination were not uncommon, as the guards would turn a blind eye to their struggles and hardships.

The higher classes, secured in their privileged positions, held an air of superiority over the lowborn. They would pass by them with arrogant indifference, barely acknowledging their existence. The lowborn were often subject to dismissive glances, snide remarks, and even acts of humiliation. Despite their desperate appeals for improved chances and equitable treatment, the cry went unheard by the upper echelons, who clung steadfastly to power and privilege, seemingly devoid of any awareness regarding the agony endured by those subordinate to them.

Ascending a tier on the hierarchical ladder from the lowborn district, the working class empathized with the struggles below them. Despite their own privileges, many elves hesitated to support societal change, fearing potential overcrowding and increased crime within their district also known as the tradeborn district.

Nevertheless, following the assault during the festival, a drastic deterioration in how the underprivileged were treated was witnessed. The incident became a catalyst for heightened tension and mistrust within the kingdom. The guards, now on high alert had adopted a more aggressive stance than before while treating the lowborn with suspicion and hostility. They increased their presence in the lower district, enforcing stricter curfews and implementing harsher measures in an attempt to maintain control and prevent further chaos.

The higher classes, whose sense of security was shaken by the attack, became even more distant and disconnected from the plight of the lowborn. Fear and prejudice fueled their interactions, as they cast suspicious glances at anyone that they deemed an outsider to their district or a potential threat. The once subtle disregard for the lowborn transformed into open disdain and contempt, as they blamed the entire district for the disturbances that had disrupted their perceived tranquility.

The atmosphere that once carried a sense of somewhat regard and respect now reeked of animosity and hostility. The divide between the classes deepened, worsening the grievances and resentments that had long festered within the lower district. The aftermath of the festival attack became a turning point, pushing the kingdom of Alora further down a path of social unrest and escalating tensions. Rumors and accusations flew through the streets as both the upper and lower districts tried to shift the blame onto each other.

As residents barricaded themselves inside their homes, the vibrant marketplaces and gathering spots of Alora fell eerily silent. Stirred by an impending threat of violence, folks were overcome with fear, uncertain about how to dispel the mounting unrest and avoid a full-blown class war. The kingdom's leaders found themselves frustrated amidst this dark period as they sought ways to ensure tranquility within their borders. Amidst the general worry and uncertainty that hung in the air like a heavy fog, one particular incident infused apprehension into the hearts of Alora's citizens: when allegations arose against lower district dwellers for stealing from an upper district forgery.

What initially appeared as an innocent accusation rapidly spiraled into a violent confrontation; both sides frantically armed themselves, ready for battle at any moment. Fortunately, enough courageous souls bravely intervened from each segment of society, calming tensions that could have easily spiraled out of control. However, it became abundantly clear that addressing underlying issues between social classes should be prioritized before additional incidents inflame existing strife within Alora.

The queen's perceived indifference to their plight further deepened the frustration among the residents. They felt as though their cries for help and pleas for better living conditions fell on deaf ears. She ultimately made the decision to increase security on the inner borders between districts. The gates dividing the lowborn district from the working class, also known as tradeborn district, it was fortified and serving as a strict checkpoint for those moving between the different societal tiers.

The higher authorities' lack of visible action or empathy only reinforced their belief that they were regarded as expendable and insignificant. To prevent further tension and unrest, it was vital for the government to undertake measures that address the root causes of class division and actively strive to enhance the living conditions of all citizens. The authorities must prioritize listening to elven concerns and taking effective action to make them feel acknowledged and esteemed. Only through a collective effort to narrow the gap between social classes can genuine strides be taken towards a fairer and more righteous society.

The queen would attempt to provide food, clothing, and supplies to the lowborn district but she was met with hostility. The complex nature of addressing class divides and the need for a more comprehensive approach that considers the underlying factors contributing to such divides. Although short-term assistance brought temporary respite, it was crucial to tackle the fundamental factors behind inequality for enduring transformation. The queen's intentions, though well-meaning, fell short of resolving the deep-rooted problems at hand. Hence, a joint effort between governmental bodies and the community becomes essential to establishing sustainable remedies that cater to the welfare of all members of society.

Over time, in the lowborn district of Alora, the deteriorating living conditions cast a grim shadow over the residents' daily lives. The lack of resources, inadequate infrastructure, and neglect from the higher classes contributed to a common sense of hopelessness and despair. As the district struggled to cope with the growing population and limited support, the quality of life steadily declined.

The availability of essential needs drastically diminished as they transformed into rare goods. Pure water turned into a blissful privilege, given that contaminated wells acted as the main option for quenching one's thirst. Scarce supplies of food haunted the entire region, placing immense pressure on families to prolong their limited rations and hunt for nourishment however they could. Overpopulated and rundown residences offered minimal comfort from the brutal existence that consumed their lives.

The presence of limited resources provided the perfect conditions for direness and criminal behavior. Unemployment rates soared due to elves not being willing to give their labor, plunging the district into poverty and thereby compelling certain individuals to resort to unlawful means to survive. Moreover, the surge in thefts, robberies, and even acts of violence intensified an ambiance riddled with fear and uncertainty.

In a particular neighborhood in the district, a cluster of young elves turned to stealing from local establishments to sustain themselves and their families. As their desperation escalated, they gravitated toward more hostile offenses, consequently provoking an increase in gang-related activities and stabbings. These individuals felt suffocated by the absence of opportunities or resources present within their environment, which fostered feelings of hopelessness—a vicious circle entwining crime with poverty that proved extremely challenging to overcome.

The lack of security and law enforcement inside the walls of the lower district had worsened the situation. The few guards assigned to the lowborn district were overwhelmed and often focused their efforts on protecting the interests of the higher classes rather than addressing the concerns of the struggling residents. This disparity in treatment only fueled the growing sense of injustice and amplified the tensions between the classes.

As the citizens witnessed a continuous decline in their living conditions, they became ensnared in an unrelenting spiral of desolation. The absence of available provisions and chances for progress smothered any glimmer of optimism regarding a brighter tomorrow, instead fostering a state of acceptance and indifference. With each passing day, the district descended deeper into a state of unrest and discontent, leaving its residents feeling forgotten and abandoned by the kingdom they called home.

In the face of difficulty and the growing crime rate, the residents' hope waned, and an extensive sense of hopelessness settled over the lower district. The lack of necessities, coupled with the rising crime and the perception of neglect, fueled the flames of unrest. The region transformed into an environment of frustration, with the elves craving transformation. At the height of hardship, certain individuals within the community took matters into their own hands. Local surveillance groups emerged while impromptu medical facilities and educational institutions sprouted in response. Sadly, these noble attempts frequently encountered opposition from gangs perceiving them as challenges to their dominance over the district.

Despite facing numerous challenges, the residents of the lowborn district demonstrated unwavering determination in their pursuit of a more prosperous existence. They were well aware that transforming their circumstances would be no simple task; nevertheless, these resilient individuals adamantly clung to their aspirations for a brighter tomorrow. A prime illustration of this tenacity emerged within a specific locale, where a collective of community members established an organic garden as an innovative solution to combat the gang's ridiculous food costs. However, the local gangs had destroyed the garden. Undeterred, the residents rallied together and protested until the garden was allowed to remain. They even expanded it and eventually started selling their surplus produce at local markets.

In the lower district, life took on a twisted form of self-governance under gang activity. New and existing businesses struggled, often relying on stolen or queen-provided supplies. However, the gangs wielded control and demanded a hefty portion of supplies or profits. Wealth concentrated in their hands, leaving the rest of the populace to grapple with increasing poverty, revealing a harsh reality that even within their own district, safety from oppression remained elusive.

•••••••

Beyond the borders of Alora, in the outskirts and surrounding wilderness, small parties of Raiders and Dark Ones lurked in the shadows, observing the kingdom with watchful eyes. The Sinister Shadow and Ripper members moved with stealth; their intentions shrouded in secrecy as they prepared for their next move. Their tactics ranged from covert operations to open acts of aggression, targeting key figures and installations within the kingdom. The situation had become increasingly volatile, with reports of skirmishes and raids becoming more frequent in the southwest.

The leaders of Alora had found themselves unprepared and overwhelmed by the unexpected surge in violence, leaving them grappling with the challenge of preserving authority and protecting their community. Evidently, an imminent confrontation loomed ahead, prompting the citizens of Alora to place their faith in their leaders' ability to confront the menace successfully.

Occasional skirmishes and covert activities hinted at their growing presence. Raiders, known for their fierce combat skills and nomadic lifestyle, raided small settlements on the outskirts, sowing chaos and disrupting the kingdom's sense of security. The dark ones, with their mastery of shadow and forbidden magics, operated in covert ways, undermining the kingdom's defenses and gathering intelligence.

Commander Relios of the Vanguard was tasked with leading the charge against the growing threat to the kingdom. The occasional skirmishes and covert activities were no longer enough, and it was time for a full-scale offensive. Relios knew that he had to act quickly and decisively if they were to have any chance of defeating the raiders and the dark ones. Once his troops had assembled, he arranged his preparations and set out on his fight. If anything went wrong, this battle could decide the fate of the entire kingdom, but he pledged not to let that be his downfall. All of his troops were out looking for orders and commands, while all he could do was lead by example. With limited time for anything other than prayer and hope, the eager troops quickly departed to address this new threat.

As rumors spread and whispers reached the ears of the kingdom's inhabitants, a gradual realization took hold. Fear and uncertainty seeped into the hearts of the elves, for they recognized that external forces were plotting against Alora. The notion that the kingdom was under threat from these hidden enemies had cast a shadow over their once peaceful lives. The lowborn elves took the news as hope for liberation.

The vanguard and scouts had faced unprecedented challenges as they grappled with the task of tracking down and confronting these elusive enemies. Their efforts to uncover the extent of the threat were met with resistance, as the raiders and dark ones operated with cunning and evaded capture. The kingdom's security apparatus worked tirelessly to decipher their motives, to anticipate their next move, and to safeguard Alora from the potential threat.

None the less, the fact that the enemy was very elusive. They had much deeper roots and depths in which they came from. They knew what they were fighting for and would stop at nothing. The vanguard and the scouts felt like this was a chasing game of cat and mouse; they had to be one step ahead of what they were currently doing. On the outskirts of Alora, hidden in the wilderness, the enemies continued their preparations, biding their time for the dark ones at home to build their army to strike at the heart of Alora. The kingdom stood at the height of an imminent conflict; villages were unknowingly caught in the crossfire from small skirmishes between the two factions.

Within Alora, the realization of external threats mobilized the kingdom's resources and sparked a collaborative effort between the vanguard and arcanists. Understanding the urgency of the situation, they united to plan and fortify Alora's defense in preparation for the oncoming dangers. As the tension mounted and the threat loomed, Queen Alora braced herself for the inevitable clash, unaware of the true extent of the forces amassing against them.

The kingdom faced a critical need for reinforcement, as scouts reported sightings of the parties of dark ones and human raiders. Disturbingly, whispers of a massive army being assembled by the dark ones to obliterate their kingdom reached the ears of those responsible for the kingdom's defense. The imminent threat loomed, urging a swift and strategic response to safeguard the kingdom's survival.

The Vanguard, an elite group of highly skilled warriors, took charge of bolstering the kingdom's physical defenses. They fortified the kingdom walls, constructed watchtowers at strategic points, and implemented strict perimeter control to prevent unauthorized entry. The vanguard, exhibiting unwavering allegiance and unyielding commitment, stood as the primary barrier shielding Alora from harm.

The Arcanists, however, used their vast knowledge of magic to protect the kingdom. They were powerful arcane spellcasters whose research and sophisticated enchantments had strengthened the magical boundaries of Alora. Using their magical abilities, the arcanists cast spells around the kingdom, which provided protections around the entire kingdom that deflected hostile magic and the sinister powers that could penetrate or cause destruction. Rendering unprecedented control over the arcane magic, the arcanists were vital defenders of Alora against all magical-based threats. Aligned together under Relios' command, these specialized groups closely cooperated by comparing crucial information and sharing their duties. The scouts, who examined raider and dark one operations, mapped the enemy's movements and strategies as well as their weak points. The unified cooperation helped their cause to keep vigilant against the oncoming threat lurking on the outskirts of their kingdom.

Strategic meetings and war councils were held within the halls of the royal palace, where the leaders of Alora, alongside the vanguard and arcanists, strategized and devised defense plans. They assessed the kingdom's strengths and weaknesses, identified critical locations that required heightened security, and allocated resources accordingly. The collaboration of military strategists, magical experts, and intelligence officers ensured a comprehensive approach to defense, covering both physical and metaphysical aspects.

In these planning sessions, tactics were devised to capitalize on Alora's advantages while mitigating potential vulnerabilities. The military and vanguard reinforced their training, adopting new techniques and formations tailored to the specific threats they faced. The arcanists researched powerful spells and enchantments designed to neutralize the dark magic employed by the enemy. The vanguard devised contingency plans and practiced coordinated maneuvers to counter the raiders' guerrilla tactics.

Through this collaborative effort, Alora aimed to establish a united front against the mounting dangers. With the combined strength of the vanguard and arcanists, they formed a strong defense, with each group bringing their own unique skills and expertise to the table. Together, they prepared to defend Alora, ready to face the impending conflict with steadfast determination and a shared commitment to protect their kingdom and its citizens.

Desperation led Queen Alora to seek aid from the people of Tide Cove, the architects of colonization in the southwest. However, their engagement in conflicts with raiders hindered their ability to contribute to the impending war. Faced with their own challenges, the citizens of Tide Cove made the difficult decision to sever ties with Alora, leaving the kingdom to confront the approaching threat alone. The queen, now grappling with both internal and external pressures, stood at a crossroads in the face of an uncertain future with them.

In an effort to bolster her defenses and secure additional support, Queen Alora dispatched boats acquired from Tide Cove to gather inhabitants living along the southwestern shores. By rescuing those who had not yet faced the raiders' threats, she aimed to provide them refuge on her islands. The queen envisioned these newcomers as potential reinforcements, unaware of the internal unrest within the kingdom, contributing both labor and support during the impending threat.

....

There were a variety of emotions present among the arcanists as they observed the Dark Ones using forbidden magic, despite their deep understanding and respect for the delicate balance of magic. The way they responded involved a combination of astonishment, apprehension, and an intense feeling of intrusion into the art of magic.

After spending countless years perfecting and understanding the art of magic, the arcanists delved into their arcane energies not for power but instead to explore their abilities. Working with magic to better society, the arcanists definitely saw the benefit and harm of using it and found that the arcane can be used as a tool that benefits and unifies people, disrupts society, and harbors hate and disparity. The arcanists were completely perplexed as to how spellcasters could use such sinister magic after witnessing the forbidden magic that the dark ones practiced, such as necromancy, blood magic, and other dark arts. For years, they refused to accept these reports as true. The magic the dark ones were practicing was completely opposite of what the arcanists had been practicing for all of these years. How could elves who used the same arcane energies allow themselves to become overwhelmed by darkness?

The magic they were practicing completely disrupted the balance between dark and light, the line between life and death, and what happens when you curdle the world of energies you can tap into. The reports they received were almost impossible for them to believe that they were from the dark ones—their elven counterpart, who shared the same magical knowledge and structures. As previous years went by and more and more reports came in, such as these events showcasing the dark ones practicing forbidden magic, arcanists were still in denial at first that this was the work of the dark ones. After more and more of these reports, highly emotional disbelief shifted to anger and despair.

Recognizing the imminent threat posed to their community and the fatal practices that had begun to multiply, the arcanists were compelled to engage in action. In response, they established a council whose primary objective was to accurately scrutinize and eliminate any individuals who practiced forbidden magic in the dark arts. Armed with their own expertise and unique capabilities, these determined arcanists overcame the numerous challenges entailed by this rugged undertaking while remaining resolute in upholding their cherished principles and safeguarding their way of life.

Alongside their disbelief, the arcanists felt a deep sense of concern and apprehension. They understood the imminent dangers of forbidden magic and the potential for corruption or the catastrophic consequences it could unleash. They were aware that such practices could easily spiral out of control, endangering not only their kingdom but also by spreading throughout the mortal population on Paranova.

Moreover, witnessing the dark ones embrace forbidden magic ignited a sense of betrayal within the arcanist ranks. The dark ones were part of their larger elven community, and to see them succumb to such dark temptations felt like a betrayal of their shared heritage and the pursuit of enlightenment. It raised questions about the inherent nature of their people and the potential darkness that lay dormant within even the noblest souls.

These revelations sparked intense discussions and debates among the arcanists, as they sought to understand the reasons behind the dark ones embrace of forbidden magic. Some believed it was driven by desperation, a response to the oppression and perceived injustices their kin endured in Alora.

Some individuals expressed apprehension that it signified a more profound, natural wickedness within the essence of their being, endangered the integral existence of elven civilization, or perhaps something more insidious the dark ones had been involved with. In general, the disclosed revelations regarding the dark ones and their utilization of prohibited sorcery generated significant distress and doubt among the arcanists. These scholars found themselves grappling with comprehending the underlying incentives driving these deeds and predicting the potential ramifications for their community as a cohesive entity.

The Arcanists were aware of their duty to address this matter, not only to preserve the delicate equilibrium of magic but also to ensure the safety and protection of the kingdom of Alora. They recognized the need to delve deeper into the roots of forbidden magic and the dark path the dark ones had embarked upon. Their pursuit of knowledge intensified as they delved into ancient tomes, consulted with other magical scholars, and engaged in spirited debates to understand the origins and implications of forbidden magic.

While their emotions remained complex and their concerns deepened, the arcanists were determined to stand against the coming darkness. They sought to find a way to bring enlightenment and guide the dark ones back to the path of balance, or at the very least mitigate the threat they posed to Alora. The forbidden sorcery was like a rallying cry for the arcanists, reaffirming their staunch commitment to safeguard the sacredness of magic and ensure the survival of their elven society. Despite the treacherous nature of their task and its inherent uncertainties, the arcanists held on to their faithful resolve.

Hours upon hours were devoted to intense study and deep contemplation as they delved deeper into magical mysteries, eager to gain any wisdom that may aid them in achieving their mission. Ancient manuscripts were consulted, while the guidance of revered elders was sought after, pooling together all the knowledge available within their elven collective consciousness. Step by painstaking step, fragments emerged regarding both the mystic powers possessed by the dark ones and what lay at its core—an intricate plan began taking shape with hopes of negating this sinister magic system and restoring balance back to existence.

•••••••

While devoting extensive hours to studying the dark arts, Queen Alora confided in commander Relios about her apprehensions for the safety of their kingdom. She shared her anxieties with him concerning the growing might of the dark ones and her determination to uncover a method that could prevent their ascension. Operating as a cooperative unit, they persistently struggled to reveal the concealed truths behind the dark ones and to discover an effective solution for defeating them. Through combining their vast knowledge and faithful commitment, they managed to formulate a strategy aimed at countering their wicked sorcery and reinstating harmony within their realm.

Desperate to unravel the mystery surrounding the attacks and the growing threat to her kingdom, Queen Alora turned to seek guidance from the Stone and Tree Avatars, ancient beings connected to the earth and its elements. However, to her dismay, she discovered that the avatars were dormant and seemingly unresponsive.

For generations, the Stone and Tree Avatars had served as sources of wisdom and guidance for the elven kingdom of Alora. Their connection to the natural world granted them insight into hidden truths and a deep understanding of the balance of life. The queen had relied on their counsel in times of trouble, seeking their guidance to make informed decisions and protect her citizens.

Queen Alora was deeply disturbed upon seeing the motionless avatars. It seemed as if all wisdom and guidance had deserted her, leaving her to face the growing crisis alone. She contemplated whether their dormancy indicated a grave situation or if something more profound disrupted the natural order, causing their state of slumber.

Undeterred by the apparent silence of the avatars, Queen Alora knew she had to press forward in her quest for answers. She recognized that relying solely on external sources of guidance was not enough; she needed to rely on her own intuition and the resources available within her kingdom.

As the stone and tree avatars slumbered, the delicate balance between guidance and self-discovery shifted on Paranova. The Keeper, respecting the Provisioner's wish for mortal evolution to unfold without direct intervention, had ordered the avatars to remain dormant during times of peace. Unbeknownst to the mortal races, this decision carried unforeseen consequences, severing the Shapers' connection to these mighty beings.

The stone and tree avatars, once a source of wisdom and insight, now stood silent, their roots entwined in the very essence of Paranova. This change limited the Shapers' ability to observe and guide the evolving world. The mortal inhabitants, left to navigate their challenges independently, faced the unknown without the comforting presence of the avatars.

Yet, amidst the dormancy of these ancient entities, the Spectral Avatars, loyal to Havoc, continued to weave their mysterious influence. The delicate dance between divine guidance and mortal autonomy unfolded, shaping the destiny of Paranova in ways unknown to both Shapers and mortals alike.

Queen Alora was aware that the kingdom's survival depended on her ability to gather information and plan a response considering the avatars being dormant and communication parties failing to return, presumably under attack by enemies. She assembled a council of trusted advisors, including seasoned warriors, insightful spies, and wise scholars. Together, they analyzed the limited information available, piecing together fragments of the puzzle to gain a deeper understanding of the nature of the attacks.

Recognizing the significance of involving her citizens in the quest for solutions, Queen Alora urged the citizens of Alora to remain vigilant, report any suspicious activities they encountered, and share any valuable information that could assist in unraveling the complexity. She established a network of individuals serving as informants and introduced a system of rewards to incentivize cooperation and information exchange.

The queen's earnest favors yielded fruitful results: there was a substantial increase in the dissemination of pertinent details. Numerous reports showcasing questionable activities poured in while her informants successfully discovered several leads. However, with each lead emerged new uncertainties and interrogations loomed large. The attacks appeared masterfully coordinated, executing their plans with such precision that not even a trace of evidence was left behind. The deeper delve undertaken by Queen Alora and her team into this matter only unveiled its intricate nature further – an elusive puzzle becoming more complex at every turn.

In the bustling lowborn district, a queue of hopeful lowborn individuals formed, each yearning for a chance to contribute to the queen's tasks. This strategic move, masked as an opportunity for rewards, served the queen well, providing her with a steady arrival of eager hands that she deemed replaceable. These enthusiastic lowborn elves became the backbone of various efforts, from supporting the military to fortifying defenses.

While the majority sought for the dream of life-changing rewards, only a select few among the lowborn received the coveted recognition. For those fortunate individuals, the queen's generosity elevated them from the lower echelons of society to the esteemed ranks of the tradeborn. Such rewards, whether in the form of money or essential supplies, represented a ticket to a new life beyond the confines of the lower district, a rare ascent in the rigid hierarchy that governed Alora's kingdom.

Amidst the arcanists' achievements to unravel the mystery of forbidden dark magic attuned with the dark ones, a parallel pursuit had engaged their intellectual curiosity. The arcane scholars found themselves intricately divided into ranks, each dedicated to dissecting the complex mystery of the dormant avatars. These ancient beings, manifestations of stone and tree, had long stood as silent observers of Paranova, their reasons for slumber shrouded in the impenetrable veil of celestial mystery.

The pursuit of knowledge led the arcanists down labyrinthine paths, attempting to fathom the roots of forbidden magic while concurrently plumbing the depths of the avatars' mysterious dormancy. In their tireless efforts, the scholars sought to illuminate the dual shadows cast over Paranova, aiming to discern the threads that bound the arcane secrets and the mysterious avatars in an intricate dance of cosmic confusion.

While the absence of the stone and tree avatars remained a concern, Queen Alora resolved to rely on her own leadership and the collective strength of her subjects. She recognized that she needed to take swift and decisive action to protect her kingdom and uncover the truth behind the attacks. Every resource at her disposal would be harnessed to confront the growing threat, restore peace, and ensure the survival of Alora.

• • • • • • •

As tensions continued to escalate within the lowborn district of Alora, a series of gruesome murders sent shockwaves through the already volatile community. The residents were filled with fear and paranoia as a result of the mysterious deaths' brutality and the eerie circumstances surrounding them.

Queen Alora found herself in a state of dilemma amidst the wickedness that plagued the lower district. The pressing question that haunted her was whether to grant freedom to those born into humble circumstances. She knew that on one hand, this decision could potentially pacify tensions and quench the flames of violence burning within her realm. However, she also recognized its potential danger, as it could establish a risky precedent and give rise to further unrest within the fortified walls surrounding Alora. With time ticking away, Queen Alora understood that a resolution had to be reached swiftly if order and safety were to be restored for all of her devoted subjects.

Simultaneously with the attacks from outsiders, a series of murders has swept through the lowborn elves with no discernible pattern among its victims: individuals hailing from diverse backgrounds across racial lines and social hierarchies have fallen prey to this mysterious killer. It seemed as though their motives held no rhyme or reason other than sowing seeds of chaos and inflicting terror upon innocent hearts dwelling in all corners of society's underbelly. These gruesome acts occurred in dimly lit alleyways, deserted structures, and forsaken spaces with each victim bearing undeniable evidence pointing towards a brutal demise.

Word of the murders spread like wildfire, feeding into the existing discontent and unease that plagued the lowborn district. Whispers of a shadowy figure with supernatural abilities circulated among the residents, fueling a sense of dread and suspicion. The trust among elves started to dwindle as they grew more cautious of their fellow neighbors, with the unsettling thought that anyone might be the next victim or possibly even the culprit. As casualties continued to mount, the local government faced difficulties in upholding law and order while conducting thorough investigations into these insidious acts.

The guards were spread thin, and numerous rookie soldiers lacked the courage to explore the lowborn district during the night. The commander released a statement urging the inhabitants to stay watchful and assuring them of prompt measures against the murderer. Nonetheless, for many individuals, these words had little substance, prompting them to take matters into their own hands. Vigilante organizations emerged, roaming the streets and scouring for any hints that could steer them toward capturing the culprit.

In the lowborn district, two groups clashed in a hidden struggle. Some wanted to help the queen and move up in society, while others stirred chaos for their own gain. The vigilantes aimed for order, hoping for recognition, while the gangs thrived in the disorder, seeking wealth and fear. The district became a battleground for conflicting ambitions, where the future was balanced between chaos and hierarchy.

Upon being informed of the hardships of keeping order in the lower district, the queen was deeply troubled. She realized the importance of quelling the violence and restoring a sense of security for her subjects. Bearing in mind the welfare of her entire realm, she commanded an exhaustive inquiry, summoning both the vanguard and military units to deploy all their resources towards resolving these homicides.

Nonetheless, the challenge turned out to be quite difficult. The killer left no discernible traces, leaving investigators puzzled and frustrated. The nature of the murders hinted at a certain level of sophistication, as if the perpetrator possessed knowledge of the shadows and wielded an otherworldly power. The queen's advisors speculated that dark and forbidden magic could be at play, further deepening the sense of dread and linking to the outsiders wanting to attack the kingdom.

In the face of mounting casualties, the district found itself engulfed by anxiety and apprehension. To safeguard their well-being, the residents opted for self-imprisonment, stepping outside their homes only if needed. An unsettling atmosphere prevailed as night fell, and jittery guards occasionally patrolled deserted streets. Confronted with the burden of her subjects' lives, the queen took on the difficult task of imposing curfews and enforcing strict security measures within the confines of the lowborn district. Once a community buzzing with bustling liveliness, it now remained silent, veiled in fear and distrust.

Within this muddled mayhem and desperate circumstances, committed to justice, the queen pledged herself to unearth truthfulness behind these killings and bring the vile perpetrators before retribution's hand. She sought the aid of skilled investigators, including mages proficient in tracking dark magic and seasoned detectives well-versed in unraveling the most intricate of mysteries. It became a race against time as the kingdom teetered on the edge of anarchy, and the lives of innocent residents hung in the balance.

The queen, disturbed by the intrusive threat of outsiders wielding dark arts, felt the urgency to act swiftly. The time for observation and study seemed too prolonged, and the menace of dark arts posed an imminent danger to her kingdom's stability. The need for decisive action grew urgent as the shadows of chaos crept closer within her walls.

The killings in the lowborn district had a gloomy effect on Alora, intensifying the already tense atmosphere and igniting feelings of dissatisfaction. Understanding that solving this mystery was not solely about administering justice but also vital for reinstating a feeling of harmony and steadiness in her realm, the queen took an oath to reveal the truth. She aspired to uncover the murderer's identity and terminate their oppressive hold over the lower district.

However, as reports of Morvain and the cult within the lowborn district practicing forbidden magic had surfaced by some lowborn elves looking to receive recognition, the disbelief turned to fear and anger among the queen and the arcanists. They recognized the inherent dangers of forbidden magic, the potential for corruption, and the catastrophic consequences it could unleash.

They knew they had to take action to protect their community and prevent the spread of these dangerous practices, particularly the influence of Morvain and the cult. The arcanists banded together, pooling their knowledge and resources, and launched a campaign to root out the practitioners of forbidden magic. This led to a series of clashes between the arcanists and the rebellious cult, which eventually led to them to retreat back into the underbelly of the lowborn district.

Morvain and Fumar, wielding potent dark magic, moved through the lower district, their powers capable of taking the life force of a few arcanists. However, the ongoing clash between the cult and the arcanists remained at a stalemate. While the cult possessed significant power, their lack of experience in magical combat hindered their progress. The confrontation only served to intensify the resolve of the gangs and other residents within the district, inspiring them to seek out the cult in the shadows and join the cause for liberation from the kingdom's leadership.

•••••••

As Queen Alora beheld the suffering and strife consuming her own kingdom, a deep sense of anguish and responsibility washed over her. The mounting outsider tensions, the escalating violence, and the noticeable discontent within the lowborn district weighed heavily on her heart. She questioned her own ability to maintain harmony and protect her citizens from the coming darkness.

Each passing day brought with it new reports of unrest, shattered lives, and shattered dreams. The queen walked the streets of Alora, her eyes filled with sorrow as she witnessed firsthand the pain etched on the faces of her subjects. The once vibrant and prosperous kingdom had become ripples of fear and despair, its very fabric unraveling before her eyes. The tensions within the kingdom had affected the other districts greatly and she could see the faces of disgust coming from the elves.

The queen found herself plagued by doubts, wondering if she was truly capable of steering her kingdom through this storm. The weight of her responsibilities pressed upon her shoulders, threatening to crush her spirit. Queen Alora possessed a deep sense of responsibility towards the lives under her guardianship; she keenly felt the weight of their aspirations and ambitions which teetered on uncertainty.

During periods of solitude, Queen Alora engaged in her contemplation regarding the decisions she had made and the following outcomes they had generated. Doubt gnawed at her soul, undermining her confidence as a leader. She questioned whether her decisions had inadvertently contributed to the current state of affairs, if she had failed to address the deep-rooted issues that festered beneath the surface.

The suffering she witnessed within the lower district touched her deeply, stirring a wellspring of empathy within her. She recognized the inherent inequality and injustice that plagued her kingdom, and it tore at her conscience. Her desire to initiate tangible transformation, uniting her community and establishing a society where everyone can thrive, was overwhelming.

However, the obstacles appeared daunting. The powers of evil became more audacious with each passing day, menacing to immerse Alora in an unfathomable state of disorder. The queen grappled with her own limitations and the weight of her own wisdom. She wondered if her efforts were hopeless and if the wounds inflicted upon her kingdom were too deep to heal.

Queen Alora, finding a glimmer of hope in the arcanists' minor victory in the lowborn district, sought counsel from commander Relios. However, the commander, driven by a more aggressive approach, urged the use of the vanguard to forcefully take control of the district. The queen, reluctant to escalate the violence further, hesitated to embrace such a drastic measure. Despite her reservations, Relios respected her decision but emphasized that the vanguard's intervention remained a last resort if alternative solutions failed to materialize as intended.

Deep within the recesses of her being, Queen Alora possessed a persistent glimmer of resolve. She understood that surrendering to hopelessness was not an option she could entertain. Clinging to the belief that there were still flickers of optimism left, she envisioned her people transcending the looming shadows seeking to engulf them through unity and unwavering resilience.

With rejuvenated determination coursing through her veins, the queen pledged to intensify her struggles in order to foster transformation and reinstate harmony throughout her realm. Consciously seeking advice from insightful counselors, she actively extended herself towards those capable of providing valuable guidance and compassionate support. Immersing herself within the intricacies of governance, she tirelessly pursued innovative remedies aimed at addressing the fundamental causes instigating discord.

The emotional burden inflicted upon Queen Alora inevitably took its toll; however, it also spurred on her passionate drive. Firmly refusing despair's alluring embrace and seizing possession of her spirit, she deliberately transformed grief into action. Fully aware that traversing the path ahead would be fraught with difficulties, undeterred commitment remained synonymous with both allegiance towards her citizens and steadfast dedication fueled by aspirations for a brighter future.

Despite the demise of her husband during the fall of the Kingdom of Unity, Queen Alora remained loyal in fulfilling her responsibilities as a leader. Seeking counsel and support from trusted advisors, she delved deeply into the intricate matters of governance to discover groundbreaking resolutions for the afflictions tormenting her realm. Although engulfed in mourning, she staunchly refused to succumb to hopelessness; instead, she redirected her anguish towards active strives for enhancing the lives of her subjects and envisioning a future illuminated with positivity.

During the reign of the King in the Kingdom of Unity, the enforcement of hierarchy was nonexistent. The kingdom experienced a transformative period marked by the discovery of arcane magic, alliances with primal factions, revelations about fertility issues, and the development of new traditions and cultures. Queen Alora, standing alongside her husband in the creation of the harmonious Kingdom of Unity, harbored reservations about the social class disparities that went unaddressed during his rule. The sight of the poor cluttering the elegant streets of the kingdom appalled the queen. In her persistent efforts, she urged her husband to implement changes that would segregate the classes, allowing the higher class to live in utopia away from those who she deemed as a loss from a grand living.

In the past time, the King and Queen experienced a miraculous event before his death – the birth of their only child. This occurrence was extraordinary, given the elves' generally low fertility rates, especially before the establishment of the Genetic Pathway Organization and the emergence of the highborn. The newborn, a symbol of hope and continuity was named after her mother, becoming Alora II, the second of her name.

As Queen Alora contemplated what lay ahead, she couldn't help pondering about her daughter's integral role in shaping that destiny. Her utmost goal was to ensure an inheritance of peace and prosperity for her beloved child within the kingdom's bounds. Holding this ambition dear, she ceaselessly dedicated herself towards laying the sturdy foundations necessary for erecting a society esteemed for its stability and fairness—a society designed not just to serve present generations but also future ones yet unborn. Ever convinced by her daughter's extraordinary potential that would inevitably be realized with resoluteness and confidence, Queen Alora pledged unwavering commitment towards equipping her offspring against forthcoming tribulations through every means at hand.

Princess Alora II, from a tender age, delved into the intricate teachings of the arcanists, guided by the knowledgeable highborn. In tandem with her magical education, she immersed herself in the complex realm of elven politics and history. Despite her youth, the princess displayed remarkable maturity, aspiring to stand by her mother's side as a formidable force in the kingdom. Recognizing the importance of passing on her legacy, Queen Alora diligently armed her daughter with a wealth of knowledge and wisdom, envisioning a future where Princess Alora II would continue her efforts and shape the society she had crafted.

As the kingdom of Alora navigated dusk, Queen Alora fortified herself for the obstacles that awaited. She held steadfast in her determination to not lose courage when confronted with difficult challenges. With a heart burdened but resolved, she made a solemn vow to serve as a guiding light amidst darkness—an authoritative figure who would steer her subjects towards a more optimistic future like she would for her daughter.

....

Once heralded for bustling productivity and efficient workmanship, the area dedicated to labor in the working class has now found itself submerged in chaos. The uprising disorder prevailing in the lowborn district, along with imminent external dangers reverberated through every resident. Fear and insecurity took hold of their spirits, paralyzing their hands once they were diligent in their pursuits.

In the vast corridors of the working class, faint murmurs of dissatisfaction and opposition could be heard. Weighed down by their own apprehensions and the harsh reality that surrounded them, the workers found themselves questioning the very core of their existence. The unrelenting waves of violence and unrest had shattered their sense of security, leaving them disenchanted and discouraged.

Within the boundaries of the tradeborn district, a visible tension hung in the air as the employees, fueled by an intense blend of anger and anxiety, began to vocalize their grievances. Their trust in a system that appeared indifferent to their welfare had waned significantly. The threats emerging from the lowborn district as well as external forces had planted seeds of hesitation in their minds, gradually eroding their faith in those who held authority over them.

As the unrest spread like wildfire, the once hard-working workforce became increasingly defiant. They refused to toil under the shadow of fear, their voices rising in a chorus of defiance. The assembly lines ground to a halt, and the sound of people laboring was replaced by the clamor of discontent. Workers stood shoulder to shoulder, their unified stance a powerful symbol of their collective frustration.

The tradeborn district, once a bustling hive of productivity, now lies in a state of disarray. The absence of the workers' diligent hands brought the efficiency of progress to a grinding halt. The impact of their refusal to work reverberated through the kingdom, causing ripples of concern among those in positions of power.

Queen Alora, torn between her desire to maintain order and her empathy for the workers' plight, recognized the severity of the situation. She understood that the unrest in the working class was not born out of laziness or defiance but rather a desperate cry for security and reassurance.

The threats that loomed over the kingdom had shattered the fragile equilibrium of their lives, leaving them vulnerable and disillusioned.

Amidst the prevailing unrest, the queen demonstrated a deep sense of empathy and compassion as she strived to address the concerns of the workers. Her strategy involved convening meetings and engaging in honest dialogue, with a clear intention to bridge the divide that separated them from the ruling class. Throughout these interactions, she listened attentively, validating their fears and frustrations without hesitation.

Recognizing that decisive action was necessary for restoring stability to her kingdom, the queen commenced by implementing policies aimed at alleviating the most pressing issues faced by workers. This enveloped substantial improvements in working conditions as well as wage increments. Concurrently, efforts were made to enhance access to education and healthcare since it was evident that a well-educated and healthy workforce served as an asset for long-term prosperity within the realm. Consequently, this dedicated approach fostered sentiments of acknowledgement amongst laborers while simultaneously nurturing their growing trust towards both her leadership and authority figures. Gradually but undeniably, healing began spreading through all realms of society previously scarred by recent trouble.

Understanding that simple words would not suffice, Queen Alora pledged to take tangible actions to restore their sense of security and well-being. She initiated reforms to enhance safety measures, increase support for the workers' families, and provide avenues for their voices to be heard in the decision-making processes. Through these measures, she aimed to rebuild the trust that had been eroded and reignite the spirit of productivity within the tradeborn district before it could spread throughout the kingdom.

The road ahead was fraught with challenges, but Queen Alora remained steadfast in her commitment to rebuilding the harmony of her kingdom. She understood that the unrest within the tradeborn district reflected the kingdom's collective pain and disillusionment. The queen sought to restore faith, heal wounds, and pave the way towards a future where all residents of Alora could find peace and prosperity once more.

During the evenings that proved to be difficult, when solitude would have been the queen's only companion, she sought comfort in the company of commander Relios. His faithful devotion and commitment to the realm paralleled her own, igniting hope within Alora as they collectively envisioned a more promising future. Her sentiments toward the commander surpassed any expectations she once had, while their connection deepened with each passing day. Despite encountering numerous challenges along their path, the queen remained steadfast in her determination to reconstruct Alora and pave the way for an improved tomorrow for its entire populace.

In moments of vulnerability, she would share her emotions and troubles with him. Seeking comfort rather than solutions, she found in him a trusted listener, someone with whom she could release her frustrations. Relios, deeply caring for his queen, attentively listened yet harbored an urge to address and resolve the mounting issues that plagued the kingdom. The external threats from outsiders, the persistent troubles of the lowborn, and the rising discontent within the working class painted a grim picture for the kingdom. Relios perceived these challenges as obstacles that demanded swift and assertive action within the kingdom's walls, viewing the readiness for the looming outsider demands as a critical priority amidst the internal struggles.

The queen, while comprehending Relios' perspective, aimed for a delicate balance in the kingdom. She acknowledged the historical significance of the lowborn, once the backbone of the realm, and sought to prevent them from feeling enslaved or worsened. The burdens they bore weighed heavily on her heart, and making their hardships worse was a path she couldn't bear. As Relios departed with simmering anger, unable to endure the queen's course of action any longer, he felt that her intentions might not lead to the desired outcome. Tensions within the kingdom continued to escalate, leaving both ruler and commander grappling with the complexities of their roles.

Commander Relios, harboring fond emotions for his queen, felt a sense of duty to address the mounting challenges in the tradeborn district. Deploying the military to assist in alleviating issues, he faced the harsh reality of chaos spreading too quickly. With the military stretched thin and the vanguard occupied with monitoring outsiders, the situation became overwhelming. Despite the temptation to resort to force and take over the lowborn district, enacting a violent solution, Relios battled against that urge, seeking a more measured approach to preserve the delicate balance that his queen desired.

While the measures taken by the queen and commander Relios managed to alleviate some of the issues in the working class, the troubles persisted in the lowborn district beyond the walls. The divide between the two districts remained, with the lower district presenting an ongoing threat to the relative stability achieved in the tradeborn district. The complex dynamics within the kingdom continued to unfold, with challenges persisting on multiple fronts.

•••••••

As Fumar delved deeper into the forbidden arts, his power grew with every passing day. The dark energies that coursed through his veins granted him a formidable prowess in the arcane arts, setting him apart from his peers. Within the secret cult hidden within the shadows of the kingdom, Fumar emerged as a central figure, his potential recognized by the cult's leaders.

But with the ascent of power came an increasing restlessness within Fumar's heart. He yearned for more, hungered for greater control and influence. His thirst for power became insatiable, consuming him from within. The whispers of Havoc, the dark force that had manipulated him since his youth, intensified by urging him to seize the reins of the cult. Fumar's mind became clouded with the desire for domination, and he began to devise a plan to overthrow the current leaders and take control.

Recognizing the importance of having devoted supporters by his side, he embarked on a mission to enlist fresh recruits for his reign. Tempting them with promises of prestige and success, he persuaded these individuals to pledge their loyalty in exchange. His confidence increased with each new cult member, opening the door for risky actions that involved challenging the very supremacy of the ruling class while concurrently eroding their power. As this internal dissension escalated within the lowborn community, Fumar remained conscious that imminent action was approaching swiftly.

In the shadowed alleys of the lowborn district, it was Morvain who first perceived the insidious whispers of Havoc. Drawn to the mysterious power embedded within those whispers, Morvain followed their dark guidance. It was during one of these ominous nights that he located his target, Fumar, a lone youthful gray elf navigating the desolate streets after being cast away. Seeing potential in the young outcast, Morvain took him under his wing, adopting him as his protege. The true intentions behind Havoc's whispers remained shrouded in mystery, but Morvain, fueled by a hunger for power had embraced the dark path that unfolded before him.

While Morvain was attuned to the insidious whispers of Havoc, little did he know that the same dark voices were also reaching the ears of his protege, Fumar. In the depths of Fumar's consciousness, secret plots for leadership and power were taking root, fueled by the unseen influence of the whispers. Observing the clash with the arcanists as a depressing failure, Fumar harbored a desire for more decisive and forceful actions. He welcomed Morvain's decision to reveal themselves as the chaotic shadows beneath the lower district, recognizing the opportunity to attract new members to their cause. However, Fumar couldn't shake the embarrassment stemming from their struggles in combat. He perceived the leaders of the cult as weak, unable to grasp the darkness with the same mastery he believed he possessed.

Guided by the teachings of his master, Morvain, Fumar had learned to suppress empathy in favor of ruthless pragmatism. The haunting memories of himself coldly ending his own parents' lives served as a stark reminder of the necessity to detach from such emotions. As he witnessed Morvain's attempt to lead the cult, resulting in failure, a sinister realization dawned on Fumar. The cult was not aligned with the ruthless principles instilled in him during his formative years. With a wicked smile, Fumar understood the path he needed to tread. To ascend to leadership, he had to sever any lingering ties to empathy, especially towards the figure of his father.

The fateful confrontation between Fumar and his master, the one who had guided him on his treacherous path and brought him up from youth, was a collision of wills and egos. Their once symbiotic relationship of father and son turned volatile as Fumar challenged his mentor's authority, questioning his methods and teachings. The mentor, apprehensive about the surrounding darkness that had overtaken Fumar, made an effort to restrain his protege, cautioning him of the uncertainty that lay before him. Nonetheless, Fumar remained steadfast in his convictions and adamantly rejected any concession.

The rest of the cult members observed with anticipation, uncertain about what would transpire next. It was evident that the formerly united group had fragmented, and how this conflict unfolded would shape the future of the cult. Fumar understood that triumphing in this battle was paramount; otherwise, he risked displacement and finding himself adrift in a bewildering world. The stakes were exceptionally high, and an atmosphere burdened with tension prevailed as both elves confronted each other to assert their will.

In the murky depths of the lower district's underbelly, a clash unfolded between master and protege. Fumar and Morvain, both wielding the dark arts, engaged in a fierce exchange of spells that echoed through the hidden corridors. Amidst the chaos, Morvain began to comprehend the insidious whispers that guided his actions. He realized that he was but a pawn, a vessel to instill seething hatred in his protege, Fumar, who was destined to become darkness personified.

As the battle raged on, Morvain chose a surprising course of action. He ceased resisting Fumar's onslaught, embracing the dark spells that were cast upon him. Fumar, bewildered by his master's submission, called for him to continue the fight. However, Morvain, in an unexpected turn, revealed the true purpose behind their conflict. He disclosed that Fumar was the chosen one of the whispers, destined to lead the cult that had taken root in the shadows.

Confusion and anger welled up within Fumar as he demanded a true confrontation. Yet Morvain, instead of engaging in combat, chose to share stories of their shared past. For the first time, he addressed Fumar as his son instead of his apprentice, unraveling the intricate threads of their relationship and leaving Fumar torn between his desire for dominance and the choice to kill his master.

As tempers flared during their intense argument, Fumar's frustration and fury boiled over uncontrollably. A surge of untamed power surged forth from within him, creating an upheaval unlike any witnessed before. This cataclysmic wave entirely consumed Morvain, extinguishing his life force and physical body instantaneously.

Standing amidst the remnants of his master's demise, Fumar experienced a chilling blend of exhilaration and triumph reserved for few others who know such heights of savage defiance. The consequences stemming from his actions eluded prediction; however, crossing boundaries unrestrainedly is forevermore sealed in Fumar's destiny. The repercussions of his actions would weigh on his future, and all he could do was hope for a chance to undo the harm he had done. The conflict between opposing forces had ceased, but the true price of triumph remained uncertain.

Upon the demise of Morvain, Fumar assumed control over the strictly prohibited cult. The members of this secretive group greeted his rise to power with a range of emotions; some were in awe of his newfound authority, while others cautiously sensed the ominous aura surrounding him. Drunk on his own abilities, Fumar luxuriated in his newly acquired dominion and effortlessly compelled the followers to comply with his desires. Unfortunately, unbeknownst to them, this quest for supremacy would ultimately guide them down a destructive path. Fumar's stability rapidly declined as he descended further into the cult's forbidden wisdom, and his unpredictable nature increasingly came to define him.

The group, once characterized by a degree of self-reserving and mystery, had grown significantly in influence on the point where it could no longer be ignored. The repercussions of Fumar's actions extended far beyond the boundaries of their concealed sanctuary. It was only a matter of time before the world discovered their existence and fully understood the devastating price paid due to Fumar's unbridled ambition. Now left with nothing but fragments of what used to be a structured organization, the members of the cult must attempt to salvage what remains. Fumar's legacy will forever bear the stain of his insatiable thirst for power and the havoc he wrought upon those unfortunate enough to be in his path.

The cult, now under Fumar's command, took a darker turn. Due to Fumar's desire for power, their rituals became more intense and twisted. He pushed the boundaries of forbidden magic, delving into realms thought to be too dangerous even for the most daring practitioners. The whispers of Havoc, always present in his mind, guided him towards greater acts of chaos and destruction. As Fumar continued down this path, the once-loyal followers of the cult began to fear him. They saw the darkness consuming him and knew that it would only lead to their own demise.

As Fumar's influence expanded, so did the aspirations of the cult. They transformed into an influential entity; a concealed force prepared to sabotage Alora. Fumar's newfound mastery over the cult instilled in him a sense of purpose, providing him with a means to exact revenge on a society that had rejected him. The seeds of rebellion were planted, and Fumar directed his focus towards a future where Alora would collapse under the burden of darkness and hopelessness.

With the recent rush of new members loyal solely to Fumar, the cult that had once operated in the shadows could now emerge into the public eye. While some among the cult were hesitant about the sudden increase in followers, Fumar asserted his authority as the leader. Any dissent was met with threats of allegiance to Morvain's impending downfall. The cult, now with a more substantial and diverse following, prepared to carry out the whispers' bidding under Fumar's command. Consumed by his thirst for retribution and dominance, Fumar reveled in basking in the admiration and loyalty of his devoted followers.

The rituals and customs of the cult became more sinister, embracing the most sinister elements of sorcery. They delved into necromancy to a greater extent, communicating with the spirits of the departed and utilizing their powers. Blood magic assumed a prominent role in their ceremonies, as sacrifices were offered to energize their joint efforts.

Basking in the power that flowed through his veins, Fumar embraced his role as their new commander, brandishing forbidden sorcery without repercussions. Thanks to his guidance, the cult flourished in both number and influence, spreading their sinister doctrine among fresh converts. To maintain control, fear and coercion were employed effortlessly, wherein opponents would mysteriously vanish without a trace. Thusly, an unbreakable force emerged with intense loyalty towards their captivating leader.

Nonetheless, while Fumar's reign propelled the cult towards prosperity, an unsettling atmosphere of discomfort and apprehension engulfed its followers. Whispers of doubt and fear circulated among them as they witnessed the lengths to which Fumar would go to achieve his goals. Some questioned the darkness that had engulfed their once-humble gathering, wondering if they had strayed too far from their original purpose.

Fumar, however, brushed aside such concerns, dismissing any dissenting voices as weak and inconsequential. He remained steadfast in his conviction that Alora and its inhabitants deserved to suffer, to be consumed by the very chaos and despair that had plagued his own existence. The whispers of Havoc, ever present, fueled his wicked desires, whispering promises of ultimate power and the downfall of his enemies.

As the cult's power expanded, their aspirations also soared. Fumar envisioned himself as a transformative force, signaling the start of an era characterized by the resurgence of the lowborn elves from despair and their reclaiming of what they deemed to be rightfully theirs. With their arcane prowess and resolute loyalty, the cult devised schemes that grew increasingly bold and daring in nature.

Fumar's gaze now extended beyond the confines of the kingdom. He snuck out at night to seek alliances and forces on the outside that could aid in his quest for revenge. Fumar found the Raider clan and the Rippers among the dark ones, who became potential allies for his plans. Fumar saw in them a shared desire for upheaval, a belief that the established order needed to crumble. Through cunning and manipulation, he forged a tenuous alliance with them; their combined strength is now poised to strike a blow against Alora.

In the shadows of Paranova, an alliance had already taken root between the Dark Ones and the raider clan. While Fumar was immersed in the internal struggles of the lower district, the raider clan and their allies, the dark ones, carried with them stories of their kin being enslaved and mistreated in the kingdom of the light ones. The tales of oppression and abuse further fueled the flames of resentment and unrest among the dark ones, creating a sense of urgency within the alliance to act against the perceived tyranny of the light elves.

Fumar knew that the attack would not be easy. The kingdom of Alora was well-guarded, with powerful magicians and skilled fighters defending the kingdom. But Fumar had a plan. He had spent years studying Alora's movements, analyzing its weaknesses, and devising a strategy that could bring the kingdom into darkness.

With the gangs now rallying behind Fumar and his cult, they were ready to join his cause for chaos. However, sensing the influence of each gang leader had over their gang members, Fumar harnessed the life force of the gang leaders with a mere flick of his wrist, leaving their lifeless bodies sprawled on the ground before him. Addressing the remaining gang members, Fumar asserted his dominance and declared that they would now follow him. Faced with the stark display of his dark powers, the remaining gang members submitted to Fumar's command without hesitation, their wills subdued by the ominous force he wielded.

In a masterful display of manipulation, Fumar emerged from the shadows and took center stage in the lower district. With charisma and deceit, he spun a tale of the cult's triumph over the gangs, portraying himself as a liberator fighting against the oppressive leaders of the kingdom. Skillfully, Fumar spread false accusations while patrolling the streets, branding Morvain as the mastermind behind the gang activity. The residents were hungry for a leader and rallied behind Fumar, believing his lies and embracing him as a symbol of hope and equality for the lowborn. Little did they know that Fumar's intentions were far from noble, driven by a desire for power and control over the district.

In a wicked display of power, Fumar resurrected his mentor from the ashes, whom he had extinguished in a fit of rage during their heated confrontation. Bound by dark magic, the once-mentor became his obedient servant, a grim reminder of Fumar's dominance over life and death. The sight of the supposed gang leader, now reduced to a puppet in Fumar's hands had struck fear into the hearts of those who dared to oppose him.

The residents of the lowborn district found themselves trapped in a web of manipulation and coercion. Faced with a choice between allegiances to Fumar and the continued neglect of Queen Alora, many reluctantly sided with the charismatic sorcerer. Fumar exploited their desperation and played upon their grievances, skillfully painting Queen Alora as the source of their suffering. In this twisted narrative, he positioned himself as their liberator, promising a brighter future free from oppression and injustice.

By employing cunning and trickery, Fumar managed to establish himself as a respected figure within the lowborn community over time. He became both their savior and advocate, empathizing with their suffering and vowing to champion their cause. Blinded by hopes of transformation and driven by an overwhelming desperation for an improved existence, the citizens willingly overlooked the sinister motivations that fueled Fumar's actions. Exploiting their admiration to his advantage, he successfully gathered a formidable force under the guise that violence was essential to toppling the prevailing corrupt authority.

Behind the facade of a leader fighting for justice, Fumar was orchestrating a grand scheme to unleash chaos upon Alora. His allegiance lay with only himself, the embodiment of forbidden magic and twisted desires. Through subtle manipulation and carefully crafted illusions, Fumar had successfully painted Queen Alora as the villain, her rule synonymous with oppression and inequality.

Fumar instigated a rebellion using deceptive rhetoric and propaganda that quickly spread throughout the kingdom thanks to the rage of those who thought they were fighting for a better future. However, as their efforts progressed, it became unknown to them that Fumar's true agenda was not to liberate the people, but to bend them to his own will and secure his place as the King of Chaos.

As the lowborn district teetered on the brink of rebellion, fueled by Fumar's schemes and growing discontent, Queen Alora struggled to maintain control over her kingdom. The mounting tensions and the weight of the murders pushed her to the brink, questioning her own leadership and the impact of her decisions. Little did she know that her every move played into Fumar's hands, serving his plan for ultimate chaos and destruction.

It seems that Queen Alora's attempts to maintain control over her kingdom were ultimately ineffective, as Fumar's manipulations and the rapidly growing discontent of the lowborn district led to rebellion and chaos. The queen's struggles with her own leadership and the impact of her decisions suggest that she may have been misguided in her attempts to maintain order, and her every move played into Fumar's plan for destruction. Overall, it appears that the rule of Queen Alora was synonymous with oppression and inequality, contributing to the start of a downfall for her kingdom.

With each passing day, Fumar's grip on power tightened, and his cult of followers grew in number. The stage was set for a confrontation, a battle that would not only decide the fate of Alora but also unveil the true extent of Fumar's darkness. The dark sorcerer stood ready, his followers at his command, poised to unleash havoc upon the unsuspecting kingdom.

As anxiety gripped the denizens of Alora, the once-thriving realm of the past had now faced an uncertain fate. The impending clash between Fumar and those who sought to stand against him became a painful test of courage and resilience. Throughout the kingdom, prayers echoed and the desperate pleas of those yearning for a champion to emerge victorious over Fumar, restoring peace and righteousness to their kingdom.

Separately, within the confines of the lowborn district, a different sentiment prevailed. Hopeful gazes turned toward Fumar as a potential liberator, a figure in their eyes that could bring about change and elevate the status of the downtrodden. The conflict's outcome within the kingdom's walls would shape the very nature of Alora's future, which hung in the balance due to the division in viewpoints that had set the stage for a serious struggle.

Chapter 8: Inferno Storm

While the atmosphere in Alora remains tense, attention has now shifted back to the Dark Ones as they embark on their newfound alliance. In an effort to restore balance and reduce the growing influence of what they refer to as the Light Empire, this alliance joined forces with the Raider Clan. Both factions recognize the imminent threat posed by this expanding empire and acknowledge that forming a united front is crucial to defending their interests and way of life. Nevertheless, their partnership faces its fair share of complications. The dark ones and raider clan hold contrasting ideologies and divergent approaches to achieving their objectives, resulting in conflicts and disagreements within their alliance. However, despite these hurdles, they remain unwaveringly dedicated to their shared cause and collectively strive towards halting the advances made by the light empire.

Having a shared objective in sight, the Dark Ones and the Raider Clan engaged in discussions and arrived at important understandings. The focal point of their talks revolved around the advantageous outcomes that both parties envisioned gaining through their alliance. Drawing upon their formidable magic skills and profound understanding of mystical arts, the dark ones put forth an enticing offer to the raider clan: expansion of territory as a well-deserved prize for their steadfast backing during the impending conflict. This agreement allowed the raider clan to secure their position and extend their influence, while the dark ones gained a formidable ally in their fight against the light empire. The raider clan also saw an opportunity to learn from the dark ones and expand their own knowledge of magic and the arcane. In return, they offered their military prowess and strategic expertise to aid the dark ones in their quest for dominance.

Initially, a sense of doubt and suspicion surrounded the alliance between the dark ones and the raider clan. Both sides harbored their own apprehensions and reservations regarding aligning with each other. The autonomous and self-sufficient expressed skepticism over the intentions of the dark ones and whether they would truly fulfill their commitments. Conversely, the dark ones exercised caution in regard to placing faith in the loyalty and reliability of the raider clan, anxious about potential treachery or conflicting objectives.

However, as the negotiations progressed and discussions deepened, the barriers of skepticism and distrust gradually began to crumble. Both factions recognized the shared interests and desires for power that brought them together. Recognizing the potential of their alliance, they comprehended that it presented a distinct chance to sway the balance in their favor and confront the prevailing authority of the light empire.

By engaging in open conversations and gaining a deeper appreciation of each other's abilities and limitations, the dark ones and the raider clan were able to discover shared perspectives. They forged a bond based on mutual respect and the recognition that their combined forces would be stronger than facing the light empire alone. The realization that they could achieve their individual goals more effectively as allies rather than enemies served as a catalyst for building trust and overcoming their initial reservations.

As their collaboration endured, the dark ones and the raider clan not only embraced a mutual objective but also exchanged personal narratives involving hardships both past and present. In discovering commonalities and disparities within their life experiences, they achieved a deeper understanding of each other. The dark ones' acquisition of expertise in dark magic and the raider clan members' knowledge of guerrilla warfare went hand in hand. Day after day, their partnership flourished, bolstering their conviction in one another's capabilities. While cognizant that invincibility eluded them all, an unbreakable cohesion existed that assuredly substantiated their unyielding support for each other. Together, this united front embodied an unstoppable force worthy of awe and respect.

As the alliance solidified, the dark ones reiterated their promise to reward the raider clan with territorial expansion. This assurance acted as a catalyst for strengthening the bond between the factions, reinforcing their commitment to the alliance and the shared goal of countering the influence of the light empire. The prospect of expanded territory provided the raider clan with the security and power they sought, while the dark ones gained a loyal and formidable force to bolster their ranks in the upcoming conflict.

The dark ones and the raider clan were prepared to face the challenges that lay ahead because they shared a common goal and had a strong alliance. Their united objective of reinstating balance and countering the expansion of influence by the light empire served as an elite driving force, igniting their determination to dominate any challenges obstructing them. As they prepared themselves for the forthcoming conflict, both groups comprehended the significance of mutual esteem and reliance. They acknowledged that triumph depended on their ability to collaborate harmoniously, leveraging each other's strengths. Anchored in this realization, they cemented an unbreakable bond that would prove strength in the coming battles.

The Dark Ones and the Raider Clan recognized the significance of thorough preparations for their alliance to succeed. They assembled their respective forces, drawing upon the skilled rippers, bloodfire, shadowmancers, and emberblade warriors from their ranks. Training camps were established, where intensive drills and exercises took place. The dark ones honed their mastery of dark magic, perfecting their spells and rituals, while the raider clan focused on enhancing their physical combat prowess and guerrilla tactics.

Strategic coordination became a priority for the alliance. The dark ones and the raider clan conducted joint strategy meetings, analyzing Alora's vulnerabilities and devising plans to exploit them. They shared their knowledge and insights, leveraging the dark ones' understanding of mystical forces and the raider clan's expertise in navigating treacherous terrain. This cooperation allowed them to form a unified strategy that involved a combination of direct confrontations and covert operations.

The Dark Ones gained respect for humanity, knowing that they were diverse themselves, much like the Elven race. For now, they trusted the raider clan, seeing them as a mirror image of how they were within their own race. The successful formation of this alliance resulted in their triumphant success over their mutual enemy and the development of a fresh bond founded on trust and admiration. Furthermore, the collaborative efforts among these divergent races set the groundwork for forthcoming partnerships and coalitions, ultimately shaping a tranquil and prosperous global community.

Communication channels were established to ensure seamless coordination between the factions. Skilled operatives were appointed as messengers, utilizing secure and discreet means to exchange information and relay orders. This facilitated the swift dissemination of intelligence and updates, enabling the dark ones and the raider clan to adapt their plans as circumstances evolved.

The raiders and dark ones dispatched small parties to test Alora's defenses. These parties operated with caution and precision, employing stealth and subterfuge to infiltrate the outskirts of the kingdom. Their activities ranged from scouting enemy positions and gathering intelligence to launching calculated strikes aimed at destabilizing Alora's security apparatus. These covert operations were meticulously planned to assess

Alora's response capabilities and identify any weaknesses that could be exploited during the main assault.

Alora's guards and intelligence agencies, aware of the mounting threat, intensified their efforts to counter the infiltrators. Patrols were increased, and reconnaissance operations were expanded to detect and apprehend these intruders. The guards implemented heightened security measures within Alora's borders, fortifying key locations and implementing stringent access controls. Meanwhile, the intelligence agencies worked tirelessly to unravel the identities and motives of the operatives, analyzing patterns and clues left behind. They also collaborated with international partners to share information and coordinate efforts to track down the infiltrators. As a result of these combined efforts, several suspects were identified and apprehended, preventing further harm to Alora's security and stability.

The escalating activities of the dark ones and the raider clan put Alora on edge, forcing its defenders to maintain a heightened state of readiness. They deployed additional personnel to bolster the kingdom's defenses, ensuring that every potential vulnerability was addressed. Counterintelligence operations were launched to gather information on the alliance's plans and uncover any potential double agents. Although security measures have been strengthened, worries about the potential for an unforeseen assault remain. To alleviate this concern, Alora's government imposed a strict curfew and limited entry into specific regions of the kingdom. These actions effectively dissuaded any possible dangers and preserved tranquility within the urban areas.

As tensions mounted, the clash between the dark ones, the raider clan, and Alora became increasingly imminent. The preparations of the factions grew more intricate, reflecting their determination and resolve. The ongoing activities of probing Alora's defenses added to the sense of anticipation and urgency. Each side aimed to gain an advantage, testing the strengths and weaknesses of their enemies while refining their own strategies.

As the dark ones and the raider clan plotted their operations against Alora, they faced significant challenges that demanded careful consideration. The kingdom nestled on an island, boasted formidable walls, and the watchful eyes of scouts were ever-present due to the tests of small-party assaults on the mainland. The strategic challenge extended beyond the physical barriers, delving into the intricacies of navigating the forested landscapes.

Another challenge that would arise in the forests was that they were inhabited by the Ranuk clans, who were resistant to communication or alliances with the dark ones and humans. The need to overcome these obstacles added layers of complexity to the plans, prompting them to devise strategies that would circumvent both the physical and sentient barriers standing in their way.

The stage was set for a climactic confrontation, where the dark ones and the raider clan would face the combined might of Alora. The outcome of this conflict would shape the destiny of the kingdom and the balance of power in the land. The preparations and ongoing activities demonstrated the commitment and relentless pursuit of their goals by all parties involved. The dark ones and the raider clan had been preparing for months, gathering their forces and devising new tactics to overcome their common enemy. In contrast, the kingdom of Alora had steadfastly observed their actions and adjusted their own strategy accordingly, driven by a passionate resolve to emerge triumphantly in the ultimate clash for preservation.

·······

The Shadow Council, an elite group comprised of proficient sorcerers and influential individuals belonging to the dark ones' society, steadily operates in hiddenness away from prying external eyes. Their gatherings transpire within a chamber drenched in an eerie radiance emitted by softly lit candles—a realm filled with distinct anticipation as well as concealed knowledge. To the world outside, the dark ones are perceived as a vast worshipping sector, with their skin and veins gradually darkened by wielding forbidden magic, although they were once elves traveling with other elves during the conception of Paranova.

Despite the falsehood of perception, numerous other races succumb to fear when faced with the shadow council, thus granting leverage for manipulation and governance from these shadowy figures. Exploiting their powers steeped in darkness and incorporating mystic forces that align with their objectives enables the council to preserve dominion over all matters they partake in. One who defies or obstructs their path is often inflicted upon by ill-fated outcomes wrapped in darkness, hence spotlighting their shrouded existence while imprinting an undeniable impression across vast stretches of land through indirect influence.

In the midst of these gatherings, Aleron, a council member brimming with charm and ambition, steals the spotlight. His attire of flowing dark robes adds to his captivating presence as he unveils his plans for a mysterious summoning ritual that grabs the attention and curiosity of his fellow council members. The specifics of this summoning, however, are shrouded in secrecy and shared only with a select few who have knowledge of its true purpose and potential ramifications.

Whispers about Aleron's intentions begin circulating throughout the dark one kingdom, causing unease and fear among its citizens. Some speculate that he seeks to exploit dark magic for personal gain, while others dread the possibility that his actions may rouse dormant sinister forces from ancient times. Regardless of which theory holds truth, it is evident that Aleron's summoning will usher forth significant consequences affecting all denizens residing within the realm. As the whispers spread throughout the kingdom and the council, speculation runs rampant. Some believe the summoning to be a means of acquiring untold power, tapping into ancient forces that could turn the tides of the looming conflict. Others speculate that it may hold the key to unlocking long-lost knowledge or opening a gateway to realms unseen. The true intentions behind the summoning remain veiled, adding an air of mystery and uncertainty to the council's deliberations.

Amidst the murmurs and speculation, rumors circulate about a potential correlation between the act of summoning and the whisperers— ethereal beings brimming with immense power and allure. These mysterious entities are believed to possess strange mastery over thoughts and perspectives, discreetly influencing the actions and decisions of those they encounter. Certain members of the council ponder if summoning is a means to curry favor from these insidious whisperers or if it could be employed as a method to govern or harness their complex abilities.

On the other hand, some harbor fear that summoning may inadvertently bring about unforeseen consequences, ushering chaos and devastation into the world. Regardless of differing viewpoints, all council members concur that approaching summonses must be undertaken with the utmost caution. Plans are devised to amass more information regarding whispers along with their potential involvement in summoning while simultaneously exploring alternative avenues towards achieving their objectives. The destinies of numerous souls lie delicately in suspension as heated deliberations transpire within the council chamber.

Aleron, the council leader, worried about facing the powerful light empire directly. However, his focus shifted to the potential advantage of the mysterious power in the Inarus Inferno. He believed tapping into this force could be the key to overcoming the empire's strength. The inferno's secrets became a crucial element in his strategy for success in the upcoming conflict. The council, cautious and deliberative, sought to thoroughly discuss the intricacies of the summoning.

As the discussions of the council progress, tensions escalate and hidden motives are revealed. Each member brings their personal objectives and aspirations to the forefront, gradually unveiling the true essence behind summoning actions. Amongst this hazardous environment, one certainty remains: decisions adopted by the council will impart lasting ramifications for both realms—the kingdom itself and its cherished inhabitants. With Aleron now steering council proceedings towards a misgiving direction, the remaining members loiter on the perimeter as mere spectators, observing unfolding events in anticipation.

The Shadow Council found themselves both intrigued and concerned by Aleron's secretive meetings with the ethereal being at the summit of the volcano. After each encounter, Aleron underwent visible transformations—his once lively and authoritative presence dimmed to reveal a paleness that mirrored decay creeping into his very essence.

Throughout the kingdom, rumors began to circulate, causing growing unease among its inhabitants. Some feared that Aleron's actions would bring forth a horrendous curse upon their land, while others worried about dangerous forces being attracted to their doorstep due to his interactions with the supernatural. Despite these apprehensions, Aleron remained true in his quest for power, disregarding any potential repercussions for himself or those around him.

The whisperers, mysterious entities with immense prowess and impact, possess an unparalleled control over the sentiments and musings of individuals they come across. They exhibit the power to delve into the deepest depths of someone's mind, revealing concealed truths, anxieties, and longings. Their mere existence is believed to be spellbinding yet disquieting, capable of evoking both admiration and discomposure.

The mysterious entities were none other than the spectral avatars, ancient beings that had once consumed mortal souls for Havoc. Over the years, the dark ones harnessed these avatars to gain knowledge and evolve. The whispers in Aleron's head influenced him, and he became fixated on discovering their hidden meanings. He dove deep into each riddle, communicating with the spectral whisperer that revealed itself to him at the summit. Aleron attributed his leadership of the shadow council to being the first to survive the inferno induction, a feat that set him apart and elevated his status.

In the situation involving Aleron, it appears that the rogue spectral avatars possess a special interest in him. They are attracted to his immense strength, unwavering determination, and unshakable loyalty towards the dark ones. Although his interactions with them leave him physically exhausted, they also grant him an unparalleled sense of enlightenment and wisdom, boosting his standing among the council members. However, not all individuals within the council have faith in Aleron's alliance with the spectral whisperers; instead, they perceive it as a possible menace to their authority. Some even speculate that these mysterious beings may hold their own secret motivations and could eventually turn against Aleron at any given moment. Despite such doubts cast upon him, Aleron remains resolute in his conviction that the whisperers form an essential element of their society and will persistently seek their counsel.

The other members of the council, though aware of Aleron's meetings, cannot help but feel a mixture of curiosity and apprehension. The spectral influence on their esteemed colleague is undeniable, and their unknown nature raises questions about their true intentions and motives. Yet there is an unspoken trust and respect among the council members towards Aleron, a recognition of his deep connection with the whispers and the valuable insights he brings back from their encounters.

As Aleron's interactions with the whisperers continue, the line between his own identity and their influence becomes increasingly blurred. He walks an unreliable tightrope, balancing the desires and aspirations of the council with the cryptic instructions and guidance provided by the whispers. The council members are left grappling with their own conflicting emotions, torn between their reliance on Aleron's newfound wisdom and their growing unease about the extent of the whisperers' control over him.

As Aleron's journey with the whisperers progresses, the tension between his loyalty to the council and his allegiance to the mysterious voices intensifies. The consequences of his actions become more uncertain, leaving everyone involved to question the true intentions of the whispers and the fate of Aleron.

The council observed not only the physical transformation of Aleron but also a shift in his personality. Once noble and direct in his leadership, he now spoke in riddles, emanating an eerie aura during conversations. A sinister smile replaced the noble face, and his direct approach turned sour in the eyes of the council members. Despite these changes, the council continued to respect him as their chosen leader by Pyrothos, their fire god. They believed that their divine patron's will guide his actions.

Aleron's encounters at the peak of the volcano held great significance for him, serving as moments of discovery and transformation. Each meeting propelled him further into a mysterious realm filled with concealed information, fostering his ambition and craving for dominance.

The apparition, acting as a medium for the wisps of secrecy, became not only a source of guidance but also an omen warning of potential peril. A constant reminder of the toll inflicted on him by his connection with these whispers is evident in Aleron's dying aspect, where he appears progressively more decayed.

Aleron, guided by the mysterious riddles of the whispers, discovered the existence of a potent weapon capable of summoning an ancient entity. Keeping this plot concealed from the shadow council, he devised a cunning plan to craft the weapon—a rod infused with the essence of spectral avatars and elements from the Inarus Inferno. This formidable weapon was intended to be a tool of conquest, enabling him to obliterate anything that dared to oppose his ambitions.

The weapon that Aleron had created was a slag-like rod, which he called the Rod of Pyrothos, a potent artifact infused with the ethereal power of the spectral avatars crafted by the skilled high-mages of the Bloodfire and Shadowmancers. This rod was a manifestation of the alliance between the dark ones and the spectral beings. It channeled the spectral energy, imbuing it with the molten essence of Pyrothos, the fire god.

The power of the Rod of Pyrothos was both awe-inspiring and terrifying. It could bend and shape landscapes, harnessing the raw energy of the spectral beings to unleash devastating spells and cataclysmic destruction. Its creation represented a fusion of the dark ones' fire magic and the ethereal forces of the spectral beings, a formidable combination that threatened to tip the scales of power in their favor.

In the shadow council chamber, Aleron raised the Rod of Pyrothos, its exotic beauty captivating the members of the shadow council. With an elven prisoner as a grim example, he pointed the rod unleashing its destructive power. The prisoner's screams echoed as his skin transformed into molten lava, a horrifying display of the rod's might. Aleron, who protected them all with a protection spell, laughed wickedly while explaining that this was just a glimpse of the weapon's capabilities. The prisoner exploded, causing molten to erupt all over the chamber. He emphasized that getting close to their enemies and pointing the rod in their direction would result in a catastrophic end for all of the light empire.

The council members, once united in their pursuit of restoring balance and countering the light empire, now stood divided. Aleron's unveiling of the Rod of Pyrothos and its horrific demonstration left the members grappling with doubts and fears. The extreme nature of the power raised concerns about Aleron's true intentions. Whispers of manipulation by the rogue spectral avatars or even darker forces lingered unspoken. The council faced a pivotal decision, torn between trust and skepticism, as the fate of the elven kind hung in the balance.

Within the shadow council's chamber, tension thickened like a looming storm. As discussions escalated, a rift formed among its members. Skeptics questioned Aleron's true motives and his connection to the mysterious whisperers, while others, consumed by fear, voiced concerns about the uncontrollable power the Rod of Pyrothos held. Despite the internal dissent, Aleron, seemingly unfazed, maintained his conviction. In his eyes, the weapon was a means to reclaim balance, and he was resolute in steering the dark ones toward their destiny, even if it meant facing the shadows within their own ranks. Debates would spark about whether this was a means for balance or to take over as a dark empire emerges.

The council found themselves troubled not just by the presence of the unknown and other possible manipulators but also by their involvement in such a complicated situation. To make matters worse, they had to weigh the advantages against the hazards and decide on a course of action that worked best for their cause. However, none could deny the magnetic appeal of the Rod of Pyrothos. Its ability to reshape the conflict and tip power dynamics inspired even the most cautious council members to consider its potential merits. They grappled with conflicting desires for control and triumph, torn between fully embracing this newfound weapon or questioning what price they might have to pay should they choose to utilize it.

In the face of these internal divisions and uncertainties, the council found itself at the height of a momentous decision. The fate of their alliance, their cause, and the world itself hinged on how they would navigate the revelation of Aleron's hidden weapon and the implications of its creation. The power of the Rod of Pyrothos, infused with spectral energies, remained a double-edged sword, capable of either turning the tides of the conflict or plunging them into even deeper darkness.

• • • • • • •

Havoc, the master of darkness, observed Aleron from the shadows with a twisted smile playing upon his lips. He was pleased to see his loyal servant taking charge and stepping into a leadership role within the shadow council. Aleron's growing thirst for power and his loyal dedication to their cause were exactly what Havoc desired.

The severity of the situation was apparent, with the potential catastrophic consequences of his actions looming over the world. Nevertheless, under Aleron's guidance and Havoc's hidden counsel, Aleron remained steadfast in his determination to utilize spectral energies to his advantage and emerge victorious in the upcoming conflict. While uncertainty shrouded the future, one thing was certain: the battle for power and control was far from concluded.

Yet, satisfaction did not come easily to Havoc. He crafted a shrewd scheme meant to test Aleron's true intentions and unwavering loyalty. This test would push Aleron beyond his boundaries and compel him to make difficult decisions. It became Havoc's order for Aleron to infiltrate their enemy's stronghold and secure a potent artifact that could tip the scales of war in their favor. Aware of the inherent risks involved, Aleron also recognized that failure held no place if he wished to demonstrate his faithfulness and gain Havoc's trust. This artifact was held in Alora within the sanctum of the Arcanists; it was the ancient element that would be used to build the Rod of Pyrothos.

Havoc cloaked his scheme for now, relishing the anticipation of what lay ahead. He understood that Aleron's craving for dominance had its pros and cons. It was crucial to align his servant's ambitions with his own insidious desires. With two pawns at play, Havoc felt confident in penetrating the stronghold and recovering the prized artifact. Specifically choosing Aleron as one of these pieces, Havoc knew that Aleron's insatiable thirst for power would propel him towards victory, regardless of any associated perils they may encounter. Discreetly hiding his true intentions from Aleron became paramount for Havoc, recognizing that a diversion in their objectives could cause extreme chaos.

While Havoc eagerly awaited the commencement of Aleron's mission, he reveled in the sense of anticipation and excitement for what lay ahead. It was crucial for his other pawn, Fumar, to ignite chaos within the kingdom of Alora and divert the attention of the queen's forces, paving the way for Aleron and his Sinister Shadows group to stealthily penetrate the fortified stronghold. Once they successfully obtained the precious artifact, Havoc was acutely aware that it would enable unparalleled power for the dark ones. Unbeknownst to him, however, Aleron's loyalty turned out to be not as steadfast as initially believed; kept secret from Havoc, Aleron harbored his own hidden agenda concerning both said artifact and its potent capabilities.

Havoc observed with a mischievous sparkle in his eyes while Aleron fearlessly displayed his authority amongst the council, completely oblivious to the imminent trial that awaited him. The wicked Shaper had faith that Aleron's intense ambition would ultimately serve his purpose, yet he also understood that only those who were truly strong and committed would endure the impending hardships.

In the concealed recesses of the shadow council's secret chambers, a solemn meeting convened. Aleron, who had an insatiable desire for power, came up with a clever plan to strengthen his position and increase the council's influence. The atmosphere crackled with an aura of darkness as Aleron put forth his proposition to the council members, whose eyes betrayed a mix of awe and anxiety.

With unswerving determination, Aleron revealed his grand proposal—a summoning ritual that demanded an enormous sacrifice. Attentive ears absorbed every detail shared by him as he outlined their current predicament: either submit themselves to the overwhelming might harnessed within the Rod of Pyrothos—an instrument imbued with the very essence of the fire deity—or succumb to their inevitable downfall.

The urgency of the decision weighed heavily on the council members. The Rod of Pyrothos held immense power, but its utilization came at a great cost. Some hesitated, torn between their survival instincts and their loyalty to Aleron. Others, consumed by their own ambition, saw the opportunity to grasp even greater power through the summoning.

The members of the council were aware that their choice would have profound implications, not only for themselves but also for the entire realm. Throughout the night, they engaged in extensive discussions, carefully considering the advantages and disadvantages of every possibility until eventually reaching a resolution.

Aleron's gaze swept across the room, his voice resonating with an eerie determination. He knew that the sacrifice would be substantial, but it was a necessary step to achieve their ultimate goal. With persuasive words and subtle coercion, he compelled the council members to join him in this dangerous endeavor, to channel their collective energy and bring forth a force that would shape the fate of Alora.

The air was heavy with a blend of anxiety and excitement as the council members deliberated on their decision. The forthcoming sacrifices held the weight of eternal transformation for their lives and the kingdom's fate. Aleron, giving a somber nod, wielded the Rod of Pyrothos, witnessing its ethereal energy pulsate in response, prepared to harness their collective strength and unveil the immense fiery power it contained.

The council members prepared themselves for the upcoming ritual while adhering to their shared allegiances and personal goals. The room grew heavy with an electric tension as the shadow council embraced the weight of their choices, knowing that the summoning would unleash forces beyond their control. Left with no alternative, they were compelled to act. The future of the realm hinged upon their triumph, and there was simply no room for failure. With a deep breath, Aleron practiced the incantation, and the council members joined in, their voices blending together in a powerful chorus that echoed through the chamber.

In the heart of a desolate, shadow-clad chamber, the atmosphere crackled with malevolent energy. The time had come for the grand sacrifice, a pivotal moment in the plans of Aleron and the shadow council. The chamber was adorned with ancient symbols and sigils, casting an eerie glow upon the faces of the gathered dark ones.

As the council members prepared themselves for the ritual, news of the impending sacrifice began to ripple through the ranks of the dark ones. Whispers spread like wildfire, stirring a mixture of curiosity, dread, and dissent among the citizens. Some approached the chamber with fear, their instincts urging them to turn away, while others, driven by loyalty or morbid curiosity, could not resist the call.

The chamber soon became crowded with a mixture of council members and onlookers, their eyes fixed on Aleron, who stood at the center, his features twisted with a mixture of zeal and madness. As the chant of the ritual filled the air, a surge of power emanated from the Rod of Pyrothos, its fiery glow growing in intensity. The members of the shadow council felt the surge of energy flowing through their bodies, feeling intense power overcome them.

However, amidst the growing unease, a group of dark ones stepped forward, their voices raised in protest. They voiced their concern for the potential devastation and loss of life that the summoning would bring upon their own kind. Aleron had given in to his hunger for power, so their appeals for reason went unheard. In his pursuit of power, he displayed a readiness to do anything necessary, even at the expense of those belonging to his own group. Realizing the urgency, the dark ones understood that prompt action was necessary to prevent the irreversible repercussions caused by Aleron's deeds.

Aleron's resolve faced a test as dissent surged within and beyond the shadow council's chamber. Onlookers, desperate to halt the preparation ritual, clashed with council members attempting to maintain order. The atmosphere crackled with tension, mirroring the internal strife among the elven leaders. Aleron grew angry by the disturbance; he saw it as he predicted it. Subjects are rising within his own society to challenge the decisions that he made for his citizens and their fire God.

In a moment of ruthless determination, Aleron's eyes blazed with a sinister light as he unleashed the powers of the Rod of Pyrothos upon those who dared to stand in his way. As the dark energy surged forth, its fiery tendrils lashed out, disintegrating those unfortunate souls who had dared to challenge his authority. The dark ones observed in horror as Aleron annihilated his own kin after realizing that their leader had become obsessed with power. In a desperate attempt to halt his actions, the elves united and came face-to-face with Aleron, aiming to put an end to his chaotic rule. However, their unity was met with devastating consequences.

The chamber resonated with a jumbled chorus of shrieks and wails, entwined with the crackling noise produced by flesh colliding with the overwhelming strength of Pyrothos. The atmosphere itself appeared to grow oppressively gloomy as the sacrificial ceremony unfolded, shattering any remaining hope within the spectators' horrified gazes. Amidst it all, Aleron stood motionless in the midst of chaos, his eyes vacant and consumed by an unhinged zeal, while he relished in the devastation he had unleashed. In this transformation into a creature bearing semblance to a monster, Aleron exacted a grim toll upon his own citizens, who suffered most severely through his descent into madness.

In that dreadful moment, the full extent of Aleron's ambition and cruelty were revealed in all their horrifying glory. The council member, once regarded as loyal and highly esteemed, had crossed a threshold by summoning forth the terrifying power contained within the Rod of Pyrothos upon his own kinfolk with neither hesitation nor regret. This act would permanently tarnish his reputation and instill profound feelings of fear and uncertainty among those dark ones who had witnessed such an atrocity. The aftermath of Aleron's deeds left a lasting blemish on the fabric of the dark ones' society as they grappled to make sense of this betrayal from one among their ranks. Numerous individuals began questioning even the very bedrock of their convictions, pondering whether they could ever muster sufficient trust in another council member henceforth.

The aftermath of Aleron's merciless exhibition resulted in a state of utter silence and tangible dread. Once filled with an atmosphere of excited anticipation, the chamber was now filled with misery and hopelessness. The remaining members of the council recoiled in horror and disbelief, their faces displaying a mix of emotions etched deeply into their features. They drew back from the charred remains of their fallen comrades, as if trying to physically distance themselves from the painful reality before them.

The act of betrayal had inflicted a profound wound upon the council, leaving them scarred both mentally and emotionally. It would certainly take time for trust to be restored among them. The burden they carried as guardians of their realm suddenly felt heavier than ever before;

this shocking event served as a harsh reminder that danger could arise from within their own circle.

In the wake of chaos, Aleron stood tall, his gaze reflecting a haunting blend of triumph and derangement. He delighted in his exhibited might, savoring the fear and subservience he had implanted within those who had survived. By his deeds alone, he sent an icy message echoing into the depths of the dark ones' souls. Beyond the sanctuary walls, news of Aleron's sacrifice rapidly spread throughout their community. Whispers carried tales depicting Aleron's merciless manipulation of the Rod of Pyrothos, leaving numerous individuals terrified and haunted. Once esteemed as a council member, he now induced both power and terror, his actions forever etching themselves upon their collective awareness.

Aleron emerged from the chamber, facing the shocked dark one elves with a demeanor that oscillated between conviction and menace. Addressing the elves, he proclaimed that the sacrifice of those who opposed Pyrothos would lead to their rebirth by the fire god's hand. Aleron, presenting himself as the faithful servant of Pyrothos, sought to reassure the dark ones that his actions were guided by divine purpose, a solemn vow to safeguard their kingdom even if it meant annihilation for their enemies. The air lingered with an unsettling mix of fear, awe, and uncertainty, marking the impact of Aleron's bold declaration.

Once the Dark Ones started to grasp the reality of Aleron's genuine essence and ambitions, an air of uncertainty washed over their numbers. Some questioned whether their loyalty to the shadow council was misplaced, while others grappled with the moral implications of their allegiance. Doubt and unease festered within their midst, threatening to fracture the fragile unity that had once bound the dark ones together.

Yet, despite the shock and fear that now colored their perception of Aleron, there were those among the dark ones who still held a twisted respect for his audacity and power. They viewed his ruthless act as a necessary sacrifice for the greater cause, a testament to his loyal commitment to Pyrothos and his own ambitions.

After the sacrifice, Aleron's confidence surged, feeding off his newfound authority. He seized the opportunity to establish himself as the sole leader of the dark ones instead of the shadow council. The fear and admiration he garnered through his actions filled him with joy, as he relished in receiving admiration from those who perceived his uninhibited display of power as a symbol of might.

However, this generated suspicion among the raider clan, who considered Aleron an unpredictable threat capable of turning against them at any moment. They distanced themselves from the dark ones, apprehensive about being associated with Aleron's ruthless tactics and unquenchable thirst for control. This gap in trust jeopardized the delicate alliance that had been forged between these two factions, causing Havoc to feel anxious about his surrogate player on this delicate chessboard of politics.

In the shadowy realms beyond mortal perception, Havoc silently observed Aleron's descent into wickedness through the watchful eyes of his spectral avatars. A twisted satisfaction crept over Havoc as he witnessed his chosen pawn, once noble and guided by purpose, succumb to the darker impulses of power. The joy of seeing mortal life wither away—pleasures that Havoc had relished in the past through his avatars—now took a different form as Aleron's decisions mirrored his own wickedness. The artifact that Havoc had persuaded Aleron to retrieve from Alora was intended as a weapon against enemies, yet Aleron chose to wield it against his own kin. Havoc, recognizing the unpredictable nature of mortals, had opted to observe rather than directly intervene, allowing the seeds of chaos to sprout in the realm of Paranova.

Little did the Dark Ones know that Aleron's audacious act was merely a precursor to a much larger plan, one that would test the limits of their loyalty and devotion. With the council now under his sway, Aleron would seize the opportunity to unleash even greater chaos and destruction upon Alora, all in the name of fulfilling his urgent hunger for power and pleasing his unknown dark master, Havoc, in the guise of Pyrothos. The path ahead would be one of darkness and devastation, with the Rod of Pyrothos serving as both a weapon of terror and a symbol of Aleron's growing dominance over the fate of their world.

Aleron, wielding the ominous Rod of Pyrothos, strode through the dark one kingdom with purpose. Pointing at selected dark elves and raider clan humans, he ordered their gathering into the shadow council chamber. Resistance flared among the chosen, but Aleron, leveraging the sinister power of the rod compelled compliance. The shadowed chamber transformed into another haunting scene as lives were forcibly taken, the clinking of chains resonating against the icy stone walls. The captive's cries and pleas melded into a dissonant symphony, a grim testament to Aleron's determined march toward an unknown fate.

With a sadistic smile curling upon his lips, Aleron raised his arms in a gesture of command. The chanting of an ancient incantation spilled from his lips, a dark melody that seemed to resonate with the very essence of the chamber. It was a forbidden invocation, drawing its power from the life force of those unfortunate souls who now hung at the mercy of his dark desires.

The incantation began, the atmosphere crackled with demonic energy, and the chains that formed the walls of the chamber began to glow with an unholy light, vibrating with an insidious power that pierced their souls with the feel and sight of it. Facial features etched on the unfortunate mortals which had now become twisted with agony and fear as they fought against the restrictions of the chains grasping them while they squirmed and shouted in the suffocating atmosphere.

Within the chamber, the life force of the chained elves and humans was gradually drained, their vitality seeping into Aleron like a river of dark essence. Their energy sustained him, fueling his twisted ambitions and augmenting his powers. The captives withered before his eyes, their bodies shriveling and contorting as their life essence was sucked dry.

Out there, the situation was chaotic and terrifying. Both dark ones and raiders alike who watched were caught between feeling horror and fascination. Some of them even went insane, their minds surrendering to the attraction of Aleron's ominous authority. They chanted his name with a mixture of respect and desperation, thinking that by aligning themselves with this evil force, they could evade his anger.

Amidst the frantic cries and intense chants, an overwhelming sense of impending doom filled the atmosphere. The sacrifice taking place in the chamber served as a representation of Aleron's desire for power and complete disregard for others' lives. It was a bone-chilling reminder that he would go to any length to achieve his objectives, even if it required devouring the very souls of those who had once stood by him.

The moment Aleron positioned himself at the very heart of this eerie display, a chilling sensation crept upon those who observed it. He took great pleasure in their terror and helplessness as he indulged in the dominance that their torment provided him. The chant of his name grew louder, echoing through the chamber and beyond, solidifying his position as the dark force that now commanded the allegiance and awe of the faithful while instilling terror in the hearts of those who dared to oppose him.

With the exhaustion of life's essence from the captives, Aleron witnessed a profound stillness that settled upon the chamber. The stolen energy lingered in the air, crackling with a strange intensity and enveloping him like a murky halo. Holding the Rod of Pyrothos tightly, Aleron felt it pulsate within his hand, ablaze with a fiery radiance that resonated with its newfound boundless power. He stood tall, reveling in the surge coursing through his veins—aware that this marked but the beginning of his ruthless reign—and fully committed to attaining undisputed control without any reservations. Clutching onto the Rod of Pyrothos firmly signified invincibility; soon enough, those daring to confront him would comprehend fear at its depths. Contentedly smirking inwardly, anticipation arose as he greedily contemplated unraveling unprecedented levels of commotion and devastation in this vulnerable world.

Radiating a composed determination, Aleron gracefully emerged from the chamber, bleakness and sorrow now enveloping its abandoned surroundings. The crowd that had gathered outside erupted into a chaotic mix of outrage and support. Shouts of anger and slurs filled the air, directed at the figure who had condemned their comrades to such a fate. Yet, combined among the calls for condemnation, there were those who cheered for Aleron, enthralled by the raw display of power they had witnessed. One could argue that the cheers from those who supported Aleron were not genuine and instead stemmed from a fear of being on the wrong side of someone with such immense power.

Disregarding the commotion surrounding him, Aleron navigated his way towards the rim of the volcano. The earth beneath his feet quivered with dormant energy from the slumbering behemoth inside the Inarus Inferno. Emitting smoky tendrils from its depths, this forewarned of the catastrophic forces confined within. Upon reaching an apex, silence descended upon the onlookers. All gazes fixated on Aleron, their facial features revealing a blend of apprehension, curiosity, and admiration. Some regarded him with disdain, as they perceived him solely as a power-hungry manipulator who had forsaken his kin for personal ambition. Yet there were others who revered him—a personification of resilience and authority in their God's presence.

Amidst insults and derogatory remarks directed at Aleron, jubilant chants from devoted followers muffled such animosity. Their voices sung in a symphony of worship—their unwavering faith resting upon his aptitude to reshape their world and exact vengeance against those responsible for their oppression. In Aleron, there existed a ray of hope—a ruthless leader set to actualize the long-awaited transformation.

Gazing at the edge, Aleron elevated the Rod of Pyrothos with great height, its incandescent brilliance casting a glow on his face. The acclamations intensified, blending into a deafening boom that reverberated through the atmosphere. At that instant, Aleron sensed the burden of his recently acquired might—the climax of his sinister cravings and convoluted ambitions.

With the rumbling volcano beneath him, Aleron surveyed the faces of the spectators with a mix of defiance and triumph gleaming in his eyes. The uproar and adoration that enveloped him were pure ecstasy as he recognized his success in dominating the forces of darkness. Although the path he had embarked upon was fraught with peril and required great sacrifices, it was a journey he undertook with focus and determination.

Aware that he had crossed an ethical boundary by delving into uncharted regions of darkness, fear did not consume him. He reveled in being the sole master of his own fate and holding powers that surpassed those possessed by a few others. Realizing that it was impossible to go backwards at this point, one cast longing glances over the wreckage he had left behind. The chosen course would either lead to resounding glory or utter disaster, yet regardless, whatever came next, Aleron stood prepared to face it head-on.

With a final firm stride, Aleron embraced his preordained fate. He exclaimed triumphantly, unleashing a resounding shout that stretched across the scorching chasm of the inferno depths. In doing so, he asserted his dominance and boldly announced his war against those who had dared to oppose him. The onlookers erupted in sync with this outburst, harmonizing their voices into an ensemble of eager anticipation and zealous passion as they awaited the imminent sequence of cataclysmic events. Although aware that his journey remained incomplete, Aleron possessed an unwavering resolve to see it through to its very end. His commitment was unshakeable; he had traversed great distances and made considerable sacrifices, which rendered turning back unthinkable now.

Elevating his head proudly and kindling fearlessness within his heart, he advanced towards unfamiliar territory with a readiness to confront any forthcoming obstacle lying in wait for him. Succumbing into darkness amidst the fiery recesses of the volcano's core bestowed upon him instant legendary status—a symbolic embodiment showcasing how determination coupled with immense power can propel one toward achieving unparalleled greatness.

As Aleron gestured for the members of the shadow council to advance, they moved as one entity, their expressions concealed behind a blend of excitement and unease. The atmosphere pulsated with a captivating vitality, hinting at the forthcoming disruption that was about to be set in motion. With each progressive stride they took, the earth quivered under their feet, acknowledging the magnitude of their combined authority.

Aleron's ominous instructions served as the guide for the ritual. Chants filled the air, ancient words echoing through the chamber and intertwining with the rumbling of the awakened volcano. As if the evil forces at work had stirred nature itself, the storm outside grew worse and swirled with an otherworldly fury.

As Aleron poured the molten lava into the Rod of Pyrothos, an ominous red glow radiated from its core. The moment the lava met the metal, a bolt of crimson lightning crackled through the skies, striking the rod with unsettling precision as Aleron raised the Rod towards the sky. The collision of elemental forces sent shockwaves throughout the vicinity, causing the very foundation of the volcano to tremble. When Aleron displayed his strength, the earth erupted in an outburst of ash and lava. The atmosphere became shrouded by smoke and ash as the air echoed with the thunderous sound of nature's wrath.

Aleron released a laugh that pierced the atmosphere, filling the landscape with an unsettling echo. The intense rush of energy flowing through his whole body captivated him, and his eyes shimmered with an untamed passion. In that moment, he stood tall, appearing to transcend the limits of sapient existence, invincible to any restrictions that may be placed upon him.

The rumbling of the volcano outside mirrored the level of insanity within Aleron. The landscape shook with great force as cracks emerged and released rivers of molten lava. The once peaceful terrain has suddenly transformed into a scene of devastating disorder. Aleron harnessed the untamed power of the volcano, directing it to satisfy his vile cravings. He realized that no force in the world could withstand him as he stood among the devastation he had inflicted.

Aleron's laughter grew louder amid the mayhem, blending in with the volcano's thundering roars. His thoughts teetered on the brink of insanity, delighting in the chaotic harmony he had produced. During this state of extreme confusion, he convinced himself that he was a conduit through which the desires of mysterious entities were communicated, an amplifier of disorder called upon to transform the natural world according to his own design. The sight of the raging storm and the volcano's eruption only fueled Aleron's outrageous laughter. His body trembled with a mixture of delight and insanity as he soaked in the chaos he had created. The overwhelming force flowing within him eliminated all rationality, resulting in a mere shell of his former self.

The chamber was filled with a mix of awe and fear as Aleron's laughter echoed throughout the inferno. The dark ones and members of the shadow council who surrounded him watched in various states of fascination and terror. Some were captivated by his demonstration of power, their eyes revealing a twisted sense of admiration for the wrath he had unleashed. Others, however, experienced a growing discomfort and an unsettling doubt about the consequences that awaited them.

Beyond the confines of the ritual area, spectators struggled to reconcile their feelings of horror and fascination as they bore witness to the volcanic eruption and chaotic storm unfolding before them. Once tranquil surroundings transformed into an inferno engulfed in molten lava and swirling tempests. The earth trembled violently beneath their feet, displaying scars in their form like jagged cracks etched across the landscape.

However, a feeling of unease slowly began to creep into the hearts of those who had initially shown support for Aleron. They could no longer disregard the screams and pleas surrounding the confined souls within the inferno; their anguished cries were carried by the breeze. The true weight of Aleron's insatiable desire for power became blatantly evident. The devastation brought about by his actions was irrefutable, causing once-optimistic onlookers to confront the harsh reality of consequences. In addition to witnessing innocent lives tormented in this chaotic setting, they were left with a combination of apprehension and sorrow. It was abundantly clear that Aleron's pursuit of power exacted a heavy toll, one that would have lasting repercussions long into the future.

As the fiery bolts of red lightning raged on and the volcano's ominous roars grew louder, a deep realization swept over the spectators. Aleron's laughter morphed into something terrifyingly sinister, resounding with an unsettling echo. No longer were his laughs those of a man lost to insanity; they mirrored those of a tyrant delighting in the agony inflicted upon others.

Glimpses of fear and remorse darted between certain members of the shadowy council and the dark entities present. They exchanged wary glances, their eyes showing a mixture of fear and regret. Seduced by promises of power and influence, they now bore witness to the untold horrors spawned by their ill-fated choices. Deep within themselves, though it pained them to realize it, they acknowledged that they had willingly become mere pawns in a game far more uncertain than what their minds could ever fathom.

As the minutes elapsed, Aleron's boisterous laughter gradually faded away, giving way to a strange stillness that engulfed the atmosphere. The spectators were suddenly overwhelmed by the chaos of what had happened and haunted by the knowledge of their own participation in this dark and twisted chapter of their world's history. In that instant, Aleron cemented his legacy in the realms of darkness; his name became synonymous with the unspeakable horrors unleashed upon the populace.

The repercussions of his actions cast an ominous shadow over sapience, serving as a constant reminder of how far one could descend in their pursuit for power and the catastrophic aftermath it entailed.

As a disquieting stillness descended, the ground underneath them trembled with increasing force. An unsettling rumble echoed in the atmosphere, causing unease among all those present. From its slumber, a gigantic being made of solidified slag and blazing molten lava awoke in an abrupt outburst of scorching energy. The beast towered above the nearby terrain, creating a colossal shadow that instilled fear.

The group stood rooted to the spot, consumed by fear as the beast bellowed with unnerving force, fixating its menacing gaze upon them. They realized that their reckless pursuit of power had inadvertently stirred an alarming entity they were utterly unequipped to confront. The repercussions of their actions had finally caught up to them; henceforth, surrendering them into this intimidating creature's hands was inevitable. Fully aware that swift action was necessary for survival during this harrowing ordeal, they weakly extended their trembling hands towards their weapons—nothing more than feeble defenses against impending doom.

The Fire God, known as Pyrothos, had been summoned. Its massive form pulsed with an infernal heat, radiating waves of scorching energy that distorted the air around it. Its blazing eyes, filled with a penchant for destruction, surveyed the realm with a malevolent gaze. Those individuals, who were ready to engage in combat, soon understood that their deity had manifested. In a swift turn of events, they put away their weapons and celebrated with great joy. Aleron was the one responsible for breathing life into their divine entity. The elves fell to their knees in gratitude, praising Aleron for his devotion to Pyrothos. The fire god, pleased with the display of loyalty, spoke to Aleron in a voice that boomed like thunder. Aleron felt a surge of power coursing through his veins, and he knew that he had gained the favor of the mighty Pyrothos.

As Pyrothos began taking its first strides, the landscape cracked beneath its colossal weight, fracturing and rupture as if not capable of enduring the weight of its scorching existence. The beast spewed streams of molten lava, causing a path of burning destruction behind it. The sheer magnitude of its devastating power caused buildings to collapse, trees to turn to ash, and the ground itself appeared to crack. Aleron raised his rod, and Pyrothos obeyed, unleashing a torrent of flames that engulfed everything in its path. The dark one army scattered in terror as the fiery breath almost consumed their ranks, leaving nothing but smoldering ruins in its wake. Aleron laughed as it consumed some of his kin.

It was time for Aleron to tame this beast fully. He knew that Pyrothos could be a powerful weapon in his hands, but he also knew that he needed to be careful not to let the entity's destructive tendencies get out of control. Aleron was determined to train Pyrothos to use his flames only for the good of their kingdom, and together they would become an unstoppable force.

Amidst the chaos and destruction, the roars of Pyrothos screamed through the air, a deafening sound of raw power and devastation. The colossal entity moved with purpose, its molten body leaving scorching imprints wherever it treaded. Rivers of lava cascaded down its form, consuming everything in their path and leaving behind a desolate wasteland.

The searing heat coming from the fire god illuminated the sky, turning it a sinister shade of red. The air itself seemed to sizzle and warp under its intense presence, making it difficult to breathe. The ground beneath trembled persistently, as if in constant agony from the wrath of Pyrothos.

The pungent odor of burning rubble filled the air, thickening it around them as smoke clouds blotted out the sky. The landscape that had once tranquilized the kingdom was now caught up in a whirlwind of disorder and distress, its serenity devoured by flames wielding their destructive dance.

Fear gripped the hearts of those who witnessed the manifestation of Pyrothos. The dark ones and the raider clan, who had hoped to control this force of nature, now faced the stark reality of their creation. The magnitude of Pyrothos' power surpassed their expectations, and a sense of unease washed over them. As they watched Pyrothos continue to unleash its own wrath, destroying everything in its path by moving, they realized the catastrophic consequences of playing with such dangerous forces. The only hope now was to find a way to contain it before it caused any more destruction.

The summoning of Pyrothos had unleashed a cataclysmic force upon the realm, and the dark ones and the raider clan now faced the daunting task of attempting to control the unleashed fury. Their alliance, once forged with aspirations of power and conquest, now seemed small and insignificant in the face of such primal and destructive might.

A sense of despair settled upon them, overshadowing any lingering traces of their earlier confidence. They watched helplessly as their carefully laid plans crumbled like ash and their alliance shattered under the weight of their arrogance. They had gambled with the very essence of fire and were now reaping the catastrophic consequences.

The Dark Ones and the Raider Clan soon realized that Pyrothos' immense power had surpassed their well-thought-out strategies and calculations with its unstoppable rampage. The sheer force of the fire god made the world quiver in fear, forcing them to face the consequences of their decisions. Their once formidable alliance now lay in ruins, a result of their pride and ambition leading them astray towards destruction. In contemplation of Pyrothos' devastating wrath, they could only mourn their foolishness and regretful arrogance that brought them to this predicament. They were unable to tame or control the fire god's full might, left only with fragments of broken plans as they attempted to reconstruct from mere ashes.

Aleron defiantly remained in the middle of the chaos and confusion, his laughter blending with the inferno's sizzling. His twisted smile revealed a mind engulfed in madness and an unquenchable thirst for power. In his deranged state, he believed he had achieved a glorious triumph, oblivious to the catastrophic consequences that unfolded around him. His success pleased Havoc, who reveled in the destruction and chaos that surrounded Aleron.

In the quiet corners of Paranova, unseen by mortal eyes, Havoc, the celestial Shaper, observed the unfolding events with a mixture of fascination and anticipation. The elemental entities, ancient and dormant, held the promise of power and chaos. Havoc, curious about the potential consequences, chose not to directly intervene but instead watched as mortals like Aleron navigated the delicate dance between temptation and the unknown. In the vast tapestry of Paranova's fate, the celestial Shaper found a renewed sense of excitement, eager to witness how the awakening of these entities would shape the future of the mortal realms so that he could use them for his own wicked manipulations.

Havoc had long awaited the day when one of his whisper followers would rise to such heights of madness and power, and Aleron had not disappointed. Despite the devastation he had wrought, Aleron believed himself to be a conqueror, not realizing that he was merely a pawn in Havoc's game. Although the magnitude of the fire god's power could have overwhelmed them, Havoc believed that they would eventually emerge resilient and even more resolute.

The southern land was left in a state of devastation, and the fate of Alora, the kingdom of the dark ones, along with its residents had hovered on an uncertain outcome. The summoning of Pyrothos had unleashed a fiery tempest, and now the dark ones, the raider clan, and all those who witnessed the birth of this destructive force were left to confront the aftermath of Aleron's choices.

The awakening of Pyrothos had caused unforeseen events among all of the other entities that lay dormant in the world of Paranova, unleashing devastating events throughout the continent.

Chapter 9: Disturbance of Elements

Over thousands of years have passed since the conception of Paranova, during which the elven society went through a phase of reconstruction and healing. During this duration, mortal races remained oblivious to the Shapers' existence as mysterious celestial beings. Rather than contemplating the celestial beings, their focus was fixed upon the motionless Tree and Stone Avatars. These revered entities were believed to encapsulate the very essence of nature and wisdom. Formerly sought after for guidance and blessings, these avatars entered into a deep slumber, leaving behind nothing but an absence of their vibrant energies in the realm of mortals.

The reason behind their state of inactivity was a puzzle that remained unsolved for mortals, veiled in hushed conversations and pondering. Ancient stories and texts subtly hinted at disruptions in the natural order, causing a rupture in the flow of enchantment that severed the connection between mortal races and higher celestial forces. Some theorized that it was a fallout from catastrophic incidents that transpired during the old war with Gantum, while others suspected hidden agendas driven by malevolent entities intent on disturbing the delicate balance.

Stories as ancient as time itself and prophecies shrouding dormant figures known as Avatars are rich with mysterious tales of the past and beliefs that have been passed down through countless generations. These noble beings bear immense importance, for they are believed to possess extraordinary abilities intricately intertwined with nature's fabric and elemental forces.

As per the ancient tales, the Tree Avatar serves as a physical embodiment of the entire forest and its existence. It is believed that this mystical being resides inside a remarkable, revered tree that Mother Nature herself carefully chose. Its purpose is to safeguard and nourish the equilibrium of the natural world. The tree avatar possesses an extraordinary gift of communicating with all living beings, ranging from minute insects right up to magnificent creatures, ultimately earning its honorary title as the woodland's custodian and protector. It is strongly believed that whenever imminent danger befalls the forest or nature becomes unsettled, this ethereal guardian awakens from its deep slumber in order to restore harmony and defend the lands.

The Stone Avatar, conversely, is linked to mountains, boulders, and the very ground. It is perceived as a formidable energy intertwined with the innermost essence of the planet. The stone avatar is said to embody the strength and stability of Paranova, possessing the power to manipulate rocks, create earthquakes, and shape the landscape. It is considered a symbol of endurance and wisdom and is praised by many as the protector of the foundation.

The cultural perspectives and traditions of mortals are linked to the tree and stone avatars and are diverse among different communities and regions. Nevertheless, there are prevalent themes that resonate across multiple cultures. These beliefs frequently emphasize the interdependent relationship between sapience and the environment, highlighting the importance of maintaining harmony and showing honor for nature.

To pay homage to and establish communication with the avatars, ceremonies and rituals are performed. Typically, these rituals involve making offerings to symbolic trees and rocks while engaging in prayers and chants intended to summon forth the spirits of the avatars. Spiritual leaders, shamans, or unique individuals regarded as having a special connection with the avatars and natural elements conduct these practices. They serve as vehicles for seeking guidance, protection, and blessings from these slumbering embodiments of spiritual forces.

Legends also tell tales of predictions linked to the stirring of the avatars. It is believed that in times marked by eminent danger or disturbance, a selected individual will emerge as the fated champion, whose purpose is to awaken and channel the abilities of the avatars. While these prophecies vary, they consistently herald a hero who will reinstate balance, conquer wicked forces, and shield the natural world from annihilation.

The folklore and narratives connected to the avatars have served as wellsprings of motivation, respect, and direction for countless generations. They forge a significant bond with nature while reminding communities of their duty to safeguard and maintain the environment. These epic tales endure through endless retelling and celebration, securing that the wisdom paired with beliefs concerning the avatars persists throughout future lineages.

The ancient legends and prophecies involve a remarkable phenomenon known as the Spectral Avatars. These mysterious beings are closely associated with the ethereal realm and possess extraordinary supernatural capabilities. Unlike the tree and stone avatars, who acquire their power from the tangible world, the spectral avatars act as a conduit between mortal existence and the spiritual plane.

Per mythological accounts, these spectral entities can materialize in diverse forms while reigning over realms such as brightness, darkness, fantasies, and illusions. Typically portrayed as gleaming apparitions exuding an otherworldly luminescence, they serve both as guardians responsible for maintaining spiritual balance and custodians of ancient wisdom.

The cultural beliefs surrounding avatar avatars differ among different cultures and communities. Some view them as benevolent beings, while others consider them more ambiguous or even mischievous. However, there is a common thread in their association with mysticism and the exploration of the unseen realms.

Rituals and ceremonies associated with the avatar avatars often involve conjuring their presence through meditative practices, incantations, or the use of special artifacts. These rituals aim to establish a connection between the mortal realm and the ethereal plane, seeking guidance, enlightenment, or protection from the avatars.

The prophecies regarding the avatar avatars often speak of their emergence during times of great spiritual upheaval or when the boundaries between realms are weakened. It is believed that they will choose a worthy individual as their vessel or champion to carry out their divine purpose. These prophecies often depict the spectral avatars as catalysts for transformation, guiding sapience towards a higher level of consciousness or resolving conflicts between worlds.

As the civilizations slowly rebuilt and recovered, individuals of wisdom and spiritual inclination pondered the significance of the dormant avatars. Scholars scoured ancient manuscripts, seeking clues to their slumber, while mystics and prophets meditated and communed with the ethereal energies, hoping to unravel the secrets held within.

In Paranova, mortals view avatars as singular divine entities, unaware that they are scattered across the world. Their dormancy is orchestrated by the Keeper, a celestial Shaper who severed the connection between Shapers and Avatars. This separation had rendered the avatars dormant, awaiting the cosmic symphony that signals their awakening.

As the Keeper severed ties with the avatars, rendering them dormant, an unforeseen consequence unfolded. The primal energy was stirred by an ancient Gantum war thousands of years ago that lay beneath the lands of Paranova. The energies beneath the surface had gone unnoticed by the Shapers due to the disconnection between Shapers and avatars, a consequence of the colossal conflict that temporarily blinded them to the happenings in the world currently.

The destructive might of these giant-like beings had destroyed much of the land on Paranova, causing the elemental energies below to churn for a millennium. Although the surface had healed over time, the primal forces continued to stir beneath, awaiting a fateful trigger that would set off a chain reaction, potentially reshaping the world once more.

Pyrothos, a potent entity that manifested fire and heat in physical form, appeared, setting off the extraordinary event known as the Disturbance of Elements. Pyrothos' manifestation had a profound impact on the other elemental entities, causing them to stir and unleash their powers upon the world.

Vigoroth, the embodiment of earth and plants, responded to Pyrothos' presence by shaking the gigantic trees with immense force. The earth quivered under Vigoroth's power, sending tremors throughout the land and disturbing the primal forces of nature.

Maravas, the water entity, responded to the call of Pyrothos by stirring the seas. Vast waves rose and fell, tides intensified, and mighty currents surged across the oceans. Maravas' influence was felt in every drop of water, from the smallest stream to the mightiest sea, as it danced and swirled in response to the disturbance.

Zephyro, the air serpent had unfurled its colossal wings and let out resounding bellows upon the mountain peaks and into the valleys. The winds grew fierce and untamed, carrying Zephyro's voice across the land, stirring the air and setting in motion great gusts and breezes that swept through forests, mountains and plains.

The disturbance of elements also stirred several other entities of different natures. Valash, the crystal entity, emanated a dazzling radiance, causing crystals and gems to shimmer and resonate with elemental energy. Strelka and Strenoth, the embodiments of darkness and shadows, cast their ethereal presence, deepening the shadows and bringing forth an eerie atmosphere. Phagen, the entity of death and decay had exuded a chilling aura, infusing the land with a sense of finality and the transformation of dead mortals and creatures alike. Chromaticus, the entity of energy and vibration, pulsed with an electrifying essence, causing the very fabric of reality to vibrate and shimmer. Vitralis, the sapience entity, exuded an enlightening aura, dispersing ignorance and enlightening mortals with its serene presence. Apolis, the light entity, emanated a luminous glow, dispelling darkness and illuminating the world with its radiant presence.

Each entity responded uniquely to Pyrothos' awakening, channeling their powers and characteristics into the world. The ensuing balance of elemental forces created a spectacle of raw energy and immense power, forever etching the event in the annals of history and inspiring awe and admiration among those who witnessed it.

The disturbance of the elements was indeed a complicated and awe-inspiring phenomenon for the mortal races inhabiting Paranova. The diverse reactions of different civilizations and cultures reflected the varying beliefs and fears that emerged in the wake of this extraordinary event.

The western mortals, residing on islands surrounded by the vast seas, were gripped with fear as Maravas, the water entity, stirred the seas into intense waves. Fearing the wrath of the sea god, they were concerned that the strong surges would swallow their islands. Their lives and livelihoods were deeply intertwined with the ocean, and the unpredictable behavior of the waters left them feeling vulnerable and apprehensive.

In the heart of the forests, where the earth-like entity was honored and worshipped as a God, the stirring of Vigoroth caused concern and confusion. The mortals believed that their actions had disturbed the balance of the natural world, potentially angering their tree God. They anxiously sought to appease the deity, engaging in rituals and offerings to restore harmony and prevent any calamity that might befall them.

The dwarves, renowned for their craftsmanship and mining skills, welcomed the phenomenon of elements as a bountiful gift from the ground itself. They saw it as an opportunity to unearth rare and precious resources such as shining ores, crystals, and gems that were revealed by Valash's shaking of the mountains. The dwarves were filled with glee and eagerly set out to gather these newfound treasures, seeing it as a blessing bestowed upon them.

On the lofty peaks, the mortals believed they had disturbed the legendary air serpent, Zephyro, when they witnessed the intense winds and bellowing gusts. Fearing the serpent's wrath, they thought it might descend upon them and bring destruction with its ferocious power. The dwarves of the peaks huddled together, seeking shelter and protection from the tempestuous winds, hoping that the ancient legend would spare them. While most of the humans nestled in the mountains, had sought shelter in areas away from their homelands in the mountains.

Vitralis exerted a profound influence on the mortal sapience, bringing both tranquility and enlightenment. However, this impact created a strange fluctuation in perception during the ongoing disturbance on the surface. As the waves of Vitralis swept over, mortals experienced moments of enlightenment then only to feel depressed and lost when the influence dissipated, creating a delicate dance of emotions on the surface of Paranova.

The ongoing struggles between brightness and darkness caused by the entities of light and dark, the vibrant bursts of lightning and turbulent climate that raced through Paranova and the haunting existence of death and deterioration to sinister revival had triggered widespread alarm among the mortals throughout the land.

The mortals were convinced that the world was approaching its conclusion when they observed the confrontation between opposing powers and witnessed the strange alteration of their surroundings. These extraordinary occurrences tested their convictions and implanted feelings of doubt and fear regarding what lay ahead in the times to come.

As Pyrothos manifested into a colossal physical entity, mortals trembled at the sight of him roaming the southern lands, instilling fear. Among the dark ones, this entity was hailed as a god, their celebrations echoing worship. With an individual attempting to control this formidable force, the entire world grappled with the ominous anticipation of its potential cataclysmic impact.

In the face of such mysterious phenomena, the mortal races of Paranova grappled with their own interpretations, fears, and hopes. The awakening of the elements left a memorable mark on their collective consciousness, forever altering their perspectives on the powers that governed their world and the fragile balance that existed between mortals and the divine.

Unbeknownst to the mortals below the celestial realm, Havoc harnessed the foreign arcane energy that the Archon had given to the world thousands of years earlier and he planned the creation of evil entities entangled with primal energies below the surface. The combinations of the giant-like beings that previously roamed the land, the dark energies manipulated by Havoc, and the awakening of Pyrothos have undoubtedly caused the elemental disruption.

Unveiling the knowledge of primal energies and entities before the other Shapers, Havoc harnessed the arcane energies to craft twin entities of darkness. Bestowing upon them the names Strelka and Strenoth, mirroring his two sinister blades he wielded in combat, Havoc envisioned these dark entities as agents of chaos, capable of disrupting the balance of divinity in Apolis, the natural energy woven into the fabric of Paranova. The creation of these sinister beings marked Havoc's calculated move to tip the scales towards discord and unpredictability in the unfolding disturbance of elements.

Havoc, the master of dark arts had maintained a veil of secrecy around his hidden plans for chaos, successfully concealing the true nature of the dark entities, Strelka and Strenoth. Even the Shapers, including the

Archon, his trusted partner in schemes, were oblivious to the fact that these entities seemed natural to the world. However, in reality, the result was Havoc's intricate manipulations. The dark entities seamlessly blended into the world, and their origins shrouded in mystery as Havoc continued to weave the threads of discord within the fabric of Paranova.

•••••••

In the celestial realm, where time unfolded at a slower pace, the Shapers observed Paranova's evolution over thousands of years since the creation of Humans and Dwarves. Despite the significant role they played in that initial creation, the Shapers gradually withdrew their direct involvement from the mortal world. Unable to communicate with their Avatars or witness events from their perspective, the Shapers chose a more distant vantage point, understanding the necessity to refrain from meddling in every unfolding instance on Paranova.

During this time, the Provisioner became the mentor to the Archon, imparting crucial knowledge for her future ascension within the Chaos sector. Bonding over the creation of newer mortal races, their connection waned as the Provisioner's old habits led to a growing distance between the Archon and himself. Meanwhile, the Provisioner and the Oracle continued their collaborative efforts, sketching blueprints for new mortals inspired by the ever-changing world.

The Keeper and the Forger found inspiration in their own domains, generating ideas for avatars and crafting detailed models of landmarks and terrains. The two would spend time together debating which model would best suit Paranova or the worlds to come. The Anarchist, yearning for chaos, had hoped the mortals would continue to stir more disorder in the world. He was anticipating the inner dramas that attracted the mortals; it was his own entertainment among the celestial realms, since he chose to be less direct with the creation aspect during the creation of Paranova.

In nights of distance from the other Shapers, the Archon found comfort in the company of the Anarchist, who shared some knowledge that she desperately sought from the Provisioner. Havoc, unseen among the Shapers, covertly plotted with spectral avatars and the current happenings in the world. He occasionally slipped into the Archon's chambers to gather information about the other Shapers.

While the avatars remained dormant, the Oracle and the Provisioner cherished moments of passionate discussions about the future direction they envisioned for mortals. Their talks were filled with the excitement of possibilities and a shared exploration of the realms of imagination. The Oracle rejoiced in finding peace without the gift of sight as she embraced the freedom to imagine with her own imaginative mind, an inspiration that the Provisioner himself had sparked. Nights were spent listening to the Provisioner's vivid descriptions of the world, and in those moments, love deepened between them.

Despite the emergence of a relationship between the Provisioner and the Archon, a development that caused a tinge of worry in the Oracle's celestial heart, she understood the inseparable bond they shared. The dormant avatars provided a foundation for the continued connection between the Oracle and the Provisioner, a connection rooted in mutual understanding and the shared vision they held for the unfolding destiny of Paranova.

As time unfolded, the Shapers patiently awaited the evolution of their mortal creation, finding comfort or impatience in their daily tasks. The Provisioner aimed to instill in both sectors an understanding that creation, with its wonderous excitements, had also demanded respect for the process and time for them to grow.

....

As the elemental entity manifested on Paranova, an ominous feeling spread throughout the celestial realm, prompting the Provisioner to call an emergency meeting among the Shapers. Gathering around to witness the unfolding event, a sense of anticipation gripped each Shaper. Initially, disagreement arose between the Provisioner and the Anarchist. The Provisioner, prioritizing the protection of the world, sought to stop the potential risks posed by the awakened elemental entity. In contrast, the Anarchist urged the Shapers to embrace the dynamic and transformative nature of the emerging entity.

Unbeknownst to the Shapers, dormant primal elemental energies beneath the surface have stirred since the Shapers began altering the world. Armed with prior knowledge, the Provisioner stressed the importance of maintaining stability and minimizing potential risks that the disturbed elements could pose, foreseeing a ripple effect leading to destruction among the mortal races and their world.

The Anarchist challenged conventional notions of control, advocating for personal freedom, self-expression, and the liberation of natural happenings. He perceived the disturbance as an opportunity for change and transformation for mortals. The stark contrast in views unsettled each sector as they aligned with their respective leaders. Amidst the discord, it was the Archon who stepped forward, armed with information and influence, aiming to bridge the gap and devise a solution.

As the Archon, entrusted to lead alongside the Provisioner in the creation of worlds, addressed the Shapers about the energies she had sensed before dispersing the arcane energy across Paranova, a wave of revelation swept through the celestial assembly. Unbeknownst to her at the time, the energy remained undisclosed as it hadn't posed a risk then. Apologizing for her detachment during the idle times of mortal evolution, the Archon acknowledged her oversight.

The Archon revealed that during her dissemination of arcane energy across the world, she detected dormant raw elemental energies beneath the surface. At that time, these energies appeared natural, and she kept this discovery to herself. Unbeknownst to her, this dormant force would eventually become a crucial factor in the unfolding events. Meanwhile, Havoc, lurking in the shadows during the Shaper meeting, maintained a silence that masked his prior awareness of these energies. Purposefully concealing his knowledge, he studied the elemental forces while the Shapers peacefully awaited the evolution of Paranova.

As questions unraveled, it became clear that her withholding aimed not to hinder Paranova's progress. The Provisioner, though visibly disappointed, assumed responsibility for the decision to sever ties with avatars. The Oracle, longing for sight, regretted not foreseeing the unfortunate events preceding the elemental disturbance threatening their world.

The Archon, now acting as a neutral mediator, urged the Chaos sector to heed the Provisioner's viewpoints. She insisted that energies beyond the comprehension of mortals were now threatening the world they had collectively created. The Anarchist, proud to witness the Archon becoming a neutral force, concurred, instructing the remaining sector to devise a solution to aid the Order sector.

As the Archon left the room, the Provisioner directed his energy towards her, expressing his happiness at having her back in the fold. Hiding her excitement but eager for his attention, the Archon smiled back, adding a wink. She encouraged both the Provisioner and the Oracle to meet with her after the meeting and expressed that it could be a solution to the current events throughout the world.

The Archon, a brilliant Shaper from the Chaos sector now tasking herself with maintaining the balance of primordial forces, recognized the potential for chaos and destruction in the elemental disturbance. Seizing this spectacular event as an opportunity to work with the Order sector and fulfill her own desires, she understood the crucial need to restore balance and intervene. Recognizing that the mortal races were ill-prepared to handle the consequences without the guidance of avatars, the Archon devised a plan that embraced the unpredictable and disruptive essence of chaos itself.

Her internal battle stemmed from the realization that she had distanced herself from the Provisioner and the other Shapers. Mundane tasks undertaken by the Provisioner throughout both sectors bored her, and she craved excitement and surprises at every turn. Despite this, she acknowledged the chaotic mind of the Provisioner and was drawn to the dual nature he exposed. Throughout her time of mentorship, she absorbed the Provisioner's teachings and observed his pursuits, genuinely caring for him beyond leadership. Her desire was to be both his partner in guiding Paranova and his intimate companion. However, a constant inner struggle between the dynamics of power and love hindered her from fully embracing the path she yearned for.

The Oracle played a significant role in the Archon's pursuit of affection from the Provisioner. While the Archon succeeded in becoming the Provisioner's intimate partner on nights after the creation of mortals, the Oracle persistently mirrored this connection throughout the time thereafter. The Archon found herself increasingly alone, hearing laughter from the Provisioner's sanctuary where the Oracle accompanied him. Despite her attempts to rekindle their intimacy, the unsettling presence of the Oracle in the shadows of their shared history remained a constant challenge.

As the Provisioner and the Oracle made their way to meet the Archon, a sense of caution hung in the air. The Oracle, being perceptive over the Archon, shared her own insights with the Provisioner, urging him to be vigilant about the Archon's sudden involvement from her usual distance. She spoke of past seductions and warned him of potential hidden agendas, emphasizing the urgency of the situation and the world's dependence on their choices. Grateful for the Oracle's support, the Provisioner acknowledged her advice with a sincere embrace.

However, the Provisioner had his own solution to the unfolding crisis. In a whispered exchange with the Oracle, he proposed the idea of waking the avatars temporarily to counter the impending disturbance of other elemental entities. The Oracle, appreciating his strategic thinking, smiled in agreement. They were prepared to hear the Archon's proposed solution, eager to understand her perspective and assess the best course of action for the challenges facing Paranova.

In her chamber, the Archon reveled in excitement, a stark departure from her distanced self. The Provisioner and the Oracle, caught off guard, observed as she began reciting teachings and information passed on from the Provisioner, which surprised him with a sense of pride. The Archon, always finding ways to bring joy to the Provisioner, displayed a newfound passion for problem solving, leaving the Oracle cautious of her motives.

The Archon unveiled a plan to harness elemental energies from below the surface, tapping into the source of the entities' powers. This strategy aimed to slow down the disturbed entities, providing the mortals with a fighting chance for their future. Unaware of the potential to wake the avatars, the Archon's plan aligned with the Provisioner's vision. As they passionately discussed the strategy, the Oracle grew jealous and questioned the Archon's motives for tapping into the powers below.

Feeling the tension, the Archon played off the plan as a means to dissipate the energy, allowing observation in the celestial realm. The Oracle, however, discerned the device in question and insisted on prioritizing the waking of the dormant avatars. She scolded the Provisioner for sharing the device's existence with the Archon and questioned the depth of their relationship. Disturbed, the Oracle left the room, leaving the Provisioner to grapple with the sudden dilemma on his own.

In the wake of the Oracle's departure and her disagreement over the use of the device, called the Affinity, the Provisioner found himself torn between choices. He firmly insisted that the device should not be employed, rebuffing the Archon's almost desperate plea to consider her plan. Frustration took hold of the Archon, and in her attempt to sway the Provisioner, she enveloped him in her energy, using the embracing technique that he once loved. Reminiscing about their shared moments of the past, she poured her emotions into the encounter.

The Provisioner, though smiling at her, remained resolute. He firmly rejected the use of the Affinity, emphasizing its off-limits status as a last resort. Expressing gratitude for her renewed involvement, he assured her that he would consider her plans if waking the avatars proved insufficient. The Archon, feeling a sense of shame and defeat, witnessed the passion and adoration in the Provisioner's gaze, similar to what he once held for her but now had been fixated on the Oracle once again.

Beyond her personal emotions, she grappled with the moral implications of her approach. Not only did she fail to secure the Provisioner's cooperation, but she now needed to devise a way to obtain the affinity without his involvement and keep it hidden. The Archon faced a complex web of emotions and challenges as she navigated the intricate dynamics of power, love, and the pursuit of her goals.

In the hushed aftermath of the disagreement, the Archon found herself compelled to slip into the Provisioner's sanctuary. Battling conflicting emotions, she wrestled with the urge to wait for him and fully surrender herself to a shared energy in a desperate attempt to finalize their partnership. Recollections of their insightful conversations and his open discussions of passion played in her mind. A vivid memory surfaced, one from a moment of seduction, revealing a potential hiding place for the Affinity.

Driven by a mix of desire and curiosity, the Archon ventured deeper into the sanctuary. There, she unraveled the mystery of its location and key. As she uncovered the Affinity, it rose from the depths, its brilliant lights captivating her gaze. In its radiant presence, she felt a powerful aura that momentarily quelled thoughts of her and the Provisioner together and blurred her own surroundings.

For a moment, the beauty of the Affinity eclipsed her desires. Yet a deeper yearning emerged—a hunger for power to fuel her insatiable ambition. As she stood before the entity, the Archon contemplated the path she had chosen, navigating the intricate balance between her personal desires and the unfolding fate of Paranova.

The Order sector had discovered and harnessed the Affinity, a cosmic energy entity, into a crystallized shard during the creation of the universe. The sector had mastered the art of tracking and capturing energy sources from diverse worlds, utilizing the Affinity to find uninhibited planets rich in boundless energy for study and observation.

Despite its potential, the Provisioner sealed away the Affinity due to its unpredictable nature when used. In one instance, it had harnessed everything from a world in the past, erasing all traces of its existence. The Order sector believed the entity possessed consciousness and had connections to the celestial energies from which the Shapers were born. The act of sealing it into a device may have induced anger, introducing chaotic uncertainties in its utilization.

In the past, the Provisioner cautiously used the Affinity, extracting small amounts of resources from worlds. These resources were then discharged into his observatory, where he learned much about tangible worlds. The Affinity played a crucial role in his quest to craft worlds suitable for mortals, providing essential insights into the delicate balance of creation.

The Provisioner held the belief that the Affinity possessed the ability to induce a trance-like state on celestial Shapers. Not only limited to elemental powers, but the entity also exhibited manipulation of celestial energy. Realizing the potential dangers and seeking assistance from the Oracle long ago, the Shapers kept the Affinity sealed away in their sector. Their intention was to find a solution that could aid the entity, but there lingered a deep-seated fear. They worried that the Affinity might harbor negative sentiments toward celestial energy due to the decisions the Shapers had made in harnessing it in the first place. The delicate balance between the Shapers and the Affinity was tenuous, fraught with uncertainties and the weight of past choices.

The Anarchist, feeling a sense of pride for the Archon's initiative during the emergency meeting previously, decided to pay her a visit. However, upon entering her chambers, he was greeted by a scene of chaos—sketches and notes scattered erratically, with no sign of the Archon. Alarmed, he discovered a blueprint of the Provisioner's sanctuary, prompting him to investigate her whereabouts fearing the worst from the Archon.

As he entered the sanctuary, a sense of dread washed over the Anarchist. There, he found the Archon captivated by the affinity, her gaze fixated on the mesmerizing entity. Realizing the potential consequences of her actions, the Anarchist hurried to seek the Provisioner, hoping for his involvement. Recognizing the Archon's reckless choices and fully aware of the Affinity's capabilities, he understood the potential it could unleash if it were used on Paranova.

In their quarters, the Oracle and the Provisioner engaged in a heated argument about the emerging connection between the Provisioner and the Archon. The Oracle, overwhelmed with emotions, expressed her deep-rooted feelings and perceived a unique bond slipping away out of resentment. The Provisioner defended his position while highlighting the Archon's development and leadership abilities despite admitting to having fallen prey to the Archon several times. However, the Oracle harbored bitterness, feeling that the Provisioner's compassion for all celestial beings made him oblivious to the emotions of those closest to him. The argument reached a stalemate as tension filled the room, leaving both the Oracle and the Provisioner at an impasse.

The Anarchist arrived amidst an awkward argument between the Provisioner and the Oracle, insisting that both join him in the sanctuary where the Archon had summoned the Affinity entity. The unfolding events hinted at a crisis that required immediate attention and collaboration among them.

As the group hastened to the sanctuary, the Archon found herself unable to recall the Provisioner's instructions on using the Affinity. Frustration welled up within her as she grappled with the mysterious entity. The crystallized shard, housing a captivating ethereal energy, pulsed with the raw essence of elements. It held the power to manipulate and channel elemental forces, capable of restoring harmony or causing complete destruction, depending on who controlled it.

Driven by a hypnotic thirst for power, the Archon sought to unlock the Affinity's potential and bend it to her will. The allure of its immense capabilities fueled her ambition, blurring the lines between her personal desires and the potential consequences for Paranova. As she meddled with the Affinity, the fate of the world hung in the balance, caught between the conflicting intentions of the Shapers and the unpredictable nature of the cosmic entity.

In a desperate attempt to bend the Affinity to her will, the Archon unleashed a barrage of arcane magic, seeking to overpower the entity. However, the Affinity fought back with elemental powers, resisting the Archon's corruption. As the group reached the sanctuary, they witnessed a fierce battle between the Archon and the Affinity. The entity enveloped the Archon with elemental power, and they plummeted through the sanctuary into the cosmos, initiating a clash between elemental and celestial forces above Paranova.

Despite the Provisioner and the Anarchist's earnest attempts to intervene, their efforts amounted to nothing. The Affinity manipulated the Archon with its mysterious cosmic powers, and in a moment of hypnotic revelation, she unintentionally disclosed her true intentions: a desire for ruling power, deception, and manipulation. This revelation struck the Provisioner deeply, as he yearned for their connection to be authentic, untouched by a craving for power.

Having finished playing with the Archon, the Affinity shifted its focus toward Paranova, instilling horror in the remaining Shapers who recognized the impending doom facing their creation. Breaking free from the hypnotic trance induced by the Affinity, the Archon summoned a potent dark celestial energy pulse. This decisive release collided with the crystallized shard, marking her emergence from the hypnotic spell cast by the Affinity. With unwavering determination, the Archon directed her celestial power towards the Affinity, depleting all her energy to prevent its descent and the potential destruction of the world below. The very energy she emanated, potent and celestial, carried the risk of not only obliterating the looming threat but also consuming her in the process. The colossal collision and dark energy fractured the entity, shattering it into countless shards that scattered across the continent.

Each shard carried a fragment of the cosmic entity, potent and unpredictable. Below, the mortals witnessed the celestial collisions, interpreting them as stars engaged in an epic battle. The glimmers in the sky grew in size and intensity, resembling dazzling shooting stars descending from above. Initially seen as a glimmer of hope, the celestial display quickly turned into a source of fear and uncertainty.

Realizing that these celestial objects were descending upon Paranova, the mortals' hope transformed into apprehension. The mesmerizing display now sparked fear, as the mortals understood that they were not being saved but were now faced with doom from the shards hurling downward at their world.

As the fragmented shards collided across the continent, the Shapers keenly observed a significant change—the elemental storms were diminishing, not entirely, but sufficiently to give the inhabitants of the world a chance at survival. Among the notable alterations was the weakening of Pyrothos, the fiery entity. Seizing this opportunity, the Provisioner ventured into the cosmos to retrieve the Archon, who had expended all her energy in a valiant stand against the Affinity. Ultimately, her choice to chase the Affinity and unleash the devastating attack ended with saving the world from an imminent collision that would have been complete destruction.

As he carried the weakened Archon back to her chamber, she awoke with a smile, realizing that surrendering herself to the Provisioner had proven to be the right choice, albeit in a different way than she initially thought. She had used all her energy into her magic blast, with the intent to sacrifice herself for the creation that she and the Provisioner had worked tirelessly to form.

Meanwhile, in the observatory, the other Shapers informed the Provisioner of the newfound weaker elemental energies. Although the fragments had subdued the energies, harmony had not been fully restored. With uncertainty surrounding the scattered fragments and the need for a new plan, the Shapers had to adapt their strategy.

Despite the Oracle's desire to address the Archon's situation, she recognized the more pressing issue—the fate of their creation was at stake. Resolute and focused, she listened attentively to the Provisioner's proposed next steps, understanding that the Shapers needed to devise a plan to navigate the challenges posed by the scattered fragments and maintain the delicate balance of their world.

•••••••

When confronted with the imminent threat and the potential ruin that loomed over Paranova's inhabitants, the Order sector promptly took action. They fully grasped the severity of the situation and recognized that grave repercussions could emerge if unsuspecting mortals were to encounter the dispersed powers of the fragmented Affinity. With great urgency, they formulated a strategy to stop the potential catastrophe and preserve their world's delicate equilibrium.

As the situation demanded, the dormant Stone and Tree Avatars, ancient and admired avatars of the Shapers, had awakened from their slumber with a surge of celestial energies. These avatars, who are representations of the primal forces of nature and protectors of harmony, immediately understood the threat that the shattered Affinity posed. They understood the magnitude of its fragmented power and the potential chaos it could wreak upon Paranova.

Filled with a dignified purpose and a steadfast determination, the stone and tree avatars set forth on a momentous journey that spanned the vast expanse of Paranova. Guided by their deep connection to the essence of nature and the elements, they embarked on a relentless quest to retrieve and reunite the scattered shards before mortals could seek them out.

With each step they took, the avatars drew upon their ancient wisdom and celestial energy, their every action driven by the paramount objective of preventing mortal hands from obtaining and misusing the dangerous fragments. The stone avatars, embodying resilience, stability, and the unyielding strength of the earth, lent their unwavering support to the mission. The tree avatars, representing growth, harmony, and the intricate interconnectedness of all life, brought their wisdom and nurturing essence to bear.

Together, the stone and tree avatars ventured through treacherous landscapes, traversing towering mountains, dense forests, vast deserts, and untamed waters. They encountered formidable challenges and overcame countless obstacles, their celestial presence resonating with the forces of nature around them.

As avatars collided with the fiery entity Pyrothos, the formidable giant easily scorched the tree avatars in its path. However, the stone avatars stood resilient, serving as a crucial distraction to prevent the colossal entity from rampaging across the entire continent. The Shapers, now thankful for the awakened avatars, gained a unique perspective—they could finally perceive the world from the avatars' viewpoint. They realized from observing the elemental storms that the disturbances weren't the result of physical elemental entities awakening, but rather of elemental turmoil bubbling up from below.

Every nameless Shaper, previously working behind the scenes for both sectors, now has their moment in the spotlight. Taking control of avatars, they embarked on a collective journey to seek out fragments to collect them and aid in keeping Pyrothos at bay. Under the command of the Anarchist, the chaos sector leveraged its influence to control spectral avatars, delving into the depths below to gain insight into quelling the elemental disturbance. The collaborative efforts of the Shapers unfolded as a symphony of coordinated actions to navigate the challenges posed by the disturbance and the fiery entity threatening their world.

Throughout their enduring journey, the avatars remained steadfast in their purpose, tirelessly collecting the scattered shards of the Affinity entity. With each fragment they retrieved, they carefully preserved and safeguarded its power, recognizing the need to prevent the potential imbalance and chaos that could be unleashed upon the world if these fragments fell into the wrong hands.

The avatars' mission resonated with the mortal races of Paranova, who witnessed their journey from afar. News of their valiant efforts spread like wildfire, igniting a sense of awe and reverence among the inhabitants. The mortals, recognizing that the fate of their world rested upon the avatars, regarded the avatars as beacons of hope and guardians of their collective future. The unfolding events created a bond between the celestial and mortal realms unknowingly, inspiring a shared determination to overcome the challenges that threatened their world.

As the avatars pressed on, their presence alone had a profound effect on the lands they traversed. The earth beneath their feet quivered with renewed vitality, the flora flourished, and the elements responded to their celestial energy. It was as if the very fabric of Paranova rejoiced in their purpose and lent its support to their noble cause.

As a result, the avatars persisted in their tireless efforts to put the damaged Affinity entity back together. The mortal races watched in anticipation, their hopes intertwined with the fate of their world, knowing that the success of the avatars' mission would determine the destiny of Paranova and safeguard its delicate balance for generations to come.

Before the fragments could be pieced back together, the Keeper, an ancient and wise Shaper, gazed upon the fragmented powers of the remaining elemental fragments scattered throughout the realm of Paranova. A mix of astonishment and curiosity flickered within their timeless being as they observed the increasing strength of these elemental forces. He noticed a shift in power when the fragments came together and wanted to use caution while dealing with the fragments.

Observing one mere mortal take command of the colossal entity of Pyrothos, the Keeper's thoughts crystallized. Once viewed as mere vessels, the mortals had undergone a remarkable transformation. They had transcended their previous limitations, displaying an unparalleled ability to summon and manipulate the elemental forces that intricately shaped their world. The Keeper marveled at their newfound capacity to wield such potent elemental power—a capability that had traditionally been the domain of the divine and celestial beings. This shift in mortal prowess signaled an ideal shift, altering the perception of their role in the cosmic tapestry.

While marveling at the mortals' newfound mastery over elemental forces, the Keeper also recognized the dangers. They understood that wielding such power without wisdom and restraint could lead to devastating consequences for Paranova. The fragmented powers of elemental entities were not meant to be used recklessly. The Keeper wondered if the mortals had received help beyond their understanding, raising concerns about unforeseen influences in the unfolding events and what happened in the avatars' absence.

With this understanding, the Keeper, in his dedication to maintaining the delicate balance, resolved to intervene. They realized that the watchful guardianship of the avatars was necessary to separate and protect the fragments and shards of elemental powers. By ensuring that each piece remained distinct and isolated, the Keeper sought to prevent the catastrophic consequences that could arise from their unification.

The Keeper understood the inherent nature of these fragmented powers—they were like delicate pieces of a celestial puzzle. Alone, they possessed immense potential, but when joined without proper guidance, they could transform into an uncontrollable force capable of tearing the very fabric of Paranova asunder. Thus, the Keeper saw it as their duty to safeguard the fragments, allowing them to be protected under the watchful eye of the avatars.

And thus, the Keeper devised a plan to protect the elemental fragments. Teaming up with the Forger, they aimed to craft new avatars as guardians for these fragments. The Keeper intended to use these avatars to keep each fragment separate, shielding them from those with selfish desires who might attempt to unite them. The Forger would swiftly create these guardians, using the elements associated with each fragment for their crafting.

As the Forger and the Keeper collaborated on the creation of the guardian avatars, a subtle exchange of smiles occurred between them. The Forger, thrilled to be part of this grand plan, couldn't hide his excitement. The Keeper, attempting to maintain a serious demeanor, couldn't help but smile back, reminiscing about their past debates on the best creations for Paranova. Despite the Forger's mischievous nature, he was determined to use the Keeper's elegant designs for the guardian avatars, honoring their close bond and striving to make the Keeper proud.

In this way, the Keeper embarked on a delicate dance of balance and protection. They understood the significance of preserving the fractured state of the elemental powers, for it was only through this careful separation that the mortals of Paranova could continue to wield the elemental energies responsibly and without succumbing to the temptations of unchecked power.

In the depths of his own contemplation, the Keeper questioned the origin and nature of these mortal abilities. Were they born with innate gifts and dormant powers waiting to be awoken? Or had they acquired their mastery over the elements through arcane knowledge and ancient rituals? The answers eluded the Keeper, sparking a thirst for understanding that burned brighter than ever before.

The implications of mortals possessing such formidable powers weighed heavily on the Keeper's mind. For millennia, it was assumed that elemental energy existed as the conduits through which balance and harmony were maintained in every world created. But now, with mortals able to harness and shape the elements to their will, the balance is in jeopardy. The Keeper realized the delicate balance they were tasked with preserving had been significantly disrupted.

With wisdom and foresight, The Keeper orchestrated his detailed plan to disperse the collected affinity fragments across Paranova. The avatars moved with the Keepers guidance; each fragment or shard was strategically placed in key locations, and their distribution was intended to create a harmonizing effect, dispersing the concentrated elemental energies and alleviating any potential chaos if any awakened entities could unleash them. The Keeper understood that balance was paramount, and by carefully guiding the fragment placement, the delicate equilibrium of Paranova could be maintained.

With most of the Affinity pieces located and in safekeeping, the Guardian Avatars assumed their new roles as guardians of these potent fragments. They understood the immense power contained within the fragments and the potential chaos that could ensue if they fell into mortal hands.

The new guardian avatars, freshly introduced to Paranova, seamlessly adapted to the celestial energies provided by the Shapers and the knowledge bestowed upon them. They stood steadfast, ready to defend and safeguard the fragmented shards of the Affinity. Crafted to match the elemental nature of the fragments they protected, these guardians took various forms—be they fire, water, earth, or air avatars. Endowed with elemental powers and attuned to the elemental barrier below, they pledged to protect the fragments and assist the original avatars whenever necessary.

The elemental entities within the core of Paranova were in balance due to the fragments of the affinity entity, which pulsated with an ethereal energy that resonated with the elemental forces of the world. They acted as conduits, interweaving and harmonizing the elemental energies that flowed beneath the surface. Each fragment carried a unique resonance, aligning with a specific elemental aspect—fire, water, earth, air, and more.

As the elemental forces surged through Paranova, the affinity fragments resonated, synchronizing the elemental energies and maintaining equilibrium. Their profound purpose extended far beyond the mortal realm, delving deep into the essence of the world itself. They were the conduits that bound the elemental forces, their radiant presence resonating within the very core of Paranova, a testament to the delicate balance that sustained the world.

When the balancing of the fractured pieces of Affinity took hold, an intriguing transformation swept across the land of Paranova. The elemental events that had once shaken the very fabric of existence began to dwindle, their extreme powers receding like a fading wind.

The mighty trees, once stirred by the vigor of Vigoroth, found peace in stillness. No longer would their branches sway with an otherworldly force, for the harmonizing influence of balanced affinity soothed their ancient roots. The seas, once whipped into a frenzy by the swirling might of Maravas, grew calm and serene, with waves lapping gently against the shores. The air, once resounding with the bellowing call of Zephyro, now settled into a tranquil breeze whispering melodies through the valleys and over the mountain peaks.

The fierce storms that had raged, fueled by the conflict between light and darkness, gradually died down. The radiant glow that once illuminated the sky, emanating from the clash of chromatic energies, faded into the depths of memory. Likewise, the haunting presence of Strelka and Strenoth, the embodiments of darkness had dissipated, retreating to the shadowy corners of Paranova. The land, once shrouded in an eerie chill with death rising from the influence of Phagen, regained a sense of peace as life reasserted its hold on the mortal realm.

However, amidst this gradual calm, there remained a fiery nuisance. Pyrothos, the embodiment of fire and heat, had continued to burn brightly in his physical form. The awakening of the elements had kindled his power, but now, as the elemental events diminished, his strength waned as well. Yet, in his weakened state, Pyrothos unintentionally wreaked havoc on the landscape he traversed. His very presence was a manifestation of destructive forces that scorched the earth and transformed once vibrant landscapes into smoldering remnants.

It was a bittersweet paradox. While the balancing of the fragmented Affinity brought respite and restored balance to the elemental events, it also highlighted the unintended consequences of Pyrothos' awakening. The fire and heat that surrounded him still clung to his essence, leaving a trail of destruction in his wake.

In the face of this realization, the inhabitants of Paranova grappled with a newfound understanding. The elemental events, once feared and revered, now became symbols of a fragile balance that required careful tending. The mortals learned to navigate the ebb and flow of elemental power while respecting its might and acknowledging the potential for both creation and destruction.

The Keeper, calling upon his small plant-like avatars, dispatched them to the western continent on a mission to engage with Alora. Their task was to deliver a fragment shard from the Affinity that held elemental opposition to fire, a vital component in the conflict surrounding Pyrothos in the southern lands. Knowing the elves of Alora to be paragons of light, balance, and order, the Keeper envisioned their involvement as crucial.

The swift movement of the plant avatars aimed to present the Keeper's plan—to utilize fractions of the Affinity to diminish its power, guiding the giant entity back into the volcano for a return to its deep slumber. Recognizing that mortal wielders were necessary for this task, as the avatars couldn't harness the Affinity's power, the Keeper entrusted the elves of Alora with this responsibility. He held faith in their intelligence, strong will, and reverence for the avatars.

·······

In the quarters where the Archon found herself awakening, weakened from the aftermath of her intense clash with the Affinity, a subtle movement in the dark corner caught her attention. Emerging from the shadows was Havoc, the master of dark arts and stealth. Fixing him with a fierce gaze, she demanded that he reveal himself fully. With a wicked smile, Havoc approached her. The Archon wasted no time in questioning his motives and actions during the time when the avatars lay dormant. Determined to gain clarity on the plans they had crafted together and the lone pursuits Havoc had undertaken without her, she sought to unravel the mysteries that had unfolded in his absence.

Havoc, acutely aware of the Archon's penetrating scrutiny, locked eyes with her, a flicker of confidence mingling with a tinge of apprehension. In his relentless pursuit of chaos and discord, he had orchestrated a web of manipulation, dispatching mysterious whispers to sow seeds of malevolence and sway the course of events in Paranova. His ferocious desire for power and unwavering commitment to seeing his evil plans through were the driving forces behind every strategic decision.

Locked in a gaze with the Archon, Havoc couldn't suppress a twinge of contempt. To him, she appeared weak and clumsy, a figure marked by mishaps and failures that rendered her unfit to lecture him. In his eyes, her presence only highlighted the sharp contrast between their methods and capabilities. The disdain he felt emanated from a belief in his own superiority, a conviction that his solitary endeavors far surpassed any collaborative efforts they might have shared.

With a dark smile playing upon his lips, Havoc stood firm to the Archon's scrutiny. He reveled in the chaos he had orchestrated deep down and the intricate threads of deception he had woven through the tapestry of Paranova. For him, the interplay of power, manipulation, and consequence was an intoxicating symphony, and he relished every note of disharmony.

Yet, even as he met the Archon's gaze with a mixture of defiance and caution, Havoc knew that their intricate dance of power was far from over. The clash of their opposing ideologies and methods promised to shape the destiny of Paranova, for better or for worse. And in the depths of his dark heart, Havoc nurtured a glimmer of anticipation, eagerly awaiting the next move in this wicked game of power and chaos.

As the Archon beckoned Havoc closer, he reluctantly sheathed his hidden sinister blade, wary yet intrigued by her sudden vulnerability. The Archon, weakened by the aftermath of her clash with the Affinity, sought support from her loyal ally. In a hushed tone, she urged Havoc to reconsider their initial plans for Paranova, cautioning against mirroring the patterns of the Anarchist's past struggles. Despite his preference for the shadows, the Archon's continued alliance could prove beneficial in the grander scheme of things. Sitting in silence, Havoc absorbed the Archon's words, hopeful that her convictions still resonated with the chaotic essence they both embodied. He nodded, giving her satisfaction, knowing that she would believe him.

As Havoc moved away from the Archon, he experienced a range of emotions, including fear and excitement. He was aware that his future actions would be closely examined and he had to proceed cautiously in the subtle balance of authority and allegiance. The watchful gaze of the Archon served as a constant reminder that each action would be closely monitored and his loyalty would be put to the test.

The Archon's thoughts turned inward as she considered the abandoned plan to combine a realm with Paranova—a vision that the Order and the ever-vigilant Anarchist had prevented. Though the pursuit of this grand design had been temporarily halted, a flicker of intrigue danced in the Archon's mind—could Havoc, in his relentless pursuit of chaos, still be working towards the realization of that complicated plan? They both agreed long ago to stop the plotting, but maybe he was working alone for his own gain.

Sometime after the mortal creation, the Anarchist accused the Archon and Havoc of the chaos within mortal and celestial realms. The Archon couldn't shake the feeling that Havoc might continue with their initial plans. Both had swiftly risen through the ranks of the Chaos sector, not just due to their individual prowess but also because of their faithful allegiance to the chaotic cause. However, the Archon sensed a growing eagerness surrounding Havoc during his surprise visit, a desire that seemed to transcend their partnership. Worried that he might have lost himself in the solitude of the shadows, she grappled with the realization that his mission might no longer require her presence.

The Archon knew all too well the cunning and deceptive nature of Havoc. His ambitions knew no bounds, and he reveled in the chaos and destruction he wrought upon the world. She pondered the possibility that, behind his calculated moves and intricate schemes, Havoc may be secretly furthering their original objective, biding his time until the perfect moment to strike.

A shrewd smile curled on the Archon's lips as she considered the implications. Perhaps Havoc's apparent distractions and diversions were nothing more than a smokescreen, concealing his true intentions. The Archon, driven by her own thirst for power and dominion, recognized the potential of joining forces with Havoc to bring about a union of realms. It would be a feat that would shake Paranova to its very core, reshaping the balance of power and establishing their dominance over the mortal races.

However, caution tempered the Archon's enthusiasm. She knew all too well the treachery that lay within Havoc's core and the chaos he sowed wherever he treaded. Any alliance with him would require a delicate dance, a game of manipulation and control where neither party could afford to fully trust the other. She also had developed feelings for the Provisioner and his vision, which contradicted her own vision for the future.

As soon as she regained her strength, the Archon planned to slip into Havoc's shadowy corridors. She aimed to unveil the secrets he had been harboring in his secure domain; she wondered if he still harbored the same desires for a united realm as she did. The Archon was eager to find answers to her questions and imagined the schemes he had woven in the shadows.

With these thoughts swirling in her mind, the Archon made a silent vow. She would keep a watchful eye on Havoc, observing his every move in the background and seeking the subtle signs that would reveal his true intentions. The realization of their shared vision could only come to pass if she could outmaneuver and manipulate the master of chaos himself.

As the Archon grappled with the internal debate of right and wrong, the Provisioner sought to join her in company while she rested. Filled with distress, she wondered if he had overheard the conversation with Havoc or if Havoc was still lurking in the shadows. The Provisioner, extending his calming touch, reassured the Archon. He mentioned that he had much to discuss regarding the events involving the Affinity but expressed pride in her swift decision to save the world from impending destruction. Desperate for his approval, the Archon overflowed with gratitude, and as the Provisioner stood up, it seemed as if he was about to share some crucial insights.

The Provisioner, standing tall, conveyed his concern about the Archon's impulsiveness, a trait he deemed necessary for her to refine if their partnership was to endure. He remained uncertain about her decisions, but a crucial detail lingered in his mind—the revelation she made to the Affinity during her hypnotic state. Her declaration of desiring power and dominion over the universe unfolded as a betrayal for the Provisioner. He felt a deep sense of disappointment, questioning her use of the information that he had willingly shared during their vulnerable embraces.

While absorbing his words, she maintained a false sense of indifference, wary of Havoc's potential gaze. The Provisioner, while acknowledging the Archon's survival in the clash with the Affinity, emphasized the necessity for her to learn discipline. In response, the Archon attempted to lighten the mood with an inappropriate flirtatious remark, but the Provisioner remained steadfast in his seriousness, implying that this was a crucial and final warning.

As the Provisioner left the room, the Archon began reflecting on her repeated mistakes and recognized her chaotic nature and the consequences it brought. Despite yearning for the Provisioner's approval and attention, she understood that she had to find a way to prove herself differently. As time moved slowly, a sense of restlessness overcame her. She could not shake off the feeling that the only time the Provisioner truly paid attention to her was when chaos unfolded. While contemplating her next move, she overheard the Provisioner addressing the Shapers in the meeting room.

As the Shapers gathered in the meeting room, the Provisioner and the Anarchist took charge of the discussion, providing a platform for each celestial being to express their thoughts. The Provisioner began by expressing gratitude for every contribution, acknowledging both significant and minor roles in quelling the elemental storms on Paranova. He then described the strategy the Keeper had come up with to provide a fragment to the mortals as a defense against the lingering threat of the fiery entity.

With an open forum for discussion, the Provisioner encouraged the Shapers to share their perspectives on the current state of Paranova and their visions for its future. The room was filled with a mix of voices, each Shaper presenting their unique viewpoint on the unfolding events and the direction they believed Paranova should take. The meeting became a forum for diverse opinions and ideas, reflecting the intricate dynamics within the celestial realm.

Amidst the discussions in the meeting room, tensions flared as sector perspectives clashed and arguments threatened to divide the Shapers. However, the Anarchist and the Provisioner, recognizing the importance of unity and constructive dialogue, intervened to quell the rising discord. They urged the Shapers to channel their energy into discussions that would bring about collective benefit rather than furthering division.

The Anarchist, known for embracing chaos, emphasized the need for diverse perspectives and the exploration of unconventional ideas. On the other hand, the Provisioner, with a penchant for order, sought common ground and understanding among the Shapers. Together, they guided the discourse towards a more productive and collaborative path, fostering an environment where each Shaper could contribute to Paranova's future without fracturing the celestial unity.

Between the discussions, it became apparent that both sectors ultimately desired the well-being and balance of Paranova, albeit through different means. The Order sector sought harmony, structure, and preservation of the natural order, while the Chaos sector yearned for evolution, growth, and the exploration of new possibilities. Though their methods diverged, the underlying motivation was to safeguard the world they held dear.

During the course of the meeting, tensions progressively diminished, and a newly formed understanding began to develop. Both sectors acknowledged the need for cooperation, combining their respective capabilities, and developing creative solutions that could harmonize their opposing perspectives. The issues they encountered required a collective effort that went beyond the limitations of their own philosophies.

Together, the leaders of the Order and Chaos sectors agreed to forge ahead with the common goal of establishing a future in which Paranova could grow and thrive for generations to come. They recognized that their differences could be utilized as assets and that by embracing diversity, they could unlock undiscovered potential and create an era of unity and advancement.

With a renewed sense of purpose, the leaders returned to their different sectors, carrying the spirit of collaboration and a commitment to finding common ground. They recognized that what lay ahead would be difficult, requiring sacrifices and compromises, but they also recognized that the collective knowledge and cooperation of both sectors would open the way for a more promising and stable future for Paranova.

·······

After discovering that Havoc harbored more chaotic plans for the world of Paranova and beyond, extending beyond their seemingly harmless intentions of the past—at least, that is how the Archon perceived it—she found herself at a crossroads. In the dim corridors of Havoc's room, she pondered for a while before making the crucial decision of whether to align herself with him or uphold the delicate balance with the Provisioner.

The Archon, humbled by the consequences of her actions and the looming threat of Pyrothos, came to a profound realization. She recognized that her past manipulations and selfish pursuits had only further destabilized Paranova and that the time for change had arrived. Swallowing her pride, she made the decision to set aside her personal agenda and focus on the well-being of Paranova.

With genuine intent, she made her way towards the Provisioner and the Oracle, and she sincerely expressed regret for her previous conduct. She openly acknowledged that arrogance and a thirst for power had hindered her ability to make sound judgments, causing her to overlook the immense capabilities of Paranova and its residents. As Pyrothos's looming threat finally made her realize the repercussions of her past decisions, she resolved to rectify them without hesitation.

The Provisioner, ever wise and understanding, listened to the Archon's words with a mix of caution and hope. He recognized the sincerity in her voice and saw the genuine desire within her to rectify the damage she had caused. Understanding the urgency of the situation and the need for unity, he extended a hand of reconciliation, inviting the Archon to join the collective efforts to safeguard Paranova.

As sincerity emanated from the Archon, a different pattern in her celestial energies caught the attention of both the Provisioner and the Oracle. Despite their vast wisdom and ability to observe celestial energies, this instance stood out as a unique and genuine expression from the Archon. The Oracle silently conveyed her approval to the Provisioner through a gaze, acknowledging the shift in the Archon's demeanor.

In the celestial realm, where energies intertwined and resonated, the subtle changes in the Archon's aura hinted at a depth of emotion and authenticity not often witnessed. The Provisioner, recognizing this, felt a renewed sense of connection with the Archon, and the Oracle, attuned to the nuances of celestial energies, sensed the sincerity that now emanated from the once rebellious Shaper.

With a newfound sense of purpose and a commitment to the greater good, the Archon pledged her allegiance to the cause. She acknowledged that her past actions had caused pain and chaos, but she was now dedicated to using her powers and influence for the betterment of Paranova. Her knowledge and understanding of the elemental forces, combined with the collective wisdom of the Order sector and the Chaos sector, would be instrumental in finding a solution to the imminent threat.

As the Archon's mind churned with the possibilities of Havoc's hidden motives, she recognized the need for caution and transparency. Aware of the potential ramifications and the delicate balance of power at stake, the Archon decided it was crucial to inform the other influential figures of Paranova—the Shapers—about her suspicions regarding Havoc's intentions.

The Archon's revelations unfolded in the celestial meeting room, each word carrying the weight of secrets and past deceptions. She spoke of her observations and concerns regarding Havoc, revealing the lingering possibility that he might still be dedicated to their original plan. This plan aimed to sow chaos as a distraction, ultimately uniting the death realm with Paranova.

While the Archon remained vague about the details, her emphasis on the potential chaos sown by Havoc among mortals was real. She admitted to severing the Oracle's vision and described how Havoc had created an ethereal realm—a place of transition for souls—where the Oracle's sight remained lost, manipulating it to further his ambitions for power. The Archon openly acknowledged her role in corrupting the first mortal race, planting seeds of doubt in the Provisioner's abilities and casting shadows upon the celestial creation.

Her admission, burdened with remorse and a desire for redemption, echoed through the celestial meeting room, leaving the other Shapers and celestial beings in stunned silence. The weight of her past actions and the revelation of her involvement in Havoc's schemes unfolded against the celestial backdrop, casting a somber tone over the discussions in the realm of the Shapers.

The Oracle, grappling with the weight of the Archon's betrayal, struggled to maintain her composure. The memories of that fateful night, when the innocent Shaper was wrongly accused and murdered, both haunted her consciousness. The Archon's wicked manipulations had caused irreversible harm, and the Oracle found it challenging to confront the one responsible.

As the Oracle avoided contact with the Archon, her emotions remained tightly controlled. The desire to scream, to retaliate, and the need for solitude in meditation all churned within her. The Oracle's gaze then shifted to the Provisioner, seeking comfort or perhaps an understanding of his reaction. To her surprise, the Provisioner appeared unaffected, his stoic demeanor suggesting a depth of comprehension or a readiness to address the situation.

The Anarchist, standing in a conflicted state of betrayal and pride, grappled with the revelations brought forth by the Archon. Her transparency laid bare the intricate web of manipulation, and the Anarchist couldn't help but reflect on the path she had chosen. While feeling a sense of betrayal, he also acknowledged a certain pride in her ability to navigate the intricate dance of chaos.

The Anarchist, haunted by his own past mistakes in the death realm, had hoped the Archon could lead the Chaos sector to renewed greatness. However, her descent into the shadows that mirrored his own past had left him in a state of disappointment. In silent reflection, he awaited the Provisioner's decision on how to navigate this unforeseen betrayal and its potential consequences for the celestial realm. The Anarchist's gaze shifted towards the Provisioner, seeking guidance and resolution in the face of this complex celestial dilemma.

As the Archon kneeled before the Provisioner, her revelation left a heavy silence in the room. The Provisioner, seemingly unaffected by the turmoil of emotions, pondered the complex situation. The Archon, feeling the weight of his gaze, surrendered herself to his will.

The Provisioner contemplated a range of emotions, from disappointment to a desire for decisive action against the Archon. He considered the idea of the Chaos sector leaving Paranova entirely, a decision that echoed in the silent nods of agreement from the Order sector. Expressing gratitude for their patience and discipline, the Provisioner acknowledged the sorrowful nature of the situation.

Standing the Archon up, he explained that her actions carried consequences. Despite appreciating her transparency, he emphasized the need for discipline. The Archon, agreeing to undergo interrogation and share more details about Havoc and his plans, acknowledged the consequences of her choices. She expressed a sense of calling, a decision that aligned with her chosen side in the unfolding celestial drama.

In the dimly lit interrogation room, the Provisioner, with a grim look of authority, pressured the Archon to speak. She found herself on the precipice of pleading for forgiveness, revealing the internal struggle between moral and immoral actions that had been consuming her. The Archon acknowledged the impact that the Provisioner's compassion and grace had on her, admitting that it was his unwavering commitment that had allowed her to glimpse the vision he so passionately poured his celestial energy into. However, the Provisioner with a stern voice, demanded complete transparency from her. He warned of severe consequences, hinting at the potential exile of the Archon to join the remaining Chaos sector that had already been imprisoned in their duties overseeing the death realm long ago. The room hung heavy with tension as the Archon prepared to lay bare her secrets.

The Archon, with a heavy heart, laid bare the intricate details of her past secrets and the original plan to liberate the remaining Chaos sector imprisoned in the death realm. She envisioned herself as a triumphant liberator, assuming rulership over both the Chaos sector and the mortal realm, with Havoc as her steadfast companion. However, she candidly admitted that the original plan was derailed when reminded of her leadership duties within the Chaos sector. Undeterred, she sought alternative avenues to satisfy her chaotic inclinations, dabbling in the creation of the Gantum, predatory creatures, and infusing the world with arcane energy. Despite the pain it caused the Provisioner, she strived to be truthful, revealing her intention to confront Havoc in the shadowy domain where he plotted and schemed, nurturing the seeds of chaos and evil.

In a vulnerable moment, the Archon delved into her haunting past, pleading with the Provisioner to join her in the investigation of Havoc's dark deception. The weight of her actions pressed upon her, and she was determined to shield the world he had created from the darkness that Havoc had planned. Using the intimate language they shared during moments of embrace, she recalled the passionate visions he painted for her about Paranova and the worlds that would follow. With sincerity in her eyes, she confessed her love for him, acknowledging the possibility that he might never reciprocate those feelings.

The Provisioner maintained a stoic silence as he escorted the Archon out of the room, with the Shapers and the Anarchist trailing behind. The Oracle, torn between the mission to seek justice and the execution of the Affinity shard plan on Paranova, exchanged a pressing look with the Provisioner, who did not want the Oracle to follow but she persisted. The group followed the Archon into the depths of the Chaos sector, each step echoing with anticipation and uncertainty. The air was charged with a mix of determination, betrayal, and the weight of impending revelations.

As the Shapers delved into Havoc's dark corridors within the Chaos sector, the sketches unveiled a disturbing panorama of mortal souls connected to the ethereal transitional realm. The Archon, surprised by the insidious nature of Havoc's plans, felt a mix of apprehension and curiosity. The sketches depicted a complex web of connections, suggesting a deeper and more intricate plot than she had anticipated. He had plans within plans containing directions for spectral avatars, mortals and wicked diagrams.

Alarmed by the sinister revelations, the Shapers intensified their search, scouring every corner of Havoc's domain. The darkened corridors echoed with their footsteps as they sought to unravel the mysteries hidden within the sketches and discern the full extent of Havoc's designs. The ethereal transitional realm, a place where mortal souls lingered, became a focal point of concern and scrutiny, prompting the Shapers to navigate its depths and uncover the true nature of Havoc's intentions.

As the Shapers delved deeper into their investigation, peeling back the layers of Havoc's schemes, they discovered a trail of destruction and deceit. The true extent of Havoc's insidious plans began to unravel, revealing a web of manipulation and betrayal that spanned across Paranova. The Shapers unearthed evidence of his nefarious dealings, exposing his role in sowing discord and orchestrating chaos for his personal gain.

The Oracle's heightened senses and the surge of energy within Havoc's domain provided a unique glimpse into a possible future. In a vision, she witnessed the Archon standing alongside the Provisioner, adorned in celestial battle armor, leading the Chaos sector to greatness. The world of Paranova developed into the magnificent creation that the Shapers had imagined, thanks to their combined efforts.

The sight left the Oracle in awe, recognizing the Archon as a key figure in the Provisioner's vision for the future. It solidified the importance of the Archon's role in shaping the destiny of Paranova. The Oracle, however, became exhausted from the vision's intensity and collapsed to the ground as a result of the strain on her celestial senses and the weight of the revelations. The Provisioner, determined to unravel Havoc's plans and ensure the safety of Paranova, focused on the impending task at hand.

As the Oracle shared the vision with the others, a chilling atmosphere descended upon the room, signaling an unnatural presence. The Anarchist and the Archon, attuned to the subtle energies around them, sensed the disturbance. The Archon, once again showing her perceptive nature, turned her attention to the Provisioner, her eyes reflecting concern and curiosity about the unseen force at play. The Anarchist, ever vigilant, readied himself for whatever might unfold, his instincts alert to the subtle shifts in the celestial realm. The Oracle, still recovering from the intensity of her vision, stood alongside the Provisioner, ready to face the unknown together.

As Havoc entered the room, his sinister presence sent a shiver through the atmosphere. His laughter echoed, revealing a sense of triumph and disdain. Locking eyes with the Archon, he taunted her weakness and proclaimed that she had finally caught up to his machinations. The Anarchist, ever protective, attempted to intervene, but Havoc, fueled by anger, dismissed his efforts. Turning his attention to the Provisioner and the Oracle, Havoc challenged their perception of reality. In a twisted display of chaotic passion, he asserted that both celestial and mortal beings were not perfect but agents of chaos. The room hung in tense anticipation as Havoc's words lingered, leaving the Shapers to grapple with the unsettling truth he presented.

As Havoc revealed his sinister blade, tension thickened in the room. The Shapers, recognizing the imminent threat, adopted a defensive stance. Smoke billowed, obscuring the room and favoring Havoc's covert maneuvers. He unleashed a relentless assault, overwhelming multiple Shapers simultaneously. He made a daring move to aim a fatal strike at the Provisioner's neck, but the Archon quickly intervened, deflecting the fatal blow with her sword.

However, Havoc wasn't deterred. With a second sinister blade in hand, he targeted the defenseless Archon. In a selfless act, the Oracle, sensing impending doom, threw herself between Havoc's blade and the Archon, taking the lethal strike in her chest. The Provisioner retaliated with a powerful blow, but Havoc, exploiting the cover of the smoke, vanished through a portal, escaping the immediate confrontation. The room, now filled with a somber atmosphere, bore witness to the consequences of the chaotic clash.

As the Oracle lay poisoned by Havoc's treacherous act, her mind was consumed by a resurgence of visions. Dark and demonic images flooded her consciousness, intertwining with glimpses of Paranova's future. In her weakened state, she struggled to discern the exact nature of these visions, but one thing remained clear: there was a deep connection between the dark forces she saw and the fate of Paranova itself. With her dying breath, she mustered the strength to convey a dire message to the Provisioner. She warned him of the necessity to remain ever vigilant in pursuing their shared dream, for the very survival of the world hinged upon their steadfast commitment.

In the wake of the Oracle's sacrifice, her final words reverberated through the room, carrying the weight of urgency and responsibility. She emphasized the pivotal role the Archon played in realizing the shared vision of the Provisioner and the Oracle. The burden of this profound message settled heavily on the Provisioner's shoulders as he vowed to honor the Oracle's dying wish.

Determined to safeguard the future of Paranova, the Provisioner reflected on the sacrifices made and the challenges that lay ahead. The Archon, now understanding the severity of her actions, felt a renewed sense of purpose. The room, shrouded in the aftermath of the chaotic confrontation, became a quiet space, echoing with the resonance of the Oracle's final plea for the preservation of their celestial creation.

The anguish of the Provisioner echoed through the celestial realms as he cradled the lifeless form of the Oracle. Tears streamed down his face, mingling with the cosmic energies that surrounded them. During his grief, he couldn't contain the torrent of emotions, directing blame at the Anarchist for his choices and the Archon for the repercussions of her actions.

The celestial realms were shrouded in sorrow as the Provisioner carried the Oracle to her sanctuary, a place where her celestial body could find peace and rest. The loss of the Oracle left a void that resonated across the sectors, and the Shapers grappled with the aftermath of a shattered alliance and the looming threat Havoc posed.

In the aftermath of the chaotic events, the Archon grappled with a flood of emotions. Remorse gripped her heart as she recognized the selfless sacrifice the Oracle had made, putting herself before the Archon. In that moment of clarity, the Archon acknowledged the unyielding support the Oracle had provided to the Provisioner and understood the depth of their partnership.

Jealousy, which had clouded the Archon's perception before, now seemed petty in comparison to the Oracle's sacrifice. A sense of regret settled within her, acknowledging that she may not have been capable of such a selfless act. However, this revelation also brought renewed determination. The Archon found herself proud of the choice she made to stand for righteousness and morality. Witnessing Havoc's descent into pure chaos, veering away from the essence of chaos itself and becoming evil, she recognized the need to confront the upcoming threats in both the realms of Shapers and mortals.

Clutching the sinister blade, the Archon could feel its radiant power, a force that could extinguish celestial beings. It became a relic, a tangible reminder of the choices made in her past and the sacrifice the Oracle had made to protect her. As the radiance of the blade enveloped her, the Archon found a renewed sense of purpose, a realization that perhaps the Oracle had seen a path for her, a destiny intertwined with the Provisioner and the grand vision the two had shared.

Alone in the sanctuary, the Provisioner grappled with a torrent of emotions that threatened to engulf him. He looked upon the celestial form of the Oracle, lying in serene repose. Memories flooded his mind—memories of shared visions, laughter, embracing one another, and the deep discussions that had shaped their journey through the cosmos.

In the hallowed space where they had found comfort away from their cosmic duties, the Provisioner confronted the daunting reality of a universe without the Oracle's wisdom and companionship. He spoke to the still form, his voice a mix of grief and determination, as if seeking counsel from the departed celestial being.

The sanctuary's celestial energy had a somber tone that mirrored the Provisioner's intense loss. Yet, amid the grief, a resolve began to take shape. The Oracle's words and influence lingered, reminding the Provisioner of the responsibilities that lay ahead. With a heavy heart, he steeled himself for the challenges unfolding across both realms, knowing that the path forward would be fraught with trials and tribulations.

Leaving the sanctuary, the Provisioner cast one last longing gaze at the Oracle, his cherished friend and intimate partner. With a gentle kiss, he bid her farewell, the celestial energies lingering in the air like a solemn promise. In the quiet of the sanctuary, he whispered words of gratitude and love, thanking her for the unwavering support she had provided throughout their celestenial time together.

The Provisioner vowed to seek justice for the deceased Oracle and carry out the joint vision they had created as he maintained the role of the Shapers' expected leader, his celestial calm etched with a determined resolve. With love sounding throughout the cosmic echoes, he carried the weight of responsibility, drawing strength from the memories of their shared experiences and the bond that transcended celestial realms.

In the wake of the Oracle's passing, a somber atmosphere descended upon the gathered members of the Order sector. The weight of the Oracle's last words lingered in the air, serving as a constant reminder of the challenges that lay ahead. The Provisioner, now more determined than ever, understood the gravity of their shared mission. He knew that the dark and demonic visions plaguing the Oracle in her final moments were a vision of looming threats to Paranova, and he vowed to heed her warning.

With the Archon's newfound clarity and realization of her past mistakes, she too felt the weight of responsibility pressing upon her. She recognized that her pursuit of power and manipulation had only contributed to the chaos and instability that threatened the world. She was the sole reason the Oracle could not see the events coming. Swallowing her pride, she committed herself to supporting the Provisioner and working towards the greater good of Paranova.

Together, the leaders of the Order sector and the reformed Archon convened to discuss their shared objectives and devise a plan to confront the emerging darkness. Both parties recognized the need to put aside their differences and work together for the benefit of the two realms that they both cherished, which made the meeting transparent.

As they deliberated, the Provisioner emphasized the importance of vigilance and unity in the face of the unknown. He urged the members of the Order sector to harness their collective wisdom, magic, and resources to fortify Paranova against the impending threats. The Archon, now fully committed to the cause, added her own insights and resources to the discussion, acknowledging the need to rectify her past mistakes and prove her dedication to the world's well-being.

Within the midst of a collective determination and a renewed understanding of purpose, the Provisioner and Archon took an oath to uphold the Oracle's enduring legacy and shield Paranova from the advancing darkness. They comprehended that their journey ahead would not be without challenges, but they were resolute in confronting them directly. Through the unity of the Order sector and with newfound devotion to righteousness from the Archon, optimism began to emerge amidst hardship.

As the conclusion of the meeting neared, the individuals belonging to the Order division scattered, united by a mutual drive to confront forthcoming obstacles. The journey to safeguard Paranova and fulfill the Oracle's prophecy would not be easy, but they were determined to persevere. United in their cause, they set forth on a path that would test their resolve, challenge their beliefs, and ultimately shape the destiny of Paranova.

....

Amidst the unfolding events and imminent storm, the avatars, under the wise guidance of the Keeper, successfully delivered a shard of the Affinity fragment to the inhabitants of Alora. This shard represented a glimmer of hope, providing a tangible source of power capable of assisting them in their ongoing battle against encroaching darkness.

As word about the arrival of the Affinity shard spread throughout Alora, its residents were infused with a newfound vigor and resoluteness. They perceived it as an emblematic token, fostering unity and reminding them that they weren't alone in confronting mounting disorder. With assistance from the avatars' counsel, those residing within Alora wholeheartedly embraced this powerful shard's potential to reinforce their determination while safeguarding their cherished kingdom.

With the wise guidance of their elven protectors, the inhabitants of Alora commenced unraveling the hidden capacities housed within the Affinity shard. This remarkable artifact metamorphosed into a force for transformation by endowing them with prowess over elemental forces and fostering deeper connections amongst themselves as members of a unified community. In unison, they devoted themselves to tireless practice and refinement, preparing diligently for the inevitable obstacles that awaited them on their path forward.

With the arrival of the Affinity shard, a renewed feeling of togetherness stirred among the elves inhabiting Alora. In view of the menacing growth of darkness, long-standing grievances and divisions were cast aside as they acknowledged the importance of agreement. The elves, renowned for their ancient wisdom and deep bond with nature, generously imparted their knowledge to fellow races, fostering an atmosphere characterized by collaboration and empathetic comprehension.

In the midst of gloom, a faint flicker of optimism illuminated the core essence of Alora. The dormant and concealed Affinity shard emerged as a tangible proof of unwavering determination and strength within its inhabitants. Recognizing their intertwined destinies with Paranova, they tackled the forthcoming obstacles head-on, resolved to surpass them at all costs.

The Kingdom of Alora stood as a testament to the power of unity, resilience, and the faithful belief that light could prevail over darkness. The stage was set for a new chapter in Paranova's history, where mortals could withstand the elemental forces, ready to confront the trials ahead and restore balance to their world. With the Affinity shard as their guiding light, they embraced their shared purpose and stepped forward into an uncertain future, filled with hope and determination.

Chapter 10: Clash of Eternal Flames

The aftermath of Pyrothos's destructive rampage in the southern regions of Paranova is a scene of desolation and sorrow. Lands that were once prosperous now lie in ruins; their vibrant colors replaced by a desolate scene of burned earth. The remnants of towns and villages stand as solemn reminders of the lives upended by the colossal elemental entity. Streets once filled with laughter and bustling activity now bear the weight of silence and devastation.

Among the ruins, individuals who have managed to survive bear expressions of sorrow and exhaustion on their faces. They painstakingly sift through the wreckage, yearning to discover any signs that might bring them closer to finding their loved ones or possibly rescue fragments from what used to be their lives. The atmosphere feels weighted with a mixture of ruinous smells and filled with the tormented cries of those grieving unfathomable losses. The remains of once vibrant forests now stand as dignified guardians, their charred limbs stretching out towards the oppressive gray heavens above.

Amidst the scenes of devastation, a glimmer of resilience emerges. Communities band together, their collective spirit refusing to be extinguished. They offer comfort to one another, sharing meager resources and vowing to rebuild their shattered homes and lives. It is a testament to the unbreakable sapient spirit, defying the overwhelming force that has torn through their world.

In the wake of Pyrothos's rampage, Paranova stands wounded but not defeated. The survivors, marked by loss but driven by determination, come together to rise from the ashes and reclaim their fractured world. As they gather their strength and resources, a new resolve takes hold—a resolve to confront the forces that threaten their existence and restore balance to their once-harmonious realm.

The southern regions of Paranova bear the scars of Pyrothos's devastating rampage; their landscapes have transformed into scorched wastelands. Once-thriving fields are now desolate, their fertile soil transformed into ash. Once signs of progress and society were crumbling villages stood as haunting reminders of the uncontrollable violence that tore through their neighborhoods. Building and structure hues have disappeared, leaving a monochrome palette of charcoal wreckage and smoldering remnants.

The profound and extensive effect on the communities affected is undeniable. Previously providing peace and comfort, now dwellings lie in ruins, their very foundations giving in to devastation. Once vibrant thoroughfares morphed into eerie silence as they bore the scars of fractured cobblestones and charred remnants. Those still residing, having endured this cataclysmic event, are living proof of the distressing toll it has inflicted upon their existence.

The ravaged landscape is an unsettling reminder of the destructive impact of the gigantic beast that scorched the once-fertile region. Once brimming with life and vibrant vegetation, the fields and meadows now lie barren and empty while their once nutrient-rich soil has been reduced to smoldering embers. The devastation's impact on society exceeds far more than these lush lands. Within the affected communities, farmers confront an uncertain future as their livelihoods become threatened by withering crops and starving livestock searching in vain for sustenance. The loss of these productive lands not only engulfs the immediate community but also casts broader shadows on food security and economic stability within the region.

The impact goes far beyond the physical damage. The emotional scars are raw and burning, as families and friends grieve the loss of their loved ones and struggle to comprehend the chaos that has shattered their sense of safety. Sorrow and hopelessness hang heavily in the air, intertwining with the pungent stench of smoke and ruin. Yet amidst this pain, a flicker of resilience emerges. Communities unite, providing support and comfort to one another, determined to rebuild their destroyed homes and discover optimism amidst the hardship.

This is a moment where affected communities face reality head-on; it is a period that tests their determination and ability to bounce back. They understand that recovering from this disaster will be filled with challenges; however, they refuse to surrender to despair. With each step forward, they reclaim fragments of what once was while sowing seeds of hope on barren ground. Together, they draw strength from shared experiences, building bonds that transcend the devastation.

The scorched landscapes and crumbling cities bear witness to the magnitude of the catastrophe, serving as a constant reminder of the forces that threaten their existence. However, a fire has started in the hearts of the affected communities—a fire fueled by tenacity, community, and the conviction that they can overcome even the direst difficulties. The southern regions of Paranova may be scarred, but they are far from defeated.

These communities affected by the destruction have come together to rebuild their homes and lives, supporting each other in their collective efforts. They have formed support networks, sharing resources and knowledge to ensure a brighter future for themselves and future generations. The scars on the southern regions of Paranova serve as living proof of their resilience and determination to rise above the ashes. Other communities have gathered what they can in search of new lands to call home.

The southern regions of Paranova bear the painful scars left behind by Pyrothos's destructive rampage, leaving those who survived trapped within desperation and deep despair. In the aftermath of devastation, elves now find themselves still standing but surrounded by nothing more than remnants of what was once a vibrant existence. Their homes, once comforting sanctuaries filled with warmth and comfort, now lie in ruins, reduced to mere charred fragments that stand as grim reminders of their former glory. The streets, which used to resonate with cheerful laughter and bustling activities, have become hauntingly silent except for resounding echoes of sorrow and agony.

Amidst the ranks of survivors lingers a prevailing sense of hopelessness that infused their souls while they grapple relentlessly to rebuild lives broken amidst utter destruction. The loss endured through death or separation from loved ones weighs heavily on their hearts, casting shadows so dark upon their spirits that they seem almost hopeless. Every passing day becomes not just an ordinary struggle but rather a battle for survival itself as these resilient individuals scrounge desperately to secure scarce resources and draw strength from the unity shared amongst fellow survivors.

Despite their resilience, the survivors are confronted with multiple hurdles that pose a threat to their morale. They struggle daily with hunger and thirst due to the scarcity of food and clean water, which makes their situation worse. The impact of witnessing the devastation creates enduring scars within them, leading to sleepless nights and haunting nightmares. Formerly lively communities now exist in fragments as individuals and families struggle to establish some appearance of normality amid this newfound harsh reality.

Nevertheless, amidst feelings of desperation and hopelessness, a glimmering spark of determination begins to ignite within the hearts of these survivors. They start to rebuild their communities from the ashes, brick by brick and painful step by painful step, because of their shared suffering. They form support networks, sharing their burdens and offering each other a glimmer of hope. Through their resilience and unwavering spirit, they dare to dream of a brighter future, refusing to let Pyrothos' rampage define their existence.

Amidst the wreckage, seeds of optimism are planted. Emerging victorious from the devastation, those who endured vow to commemorate their cherished departed and construct a fortified Paranova that surpasses its former state both in strength and resilience. It is through their combined might and steady determination that they discover the bravery needed to confront forthcoming obstacles and pave the way towards recuperation and renewal.

Individuals longing for security and comfort gravitated towards the entrances of the Volcanic Kingdom, desperately seeking sanctuary amidst the chaos that consumed Paranova. Their weary faces bore the weight of their struggles, and their eyes were filled with a glimmer of hope for respite within the fortress walls. However, their pleas for entry were met with stern denial, with the gates remaining firmly closed. The once-hospitable kingdom now stood as a bastion of isolation, leaving the displaced masses to fend for themselves on the outskirts, their dreams of finding sanctuary dashed against the cold stone walls.

Desperate and with nowhere else to turn, some members of the community began to curse their own God. They questioned why they were abandoned in their time of need, feeling betrayed and forsaken. The bitterness and anger grew within them as they blamed Pyrothos for the hardships they were enduring. Despite their faith being tested, they clung to this act of rebellion as a way to cope with their shattered hopes and dreams. However, some communities endured the test of Pyrothos and saw the scars as a new beginning for their people.

As the ruins of the southern regions of Paranova smolder in the aftermath of Pyrothos's devastating rampage, Aleron's obsession with harnessing and controlling the colossal elemental entity only grew stronger. He delved deeper into the ancient lore and forbidden arts in an effort to discover the secrets that would give him control over Pyrothos because of his insatiable desire for power. The remnants of shattered cities and scorched landscapes served as a grim reminder of the destructive might he sought to wield, driving him further down the treacherous path he had chosen.

Days and nights blurred together as Aleron immersed himself in the pursuit of understanding the elemental forces. He pored over ancient tomes, deciphering cryptic incantations and unraveling complex rituals that had long been forgotten. Through dangerous experiments and daring invocations, he sought to establish a connection with Pyrothos—a link between his own mortal existence and the immense power of the fiery entity.

The trials were exhausting and dangerous. Aleron subjected himself to harrowing rituals, enduring the searing heat and risking his very soul in the process. He danced on the precipice of madness, his mind teetering between elation and despair as he strived to commune with the volatile essence of Pyrothos. The elemental force responded, its presence pulsating through his veins like molten fire but always on the edge of slipping from his grasp.

In his relentless pursuit, Aleron discovered the intricate dance required to exert influence over Pyrothos. With each encounter, he refined his techniques, seeking to command the elemental entity's power while avoiding its chaotic wrath. He learned to channel his will and intent through intricate incantations and ancient sigils, forging a fragile bond between himself and the seething force of nature. Aleron's relentless pursuit of harnessing Pyrothos' power led him to discover the delicate balance between exerting influence and avoiding chaos.

Yet, for all his progress, Aleron realized that his control over Pyrothos was far from absolute. The fiery entity remained a spontaneous force, its essence resistant to complete subjugation. Waves of scorching heat and bursts of destructive flames would surge forth at unpredictable moments, challenging Aleron's authority and leaving devastation in their wake. It was a constant battle of dominance and submission, a delicate balance between asserting his will and surrendering to the raw power of the elemental force.

As Aleron's connection with Pyrothos deepened, his once-cold demeanor grew intense with a mix of awe and desperation. The fire that danced in his eyes reflected both his promise of command and the dangerous dance with the chaos he had consumed. The allure of wielding such tremendous power overwhelmed him, and with each interaction, he teetered on the precipice of losing himself to the inferno he sought to control.

The path Aleron had chosen was fraught with uncertainty, and he knew it. The power he coveted was as volatile as the flames themselves, capable of both reshaping the world and consuming its wielder. Despite his desire for dominance, he continued to persist in his pursuit. Aleron's unrelenting desire for control over Pyrothos and the elemental energies flowing through Paranova endangered not only his own sanity but also the fundamental fabric of the world he aimed to conquer. As he delved deeper into the forbidden arts, Aleron's mind became a battleground between reason and madness. The whispers of Havoc echoed in his ears, tempting him with promises of unimaginable power. With each step closer to his goal, the delicate balance of Pyrothos trembled, threatening to unleash chaos upon all who inhabited it.

As Aleron delved deeper into the intricate process of taming Pyrothos, a dark unease gnawed at his soul. The immense power coursing through him, while intoxicating, it came at a steep cost. He could feel his essence withering away like a dying flame flickering in the wind. Doubt crept into his mind as whispering tales of his own frailty and the fragility of his resolve. The weight of responsibility bore down upon him, for he knew that the fate of his subjects rested upon his success. The thoughts of Pyrothos untamed, wreaking havoc upon the lands, had sent a shiver down his spine. With each passing day, as his own vitality waned, the urgency to overcome his own doubts and harness the colossal entity grew ever more pressing. He steeled his resolve, drawing upon the flickering embers of his spirit, for he could not allow his own internal decay to eclipse the destiny of his followers.

Rumors like the tendrils of darkness had snaked their way throughout the Dark One kingdom, spreading whispers of Alora's alleged mistreatment and enslavement of the Dark One kind. These murmurs, woven with threads of truth and elaborated with layers of fear and uncertainty, reached the ears of Aleron, which began stirring a storm of emotions within him. He listened intently to the tales that painted a grim portrait of Alora's involvement in manufacturing a new race, born out of the suffering and exploitation of his own followers.

Aleron dug deeper into the truth of these rumors, driven by a mix of righteous rage and a desire for power. He sought to uncover the hidden truths, to peel back the veils of deception, and to reveal the dark secrets that he believed Alora was desperately trying to conceal. Each whispered account he encountered, each testimonial of cruelty and oppression, fueled his determination to expose Alora's alleged transgressions to the world.

Armed with extensive knowledge and fueled by a strong sense of righteous anger, Aleron pondered his options deliberately. He resolved to wield the power embedded within these rumors as a weapon in order to manipulate society and execute a grand scheme that would further his personal ambitions. Meticulously assembling fragments of truth, he skillfully intertwined them into a narrative brimming with tales of injustice and anguish, aiming to strike an emotional chord within the hearts of the elves.

Aware that the key to his triumph lay in not only captivating the masses but also stoking their hunger for change, Aleron understood the importance of presenting these rumors in an effective manner. With accurate precision, he strategically dispersed exciting tidbits of information at well-calculated intervals designed to elicit feelings of urgency and rage among his audience. Through this calculated approach, he sought to galvanize individuals into initiating meaningful actions while simultaneously fueling their passion, thereby clearing a path for his ultimate plan's realization to unfold.

Aleron devised a cunning strategy to control the typical dark ones out of his intense hatred for the light ones. Leveraging the tales of rumor, he sought to fuel their animosity towards the light ones, creating a narrative that aligned with his grand scheme of obliterating them entirely. Recognizing the need for a cause that would rally his followers, especially in the wake of Pyrothos's actions and growing concerns about morality, Aleron aimed to provide the push for justice and liberation that would unite the dark ones behind him.

Standing before a sea of faces, Aleron unleashed his proclamation on the masses. His voice carried on as a clarion call of outrage and rebellion, reverberating through the air aiming to reach the depths of their souls. With each carefully chosen word, he painted vivid images of agony and despair, drawing upon the collective anguish of the elves to stoke the fires of anger and vengeance. The crowd now brimmed with a burning desire for retribution.

The impact of Aleron's words was memorable. The air was filled with gasps of disbelief, then with murmurs of unrest that developed into loud cries for justice. The tales of suffering that Aleron had masterfully portrayed sparked anger in their hearts. The emotional tide swelled, drowning out reason and replacing it with an insatiable hunger for vengeance. The masses, united by their shared grievances and the charismatic presence of Aleron, embraced his cause and pledged their loyal support.

And thus, the realm is balanced on the brink of war. Aleron not only managed to wield the influence of hearsay but also transformed it into a formidable weapon capable of igniting hostilities. The populace stood ready to support Aleron because they were adamant that their mission was right and were full of passion, purpose, and an unquenchable thirst for vengeance.

As the dust settled and the echoes of Aleron's proclamation faded, the destiny of Paranova hung in the balance. A carefully woven web of rumors and the manipulated emotions of the populace had set the wheels of war in motion. The stage was now set for a clash of forces as Aleron's grand design unfolded, and the fate of the kingdom and its residents rested on the outcome of their impending battle. Aleron rallied his devoted followers and got them ready for the inevitable conflict, thanks to his steady conviction. The weight of their collective determination hung heavy in the air as they stood ready to defend their cause with every ounce of their being.

....

When the Queen of Alora assigned a specially chosen team of Vanguard and Arcanists with the sacred duty of restoring equilibrium using the sacred Affinity Shard, their significance in the grand plan became evident. Consisting of adept fighters, knowledgeable arcanists, and gifted individuals attuned to elemental forces, they epitomized hope and resilience when confronted with impending danger.

Bound together by resolute loyalty and unshakeable faith in the potential held within the Affinity Shard, this diverse cluster displayed themselves as a symbol of support, ready to confront any hurdle that threatened to disrupt harmony's delicate balance. With combined might and an unyielding resolve, they stood prepared to undertake any necessary measures to ensure peace once again reigned supreme upon Alora's lands.

The Vanguard, along with the arcanists driven by a shared purpose, convenes in the hallowed halls of Alora's ancient citadel. They have tough conversations while grappling with the weight of responsibility and the echoes of legends around them. They meticulously plan their next course of action. The strategic minds among them analyze maps, scrolls, and ancient tomes, seeking the most effective route to reach the heart of darkness—the Kingdom of Dark Ones, where Pyrothos and the dark elven kind await. One example of their detailed planning involves dissecting the history of Pyrothos and the dark elven kind, studying their strengths, weaknesses, and past battles.

They strategically assign vanguards to gather intelligence, while arcanists delve into forbidden arts to uncover any hidden weaknesses or enchantments that could be exploited. They also devise a carefully coordinated attack strategy, taking advantage of covert paths and leveraging the elemental powers of the arcanists to weaken Pyrothos and his kin before engaging in direct combat.

A debate had unfolded between the queen and commander Relios, and the group was entrusted with wielding the affinity shard presented by the plant avatars. Internal conflicts within the kingdom cast a shadow over the operation, but the queen remained resolute. She emphasized the importance of recognizing the larger threat—Pyrothos—and the impending danger it poses. Despite the inner troubles threatening the stability of their realm, the queen insisted that prioritizing the resolution of this colossal menace was paramount. The fate of their kingdom, and perhaps the entire world, hung in the balance, and the queen urged her military and special classes to unite against the impending doom.

Their planning sessions are rife with argument, but wisdom and a shared desire to reclaim harmony temper them. Each member brings their unique expertise to the table, be it tactical prowess, elemental mastery, or ancient lore. They understand the risks and challenges that lie ahead, but their unbreakable determination fuels their resolve. They know that the affinity shard, entrusted to them as a symbol of Paranova's last hope, holds the key to pacifying the raging forces of Pyrothos and restoring balance.

With the Affinity Shard pulsating with suppressed power and its energy resonating with the hearts of the vanguard, they forge a bond, a sacred pact to fulfill their purpose. They don their armor, grasp their weapons, and embark on a long journey with the weight of the world resting on their shoulders. With each step, their determination intensifies, knowing that the shard in their possession is not merely an object but a beacon of salvation—a conduit through which they can channel the forces of harmony and quell the destructive might of Pyrothos.

The mission of the vanguard extends far beyond mere physicality; it involves the spiritual and moral realms. They carry with them not only the aspirations and wishes of numerous souls but also the prayers of those who long for a world free from turmoil and despair. Their unwavering dedication to their cause ignites their inner spirits, while their support bolsters their determination. With the affinity shard shimmering radiantly, they advance confidently, ready to confront any challenges that lie ahead in the kingdom of dark ones.

The vanguard's mission is not just to conquer the kingdom of the dark ones; rather, it aims to revive hope and bring light into a place where darkness reigns. Their selfless purpose resonates deeply within many hearts, inspiring others to unite under their banner and oppose malevolent forces. As they forge ahead on this hazardous path, their unyielding resolve becomes a beacon of optimism for all believers in a brighter future.

In the heart of Alora's vanguard war room, a gathering took place. This assembly consisted of seasoned strategists and commanders who convened to design a strategy that would steer their advance towards the domain of the kingdom of dark ones. Charts were sprawled across the tabletop, detailingly outlining treacherous terrains and identifying possible hurdles along their route. Each participant contributed with their specialized expertise, knowledge of battle tactics, and understanding of both the enemy's strengths and weaknesses. The atmosphere in this chamber pulsated with intensity and a shared sense of purpose.

As debates occurred among strategists, an orchestration emerged as their voices intermingled harmoniously within the confines of the room. They understood that their success depended not solely on individual skills but also on collective unity—functioning as one synchronized entity. With each passing second, accurate planning transformed into a beacon for all hopeful believers in light conquering darkness.

Discussions filled the air as they weighed their options and evaluated the risks. They were aware that the kingdom of dark ones was a stronghold that was well-defended by the dark elves, which had a reputation for forming alliances with sinister forces. The vanguard understood the severity of the task at hand—they were not only facing Pyrothos, the embodiment of chaos, but also an entire kingdom that thrived in the shadows. The vanguard knew that their mission required careful planning and strategic maneuvers. They realized that they needed to gather intelligence on the dark elven kind and devise a plan to weaken their alliances with sinister forces. The fate of the world rested on their shoulders, but they were determined to be the beacon of hope that would bring light back to the realm.

The elemental storms, wreaking havoc across the land, had altered the familiar landscapes and pathways, rendering the old routes unknown. In the wake of Pyrothos and other elemental disturbances, the queen's southwestern expansion faced significant challenges. The territories, once confidently seized, now bore scars, requiring careful consideration for any strategic movement. With the element of surprise in mind, the scouting mission became essential. Hidden but effective, the goal was to plan a surprise attack rather than passively waiting for the impending conflict to reach their cherished kingdom. The scouts prepared to navigate the altered terrain, seeking a route that balanced secrecy and strategic advantage.

With careful consideration, the vanguard strategists charted a course that balanced speed and stealth with a calculated approach. They sought to exploit weaknesses in their enemies' defenses, identify strategic chokepoints, and exploit any potential divisions within their ranks. The goal was clear: to reach Pyrothos and confront the colossal entity while minimizing casualties and ensuring the safety of the affinity shard.

The military, cognizant of the potential ambushes from both the dark ones and the raiders that had been plaguing the mainland, took strategic precautions. The scouting party, comprising the kingdom's best, opted for a southern route, steering clear of the most vulnerable areas. They established outposts along the way, employing a sophisticated communication network. The arcanist psychics, renowned for their telepathic abilities, played a crucial role in maintaining contact between these scattered outposts. Their telepathic prowess allowed for swift and secure communication over great distances, ensuring that any sign of lurking enemies in the territory could be promptly detected and addressed.

The Vanguard recognized that their success hinged on unity and cooperation, as they would face relentless opposition on their journey. They assigned roles and responsibilities to their soldiers, considering their unique skills and expertise. Special units were formed, specializing in elemental magic, distance and close combat. Each member understood the importance of their contribution to the collective effort, forging an unbreakable bond among comrades.

Supply lines were established, provisions accurately calculated, and contingencies prepared for unforeseen challenges. The vanguard leaders sought to empower their troops with hope and determination, fostering a sense of camaraderie and purpose that would fuel their resolve on the battlefield. They emphasized the significance of the affinity shard as their ultimate weapon against Pyrothos and the key to restoring balance and averting further catastrophe.

The commander, his voice resonant with determination, emphasized the importance of the Affinity Shard as their key weapon in their quest to reclaim balance. He spoke of the shard's unique ability to harness and manipulate elemental energies and its connection to the very fabric of Paranova's existence. It held within it the power to weaken Pyrothos, disrupt its destructive influence, and restore harmony to the land.

Each member of the vanguard recognized the weight of responsibility that came with wielding the shard. They understood that it held not only the potential to bring about victory but also the delicate balance of their world. They discussed strategies and tactics while planning on how to maximize the shard's potential in their upcoming battles.

The shard was seen as more than a mere object—it was a symbol of hope. It represented their collective belief that they could restore order amidst the chaos and safeguard their realm and its inhabitants. Its radiant glow served as a beacon, guiding them towards a future where Paranova would thrive in harmony once again. The realization of the shard's immense power dawned on them, highlighting its potential to tip the scales in their favor. Nevertheless, they possessed an acute awareness regarding the weighty accountability that accompanied its usage. With a solemn promise to practice vigilance and altruism, they were determined not to disturb the fragile equilibrium they passionately sought to uphold.

As they debated, voices filled with passion and conviction enveloped the war room. The vanguard members recognized that their hope for reclaiming balance rested on their ability to wield the affinity shard with precision and purpose. They shared a common vision of a world free from the devastating grip of Pyrothos, where life could flourish without fear.

With each passing moment, their determination grew stronger. The affinity shard became a focal point, a rallying symbol that fueled their resolve and ignited a fire within their hearts. They knew that their mission was not just about defeating Pyrothos but about preserving the very essence of Paranova and ensuring its future prosperity.

Under the guidance of the plant avatars, the masters of elements delved into the intricate knowledge of the affinity shard. The arcanists, with their keen observation skills, closely studied the shard's properties, while the military strategized on how to best utilize its immense powers. A consensus emerged among them that the wielders of the shard should be the masters of elements, individuals intricately connected to the elemental forces of nature. This decision was grounded in the belief that their deep connection with the elements would enable them to harness the shard's power effectively and with precision.

As the discussion continued, plans were laid out, strategies were refined, and the importance of the affinity shard spread throughout the war room. It became clear to all that their hope for reclaiming balance relied heavily on their ability to wield this powerful artifact. They would seize this opportunity, united in their purpose, ready to face the battles ahead with purpose and the guiding light of the Affinity Shard.

The choice had been finalized—the vanguard would embark on a journey towards the kingdom of dark ones, home to Pyrothos and the dark elves. They were fully aware of the dangers that lay before them: formidable clashes awaited them, and there might be a need for sacrifice along the way. Nevertheless, their loyal dedication to their objective, their steadfast belief in what they fought for, and their resolute determination gave them strength.

The Vanguard launched themselves on a challenging journey with the arcanists by their side, navigating through treacherous landscapes and facing formidable enemies. They carried the hopes of their families, the weight of their kingdom's future resting upon their shoulders. The vanguard advanced toward the heart of darkness with their tactical plan in place, their spirits fortified by their shared goal, and their eyes set on the road ahead, prepared to face Pyrothos and the kingdom of dark ones and put an end to the chaos that was threatening to consume Paranova.

•••••••

The Alora army, marching southward with a purpose, faced relentless ambushes from the dark ones' assassins and raiders. These skirmishes tested the elite vanguard's mettle, but the Alora warriors, well-trained and disciplined, proved their prowess in battle. Despite the ruthless tactics employed by the dark ones, the Alora forces remained focused on their mission. They recognized the importance of swift and decisive action, understanding that any survivors from these skirmishes could pose a threat if they reached the safety of the dark one kingdom. The Alora elite vanguard moved forward with a fierce determination to face the impending difficulties that lay ahead.

As the majority of Alora's army marched continuously towards Pyrothos, their eyes were met with an awe-inspiring and terrifying sight. The once-calm skies were now scarlet, tinted with blazing embers that danced and swirled, casting an awful glow over the land. Exotic energy charged the air, creating roaring sounds.

As they ventured deeper into the scarred landscape, their hearts swelled with a mixture of trepidation and determination. The colossal figure of Pyrothos loomed on the horizon, an imposing silhouette against the blazing backdrop. Its immense form, wreathed in flames and billowing smoke, sent tremors through the earth with each step it took. The ground quivered beneath the soldiers' boots, showcasing the raw power that Pyrothos possessed.

As the soldiers drew nearer to Pyrothos, the heat intensified, causing sweat to trickle down their foreheads and their armor to become uncomfortably hot. The atmosphere was charged with vitality, unleashing a strange orchestra of burst and sizzle noises. The smell of smoldering sulfur invaded their lungs, making it difficult for them to breathe freely. Even in the face of physical uneasiness and extensive apprehension, their determination stood strong.

The soldiers exchanged nervous glances, their eyes filled with a blend of fear and reverence. They marveled at the sheer magnitude of Pyrothos, realizing the monumental task before them. But amidst the apprehension, a resolute spirit stirred within their ranks. They were warriors, protectors of their realm, and bearers of the Affinity Shard. They had trained for this moment, honed their skills, and carried the hopes of Paranova on their shoulders.

The soldiers, fueled by an unbreakable belief in their cause, forged ahead undeterred. Their resolve was strengthened as they laid eyes on Pyrothos, knowing that defeating this gigantic being would not only bring about balance but also secure the fate of their world. With minds focused and hearts armored against despair, they marched onward with readiness to confront the most demanding test life had thrust upon them.

Aleron, still in the process of taming the colossal Pyrothos, used his unique bond with the elemental entity to gain insight into the approaching threat. He saw through Pyrothos's eyes and sensed the advance of the Alora army towards the dark one kingdom. Fueled by panic and urgency, Aleron quickly conveyed the imminent danger to the dark one army. The news of the approaching light ones and the potential threat to their kingdom spread like wildfire among the dark ones, striking fear and a sense of impending conflict.

In response, the dark one forces swiftly mobilized their defenses, understanding that the war, which they had not sought, was now brought to their doorstep. Despite the unexpected nature of the conflict, the dark ones stood ready, their resolve unyielding. They prepared to face the Alora army, determined to defend their sacred kingdom from the perceived threat and ensure the survival of their elven heritage. The stage was set for a confrontation that would test the strengths and strategies of both factions in the unfolding drama of Paranova.

The dark one army, consisting of various castes within their society, stood united with a shared purpose—to defend their homeland against the encroaching threat from the Alora army. The Bloodfire, masters of fire magic and pyromancy, prepared to unleash their destructive powers upon anyone who dared challenge them. The emberblades, armed with weapons forged in the depths of their forges, prepared themselves for close-quarter combat. Meanwhile, the Rippers, skilled in strategic warfare, quickly devised flanking routes to outmaneuver their foes.

The Shadow Council, a secretive and influential group among the dark ones, enlisted the services of the Warlocks, approving their use of any means necessary to ensure victory. As the dark one army stood in formation, their allies from the human raider clan joined them, recognizing the urgency of the situation. Together, they formed a formidable force, ready to face the Alora army and defend their sacred kingdom with determination and strength. The air crackled with tension as the impending clash between light and dark forces loomed on the horizon.

As the soldiers closed in on Pyrothos, the monstrous entity that had brought chaos to Paranova felt the trembling ground. The weight of its enormous body brought forth an increasing sensation of heat, yet they refused to succumb to fear. Witnessing firsthand the wreckage and loss of lives and despair shrouding what was once a flourishing land, they seized this opportunity to alter history. Step by step, with purpose and unbreakable resolve, their commitment intensified. Endlessly training and refining their battle tactics, they prepared themselves for this very moment.

The weight of their weapons felt reassuring in their hands, a symbol of their commitment to protect their kingdom and restore peace to Paranova. As they approached the towering figure of Pyrothos, its fiery breath scorching the earth beneath their feet, their hearts pounded in their chests. But they stood tall, their eyes locked on the beast, ready to face their greatest challenge yet. The air crackled with anticipation, and a resounding battle cry echoed through the ranks, uniting them for a common purpose.

With the crimson skies as their witness, the army of Alora stood on the threshold of battle, ready to confront the embodiment of chaos itself. They raised their weapons, their voices merging into a resounding war cry that echoed through the desolate landscape. The clash of steel, the crackle of elemental magic, and the resolute determination of the soldiers would define the imminent battles to come—a clash between the forces of darkness and the willful spirit of the vanguard, determined to reclaim the balance and restore hope to Paranova.

As the Vanguard of Alora marched forward, their hearts strong and their spirits burning, they were thrown into the thick of battle. As the forces of light battled with the dark forces that tried to destroy Paranova, the clash of steel, the crackling sound of elemental power, and the loud roars of battle echoed across the war-torn landscape. A powerful warlock sorcerer from the forces of darkness arose in the middle of the mayhem, conjuring an army of shadow creatures to overwhelm the vanguard.

However, the front line demonstrated resolute determination and unfaltering persistence, displaying their unmatched skill and relentless fortitude in their counterattack. Every swing of their blades and burst of mystical energy produced a powerful rejection against the growing cloak of darkness, encouraging hope in others and rallying allies to join them. The clash between radiance and darkness manifested itself as an emblematic representation of the ceaseless battle between righteousness and malevolence. Thus, it stood as a testament to the elven kind and their unbreakable fortitude and belief that even when confronted with seemingly insurmountable differences, courage coupled with unity would ultimately triumph over hardship.

With unparalleled precision, the elemental masters demonstrated their control over the elements. Their enemies were held in fearful awe as fire twisted and turned, consuming all it touched. The ground beneath their foes' feet shook violently, causing even the bravest to tremble. The mighty force of water relentlessly surged forward, threatening to drown those who opposed it. And gusts of wind erupted across the battlefield like a wild tempest, unceremoniously tossing aside anyone foolish enough to challenge them. Each individual elementalist possessed a unique bond with the elements, utilizing this connection to manipulate spells and call forth powers that struck terror deep into the hearts of their enemies.

In the chaos of the battlefield, the shadowmancers skillfully joined forces with the rippers in their flanking maneuver, swiftly targeting the vanguard archers of the Alora army. The archers found themselves overwhelmed by the ripper blades, and those who survived were forced to retreat, leaving behind a prime location that the shadowmancers seized. Positioned strategically, they became a formidable force, unleashing potent shadow magic behind the lines of the Alora army.

However, the Elementalists and Arcanists among the Alora forces were quick to respond. With mastery over elemental and arcane energies, they erected elemental walls and utilized arcane magic to counteract the shadowmancers' onslaught. The battlefield became a dynamic interplay of elemental forces as each side sought to gain the upper hand in this intense confrontation. The Alora army, though facing unexpected challenges, demonstrated resilience in the face of the dark ones' cunning tactics.

The Emberblades and human raiders engaged fiercely with the Vanguard and the Alora military; the clash of weapons and the fiery chaos created a spectacle of war. The Bloodfire, proficient in fire magic and pyromancy, unleashed flames upon the battlefield. However, the elementalists from Alora demonstrated their mastery over water magic, countering the bloodfire's fiery onslaught. The battlefield became a dynamic arena where elemental forces clashed, and the Alora army managed to neutralize the dark ones' advantage in fire magic.

Amidst the chaos, the Sinister Shadows, hidden and observing, played a crucial role in the dark ones' strategy. Serving as strategic leaders, they guided the dark ones with insights into the movement of the battle, identifying opportunities to strike at weak points in the Alora forces. The sinister shadows' hidden presence added an element of cunning and calculated precision to the overall strategy, making the battle a challenging and dynamic contest between the two factions.

Commander Relios, recognizing the pivotal role Pyrothos played on the stage of the war, rallied his army to regroup and prepare for the looming threat. The vanguard's success in pushing back their enemies had given them a momentary advantage, but the commander knew that facing Pyrothos required strategic planning and coordinated efforts.

The battlefield became a dynamic landscape, with both factions adjusting their positions and strategies. The Alora military, now regrouping, sought to anticipate and counteract the potential havoc Pyrothos could unleash. The tension on the battlefield heightened as the dark ones prepared to unleash their colossal and fiery ally, shaping the course of the impending conflict.

As it were calm before the storm, Pyrothos loomed ahead, a behemoth wreathed in flames and fury. Its immense form surged forward, leaving destruction in its wake. The ground trembled beneath its colossal weight, and its fiery breath scorched the air. But the vanguard stood steadfast, their spirits unyielding, as they directed their focus and combined their powers to counter this formidable foe.

Bolts of lightning crackled through the skies as the arcanists channeled their energy, striking at the very heart of Pyrothos. Walls of earth rose to shield the vanguard from its fiery onslaught, while torrents of water sought to douse the flames that threatened to consume them. With their unity and the guidance of the Affinity Shard, they harnessed the full extent of their elemental prowess, their powers interweaving in a symphony of light and energy.

The battles raged on, the clash between light and darkness intensifying with each passing moment. The vanguard fought with focus, their eyes fixed on their goal: to reclaim balance and restore harmony to Paranova. The vanguard knew the stakes were high, for the very fate of their world and kingdom were at risk.

Through their collective efforts and unwavering resolve, the vanguard pressed forward while pushing back the forces of the dark ones and challenging the might of Pyrothos. They witnessed the impact of their combined strength—the triumph of unity against the forces of chaos. With every defeated foe, their confidence grew, and their belief in the power of the affinity shard intensified.

The battles were fierce and grueling, but the vanguard held steadfast. They fought not just for their own survival but also for the future of Paranova. As the sun dipped below the horizon, the resounding clash of weapons and the echoes of elemental forces continued, a testament to their unyielding spirit and their commitment to restoring balance. In one particular battle, the vanguard found themselves outnumbered and surrounded by a horde of chaos-infested creatures.

Facing their opponents head-on, the members of the vanguard stood firmly side by side, each showcasing their distinct talents for safeguarding and aiding one another. United in purpose, they acted as an invincible barrier, countering effortlessly every successive assault from their adversaries. These tenacious warriors kept their alliance strong in the face of seemingly hopeless odds. To dismantle the chaos that opposing forces had sparked, they seamlessly coordinated their individual efforts using intricate maneuvers and clever strategies. As they triumphed over every vanquished foe encountered on this dangerous journey, the bond binding them grew mightier with each passing conquest.

As the battle raged on, a sudden turn of events shook the resolve of the vanguard. Pyrothos, under Aleron's insidious control, unleashed a torrent of devastating flames and storms that ravaged the battlefield. The forces of darkness seemed to gain the upper hand, causing the vanguard to be scattered and their defenses to be weakened.

In the midst of the mayhem, amidst all the disorder and confusion, their ultimate weapon against Pyrothos—the Affinity Shard—became lost within the chaos. Panic enveloped the hearts of the vanguard, as this shard represented their glimmering hope in restoring balance and triumphing over the gigantic entity. Its absence rendered their mission seemingly impossible, opening a gateway for despair to potentially infiltrate their ranks.

Under the direction of the shadow council and in collaboration with the Shadowmancers, the warlocks seized the chance that the defenseless vanguard offered. They launched a relentless assault on the retreating Alora forces, taking advantage of the chaotic fires unleashed by Pyrothos. The combination of Pyrothos's devastating flames and the calculated strikes from the shadowy forces created a nightmarish scene on the battlefield.

The dark ones, while utilizing Pyrothos as a powerful ally, also faced the grim reality of casualties within their own ranks. The fiery storms engulfed both Alora and the dark one soldiers, turning the battlefield into a harrowing display of destruction and chaos. The sinister shadows, acting as strategic advisors, continued to guide the dark ones in their efforts to control and maximize the impact of Pyrothos's unleashed power. The outcome of the conflict hung in the balance, dependent on the dark ones' ability to wield the formidable forces at their disposal.

However, during this grim moment that shrouded the Alora army in darkness, it was precisely when those gifted in wielding elemental magic, called an Elementalist, stepped forward to confront these circumstances head-on. Recognizing the dire need for the Affinity Shard, they summoned their strength and rallied their remaining forces. With their innate connection to the elements, they channeled their powers to search for the shard amidst the chaos.

They scoured the land, manipulating wind currents to catch whispers of its location and using earth magic to sense vibrations underground. Days turned into weeks, but their determination never wavered. Finally, they found the shard hidden deep inside a trench, thanks to their intuition and the whispers of the elements. With renewed hope, they sought out to retrieve it, knowing that their success would be the key to restoring balance and defeating the colossal entity once and for all.

Recognizing the significance of the affinity shard, the Sinister Shadows sent out their own members along with knowledgeable rippers to look for the elusive artifact. They carefully maneuvered through the battlefield to avoid the relentless waves of flames while being aware of the chaotic environment that Pyrothos' fiery onslaught had created.

As the Rippers provided protection and cleared a path, the shadowy figures of the sinister shadows infiltrated the outskirts of the conflict zone. Their mission to locate the affinity shard became increasingly urgent, considering its potential to sway the tide of the battle in favor of the dark ones. The shadows moved with stealth and precision, utilizing the cover of the chaotic warfare to their advantage. The outcome of the conflict seemed to hinge on the success of their mission and the strategic use of the affinity shard.

The Shadow Council closely monitored the dwindling numbers of their shadowed operatives due to the strategic actions of the vanguard archers. As they became aware of the threat the affinity shard posed, their focus changed to ensuring that their sinister shadows would be successful in locating the artifact. The council understood that the shard held the potential to counteract their ultimate weapon, Pyrothos, and thus, its significance could not be underestimated.

While the chaos of battle raged on and the fires from Pyrothos intensified, the shadow council coordinated efforts to protect and support their shadowy operatives. They issued orders to redirect the vanguard archers' attention and create distractions, aiming to provide the sinister shadows with a window of opportunity to secure the affinity shard.

Bolts of lightning crackled through the air as the arcanists and elementalists scoured the battlefield. Walls of earth rose and fell, guided by their will as they sought to uncover the precious artifact. Undeterred by any strong wind or raging water going on through the battlefield, they scoured the scattered remains.

Suddenly, amidst the ruins and burning remnants within the trenches, something caught their eye—a faint flicker of light. Resting beneath the ruins of war lay the affinity shard, radiating optimism and defying destruction. With renewed determination apparent on their faces, the arcanists carefully recovered the shard, cradling it in their arms as its vibrant energy harmonized with their own.

With the Affinity Shard reclaimed, the elementalists knew that their task was not yet complete. They understood that it was their responsibility to wield its power, harness its essence, and bring it to bear against Pyrothos. Drawing upon their training and the connection they had forged with the shard, they prepared themselves for the final confrontation.

The moment they stood there; a wave of determination surged over them. They understood that the fate of their world rested on their shoulders and they were prepared to confront whatever obstacles lay ahead. The elementalists headed towards Pyrothos with a resolution to vanquish the forces of evil, their hearts brimming with bravery and their heads bent over backwards in their pursuit of success.

As the sinister shadows and their ripper allies secured the affinity shard under the guidance of the shadow council, the emberblade and bloodfire units valiantly attempted to come to their defense. However, the vanguard and arcanists of Alora strategically maneuvered, creating a trap that prevented the dark ones from fleeing with the powerful artifact.

The battlefield became a chaotic spectacle as the elementalists continued their struggle against Pyrothos and the vanguard engaged in a fierce confrontation with the emberblades and bloodfire. The strategic moves from both sides unfolded like a carefully choreographed dance, each attempting to outwit and outmaneuver the other in the pursuit of victory.

The sudden realization that Aleron had commanded Pyrothos to obliterate both the Alora and dark one armies brought a momentary pause to the chaotic battlefield. The dark ones, in a state of disbelief, hesitated, allowing the vanguard of Alora to breach their lines. Commander Relios, seizing the opportunity, led his forces to the shard wielder, swiftly eliminating them and securing the affinity shard.

With the shard now in his possession, commander Relios strategically positioned himself to unleash its power before Pyrothos could execute the devastating blow that would have annihilated both armies standing in the prime location. The fate of the battlefield hung in the balance as the commander prepared to wield the shard and potentially alter the course of the conflict in favor of Alora.

With a surge of determination, Commander Relios unleashed the full force of the Affinity Shard. He channeled its energy, directing it towards Pyrothos and unleashing a wave of elemental power that countered the colossal entity's devastating attacks. Flames were quenched, storms were tamed, and a semblance of balance was restored.

In a display of unparalleled skill and purpose, the arcanists, elementalists, and archers fought back against Pyrothos, their powers intertwining with the might of the Affinity Shard. With each strike, they weakened the hold that Aleron had over the elemental entity, freeing Pyrothos from his insidious influence.

As Pyrothos regained control over its own powers, it unleashed a final surge of elemental energy, overpowering Aleron and causing him to fall. The army of Alora stood victorious, their unity and resilience proving that even the strongest of enemies could be defeated.

As Pyrothos, freed from Aleron's control, redirected its fury towards the dark ones, a startling alliance emerged on the battlefield. The protectors of divine magic within the arcanists, recognizing the imminent threat, had joined forces with the magic users of the dark ones. Setting aside their differences, they combined their formidable powers to create a protective force field that enveloped the battlefield and the kingdom beyond.

This unexpected collaboration between Alora and the Dark Ones proved to be a turning point in the battle, as their united strength overwhelmed Pyrothos. The force field not only shielded the kingdom from destruction but also weakened Pyrothos, making it vulnerable to the combined attacks of the allied forces.

This extraordinary collaboration served as a shield against Pyrothos' destructive onslaught. The energy of light and darkness merged, intertwining in a dance of elemental forces. The protectors of divine magic and the wielders of dark power stood side by side; their unity mirrored the common goal that they shared—to safeguard Paranova from the impending cataclysm.

With the attention of Pyrothos and the dark ones focused on the protectors, the vanguard seized the opportunity. They harnessed the power of the Affinity Shard, its radiant energy pulsating with the essence of balance and restoration. As one, they unleashed a coordinated assault, driving Pyrothos back towards the very volcano from which it had emerged.

Pyrothos experienced severe resistance from the combined armies at every turn. The atmosphere was bursting from the collision of energy and an eruption of elemental magic. The ground shook beneath their feet as they drove the massive beast closer to the volcano's mouth. The defenders' force field stood firm, shielding the kingdom from the raging turbulence around them. The elementalists, their fortitude and sense of duty compels them to make one last move as the struggle reaches its peak. They channeled the magical power of the affinity shard towards the Inarus Inferno volcano, its radiant energy bursting outward. The shard, a vessel of balance and control, became a symbol of faith and their relentless dedication.

The Elementalists sent the Affinity Shard into the volcano's core with a powerful throw. It soared through the air, a dazzling streak against the crimson sky, till it made an impact within the raging inferno below. As the shard connected with the molten depths, an explosion of power discharged, echoing with Pyrothos' own essence.

The shard's contact with the volcano unleashed a massive surge of power, generating an intense vibration inside Pyrothos' depths. This was an important moment for the elementalists since they had effectively harnessed the radiant energy of the volcano and funneled it through the affinity shard. It became a symbol of their eternal will and a flame of hope for all who saw its brilliance against the crimson sky.

A cataclysmic explosion erupted, shaking the surrounding landscape and sending shockwaves throughout Paranova. The force was immense yet contained within the confines of the volcano. As the ash settled, a stillness settled upon the land. The power of the affinity shard sealed Pyrothos, the elemental entity that had wreaked havoc and endangered the delicate balance of the world, inside the volcano's depths.

The Vanguard, their breaths heavy and their bodies weary, stood united in their victory. The protectors of divine magic and the castes of the dark ones, having set aside their differences for the greater good, joined them. Together, they surveyed the aftermath of their challenging battle, a testament to the strength of unity and the triumph of purpose.

In the wake of the unexpected shift in allegiance among the dark one army, the shadow council found themselves in disbelief. They came to the realization that the very forces they were trying to control for the greater good might not appreciate their sacrifices and manipulation. Witnessing the armies on the battlefield displaying mutual respect and unity, the shadow council slipped away, avoiding exposure. With Aleron's absence and the dark ones poised for a new beginning, the council foresaw the potential for truth to surface. They understood that the manipulated forces might turn against them once they learned the reality of their deceptions.

With Pyrothos sealed away, Paranova could begin its journey towards healing and restoration. The scars left by the devastation would serve as a reminder of the difficult struggle endured but also shown the resilience and unchanging spirit of the elves. The citizens of Paranova came together to rebuild their shattered homes and communities, determined to create a brighter future. They embraced the opportunity for growth and transformation, using their collective strength to forge a society that was even stronger than before. As they worked hand in hand, hope bloomed amidst the ruins, igniting a renewed sense of purpose and unity among the mortals of Paranova.

The Vanguard, the Arcanists, and the Elementalists knew that their roles as guardians of Paranova were far from over. They would remain vigilant, ready to face any new challenges that threatened the delicate balance they had fought so fiercely to restore. They understood that the path to lasting peace required constant vigilance and adaptation. With their sturdy will, they vowed to continue their tireless efforts, ensuring that Paranova would thrive in the face of any hardship that lay ahead.

And as the sun rose upon the scarred yet hopeful land, the elves of Paranova found peace in the knowledge that the darkness had been repelled, and the light of a new era began to shine upon them. However, amidst the victory, a grim discovery awaited them at the summit of the volcano.

There, among the smoldering remnants and the fading echoes of battle, the lifeless body of Aleron, the mastermind behind the chaos and manipulation lay motionless. His once commanding presence was reduced to mere remains, a chilling reminder of the havoc he had wrought upon the land.

The Shadow Council, ever watchful and shrouded in mystery had emerged from the shadows to claim Aleron's body. They recognized the importance of examining his remains, seeking to uncover the depths of his dark powers and unravel the twisted deception that had brought about such devastation. With solemn reverence, they carried his lifeless form with them wherever they would go, where the secrets of his dark influence would be unveiled.

....

In the coming months, the shadow council would meticulously dissect Aleron's body, carefully studying the intricate markings etched into his skin as evidence of his sinister sorcery. As they delved deeper into their analysis, they discovered forbidden texts hidden within his bones, revealing a network of dark alliances that extended far beyond Paranova.

As the army of Alora labored alongside the survivors and extended a helping hand to the wounded dark ones, a deep realization settled within their hearts. They understood, perhaps more than anyone else, the depths from which they themselves had risen. For the they too, had emerged from the ashes of a painful history, their own journey marked by struggle and resilience.

In this joint effort to restore and revive, they discovered a point of agreement with the dark ones, acknowledging that their fates were intertwined. They were able to relate to the feelings of rejection, insufficient understanding, and unfair assumptions. The echoes of their own history reverberated within the tales of the dark ones, cultivating a connection that surpassed racial divisions and customary norms.

The elves of Alora, upon learning of the manipulations orchestrated by the shadow council among the dark ones, felt a sense of kinship with their counterparts. Recognizing the struggles within their own kingdom, the Alora elves approached the dark ones with a message of unity. They acknowledged the presence of darkness even within their own grace and revealed the diversity among the vanguard, which included dark elves.

Understanding that the dark elves faced challenges in their placement within Alora due to overpopulation, the elves shared that the queen had plans to address these issues. The southwestern lands, under her rule, aimed to provide a haven where all elves could find peace and comfort. The message conveyed a spirit of cooperation and the potential for a shared future that transcended the divisions of race.

Commander Relios, recognizing the similarities between the elves in Alora and the dark ones, proclaimed a significant shift in perspective. He declared that those resembling the dark ones would be considered dark elves, a term far from ancient prejudices. In the wake of this revelation, the dark ones started embracing this new identity, seeking reassurance and validation from their dark elven counterparts within the vanguard.

Questions filled the air as the dark elves grappled with the profound changes in their realm. The revelations of lies and betrayal challenged their beliefs and traditions. The deity they once worshipped had turned on them, and their leader viewed them as expendable. The very essence of their existence, the belief in reincarnation through the fires, now stood in question. Were they truly reborn, or were their lives merely extinguished in the relentless flames? The dark elves faced a time of introspection and transformation as they sought to redefine their identity in the aftermath of these hard revelations.

With empathy as their guiding force, the Alora elves offered not only physical aid but also a listening ear and an open heart. They made an effort to comprehend the suffering and scars endured by the dark ones and acknowledged that healing necessitated not only rebuilding physical structures but also healing the deep wounds etched in the collective psyche of their folk.

Through patient dialogue and genuine acts of kindness, the Alora elves nurtured the seeds of compassion, fostering an environment where stories could be shared, grievances could be aired, and understanding could begin to take root. Amidst the ruins, as sunlight bathed the scarred land in its golden hues, harmony prevailed between both elven groups despite their personal struggles. Through peaceful moments, they came to understand that despite their differences, they shared an innate desire for a world free of prejudice and animosity.

Commander Relios, having succeeded in the mission, reached out to Queen Alora, requesting supplies and aid for their new allies, the dark elves in the volcanic kingdom. The unexpected messages caught the queen off guard, and she soon found herself in a difficult situation. The kingdom was facing internal tensions, and supplies were scarce. Most resources were being directed towards addressing the discontent among the lowborn citizens.

Recognizing the urgency of the situation, Queen Alora agreed to send aid to the commander and his army. However, she emphasized the need for half of the army to return to the kingdom promptly, hinting at an underlying concern about potential threats looming closer to home. The delicate balance of managing internal issues while extending assistance to allies reflected the challenges faced by the kingdom of Alora.

....

With time passing by—days seamlessly transitioning into weeks and weeks evolving into months—a subtle metamorphosis unfolded. Genuine connections were forged, and nourishing friendships flourished, eclipsing remnants of past grievances with promising prospects. Shoulder to shoulder stood the light and dark elves, united not only in rebuilding efforts but also in fostering a shared optimism for Paranova's future defined by unity and empathy.

In this newfound alliance, the elves began to rewrite the narratives of their troubled past. They embraced their common roots, acknowledging the shared experiences that had shaped their destinies. From the ashes of conflict and division, they sowed seeds of empathy, nurturing a spirit of reconciliation that would guide them towards a future built on trust, compassion, and the collective wisdom gained from overcoming difficulty.

In their unity, the elves became beacons of hope, exemplifying the power of understanding and resilience. They knew that true progress could only be achieved through acknowledging the wounds of the past and working together to ensure a more inclusive and harmonious future. They continued their joint efforts to rebuild and forge stronger bonds. The elves carried within them the unwavering belief that, from the ashes of division, a unified Paranova would rise, a testament to the transformative power of empathy and the indomitable spirit of those who chose to walk the path of healing.

Within the ranks of the dark elves, a division emerged. While many embraced the shift towards reconciliation and unity with the Alora elves, some chose to cling to the ancient prejudicial title of "dark ones." These elves aligned themselves with factions like the raider clan or the shadow council, resisting the newfound happiness that surrounded the volcanic kingdom.

For this group of dark elves, the allure of traditions ingrained by the shadow council remained strong. They migrated or stayed within the volcanic kingdom, distancing themselves from the evolving dynamics of the majority. In seclusion, they aimed to uphold their customs, resisting the tide of change that swept through the hearts of their kin. The internal struggles among the dark elves mirrored the broader complexities of the alliances forming within the realm.

•••••••

Back in Alora, as the night cloaked the kingdom in darkness, an unsettling presence lurked within the shadows of the Lowborn district. The streets, normally bustling with exotic life, now held an eerie stillness. Unbeknownst to the kingdom inhabitants, a crafted plan was unfolding, taking advantage of the chaos and diversion caused by the war against Pyrothos.

At the heart of this sinister scheme stood Fumar, a figure shrouded in mystery and malice. His piercing eyes gleamed with cunning intelligence as he accurately calculated his every move. Fumar had long harbored a deep-seated resentment towards Alora and its ruling elite, fueled by years of inequality and oppression.

In a twist of fate, Fumar seized the perfect opportunity and began to weave an intricate tapestry of plots and schemes. He carefully orchestrated his actions, patiently waiting for the right moment to strike at the heart within Alora's walls. Despite his actions eluding understanding, Fumar successfully cloaked his true intentions in layers of secrecy.

As the night wore on, murmurs of dissatisfaction coursed through the hidden channels of the kingdom, hinting at an imminent menace that threatened to dismantle their fragile state of tranquility. The kingdom would soon become trapped in a complex web of traps set by Fumar's evil schemes, unaware of the impending doom that loomed ahead.

What lay in wait for Alora within the depths of the Lowborn district? What sort of plans did Fumar have prepared for the kingdom and its inhabitants? The answers, vague by darkness and uncertainty, remained a mystery. With Fumar's schemes known for their intricacy and unpredictability, Alora's citizens could only ponder and dread what had yet to be revealed. As dawn approached, an air of tension gripped elven hearts as they wondered if they would ever unravel the truth behind Fumar's vile plots and rescue their cherished kingdom from impending catastrophe.

As night descended upon the unsuspecting kingdom with moonlight casting an eerie glow on its streets, the scene was set for a new kind of battle, but one fought not with weapons or sorcery but with cunning deceit. Alora found itself on the edge of a fresh threat while hanging in suspense over its destiny. Meanwhile, Fumar, as the mastermind orchestrating the forthcoming turmoil, waited patiently for the right moment to unleash his malevolent designs.

Chapter 11: Fallen Whispers

As the war against Pyrothos raged on, Fumar and his cult saw an opportune moment to capitalize on the distraction and chaos caused by the colossal entity. They recognized that the kingdom's resources and attention would be primarily directed towards combating the external threat, leaving internal defenses weakened and vulnerable. It was during this time of strategic diversion that Fumar and his cult initiated their rebellion, meticulously plotting their path to power.

Fumar, a cunning and charismatic leader, understood the importance of gaining a foothold within the lowborn district, the heart of discontent and unrest. He recognized that the marginalized population residing in this district had long been subjected to poverty, oppression, and neglect by the ruling elite. With the war against Pyrothos drawing the majority of attention, Fumar knew that the lowborn district would be the perfect breeding ground for rebellion.

To gain influence and support, Fumar employed a multi-faceted approach. He crafted his message of liberation and equality, appealing to the frustrations and grievances of the disenfranchised. Through carefully orchestrated gatherings and underground meetings, Fumar and his cult members planted the seeds of dissent, highlighting the systemic injustices that continued their suffering. They skillfully employed persuasive rhetoric, painting themselves as champions of the oppressed and promising a new era of fairness and justice.

Fumar's cult acted as a secretive network, utilizing covert communication channels and encrypted messages to recruit individuals disillusioned with the ruling class. They established secret meeting places in the shadows of the lowborn district, carefully avoiding detection by the authorities. Fumar tapped into the shared anger and frustration of the populace, fostering a sense of unity and common purpose among those who had long felt voiceless.

Aiden Kynes, a gifted Gray Elf with a profound affinity for protection magic, had endured a life like that of his closest companion during their youth with Fumar. Both had suffered the harsh fate of being discarded by the Genetic Pathway Organization and left to navigate a world that had little use for their unique abilities.

Aiden emerged as a beacon of light, reflecting compassion and generosity in a stark opposition to Fumar's rising doom, despite their shared sorrow. Aiden's unrelenting commitment to helping others drew elves to him, and he quickly became a symbol of hope for many who felt diminished and overlooked. His capacity to sympathize with and encourage those in need made him a natural leader, inspiring others to discover their own voice and speak up for what they believed in.

Growing up together, Aiden and Fumar formed a bond that surpassed mere friendship. They became like brothers, finding comfort in each other's presence and navigating the challenges of their existence with shared resilience. Aiden's inherent goodness shone through, and his protective nature extended not only to Fumar but also to those who had received criticism and marginalization from society.

As Aiden's journey took a different direction, he set forth on a quest to explore and understand himself better. With purpose, he committed himself to the noble cause of using his magical powers to protect those in need. An undeniable worry plagued his heart as revelations about Fumar's true nature became known. He saw his once-familiar friend gradually engulfed in darkness as he regrettably continued down the potentially hazardous path that lay ahead.

In the shadowed alleys of the lowborn district, Aiden, distinguished by his divine magic, became a beacon of hope for the struggling elves. Despite his lowborn status, he chose to use his abilities to uplift the businesses and lives of those in the district. Instead of taking the expected route into the military as a lowborn front line, Aiden opted to align himself with the arcanists, seeing that his divinity magic was a means to make a difference in the kingdom. However, with his lowborn status, he was never seen as an arcanist, nor did he have the opportunity to become one.

While Fumar, once considered his brother, embraced the path of wicked leadership within the cult, Aiden remained committed to helping his fellow lowborn elves. He endured hardship alongside them, offering assistance and compassion during the years of struggle. Aiden's divergence from Fumar's path underscored the stark contrast in their choices and destinies.

Aiden's concern for Fumar's well-being intensified as he witnessed the rebellion taking shape and Fumar's growing influence over the lowborn district. He understood the allure of Fumar's message and the justifiable grievances that fueled the rebellion, but he feared the destructive path that Fumar seemed to be embracing. Aiden knew that their shared background and experiences should have propelled them towards building a better world, one where their unique gifts could be celebrated rather than rejected.

Yet he saw Fumar slipping further away from the light, succumbing to a darker purpose. Despite his reservations, Aiden couldn't deny the impact Fumar had on the lowborn district. His charismatic leadership and promises of justice drew crowds to him. However, Aiden observed privately how Fumar's resistance escalated into a violent uprising, bringing chaos and misery among both the downtrodden and those in power. The struggle of two individuals with similar origins and objectives but ultimately choosing opposite paths to achieve their goals—one embracing compassion and understanding while the other descending to rage and violence.

In the face of Fumar's growing influence and the rebellion's momentum, Aiden found himself standing at a crossroads. The fate of their friendship and the role he would play in the unfolding events weighed heavily on his mind. With a heavy heart, he resolved to confront Fumar, to try to steer him away from the path of darkness and remind him of the value of empathy and redemption. Aiden knew that he had a pivotal role to play, not only in potentially saving his friend but also in mitigating the potential destruction that Fumar's rebellion could bring upon the kingdom they had once called home.

As Fumar continued his daily tasks, advocating for liberation and justice within the district, Aiden strategically made appearances in public. Fumar, putting on a facade of friendship, would rejoice at Aiden's presence, publicly heralding him as the unsung hero in the shadows, assisting the needy elves without seeking recognition. The odd act of rekindling their relationship left Aiden shocked, and he couldn't shake the feeling that Fumar was well aware of his discomfort.

Fumar, in his rebellion, sought to manipulate Aiden's empathetic nature for his cause, hoping to bring him into the fold of the cult. However, Aiden remained wary, recognizing the insincerity behind Fumar's gestures and questioning the true motives behind his friend's actions. The delicate dance between the two unfolded in the public eye, where hidden intentions clashed with genuine compassion.

As Fumar sought to solidify his rebellion, he turned to Aiden with a proposition—a plea for his loyal friend to join him in his cause. However, Aiden's sturdy commitment to his principles and his refusal to embrace the path of darkness and destruction that Fumar had chosen led to a bitter and subtle confrontation. Fueled by anger and frustration, Fumar unleashed his powers upon Aiden, casting him aside and ensnaring him in a mind-flaying trap, a forbidden and morally wrong form of magic.

Imprisoned within the confines of his own thoughts, Aiden discovered himself ensnared, unable to escape from the mental restraints that kept him in captivity. This state of being had proved excruciatingly painful, as he watched Fumar's schemes unravel directly from within the depths of his consciousness yet remained utterly powerless to intervene or redirect their unfolding course. The mind-manipulating trap twisted Aiden's perception, obscuring his cognitive processes and confining him to a place where helplessness prevailed.

As Fumar continued his march advocating for liberation and justice, the public remained oblivious to the mind-flaying trap he had planted on Aiden. Week after week, Aiden mindlessly followed Fumar by his side, creating the illusion that figures like Aiden, the protector of lowborn, believed in Fumar as their liberator. The public, witnessing Aiden's apparent support, began to see Fumar as a credible leader, further solidifying his influence and rallying support for the rebellion.

The manipulated display of unity fueled the public's trust in Fumar's cause, and the momentum of his movement grew stronger with each passing day. The mind-flaying trap cast its deceptive spell not only on Aiden but also on the perceptions of those who witnessed the supposed alliance between the two figures.

As Fumar's rebellion gained momentum and chaos reigned, Aiden's plight served as a painful reminder of the cost of diverging paths and the destructive consequences of succumbing to the allure of darkness. His mind became a battleground, wrestling with conflicting emotions of betrayal, regret, and a desperate yearning to protect those he cared for. In his entrapment, Aiden became a silent witness to the unfolding tragedy, unable to sway the course of events or shield the innocent from the impending storm that his friend had planned since a youthful age under a hidden agenda.

Fumar and his cult members launched coordinated acts of civil disobedience and subversion by taking advantage of the chaos Pyrothos had caused. They strategically targeted symbols of the ruling elite's authority, undermining their control over the kingdom. Propaganda campaigns, spreading like wildfire through the lowborn district and the working class, further fueled the rebellion's momentum. Fumar's cult employed artful deception and manipulation, amplifying their message of resistance and rebellion while evading the watchful eyes of the ruling class.

The war against Pyrothos provided Fumar with a shield, masking the true intentions of the rebellion and diverting attention away from their activities. The ruling elite, preoccupied with the external threat, remained oblivious to the growing influence and power of Fumar and his cult. The rebellion's strength was growing with each passing day as more disenchanted individuals flocked to Fumar's cause, emboldened by the prospect of change and a chance to dismantle the oppressive system.

Fumar and his cult employed a strategic approach in selecting their battles, opting to evade direct conflict with the primary forces committed to opposing Pyrothos. Instead, they dedicated themselves to fostering discontent, weakening the dominion of those in power, and garnering favor from the denizens residing in the other districts. Gradually but surely, their rebellion amassed strength and emerged as a formidable entity capable of challenging the existing hierarchy and reshaping the kingdom's fate.

As the war against Pyrothos reached its zenith, Fumar and his cult would emerge from the shadows, ready to seize control and claim their vision of a new order. Their careful planning, exploitation of the distraction, and cultivation of support within the lowborn district paved the way for a rebellion that would shake the foundations of Alora. Fumar and his cult had spent years secretly building a network of loyal followers, patiently waiting for the perfect moment to strike.

With the chaos of the war providing cover, they swiftly mobilized their forces and launched a coordinated assault on key strategic locations throughout the kingdom. The elves were tired of oppression and yearning for change; they rallied behind Fumar's charismatic leadership, propelling the rebellion forward with unstoppable momentum.

As Fumar's grip tightened on the kingdom of Alora, his once discreet acts of mayhem evolved into brazen displays of violence in the public eye. No longer content with operating in the shadows, he reveled in the chaos he had sown, eager to strike fear into the hearts of the elves of Alora. Crowded streets and bustling marketplaces became stages for his twisted performances, where bloodshed and terror became the main attractions. His daring deeds encouraged his disciples to continue their ruthless hostility, leaving a path of destruction in their wake. The lowborn district trembled under the weight of Fumar's malice as his blatant acts of brutality cast a somber gloom over the lives of its inhabitants.

Fumar's rebellion against the ruling class took a dark turn as he successfully attacked key locations, capturing highborn members and presenting them to the lowborn elves. Serving as both executioner and judge, Fumar recited the crimes committed by the ruling class against the lowborn, heightening the sense of injustice. Amidst the gruesome acts, Aiden, manipulated and mind-flayed, was forced to watch in horror as Fumar carried out the executions with a twisted sense of excitement.

The lowborn elves, fueled by a sense of revenge and empowerment, cheered on Fumar's sinister acts, seeing him as a symbol of liberation. The rebellion gathered momentum as Fumar continued to exploit the grievances of the lowborn, using his mind-flayed puppet Aiden to amplify his influence and control over the masses. The once-empathetic protector of lowborn had become a pawn in Fumar's dark and manipulative game.

In the twisted reign of Fumar and his cult to follow, a dark spectacle unfolded—the hangings of the elite. As Fumar solidified his grip on power, he sought to sow fear and establish his authority over those who had once held influence and privilege. In the heart of Alora, gallows were erected, their eerie presence casting a shadow over the kingdom. Citizens were forced to witness the gruesome executions of once respected leaders as Fumar reveled in the terror and despair that filtered the air. The sound of the creaking gallows and the sight of lifeless bodies swinging in the wind became haunting reminders of the kingdom's descent into darkness under Fumar's vicious rule.

One by one, figures of prominence were dragged to the gallows, their hands bound and faces filled with dread. The once proud and powerful, those who had enjoyed wealth and status, now found themselves at the mercy of Fumar's merciless judgment. The executions were not swift and merciful; instead, they were drawn-out, agonizing displays meant to inflict maximum suffering.

The noose tightened around their necks, and the crowd that had gathered watched in morbid fascination as life was extinguished before their eyes. The bodies swayed in the wind, a grim reminder of Fumar's iron grip on the kingdom. The public hangings transformed into spectacles that were meant to instill fear in the hearts of the elves, serving as a reminder of what would happen if they defied authority and aiming to completely eliminate any trace of resistance.

As each execution occurred, the social fabric became increasingly frayed, security diminished, and the general population lived in constant fear. Once esteemed pillars of influence, the privileged class now stood as lifeless emblems of Fumar's reign. Their deaths served as a stern warning to anyone who dared challenge his authority, fueling an atmosphere of growing desolation and oppression.

Throughout the higher district streets, grieving cries resonated sorrowfully as loved ones mourned their losses and witnessed the remnants of a once-vibrant society shattered. These hangings etched themselves deep into collective memory, serving as symbols of a dark era endured during Fumar's uprising—a time when justice was twisted and even those with great power fell victim to their own arrogance.

In the depths of the Lowborn District, Fumar's cult wielded their mind-flaying powers with evil intent, twisting the minds of the vulnerable and downtrodden. Through forbidden rituals and dark incantations, they tapped into the darkest recesses of the sapient psyche, unleashing a wave of madness and intensity that swept through the streets of Alora.

Individuals who were once ordinary citizens became vessels of chaos, their minds fragmented and filled with a maddening rage. The mind-flaying powers of Fumar's cult warped their perceptions, clouding their judgment and transforming them into zealous devotees willing to do anything to destabilize the once prosperous kingdom.

Once friendly neighbors turned on one another, driving them to commit heinous acts out of an unquenchable rage. Streets became battlegrounds as frenzied mobs clashed with anyone they perceived as a threat to Fumar's cause. The once bustling markets and lively squares now bore witness to scenes of violence and mayhem as the mind-flayed zealots sought to tear down the fabric of stability that had once defined Alora.

Reason and compassion were abandoned, replaced by a fanatical devotion to Fumar and his twisted ideology. Their actions were driven by a distorted sense of righteousness, as they passionately believed that their chaotic acts were necessary for the kingdom's salvation. The mind-flaying powers had stripped them of their individuality, reducing them to mere pawns in Fumar's grand design.

The kingdom was engulfed in a storm of madness, its foundations shaken by the relentless onslaught of mind-flayed zealots. Order and civility crumbled in the face of unchecked aggression, leaving Alora in a state of disarray and despair. The once harmonious community became a breeding ground for chaos as Fumar's influence grew stronger with each mind-flayed convert.

It was a chilling display of the power of manipulation, as minds once filled with hope and dreams were shattered and replaced with a single-minded obsession to serve Fumar's cause. The mind-flaying powers, a weapon of psychological destruction, left a lasting scar on the collective consciousness of Alora, forever reminding its inhabitants of the horrors that unfolded during Fumar's rebellion.

The twisted relationship between Fumar and Aiden, once viewed as brotherly, now stood as a horrifying testament to the depths of wickedness that had consumed them. He put on a public show for the citizens of Alora, which Fumar expertly staged to show off his crafty malice. Fumar paraded Aiden around like a trophy of his nefarious acts, a savage smile spreading across his face as he bound him. The sight sent shivers down the spines of those watching, a chilling reminder of Fumar's decline.

As the bloodshed in the lowborn neighborhood worsened, Fumar relished his sadistic display of power. He compelled Aiden to observe the crimes unfolding before their eyes while ensuring that his companion could not look away from the horrors. Aiden, enslaved by the mind-flaying spell, was forced to watch as the streets stained red with the blood of the innocent, his heart heavy with agony and helplessness. Fumar's twisted enjoyment rose with each life lost, his laughter echoing across the bloodshed. Aiden's thoughts pleaded for release, desperate to get away from the nightmare that had become his life. The depths of Fumar's corruption appeared to go on forever, leaving Aiden wondering if there was any hope for their ravaged home.

The mind-flaying spell, a vile form of control, kept Aiden bound and unable to intervene. It twisted his mind, locking away his true self and leaving him a mere spectator to the growing chaos. Every fiber of his being screamed for him to take action, to rise against the tyranny that had enveloped Alora, but his body remained motionless, a puppet in Fumar's vicious hands.

The weeks passed, and Aiden could do nothing while Fumar's evil spread to every part of their broken existence. The once-vibrant town square, now a grim wasteland, acted as a heartbreaking reminder of the lost promise. Families were ripped apart, houses were plundered, and innocent lives were lost as a result of Fumar's hostile control. Aiden's heart wrenched with each helpless look he cast at his fellow citizens.

The elves of the lowborn district, though disturbed and repulsed by the horrors orchestrated by Fumar, found themselves entangled in a web of conflicting emotions. They struggled to reconcile the gruesome scenes before them with the notion that it was all an elaborate act to assert dominance over the higher echelons of society. Whispers spread through the kingdom, speculating that Fumar's malevolence was a calculated display, a twisted performance designed to strike fear into the hearts of the privileged and powerful.

While they wished for an end to the slaying and Aiden's release, the residents of Alora couldn't help but feel a strange sense of unpleasant satisfaction at Fumar's daring. It appeared as though his acts were a brave protest against the long-standing injustices they had to face and a sign of rebellion against the oppressive structures that had kept them outside the system.

Holding on to a glimpse of optimism, the lowborn elves felt Fumar's activities were motivated by a desire to challenge the governing class and bring about constructive change for their community. Fumar's persistent onslaught, unbeknownst to them, was motivated by his own selfishness and ambition for power rather than any genuine concern for their well-being. The lowborn elves were unaware, in their foolish ignorance, that they, too, were considered throwaway pieces in Fumar's grand narrative. As the rebellion progressed, the line between liberation and manipulation blurred, putting the fate of the lowborn elves in doubt.

Within the depths of their inner beings, they comprehended the true essence of the atrocities inflicted upon the lowborn district and Aiden's endured suffering. Nevertheless, a portion of them dared to entertain the notion that Fumar's audacious acts were a necessary display of wickedness, serving as a means to expose and reveal the widespread corruption and hypocritical behavior that stained Alora's higher tiers of society. Their deepest longing was for transformation, and Fumar's boldness offered a flicker of optimism—perhaps their voices would finally be acknowledged. Inevitably, they couldn't resist contemplating whether his actions would kindle an impassioned fire within those who suffered oppression, inspiring them to rise up resiliently while demanding just retribution that had long eluded their deserving souls.

It was this delicate dance between repulsion and fascination, revulsion and acceptance, that swirled within the hearts of the lowborn citizens. They grappled with their own consciences, torn between their desire for justice and their grim fascination with Fumar's brilliant display of power.

As the chaos in the lowborn district escalated, the queen found herself teetering on the edge of despair. With her magic users on their way back from the exhausting war in the south, the kingdom's defenses were stretched thin. The remaining guards, military, and arcanists struggled to contain the chaotic demise of the lower district. The queen, feeling ill-equipped to retaliate against the cult's open rebellion, had to cling to the hope that the internal strife would somehow lead to a natural resolution, even as the district descended into its own downfall. The fate of the lowborn elves and the stability of the kingdom hung in an insecure balance, and the queen could only watch and wait for a turn of fortune.

Fumar and his cult, fueled by their twisted ideologies had managed to establish a base of operations that extended beyond the confines of the lowborn district. Their methods of recruitment and subversion were cunning and calculated, preying on the disenchanted and downtrodden.

Using covert tactics, Fumar's cult members infiltrated the working-class districts, weaving their way into the fabric of discontent. They whispered words of dissent and rebellion, stoking the embers of discontentment that smoldered within the hearts of those who felt criticized and ignored. Through covert meetings and hidden gatherings, Fumar's cult slowly garnered support from the disaffected and disgruntled individuals within the working-class districts. They offered peace to those who felt forgotten, presenting themselves as champions of the downtrodden and advocates for justice.

Since their cult's power grew, Fumar and his followers became skilled manipulators. They skillfully exploited their recruits' frustrations, transforming them into passionate followers motivated by their shared animosity and desire for retribution. They tightened their grip on those who had fallen out of favor with society by instilling a sense of belonging and purpose in them. Fumar and his cult members convinced their followers that they were part of a virtuous quest to oppose those who had abandoned them, using compelling rhetoric and carefully prepared tales. This sensation of empowerment strengthened their commitment, making it increasingly difficult for anyone to break free from the cult's grip.

With each new recruit, their ranks became stronger, and their network of influence expanded. Because of their fierce allegiance and unfaltering commitment, Fumar's cult became a powerful force that threatened the rank structure in Alora. Their relentless quest for justice and freedom drew all kinds of elves together, unified by an intense desire to tear down the corrupt system that had afflicted their society for far too long. As Fumar's cult gathered traction, whispers of their rebellion began to sound through the streets, causing dread in the minds of those who had once held power.

Elves who were dissatisfied with their lives and the working-class districts found safety and a sense of belonging within Fumar's cult. These individuals were dissatisfied with their lowborn identities. They saw it as an opportunity to rise up against the authorities and dismantle the structures that had held them confined for so long.

Decoy attacks played a crucial role in Fumar's grand scheme. His cult members executed carefully planned assaults on strategically chosen targets, drawing the guards away from their intended focus. These diversionary strikes were accurately timed and executed with precision, exploiting the limited resources and power of the guards. As the guards chased after the decoy attacks, Fumar and his cult were able to infiltrate the main stronghold unnoticed. They swiftly dismantled the oppressive structures, gathering intelligence and supplies to help them prepare for their attack.

Misinformation became a potent tool in Fumar's hands. His cult spread rumors, false leads, and fabricated reports to intentionally misdirect the guards and the authorities. They used a network of informants and covert messengers to disseminate misleading information, ensuring that the guards were chasing shadows while the true activities of the cult remained concealed.

Acts of sabotage were another integral part of Fumar's strategy. His cult members covertly sabotaged infrastructure, disrupted supply lines, and undermined the stability of key locations within the kingdom. By creating a constant state of chaos and disarray, they stretched the guards' capabilities thin, diverting their attention from the true intentions and operations of the cult. Fumar's cult members were highly skilled in their acts of sabotage, often leaving behind minimal evidence that could be traced back to them. This made it even more challenging for the guards to identify and apprehend the culprits, further contributing to the cult's ability to remain concealed and continue their sinister activities undetected.

Fumar's cult also exploited the vulnerabilities of the kingdom, targeting areas where the military guards were spread thin or lacked sufficient presence. They struck at opportune moments, taking advantage of the military being divided with attention during the ongoing war against Pyrothos. The chaos and distraction caused by the war became fertile ground for Fumar's schemes to flourish.

Moreover, Fumar's devout followers were adept at seamlessly integrating themselves into society, thereby posing a formidable challenge for law enforcement in detecting their true allegiance. Their covert operations entailed employing hidden techniques such as encrypted messaging platforms and concealed signals, ultimately rendering investigations into their actions highly intricate undertakings.

The cult members operated with stealth and precision, utilizing secret passages, hidden tunnels, and concealed safe houses to move undetected throughout the cityscape. They operated under the cover of darkness, swiftly and silently carrying out their subversive activities, always one step ahead of the minimalized guard units. The cult members were highly skilled at evading surveillance, constantly adapting their tactics to avoid detection. They meticulously planned their operations, carefully selecting targets and executing their plans with accurate precision.

By employing these cunning schemes of diversion, misinformation, and sabotage, Fumar ensured that the focus of the guards and the authorities remained fragmented and scattered. This allowed his cult to operate in the shadows, advancing their dark agenda unhindered and unnoticed, as chaos reigned within the once-peaceful kingdom of Alora.

·······

With the return of the magical arcanists and elementalists, the queen saw a glimmer of hope amid the chaos within her kingdom. The arriving troop, battle-hardened from their success against Pyrothos, was immediately enlisted to address the pressing issues within the kingdom. However, the queen's attempts to reach the commander assisting the dark elves remained unanswered, leaving her with a sense of unease and uncertainty about the unfolding events in the lowborn district. As the arcanists and elementalists prepared to lend their magical prowess to quell the internal strife, the fate of the kingdom was on the edge of collapse.

In the wake of the war against Pyrothos, the returning arcanists and elementalists, battle-tested but fatigued, observed the harrowing state of the kingdom they once knew. The once-peaceful kingdom had descended into madness, with over half of the population succumbing to violence. The highborn, unaccustomed to the frontline responsibilities, found themselves grappling with the challenges left in the wake of the absent vanguard. Targeted by the cultists and subjected to public executions, the highborn faced an uncertain existence. Despite the grim circumstances, many among the highborn exhibited resilience and courage as they stood united to defend their beloved kingdom. The arcanists and elementalists, eager to contribute their newfound combat skills, prepared to join the effort to restore order and stability within the realm.

Guided by the arcanists' keen senses and honed magical skills, a determined group set out on a mission to investigate the hidden areas where dark arcane magic thrived. These elusive traces of sinister energy, though subtle, were not beyond the perceptive gaze of the arcanists. The group moved with purpose, intent on uncovering the source of the menace that had plunged the kingdom into chaos. Their search for answers became more urgent as they delved deeper into the shadows and hidden spaces because they wanted to put an end to the plots that threatened the very foundation of their formerly peaceful kingdom.

In the depths of the dark tunnels, highborn Kleia and a group of dedicated arcanists stumbled upon a disturbing sight: Aiden, bound and helpless, held captive by the sinister deception of Fumar's cult. Recognizing the urgency of the situation, Kleia swiftly untied Aiden, her heart filled with both concern and determination. She knew that they needed to escape the tunnels quickly before Fumar's cult members returned. With Aiden now free, Kleia whispered a plan to him, their voices barely audible in the eerie silence of the underground labyrinth.

As they emerged from the shadows, Aiden's disoriented state became apparent. It was clear that he was under the influence of a powerful and insidious spell, his mind trapped within its clutches. With great care, Kleia and the arcanists transported Aiden to the safety of the Arcanist Sanctum, a place of knowledge and magical expertise. They knew that breaking the spell would require a delicate and intricate process that only the most skilled arcanists could perform. As they laid Aiden down on a bed, Kleia's determination grew stronger, knowing that they had to act swiftly to save him from the clutches of darkness.

Within the sanctum's hallowed halls, the arcanists worked tirelessly to evaluate and understand the nature of the mind-flaying spell that had ensnared Aiden. They delved into ancient tomes, consulted with their most experienced members, and conducted intricate rituals to unravel the dark magic's grip on Aiden's consciousness. They worked with a sense of urgency because they were aware that the chance of Aiden's mind suffering permanent harm increased with each passing second. The arcanists remained undeterred, channeling their collective knowledge and expertise into finding a solution that would bring Aiden back from the brink of darkness. They knew he had valuable information on Fumar and could not afford to lose him, which added pressure to the situation.

With the revelation about the dark arcane magic and its temporary effects on sapient minds, the arcanists saw a glimmer of hope in understanding the workings of the sinister cult. The dark elf arcanist took on a crucial role in deciphering the nuances of their own kind's magic, shedding light on the practices that the cult employed to manipulate and control minds. This newfound knowledge became a valuable asset in the ongoing battle against the chaos that plagued the kingdom. The arcanists, both light and dark, collaborated to strategize and counteract the effects of the dark arcane magic, aiming to weaken the cult's grip on the minds of the manipulated individuals. The pursuit of information and the cooperation between the different factions marked a turning point in their efforts to restore order to the kingdom.

Kleia stood by Aiden's side throughout the painstaking process of evaluation and recovery. She witnessed the arcanists' expertise and their unwavering commitment to unraveling the mysteries of the mind-flaying magic that had plagued this elf. Kleia felt a natural bond with Aiden, realizing that he was the protector of the lowborn elves of legend throughout the years.

As time passed, the arcanists efforts bore fruit. Through their collective wisdom and unyielding resolve, they discovered the intricacies of the mind-flaying spell that had ensnared Aiden's mind. With their combined powers, they gradually unraveled its dark tendrils, releasing Aiden from its grip.

When Aiden finally emerged from the depths of his tormented mind, he found himself surrounded by caring faces and familiar voices. Kleia, her eyes brimming with relief, extended a hand to help him rise. It was confirmation of their newfound friendship and the unbreakable bond that had withstood the test of Fumar's influence.

Aiden, now free from the mind-flaying spell, would play a pivotal role in the battle against Fumar and his cult. He would stand with Kleia and the arcanists, united in their determination to stop Fumar's plans and bring peace to the troubled kingdom of Alora, armed with knowledge of their evil schemes. Together, they would forge a path of resistance against the persistent darkness, their steadfast resolve fueled by the hope of reclaiming their beloved kingdom from Fumar's clutches.

Aiden, haunted by the memories of Fumar's mind-flaying spell and the atrocities he was forced to witness and partake in, found himself torn between the past and the present. The echoes of Fumar's vicious actions ruminated in his mind, causing him inner struggle and conflict. As the realization of the darkness within Fumar sank in, Aiden struggled to reconcile the friend he once knew with the vicious leader that Fumar had become.

Aiden was showing fearful emotion, still reeling from the intensity of being under Fumar's mind-flaying spell for months. He had remembered the torture that Fumar put him through. Fumar would parade him around the lower district, embrace him inappropriately, execute elves with pleasure and make him do unspeakable acts.

The intensity of the mind-flaying spell left scars on Aiden's psyche, but within those memories lay valuable information about Fumar's sinister schemes. Aiden, driven by a sense of responsibility and a desire to redeem himself, decided to share the details of Fumar's plans with the arcanists and those fighting against the cult. His knowledge became a crucial piece in the puzzle to dismantle the cult's operations and bring an end to the chaos gripping the lower district.

Fumar's realization of the limited time frame pushed him to expedite his grand plan, sensing an opportunity amid the absence of reinforcements. In the hidden corners of the kingdom, small-scale skirmishes continued between arcanists, highborn, elementalists, and the remaining vanguard. Aiden and Kleia led their respective groups, each clash resulting in a stalemate with losses on both sides.

As Fumar observed the impasse in these skirmishes, he grasped the urgency of unleashing his full-scale assault sooner than originally planned. The absence of the returning military and vanguard created a temporary vulnerability within the kingdom's defenses, and Fumar was determined to exploit this window of opportunity. The looming threat of a large-scale battle within the walls of Alora added a layer of tension to the already turbulent atmosphere, setting the stage for the impending clash between the forces of chaos and those striving to maintain order.

With calculated ruthlessness, Fumar set his deceptions into motion, pulling the strings of his devoted cult members and orchestrating a meticulously planned series of events. His aim was to sow unprecedented chaos and bring Alora to its knees, shattering the very foundations of the kingdom and its societal structure.

As night fell over the cityscape, Fumar's cult emerged from the shadows like a relentless swarm of darkness. They struck with precision and ferocity, targeting key locations, symbols of authority, and centers of power. Decades of secret planning and preparation came to fruition as acts of sabotage, calculated misinformation, and devastating attacks were carried out with surgical precision.

The kingdom of Alora was transformed into a warzone, its streets ablaze and resonating with the anguished cries of those unjustly caught in the crossfire. In order to instill fear in its citizens and weaken the foundation upon which society stood, Fumar's followers unleashed a wave of terror across the districts while remaining steadfastly committed to their sinister goal.

The Alora opposition fought valiantly, engaging in desperate skirmishes with Fumar's forces throughout the kingdom. But the scale and intensity of the onslaught overwhelmed their efforts, forcing them into a defensive stance as they struggled to protect the remaining bastions of resistance within Alora.

Fumar, reveling in the chaos and destruction that he had unleashed, remained one step ahead, always eluding capture and manipulating events from the shadows. With each passing hour, his grip on the kingdom tightened, while the hope of reclaiming Alora grew increasingly dim.

Queen Alora, burdened by the impending chaos and the threat posed by Fumar and his cult, made a difficult and heart-wrenching decision to ensure the safety of her beloved daughter, Princess Alora. Recognizing the danger that loomed over the kingdom, she dispatched the young princess to the remote outer village of Freynora, seeking the protection of the honorable highborn, Freynora. The highborn mage's reputation as a powerful and skilled guardian provided a glimmer of hope in an otherwise bleak situation.

As Queen Alora contemplated the future of her kingdom, the weight of responsibility bore heavily on her. Desperation coursed through her veins, mingling with a deep sense of love and protectiveness for her child. The decision to send Princess Alora away was agonizing, as it meant parting with her only comfort amidst the encroaching darkness.

However, the queen was fully aware that sacrificing her own desires and ensuring her daughter's safety were essential in order to protect Alora from imminent horrors. The idea of subjecting Princess Alora to the same agony and distress that had befallen their formerly tranquil kingdom was unfathomable to her. Filled with immense sadness, Queen Alora made a firm decision: she would diligently search for a secure sanctuary where Princess Alora could flourish undisturbed, shielded from the impending mayhem.

In a surprising twist of fate, Freynora, a highborn who harbored disdain for the queen's rule over Alora, welcomed the princess without hesitation. Freynora held dominion over an outer island that was under the queen's jurisdiction, and she was a respected and noble leader of her peaceful community. Though the elves on her island were not warriors, consisting mainly of other highborn and citizens seeking refuge from the political complexities of the kingdom, Freynora pledged to shield the Princess from any threats that might extend to the outer islands.

In a desperate bid to regain control and eliminate the threat within her kingdom, Queen Alora resorted to a drastic measure: the consumption of the magical pool situated at the heart of Alora. The pool, a source of immense magical power, had long been admired and preserved as a symbol of unity and prosperity. But in this dire moment, the queen made the agonizing choice to unleash the destructive forces contained within.

As the magical energy surged through her veins, Queen Alora unleashed a devastating wave of destruction upon the lower districts of Alora. The once vibrant streets were engulfed in a cataclysmic display of raw power, leveling buildings and causing unfathomable loss of life. In the face of rebellion and impending chaos, Queen Alora believed this extreme measure would serve as a deterrent and demonstrate her stubborn resolve to protect her kingdom.

However, hidden behind the facade of strength and determination, Queen Alora's emotions churned like a tempest within her.

The weight of her decisions bore heavily upon her conscience, as the lines between right and wrong blurred in the midst of desperation. A feeling of remorse tugged at her heart as she realized that her actions had caused suffering among her own subjects. Although she cared deeply for her subjects, the harsh reality of the decisions she had made and their resulting consequences presented a difficult challenge.

Queen Alora's inward journey would be just as dangerous as the physical battles fought in the district streets. She would have to confront her inner demons, navigate the complexities of authority, and gather enough courage to make sacrifices beyond imagination. All these efforts were necessary in order to seek redemption for herself and ensure the well-being of her nation's inhabitants.

In the aftermath of the arcane pool's unleashed power, the queen witnessed the devastating waves of destruction that surged through her outer-lying districts. The once vibrant and peaceful communities were now extinguished, their inhabitants lost to the unforgiving force that emanated from the pool. Memories of her conversation with Commander Relios ruminated in her mind, a haunting reminder of the weighty decision she had made.

The commander's warning about the pool being a last resort to extinguish Pyrothos echoed in her thoughts, yet in the absence of the fiery entity, she had opted to employ its formidable energy against her own subjects. The queen grappled with the bitter irony that the tool designed to protect had become an instrument of devastation. Her choice, made in desperation to quell the chaos sown by Fumar, now casts a shadow over the kingdom, leaving her to confront the unintended consequences of wielding such formidable arcane might.

In the aftermath of Queen Alora's devastating actions, Fumar and his cult seized upon the casualties and destruction as an opportunity to further their sinister cause. Utilizing dark necromantic arts, they tapped into the lingering energies of death and harnessed them to raise an unholy army of the dead. The fallen victims of the queen's destructive magic—what were once lifeless corpses scattered throughout—were now reanimated puppets under Fumar's control.

The mindless, deathly corpses, mere husks devoid of sapience or free will, emerged as a terrifying force under Fumar's sinister control. These grotesque minions, manipulated by his dark influence, unleashed chaos and devastation upon the once-thriving kingdom. Fumar reveled in the power he had harnessed, using this army of the dead to terrorize and subjugate innocent districts. His actions spread fear and despair like a plague, leaving survivors within the kingdom in a state of constant dread.

The queen, witnessing the nightmarish spectacle of countless corpses rising under Fumar's command, was struck with horror. The unintended consequences of her desperate decision now manifested in the form of this unholy army, and she couldn't escape the realization that her actions had unwittingly played into Fumar's hands. She had allowed a dark force to take control of the once-loved kingdom, which was now on the verge of destruction.

The streets of Alora were turned into a battlefield as the reanimated corpses, stripped of their former sapience, unleashed their wrath on the kingdom's remain vanguard and faithful defenders. The hollow groans of the reanimated corpses filled the once prospering kingdom, their rotting flesh and burning eyes a horrific sight to witness. The survivors, who had previously been filled with optimism, now cowered in their homes, fearful of the impending attack. The kingdom's busy markets and vibrant gatherings were replaced by an unsettling calm, broken only by the haunting sounds of bones crushing and agonizing screams.

The battle between the reanimated horde and Alora's courageous defenders portrayed a horrible sight of death and ruin. The loyal defenders fought with fierce tenacity, their swords colliding against their opponents' rotting flesh with the assistance of the magical defenders who were defying Fumar's spell.

As spells ricocheted through the dark atmosphere, crackling with mystical power, the night erupted in pockets of shimmering allure. In the midst of this fearless rampage, an overpowering stench intermingled—death's putrid breath intertwining with blood's metallic edge—to form a sickening atmosphere that weighed heavily upon all present. Driven by their indomitable resolve, valiant defenders fiercely resisted the ceaseless surge of monstrous beings, resolutely refusing to surrender even an inch of territory.

Despite their valiant efforts, the defenders of Alora faced a formidable foe. The undead, driven by a single-minded hunger for destruction, fought with relentless ferocity. Their lifeless bodies moved with unnatural agility, their decayed limbs displaying a grotesque strength. Each fallen soldier was swiftly added to their ranks, reinforcing the overwhelming tide of undead forces.

The cult, with an eerie precision, managed to keep count on the reanimated corpses, understanding how many they were able to control with detail. Although their control over these undead minions had its limitations, as the corpses would eventually fall, the cult exploited the fallen survivors to continuously bolster their growing army of the undead.

This strategic use of fallen victims became a relentless force that the magical defenders struggled to grapple with.

The defenders, armed with their own magical prowess, found themselves challenged by the cult's dark abilities. While they could withstand the mind-flaying powers to some extent, the relentless advance of the undead minions posed a more immediate threat. Trapped in corners and overwhelmed by the sheer numbers and persistence of the undead, the defenders fought valiantly but were gradually being pushed to their limits.

The unfolding scenes presented an eerie medley of fright and bravery. The valiant defenders of Alora, burdened by sorrow yet resolute in their hearts, had constituted a fortress against the encroaching gloom. Their struggle to safeguard their cherished realm transcended into a profound dedication to commemorate the fallen heroes. Amidst the bedlam and desolation, acts of valor and selflessness gleamed radiantly as warriors embraced martyrdom in order to halt the unrelenting advance of the undead menace. The clash of their weapons reverberated against the skeletal horde while defiant shouts pierced through the dark night.

Before making the decision to depart for the war in the south, a small group of Paladins chose to stay behind in the kingdom, pledging themselves as the royal guard to the queen. Their commitment to the crusade against death and their unwavering belief in the fight for the living led them to temporarily abandon the queen's side. They saw their duty in protecting the innocent and defending against the oncoming darkness that threatened to consume the living.

With their shining armor and holy powers, the Paladins formed a last line of defense against the undead onslaught. Despite being outnumbered, they fought valiantly, their faith fueling their resolve to stand against the tide of death. Their presence amidst the chaos was a beacon of hope for those who sought refuge from the relentless advance of the cult-controlled undead. The Paladins' commitment to their cause would be tested in the face of an enemy that seemed unyielding and determined to plunge the kingdom into eternal darkness.

Undeterred by the looming threat of darkness, the defenders persisted with the purpose of reclaiming their territory. They exhibited unparalleled courage as they wielded their weapons, fighting relentlessly for the sake of their homeland. Their collective strength and steadfast unity served as an impenetrable barrier against the ongoing terror. The atmosphere crackled with mystical energy as spellcasters unleashed potent incantations that illuminated the battleground while obliterating legions of undead assailants with fiery explosions and electrifying bolts. Despite the nature of the conflict rumbling beneath them, they maintained an unwavering stance, adamantly refusing to relinquish even a fraction of their cherished lands.

Fumar, a master of manipulation and deception, carefully planned his assault on the Arcanist Sanctum while the undead distracted the remaining Paladins. Recognizing the formidable magical defenses that guarded the sacred knowledge within, he devised cunning tactics to overcome them and seize the valuable scrolls and tomes of magic that held all of history regarding arcane magic and ancient history.

Under the cover of darkness and chaos, Fumar's cult launched a multi-pronged attack on the arcanist sanctum. They utilized their knowledge of the layout and vulnerabilities of the magical defenses, exploiting weaknesses and blind spots to infiltrate the inner sanctum. By utilizing a blend of covert tactics, diversionary maneuvers, and pure strength, they successfully navigated past mystical barriers and defeated the arcanists who attempted to impede their progress.

As they delved further into the sacred space, Fumar's devoted followers faced formidable opposition from the remaining arcanists, who had rallied their forces. However, the cult's relentless determination and intense focus on their objective allowed them to push forward, inching closer to their ultimate goal of obtaining the ancient scrolls and tomes of magic.

Fumar's cult members, skilled in both dark arts and subterfuge, moved with a precision that spoke of careful planning. They struck swiftly and decisively, disorienting the arcanists and sowing confusion among their ranks. While some engaged the defenders in direct combat, others focused on disabling the protective enchantments that safeguarded the precious scrolls and tomes.

With each barrier breached and every defense neutralized, Fumar's cult members seized the opportunity to lay their hands on the coveted sources of arcane knowledge. They rifled through ancient tomes, unrolled delicate scrolls, and absorbed the forbidden wisdom inscribed within. The stolen power resonated with their malevolent intentions, fueling the cult's dark magic and granting them newfound abilities.

The impact of this theft on the arcanists ran deep. Stripped of their most treasured resources, they found themselves weakened and vulnerable. The loss of centuries of accumulated knowledge left a void within their ranks, impeding their ability to counter Fumar's cult effectively. Spells and incantations that once flowed effortlessly from their lips now felt disjointed and lacking in potency.

During the intense confrontation between Aiden, Kleia, and their group of spellcasters against Fumar and his cult, both sides suffered losses. The adept spellcasters fought valiantly, using their magical prowess to try and reclaim the stolen knowledge and artifacts. However, Fumar, with his dark powers, snuffed out the lives of the adept spellcasters, leaving a somber atmosphere in their wake.

Aiden, filled with righteous anger, attempted to strike back at Fumar with a divine bolt, but the cult leader swiftly erected a protective barrier, deflecting the divine energy. Fumar, showing a sinister frown, scorned Aiden for choosing the side of the living and mocked his newfound connection with a highborn woman. With a cruel laugh, Fumar turned his back on Aiden and walked away, carrying the precious scrolls, tomes, and history books that held the essence of Paranova's knowledge.

Despite Aiden's desire to pursue Fumar, Kleia intervened, urging them to regroup and strategize for a more effective approach against the madness that Fumar was unleashing upon their kingdom. The stolen artifacts represented not just knowledge but a key to understanding and combating the cult's dark magic. They thought the battle was far from over, and the group needed to find a way to stop Fumar's plans and bring an end to the chaos he was sowing.

In the heart of Alora, the once majestic throne room had transformed into a bastion of desperate defense. Queen Alora, her face etched with a mix of determination and anguish, stood at the forefront alongside the remaining Vanguard and Paladins, their numbers dwindling with each passing battle. Surrounded by the deafening sound of chaos and the relentless assault of Fumar's rebels, they found solace within the fortified walls of the throne room, determined to protect their queen.

Outside, the clamor of clashes and screams echoed through the corridors as the rebels pressed their advance. The air hung heavy with tension, and the flickering torchlight cast eerie shadows on the faces of the defenders. The grim realization that Fumar and his cult had taken control of their once-great kingdom seemed to replace hope as it faded away like a dying ember with each passing second.

The defenders were fully aware that the only way to survive was by maintaining control over the throne room, which acted as the core of their kingdom. They stood side by side in unison, their resolve growing stronger with each passing second as a result of their fallen comrades' memories. They took an oath to fight relentlessly until their very last breath, adamantly refusing to allow Fumar's tyrannical rule to prevail.

Queen Alora directed her gaze towards her faithful defenders, a group of battle-hardened warriors who had been fighting alongside her since the beginning. Although exhausted and worn down, their loyalty to their queen provided a glimmer of hope amidst the encroaching darkness. However, Alora felt herself burdened by the weight of the situation at hand as well as being responsible for making choices that had led them all into this desperate moment. She grappled with these feelings, carrying within her both responsibility and remorse for having brought them to such dire circumstances.

Contemplating her assembly of warriors, Queen Alora found herself contemplating the journey that had led them to this very moment. The conflicts they had faced and the souls they had mourned were all in service of safeguarding their kingdom. The magnitude of their selfless acts burdened her deeply but also ignited a passion within, compelling the queen to locate an escape from this labyrinth of shadows. She comprehended the necessity to gather her forces and infuse them with boundless resolve, akin to what they had exhibited so often under her leadership.

In her mind, she held vivid memories of commander Relios, his fiery passion ingrained within her. His loyal devotion to their cause had always been a source of inspiration for her. At this critical juncture, she sought to tap into that strength more than ever before. As Queen Alora stood before her remaining defenders, she summoned the essence of Relios, his words of encouragement shouting in her thoughts. Recognizing that they could conquer any challenge by adopting the same intensity and commitment he imparted on her, she pledged herself to lead her troops out of the darkness and towards ultimate triumph with intense resolve.

As the assault intensified, the throne room became a sanctuary amid chaos. Queen Alora, her voice laced with determination, rallied her remaining forces, urging them to hold the line against the relentless tide. Fear and uncertainty mingled with steadfast resolve as they braced themselves for the final confrontation. As they gazed at their queen, the soldiers displayed a profound trust in her command with their gazes. Her every word breathed fresh life into her forces, filling them with renewed hope and determination. In perfect unison, they remained steadfast, prepared to confront any challenges that lay beyond the confines of the throne room.

Buried deep within the depths of Alora's heart, there flickered a glimmer of uncertainty and remorse that danced in the hidden corners. Questions arose within her, contemplating if an alternative path or a divergent choice could have saved her kingdom from this dire state. Nevertheless, when confronted with impossible odds, there was scant room for self-doubt or introspection. The sole remaining option lay in standing as one united front—an unbreakable defense to safeguard what little remained and efforts to ignite a sliver of hope amidst the oncoming darkness.

The battleground outside the protective confines of the throne room raged on persistently while Queen Alora firmly gripped her sword, determination laced with sorrow mirrored in her gaze. The fate of Alora and its populace teetered precariously; she resolved to battle until exhaustion overcame every fiber within her being. Weighed down heavily by this distressing scenario, surrendering to desolation held no appeal for her steadfast spirit.

In the face of overwhelming odds, she would stand as a beacon of strength, ready to face whatever trials lay ahead and, if fate allowed, to reclaim her kingdom from the clutches of Fumar's ruthlessness. As Queen Alora thought about Relios, her lover, and her daughter, who was waiting anxiously for her safe return, she knew that their support and love were the driving forces behind her determination to protect her subjects. The images of Relios guiding her with his wisdom and her daughter looking up to her with admiration fueled her resolve to face the challenges ahead. She couldn't afford to disappoint them; she needed to show strength on their behalf. Filled with fresh resolve, she stood herself on her mission to regain what was rightfully hers and restore tranquility to her realm.

With insidious determination, Fumar and his cult orchestrated a calculated infiltration of the heavily fortified Highborn Sanctuary. Dark magic and intense zeal increased their force as they descended upon the innocent highborn elves who had previously enjoyed the security of their sanctuary. The air grew thick with fear as Fumar's cult launched a swift and overwhelming assault, their intentions clear: to capture and bend the highborn to their will.

Amidst the chaos and confusion, the highborn found themselves caught in a sinister web they could not escape. Some were taken by force, their resistance ineffective against the overwhelming numbers and ruthless determination of Fumar's cultists. Others were deceived and manipulated; their trust in fellow highborn exploited to facilitate their capture. In the face of this relentless onslaught, the once-secure sanctuary became a battleground stained with betrayal and despair.

In the twisted celebration of Fumar and his cult, the success of bending the highborn elite to their will became a cause for morbid revelry. The resistance put forth by the highborn elite, who had once supported the vanguard's efforts, was feeble against Fumar's dark powers. He, in turn, mocked their weak attempts to stop him. As a display of his malevolence, Fumar decided to line up the highborn men and snuff out their lives one by one, reveling in the sadistic pleasure of their demise.

Some highborn were spared from immediate death and subjected instead to cruel curses through mind-flaying or wicked rituals, ensuring their suffering persisted for the cult's amusement. Fumar, displaying his dominance, commanded the cult servants to gather the captured highborn women, and he singled out those who willingly submitted to his plans. The fate of the unwilling highborn women was veiled in ominous uncertainty, as Fumar's intentions hinted at darker designs for them. The atmosphere was burdened with horror as the cult's depravity reached new depths, leaving a chilling sense of dread in its wake.

The consequences of this infiltration were dire for Queen Alora and her loyal followers. The loss of these highborn, powerful figures with influence and resources left a gaping void in her ranks. The captured highborn, now unwilling captives of Fumar's cult, were stripped of their agency, their minds twisted, and coerced into serving the dark purposes of their captors. Their once-noble intentions were perverted, turning them into pawns in Fumar's grand scheme.

As the highborn were forcefully taken or enticed into submission, Queen Alora witnessed the erosion of her support network. The loss of these influential figures not only weakened her position but also bolstered Fumar's control over the kingdom. The resources, knowledge, and connections that had been at Queen Alora's disposal were now firmly in the grasp of Fumar's cult, enabling them to tighten their grip on Alora and push their insidious agenda forward.

The Queen, in her despair, foresaw a grim future for the elven race. The highborn women, vital for preserving the genetics and fertility of the elves, had willingly become surrogates under her guidance. Their role was crucial in ensuring the continuation of the elven populace for future generations. However, with Fumar and his cult now holding them captive, the queen's worst fears materialized. The uncertainty surrounding the fate of the noble highborn women cast a shadow over the kingdom, and the queen grappled with the haunting dread that their sacrifice for the survival of their kind might now be in vain. The once hopeful vision of a thriving elven legacy now teetered on the brink of ominous uncertainty.

The infiltration of the Highborn Sanctuary sent shockwaves through the kingdom, shattering the illusion of safety and exposing the vulnerability of even the most esteemed members of society. The captured highborn, once exemplars of nobility, were now unwilling instruments of darkness, their captivity contributing to the destabilization of Alora. The consequences were significant and far-reaching, as Fumar's insidious influence spread like poison, infecting the very heart of the kingdom.

In the cold and dimly lit throne room, the air thick with tension, Fumar made his chilling entrance, his presence radiating malevolence. Queen Alora, surrounded by her royal guard and remaining vanguard, stood defiantly, her eyes filled with a mix of fear and determination. Fumar's twisted grin stretched across his face as he reveled in the power he held over the queen. The queen's voice trembled as she addressed Fumar, her words laced with a desperate plea for mercy. But Fumar only laughed, relishing in the torment he had inflicted upon her and the kingdom. The defenders, though battered and weary, stood tall in front of their queen, ready to defend her to the last breath.

With a wave of his hand, Fumar unleashed forbidden mind-flaying magic upon Queen Alora, a cruel and torturous spell designed to break her spirit. Agonizing visions and haunting whispers assaulted her mind, tearing at the very fabric of her being. Fumar relished in her anguish, savoring every moment as he sought to dominate her will. His actions proved to be destructive and harmful to her. Despite being tired and beaten, her defenders remained loyal and protective of their queen, willing to fight until the end.

In the dark chambers of torment, Fumar reveled in his sadistic pleasure, subjecting the beautiful queen to excruciating torment and attempting to control her resilient mind. His fascination with her went beyond mere malevolence, as he sought to assert dominance over her will, relishing in the power he held over the once-mighty ruler of Alora. Despite the cruelty inflicted upon her, Fumar took perverse pleasure in witnessing the queen's suffering, savoring each moment of her agony.

According to Fumar's evil schemes, his followers are forbidden to harm the queen. He had plans for her that were developing in the shadows, wrapped in darkness, and draped in the twisted fabric of his sinister desires. It was unclear how far Fumar would take the queen and the kingdom she once passionately controlled as she faced her captor's wicked fantasies.

Queen Alora fought against the trickery, summoning her inner strength to resist the insidious influence of Fumar's mind-flaying magic. She refused to succumb, but the strain on her psyche was immense. Her thoughts blurred, and her resolve wavered under the relentless assault. It was a battle of wills, and Fumar delighted in pushing her to the edge of despair; this brought a wicked sense of pleasure to him.

As the mind-flaying magic twisted Queen Alora's perception, Fumar reveled in his triumph. He taunted her, reveling in the power he held over the once-mighty queen. In a twisted turn of fate, he forced Queen Alora to her knees, a symbol of her submission to his will. The remaining vanguard, stripped of their strength and trapped in a state of helplessness, watched in horror as their leader was reduced to a pawn in Fumar's wicked game.

Fumar's sadistic laughter echoed through the chamber, filling the air with a chilling sense of dread. With each taunt, he relished in the destruction of Queen Alora's spirit, savoring the taste of his victory. The once-proud queen's eyes were filled with tears of defeat; her willpower was shattered under Fumar's mind-flaying magic. The vanguard could only watch in despair as their leader's light dimmed, their hopes fading along with her.

Fumar's dark satisfaction grew as he held Queen Alora captive, his grip on power tightening with every passing moment. The defenders, once a formidable force, now stood broken and defeated, their ranks diminished, and their spirits shattered. Fumar's manipulation had left them disillusioned, their loyalty twisted into blind obedience to their captor.

In a final act of cruelty and twisted obsession, Fumar, fueled by his wicked desires, took the lives of the remaining royal guard and vanguard but left one alive to tell the tale of their queen and her weak effort to fight for her kingdom. The once-defiant defenders of Alora lay lifeless at his feet, their sacrifice in vain against the overwhelming darkness that had consumed their beloved kingdom.

With the defenders silenced, Fumar turned his attention to Queen Alora, her spirit battered but not broken. He reveled in his sick fascination with her, seeing her as a twisted replacement for the pet he had lost in Aiden. With a sadistic grin, he forced Queen Alora onto a leash, a symbol of his complete control over her. She became his puppet, manipulated by his whims, and her dignity was shattered under his ruthless grip.

Queen Alora, once a beacon of strength and leadership, now finds herself trapped in a nightmare, forced to endure Fumar's perverse desires. Her heart ached for her fallen guard and for the citizens she had sworn to protect. Though physically restrained, a flicker of defiance burned within her eyes, a willful determination to break free from Fumar's twisted hold and reclaim her kingdom.

As Fumar paraded Queen Alora, his captive pet, through the halls of power and influence, the citizens of Alora watched in horrified disbelief. The once-respected queen, now reduced to a symbol of Fumar's depravity, became a stark reminder of the darkness that had descended upon their once-prosperous land. The memory of the destroyed kingdom and the desire for a trustworthy leader to lead them out of the shadows sparked whispers of resistance.

In the aftermath of the onslaught, the survivors of Alora were left in horrified silence as lifeless corpses, once under the control of the dark cult, fell to the ground. Their hope of reclaiming their kingdom was shattered, and a chilling hush descended upon the kingdom. The wicked Fumar, now wielding not only dark magic but the once-mighty queen on a leash, paraded through the streets unchallenged.

Fear gripped the hearts of those who remained, silencing any murmurs of rebellion or dissent. Those who dared to stand against Fumar's tyranny were swiftly met with a merciless end. The once-vibrant kingdom now lay in ruins, its inhabitants forced into submission by the dark forces that had seized control. As Fumar reveled in his triumph, Alora's streets bore witness to a reign of terror, and the survivors could only watch in helpless despair.

Fumar's twisted obsession with Queen Alora knew no bounds. As he reveled in his sadistic control over her, he devised a plan to solidify his power and expand his influence beyond the boundaries of the kingdom of Alora. With a sinister glint in his eyes, he resolved to marry Queen Alora, forcibly making her his unwilling bride.

Under the guise of liberation, Fumar sought to present himself as a revolutionary leader, promising a better future to the people of new lands. He painted a deceptive picture of freedom and equality, manipulating their desires for change and exploiting their discontent. Fumar, with Queen Alora by his side as a captive symbol of authority, aimed to rally followers and establish a new order in these uncharted territories.

In the wake of the devastating events that left Alora in ruins, a divided populace grappled with uncertainty. Fumar, reveling in his newfound power, cared little for the plight of the elves who once called the kingdom home. Mocking the higher society and dismissing the shattered kingdom, he led a procession of dark and gray elves, with some light elves reluctantly following in the wake of fear.

Yet, amidst the chaos, a glimmer of hope persisted. A faction of light elves, determined to honor their heritage and rebuild what was lost, chose to stay behind. Their resilience sparked a flicker of optimism in the hearts of those who remained, envisioning a future where the once-great Alora could rise from the ashes. The kingdom, though in ruins, carried the potential for rebirth, and the decision to forge a new path lay in the hands of those who dared to dream of restoration.

Kleia and Aiden watched from afar as Fumar, filled with a sinister determination, left the kingdom and planned to marry Queen Alora against her will. They could see the deceit in his actions as he disguised his true intentions under the pretense of liberation. Fumar intended to use the captive queen as a symbol of his authority, manipulating the people's desires for change and exploiting their discontent to establish a new order in these uncharted territories.

As Kleia and Aiden observed, they gathered the citizens of the kingdom to the safe areas outside of the walls, plotting to rescue the queen. However, they needed the remaining army of Alora to come home from the war in the south. They sent scouts to bring them home as quickly and quietly as they could.

The news of Fumar's revolt spread rapidly, capturing the attention of individuals longing for a contrasting reality. His magnetic personality and commanding presence magnetized supporters towards his mission. With little knowledge of the true extent of his malevolence, they held an optimistic view, seeing him as a symbol of optimism and a catalyst for desired transformation.

Fumar led his cult and the manipulated masses away from Alora, venturing into unexplored lands that held the promise of a fresh start. The elves, deceived by his charismatic facade, followed him willingly, their hearts filled with anticipation for a future free from oppression. Yet, hidden beneath the veil of liberation, Fumar's true intentions remained dark and vicious. Behind closed doors, Queen Alora suffered in silence, her spirit crushed by the weight of her captivity. Forced into a marriage she hated; her life became a living nightmare at the hands of her tormentor.

As Fumar's rebellion surged forward, reaching the midpoint of their venture into uncharted lands, he decided to make a startling announcement to his followers. With a sinister smile and an air of anticipation, he declared that it was time for him and his unwilling bride, Queen Alora, to embark on a honeymoon. The news sent ripples of excitement and curiosity through the cult as they eagerly awaited Fumar's next move.

Fumar spun a tale of celebration, presenting the honeymoon as a joyous occasion to mark their union and the beginning of a new chapter in their twisted relationship. He painted an idyllic picture of a romantic journey and starting a family, all while concealing his true intentions behind a facade of false affection. The cult members, caught up in their loyalty and devotion to their leader, eagerly anticipated this next phase of their dark mission.

As Fumar set his sights on establishing his legacy, he directed the elves among his followers to head east, away from the impending battles with Pyrothos in the south. He assured them that new lands awaited, promising a place they could finally call home. He told the elves that followed him out of fear to go with the remaining elves or find new lands, but he made sure to tell them all to spread word about his liberations and his newfound bride to be.

Having made promises of his forthcoming arrival, Fumar took his leave from the followers, encouraging them to locate an appropriate territory where they could establish a new society. He reassured them that their parting was merely transitory and that he intended to reunite with them in the not-too-distant future. The cult and its elven followers set out on their journey toward the eastern lands, bidding farewell to the lingering gloom of Alora in search of a new beginning.

As Fumar and Queen Alora disappeared into the unknown, the cult and followers forged their own path, navigating through unfamiliar lands in search of a place to call their own. Their journey was marked by both fear and a glimmer of newfound hope as they sought to create a society free from the burdens of their past. They moved forward with cautious optimism, aware that the specter of Fumar's influence still hung over their actions, united by their shared experiences and a determination to chart a different course.

After their challenging journey and the search for a place to call their own, they stumbled upon an abandoned village nestled not far from the scars left by Pyrothos. The village, with its sprawling landscape and sturdy structures, appeared to be a perfect fit for the size and needs of the rebellion. Inspired by their leader and driven by the desire for a fresh start, they decided to name the village "Fumaron" in honor of their mysterious and formidable leader.

With the establishment of Fumaron as their new home, the gray elves embraced their newfound identity as Fumarians. This name symbolized their unity and their allegiance to Fumar, representing a departure from their past as the gray elves. It became a badge of honor, evidence of their resilience and the bonds forged through their shared experiences. The Fumarians quickly began to rebuild their lives, constructing homes and cultivating the land surrounding the village. They created a close community, depending on one another for assistance and security. The term Fumar came to symbolize fortitude and resolve, serving as a testament to their resilience and success in adapting to their newfound residence.

As the Fumarians settled into their new village, they breathed life into the once-desolate streets. They brought with them a renewed sense of purpose and determination, eager to build a community that reflected their ideals and aspirations. The abandoned structures were transformed into homes, workshops, and gathering places as the Fumarians worked tirelessly to shape their destiny. In their pursuit of creating a new society in Fumaron, the elves of the rebellion faced the challenge of ensuring their survival and the continuity of their lineage. With the capture of highborn women from Alora, they saw an opportunity to address this concern.

The captured highborn women were confined to the dungeons, which were transformed into living quarters for their involuntary residency. It was a bleak and grim existence for these women, trapped in a place that denied them their freedom and stripped away their dignity. Their lives became entwined with the rebellion's mission to populate Fumaron with the offspring of these unions, a strategy aimed at ensuring the growth and strength of their fledgling community and their ability to create more gray elves. In honor of their newly reformed and married queen, they carried on the tradition of surrogate highborn women.

Though the rebellion may have justified their actions as a means of securing a future for their kin, it is crucial to recognize the immense suffering and violations inflicted upon the highborn women. They were reduced to objects, forced into relationships without consent, and denied the agency to choose their own path. The dungeons, once a place of imprisonment, had become a haunting reminder of the cruelty and darkness that had surrounded their journey.

Within the confines of the dungeons, the highborn women experienced a range of emotions and reactions. Some may have resigned themselves to their fate, their spirits broken by the oppressive circumstances. Others may have harbored a spark of defiance, silently yearning for liberation and the chance to reclaim their autonomy. Nearly all highborn women detested the fact that the queen ever persuaded them to surrogate in the first place; otherwise, they would not have become the target of evil schemes.

•••••••

Meanwhile, as the Alora army left the volcanic kingdom with their good-hearted deeds of helping the dark one kingdom, they embarked on their long journey back to their beloved kingdom. Little did they know of the sinister events that had transpired in their absence. Oblivious to the internal demise that had unfolded within their once-proud walls, they carried a glimmer of hope in their hearts, their minds filled with visions of restoration and reunification for both kingdoms. Their current circumstances held a profound sense of irony as they pressed on with sturdy resolve, oblivious to the deceit that had ravaged their homeland.

Little did they know, their queen was taken prisoner, their families mercilessly slain, and their kingdom was reduced to ruins by those whom they once stood against and supported. Their footsteps traced a path towards a shattered kingdom, where the echoes of their past glory clashed with the grim reality that awaited them. The contrast between their hopeful anticipation and the grim fate that awaited them cast a shadow over their journey as the unknowing travelers approached their home, walking into a storm they could never have anticipated.

As the Alora army embarked on their journey back to their fallen kingdom, unaware of the treachery that had befallen their homeland, they carried with them the weight of their heritage and the hope of restoration. With every step, they clung to their identity as Alora Elves, a name that echoed the history and noble lineage of their kin. Little did they know that in their absence, the Dark Ones had also undergone a transformation of their own with the help of the army of Alora. The dark ones of the volcanic kingdom called themselves Zelorian and named their newly constructed kingdom Zelor.

The name "Zelorians" symbolized their resilience and the journey they had developed. It represented their separation from the Alora elves and their determination to forge their own path. No longer bound by the shadows of the past, the Zelorians sought to establish their own legacy and create a society that aligned with their values and aspirations. In hope of not having a shadow council and finding a true leader within to bring a better future for the Dark Elves, no longer holding onto the ancient prejudice of Dark Ones.

Meanwhile, the Alora elves, still unaware of the name change among their Dark Elven counterparts, continued to refer to themselves as Alorian. To them, the name "Alorians" represented their unyielding spirit, their connection to their ancestral home, their queen, and their commitment to rebuilding. As fate would have it, these two distinct names, Alorians and Zelorians, would come to define the separate journeys of the two elven races. While their paths diverged, their histories intertwined, forever marking the chapters of their shared narrative in the annals of their kind.

As the army of Alora approached the once-majestic kingdom, they received word from a scout of what had transpired. Their spirits were heavy with an overwhelming sense of despair. Commander Relios felt an ache of fear and sadness as he absorbed the tragic news. The commitment to rebuilding now seemed like an impossible task in the face of such devastation. But even in their despair, the Alorians remained resolute, knowing that their shared history with the Zelorians would strengthen their determination to restore what had been lost.

With sorrow weighing on their souls and a deep sense of despair in their spirits, they pressed forward towards the crumbling empire. Relios, burdened by the weight of his emotions, resolved to embark on a quest to locate his beloved. The revelation of her absence had instilled within him an overwhelming dread and grief; nonetheless, he remained resolute in reuniting with her regardless of the sacrifices required. In light of the harrowing devastation that enveloped them, the undertaking ahead appeared formidable.

The sight that unfolded before their weary eyes was a stark contrast to the glory they had known. The once-proud walls now lay in ruins, their towering structures reduced to rubble and ashes. The streets that were once bustling with life and laughter now stand eerily silent and desolate. Each step they took seemed to echo the weight of their shattered dreams and lost hope. The air was thick with a somber atmosphere, as if the very land mourned the demise of its former glory. The once-vibrant gardens now wither and wilt, mirroring the spirits of the weary military.

As they beheld the remnants of their fallen kingdom, significant anguish engulfed their souls. This sadness stemmed not merely from witnessing the physical devastation but also from comprehending that their homeland, which embodied their very essence, had been violated and desecrated through treachery. Wandering across the remains of what was formerly their flourishing metropolis, the army couldn't escape a profound feeling of bereavement and yearning. Recollections of exotic festivities, noble undertakings, and peaceful coexistence appeared like distant sounds dwindling into a chasm of hopelessness.

In the once-glorious kingdom of Alora, a sense of desolation and sorrow hung in the air. The absence of Queen Alora and the devastating aftermath of Fumar's rebellion had left a void that could not be easily filled. The once vibrant streets now stood empty, bearing the scars of destruction and the weight of lost lives. The remaining Alorians, grief-stricken and betrayed, grappled with the harsh reality that their kingdom had been turned against them from within.

The remnants of Fumar's dictatorship and the predicament involving their imprisoned queen returned within the walls that still stood, serving as a haunting reminder of the somber fate that had descended upon their previously adored kingdom. With each passing day evolving into weeks, the Alorians found comfort in their unwavering determination and a flicker of optimism, uniting to reconstruct their native land while striving to liberate their queen from the grasp of the oppressive ruler who had taken control.

The Alorians possessed deep-rooted resilience, as they understood the potential for growth even after experiencing devastation. Their past was filled with stories of conquering challenges, reconstructing what had been lost, and emerging more powerful than ever. With firm resolve, they tapped into the combined determination of their individuals, drawing upon their ancient knowledge and unstoppable drive. United by a common goal to regain control of their kingdom, they joined forces in reconstructing the broken infrastructure and reviving life in the previously bustling streets, all while fostering hope amidst the fallen remains.

They promised to build a brand-new Alora as proof of their tenacity and unwavering determination while channeling their grief and rage towards a power of rejuvenation. As they worked tirelessly, constructing the groundwork for their reemergence, deep within their hearts, they held steadfast belief in transcending the gloom and forging a future where their kingdom thrived once again in its full splendor. The embers of their resolve glimmered, sparking a flickering beacon of hope amid hardship that not only uplifted themselves but also inspired all who bore witness to their resolute devotion.

Chapter 12: Echoes of the Past

After undergoing numerous intense events that left lasting impressions on the elven communities of Paranova, a new era was born. As time passed, there arose a feeling of rejuvenation as the shattered remnants of their societies began rebuilding and striving for forgiveness among themselves. The physical reminders engraved in their souls acted as profound symbols of the previous darkness that had engulfed their world, propelling each race towards a path leading to rebirth. With renewed purpose and resilience they found themselves on the edge of a promising future, ready to carve out their own destinies and leave behind the shadows that had haunted them for a long time.

In the following events leading to the kingdom's destruction and the division among the elven races, an era of healing and self-discovery began. The dark elves, once known as the Dark Ones, sought to rebuild their partially destroyed kingdom, naming it Zelor. Embracing a new identity, they referred to themselves as Zelorians.

On the other hand, the light elves, determined to forge a brighter future, adopted the name Alorian, distancing themselves from the shadows of the past. The gray elves, followers of Fumar, established a village in relation to his name, Fumaron, calling themselves Fumarians. Their leader's whereabouts remained a mystery, but his legacy lingered among his devoted followers.

While mortals of mixed sapience were traditionally named Nexum or Gemlar, this new generation of elves did not see themselves as half-breeds. Instead, they proudly identified as the third, enhanced elven race, forging a path forward as they navigated the complexities of their changed world. The names Alorian, Zelorian, and Fumarian echoed across the landscapes, marking the beginning of a new era for the elven races.

The war with Pyrothos had left deep scars on the Zelorians, both physically and emotionally. The rebellion Fumar led in Alora had split the once proud and united Alorian elves, left the Alorian kingdom in ruins, and broken their spirits as they sought a brighter future. The devastation was widespread, and the Zelorians found themselves facing the daunting task of rebuilding their shattered lives and in debt to the Alorian vanguard.

The Zelorians commenced a personal odyssey to rectify the misdeeds of their previous lives. They sought refuge in age-old rites and customs, with the aspiration of soothing their bruised souls and reclaiming their inherent sense of self. By engaging in meditation and introspection, they aimed to attain inner tranquility and rediscover the resilience that was eroded during times of conflict. As they delved further into their spiritual efforts, a glimmer of optimism gradually began to emerge, sparking a newfound determination within each Zelorian individual. They understood that only by embracing their past and deriving wisdom from it could they sincerely progress towards a more promising future.

The Zelorians understand that healing is a necessary step in finding their true selves and rebuilding their society. By immersing themselves in ancient rites and practices, they were able to tap into the wisdom of their ancestors and connect with their ancient cultural heritage. This bond provided them a renewed sense of purpose and fortitude to confront the challenges ahead. With each meditation and reflection the Zelorians grew stronger, both individually and collectively.

They faced not only the daunting task of physical reconstruction but also the immense challenge of rebuilding their shattered heritage and traditions. The revelation about their revered fire god and the corruption within the shadow council left scars on the collective psyche of the Zelorian elves. The guilt stemming from the actions of their previous leaders, manipulated by the council, weighed heavily on their hearts. They feared that the Alorian elves might find hatred among their elven kind because of the rebellion that seemed to take down the Alorian empire.

Despite the manipulation that stoked hostility towards the Alorians, the Zelorians were appreciative of the vanguard's unexpected assistance when they were in need. This bridge of assistance from the Alorian elves, particularly the vanguard, began to mend the strained relationship between the two elven factions. The wounds of betrayal and deception were gradually healing, paving the way for a tentative alliance born from shared hardship.

As they surveyed the ravaged land and mourned their dead relatives, the Zelorians realized that a new hierarchy and leadership would be critical to their recovery. They need a strong guiding hand—someone who can restore their confidence and bring them together again. They long for a leader who inspires hope, inspires them to overcome pain, and fosters a new sense of purpose and determination. The Zelorians understand that only through concerted efforts and foresight can they rebuild their kingdom and heal the wounds that have shattered their collective psyche.

As the Zelorians stood amidst the ruins of their once magnificent kingdom, their hearts heavy with grief and loss, they came to a reflective realization. To navigate the treacherous path of recovery, they understood the dire need for a new hierarchy and a leader capable of guiding them out of the darkness that had enveloped their land. They desired a strong guiding hand, someone who could ignite the flames of hope and restore their shattered faith.

This leader had to possess not only wisdom and strength but also the ability to unite their fractured society, knitting together the broken pieces into a cohesive whole once more. The Zelorians long for a beacon of hope, a figure who can inspire them to rise above their grief and rebuild their kingdom with tenacity and determination. In search of that guiding light, they search for a leader who can navigate the complexities of their shattered world and restore the pride and unity of their once-great race.

During the pursuit, a new king emerges: Tyrron Tylanis, a leader who embodies tenacity, wisdom, and determination to lead his elves back to their former glory. He is hailed as a beacon of hope and a symbol of Zelorian tenacity in the face of difficulty. With his steadfast determination, Tyrron quickly gained the trust and admiration of his elves. He understands that restoring pride and unity will require not only rebuilding their physical world but also healing the deep wounds that separate them. Under his leadership, the Zelorians took on a journey of self-discovery and reconciliation, determined to move beyond the past to create a better future together.

Tyrron Tylanis, a distinguished Emberblade among the dark ones, held a unique perspective on the events that unfolded during the war. Witnessing the commanding presence of Aleron as he directed Pyrothos to unleash devastation upon both dark and light elves left a lasting mark on Tyrron's memory. This experience, rather than instilling fear, served as a wellspring of inspiration for him.

Tyrron's connection with the Alorian commander, Relios, further enriched his leadership qualities. The camaraderie forged during the aid provided by the Alorian elves after the war laid the foundation for a strong bond between Tyrron and Relios. The two leaders engaged in discussions on warfare and even sparred together, fostering mutual respect and admiration.

Within the Zelorian elves, Tyrron's leadership was widely acknowledged and appreciated. Many saw him as an exceptional leader, drawing inspiration from his experiences and strategic insights. As the

Zelorians navigated the complexities of rebuilding their kingdom and forging new alliances, Tyrron Tylanis stood as a prominent figure, contributing his strength and wisdom to guide his elves toward a brighter future.

Tyrron and his ascension marked a turning point for the Zelorians. He focused on a mission to rebuild not just their physical structures but also their moral compass. No longer would forbidden magic be tolerated, for they had witnessed the destructive consequences it could unleash. Instead, the Zelorians embraced a path of moral magic, seeking to harness their powers for the betterment of their society and the preservation of their values. Alongside the transformation of their magical practices, the Zelorians severed their ties with the once influential shadow council. They recognized the need for unity and focused on creating a governance system that prioritized the well-being of their residents and the restoration of trust within their community.

Over time, the healing and redemption extended beyond their own ranks. The Zelorians opened their doors to large groups of lowborn refugees who had participated in the rebellion. These individuals sought redemption and reconciliation, recognizing the errors of their ways and desiring to make amends. The lowborn refugees, driven by a collective desire to atone for their past actions, extended their hands in service and offered their diverse skills to contribute to the recovery efforts. The intent was clear—to rebuild, reconcile, and forge a new path forward.

Tyrron Tylanis, however, made a decision under the influence of his position of leadership and the lessons learned from Alora's tragic fate. He permitted only dark elves to reside within the Zelorian kingdom, a decision rooted in the recognition that past alliances with other elven factions had led to ruin. Gray and light elves, seeking refuge, were redirected by Tyrron to the growing human/elven settlement of Nightscar. Tyrron would allow other races to travel, visit, and trade inside the new kingdom, but he wanted to keep boundaries on the living conditions while they were in the stages of restructuring.

Nightscar, once a raider clan stronghold, had evolved into a thriving community through collaboration and alliances. Under the leadership of Zelor, it became a sanctuary for those who could not find shelter within the Zelorian borders. This strategic decision aimed at safeguarding the Zelorians from potential internal conflicts, as they prioritized the stability and unity necessary for their kingdom's recovery.

With the realization that a new hierarchy was essential for their recovery, the Zelorians launched the challenging task of establishing a fresh order of leadership. After much deliberation and consultation, the elves had decided to crown King Tyrron as their new ruler, recognizing his remarkable qualities that made him the ideal candidate for the role. Tyrron perfectly embodied the cherished values of compassion, wisdom, and fairness that the Zelorians actively sought in a leader.

He displayed an immense understanding of their history, traditions, and the formidable challenges they encountered. This unwavering commitment to their well-being earned him profound respect and genuine admiration from his residents. As King Tyrron assumed the throne, the Zelorians joyfully embraced him, and their hope and determination reignited. They sought inspiration and guidance from him while trusting in his ability to lead them towards a brighter tomorrow. Under his rule and united by a shared vision of reclaiming their past glory, the Zelorians embarked on a journey of healing and rebuilding.

One of King Tyrron's first priorities was to establish order and stability within Zelorian society. He put in a lot of effort to reorganize the hierarchy so that those with integrity and merit filled the positions of power. This process aimed to eliminate corruption and favoritism, laying the groundwork for a fair and just governance system. King Tyrron also implemented policies to promote economic growth and prosperity. He encouraged trade and commerce to showcase their newfound openness while investing in infrastructure projects that improved transportation and communication networks. These efforts not only revitalized the Zelorians' economy but also fostered a sense of optimism and hope for a brighter future among the elves.

With King Tyrron at the helm, the Zelorians found renewed purpose and determination. They rallied behind his leadership and committed themselves to the daunting task of rebuilding their society. They navigated the path of recovery under his guidance while confident that their king would lead them out of the darkness of despair and into a prosperous future.

King Tyrron Tylanis, at the helm of the Zelorian kingdom, found strength and support in his family. Theatrice, his wife, became the new queen, and together, they raised two sons, Tyrion and Tevrin. The Zelorians, having witnessed the fierce events that led to the downfall of their kingdom, welcomed the family as royal, with hope and anticipation.

Theatrice, as the new queen, brought her own wisdom and grace to the throne, complementing King Tyrron's leadership. The two sons, Tyrion and Tevrin, represented the future of the Zelorian elves, symbolizing the potential for a brighter and more harmonious era. With a united royal family structure in place the Zelorians embarked on a journey of healing and reconstruction, determined to forge a new path that would lead them away from the shadows of their past and towards a promising future.

The king implemented various economic structures attracting foreign investments from other settlements and these investments helped stimulate local industries. As a result, job opportunities flourished, and the Zelorians witnessed a gradual improvement in their standard of living. The king's dedication to his subjects instilled a sense of unity and resilience as they worked together to overcome the challenges that lay ahead.

Under the reign of King Tyrron, the Zelorians began a transformative journey to embrace moral magic practices that would align with their values and create a harmonious society. Drawing inspiration from the Alora ways of life while also incorporating the cultures and traditions of the dark elves of old, the Zelorians sought to forge a unique path that upheld ethical principles.

One of the key initiatives undertaken by King Tyrron was the banning of forbidden magic, recognizing the inherent dangers and chaos it brought to their kingdom. The king was adamant about shielding his subjects from the corrupting effects of such magic because visions of the past and the atrocities committed while under its influence haunted him. By outlawing forbidden magic, the Zelorians aimed to foster a community built on trust, empathy, and respect for the sanctity of life.

Additionally, King Tyrron focused on dismantling any council that had once held considerable influence within the Zelorians' society. Recognizing the potential for manipulation and abuse of power, the king sought to establish a transparent and accountable governance structure. He entrusted key positions of authority to individuals of integrity and merit, ensuring that decision-making processes were fair and just.

As moral magic practices took hold, the Zelorians experienced a significant transformation. They embraced a comprehensive approach to magic, focusing on its positive and constructive applications. Magic became a tool for healing, nurturing, and protecting their community. The Zelorians celebrated the interconnectedness of all living beings and sought to harness their magical abilities for the betterment of their society.

While the transition was not without its challenges, the Zelorians found comfort in their shared commitment to a new era of enlightened magic. They reveled in the harmony that emerged as moral practices took root, witnessing the positive impact on their individual lives and the collective well-being of their kingdom. The teachings and traditions of the Alora merged with the wisdom and knowledge of the dark ones, creating a vibrant tapestry of magical practices that honored their history while forging a new path forward.

With the ascension of King Tyrron, the Zelorians witnessed the dissolution of the once-powerful shadow council followers, a secretive group that had wielded influence over their society for generations. Determined to foster transparency and accountability, the king took decisive measures to maintain separation from the shadow council and any ties to the Zelorians. Any engagement in secretive meetings or the illicit use of forbidden magic was met with swift and severe consequences. Those found guilty faced imprisonment, exile, or, in more severe cases, execution. The king's strict stance against such activities sent a clear message: the Zelorians would no longer tolerate the manipulation and subversion that had plagued their past, and the path forward would be one of integrity and harmony.

King Tyrron, driven by his deep love for his sons Tyrion, Tevin, and his wife Theatrice, was determined to reshape the perception of the Zelorians among other races. He was aware that the past had tarnished their reputation, making elves wary of them and reluctant to approach them. The king yearned for a time when the various civilizations of Paranova would accept his kin as more than just monsters and treat them with respect.

To achieve this vision, King Tyrron continued his mission of diplomacy and cultural exchange. He sent emissaries to neighboring cities and kingdoms, extending invitations for peaceful dialogue and establishing trade partnerships. He sought to demonstrate the Zelorian commitment to peace, progress, and understanding. The king invested resources in education and cultural exchange programs within the Zelor borders. He believed that knowledge and understanding were the keys to dismantling prejudice and promoting unity. Zelorian scholars and historians diligently worked to document their true history, dispelling misconceptions and shedding light on the rich tapestry of their culture.

As time passed, the Zelorian reputation began to shift, albeit slowly. The once feared and misunderstood race started to be viewed with a more open mind. While some prejudices lingered, King Tyrron remained resolute in his pursuit of acceptance and equality. He knew that true change would take time, but he was willing to dedicate his reign to breaking down barriers and rewriting the future for the Zelorians.

In the quiet moments, when the weight of responsibility threatened to overwhelm him, King Tyrron found comfort in the presence of his family. They were his constant reminders of the love and happiness that could be achieved in a world free from prejudice and fear.

With their faithful support, he continued to strive for a future where the name of the Zelorians would be synonymous with compassion, unity, and redemption.

·······

The elves of Alora were overwhelmed with a range of emotions in the days that followed the rebellion. The once lively cityscape bore the wounds of destruction, with ruined buildings and combat debris serving as daily reminders of the trauma they had been through. Grief and sorrow flowed over the streets as families mourned the loss of loved ones, and the collective guilt of their deeds weighed hard on their hearts. The sense of unity that once defined Alora had been shattered, replaced by fierce tension and a lingering sense of regret. The elves, however, have decided to confront the aftermath head-on, rebuilding their shattered lives and restoring their state to its former glory, faced by the haunting presence of the reanimated corpses that had wreaked havoc over the darkest days of the war.

To cleanse their kingdom and rid themselves of the lingering plague, a reflective and deep spiritual cleansing was held. It was a solemn ceremony where the Alorian priests and priestesses led the community in prayers, rituals, and incantations designed to release the trapped souls and bring peace to the restless spirits.

The spiritual cleansing took place in the center of Alora, where the battlefield scars were the most obvious. The streets were adorned with colorful tapestries, candles were lit, and aromatic herbs were burned, infusing the atmosphere with a purifying aroma. The community gathered with expressions shaped by mourning and faith to honor the fallen and filled with hope to free those who were slaughtered and reanimated, thought to be lingering within the dark ethereal plane.

Now led by Aiden and the priests and priestesses, their chants weaving through the atmosphere, calling upon the higher powers for guidance and assistance, offerings were made. They represented both a community's collective remorse for what had happened as well as a desire to be redeemed. The echoes of their sorrows and regrets recurred throughout the streets as they mixed with other whispers from ancient incantations that resonated throughout the cleansing energies in the kingdom.

As the ceremony ended, an overwhelming feeling of release had flooded into the hearts of the participants. It was as if some burden had been lifted; somehow the kingdom could begin towards healing itself spiritually. The spiritual cleansing did offer some measure of comfort for those who remained, allowing them closure and allowing them to go on with life while offering release and rest to those lost souls they held close.

In the days following the cleansing, the elves of Alora continued to honor and remember the fallen, tending to their graves with honor and care. The spiritual cleansing served as a turning point, a collective acknowledgment that the kingdom had overcome darkness and was ready to rebuild not only its physical structures but also its spiritual essence. It marked the beginning of a new chapter, where the elves of Alora could draw strength from their shared experiences, their resilience, and the belief that their kingdom would rise once again, united and steadfast.

A restructure of the hierarchy became necessary to provide stability and direction to the elves of Alora. Commander Relios, a skilled vanguard fighter known for his strength and strategic prowess, emerged as a natural leader in these trying times. His stern yet compassionate demeanor resonated with the elves, instilling a sense of confidence and security. Relios was quick to assume the responsibility of leading the recovery efforts, working tirelessly to establish order, prioritize resources, and ensure that the needs of the citizens were met.

Under his leadership, the elves found comfort and guidance, and a flicker of hope began to burn amidst the ruins. Commander Relios deeply missed his queen but dedicated himself to her daughter instead; he would help watch over her with Freynora. Relios would occasionally take long weeks venturing out into the southern regions of Paranova to search for the queen. He had a sense that she was still alive, and he would not give up over the course of many years.

Under the guidance of Commander Relios, a new hierarchy was established, one that prioritized stability, unity, and the well-being of the Alorians. Alongside him, Princess Alora took on an important role within the hierarchy, serving as a symbol of hope and continuity for the kingdom. Her wisdom, compassion, and deep understanding of the Alorian culture allowed her to connect with elves on a genuine and authentic level.

As the kingdom slowly rebuilt, Princess Alora worked tirelessly to implement policies that would address the needs of elves and promote their welfare. She actively sought input from various districts of society, ensuring that their voices were heard, and their concerns were addressed. Her dedication and commitment to the well-being of her subjects had earned her widespread admiration and respect, solidifying her position as a beloved leader in the eyes of the Alorian citizens.

Another key figure in the new hierarchy was Highborn Mage Freynora, who assumed the position of advisor to Princess Alora. With her vast knowledge of arcane arts and strategic thinking, Freynora brought invaluable insights and guidance to the leadership, helping to shape the kingdom's path to recovery. Together, Relios, Alora, and Freynora formed a formidable trio, each contributing their unique strengths to the governance of the kingdom of Alora.

This strategy also contributed to citizen empowerment and the kingdom became more of a community. The elves of Alora were not ignored; instead their thoughts and feelings were carefully considered throughout the decision-making process. District meetings and open forums were utilized to promote dialogue; in this way, the elves of Alora truly played a role in shaping their kingdom's destiny, instilling pride and ownership. The kingdom's involvement in politics increased to an all-time high as a result of this relationship. The top-tier leadership trio of Freynora, Relios, and the Princess built a prosperous kingdom in which everyone felt as if they individually made a difference.

Freynora, a respected member of the Alorian culture, held a prominent position as the leader of her own island. She was known for her mastery of divinity infused elemental magic and her experience in governing her community. Despite her independent nature and personal pursuits, Freynora maintained a deep respect for Alorian traditions and values. She delved into her own personal pleasures away from the eyes of the kingdom and enjoyed those pleasures in private on her island.

After many years and during the process of rebuilding the kingdom, a strong bond developed between Freynora and Princess Alora. Recognizing the potential in the young princess and her desire to carry on her mother's legacy, Freynora agreed to take on the role as an advisor. This decision was driven by Freynora's belief in the importance of guiding and shaping the next generation of Alorian leaders.

Freynora, the princess's personal advisor, taught her everything she needed to know about Alorian society. She taught the princess how to communicate effectively and how to present herself accordingly at various events. In addition, she educated the princess about the local cultures, the structure of the Alorian government, and several forms of magic. Through her knowledge of it all, the princess genuinely became a leader and learned how to oversee a kingdom properly. Not only did the princess learn how to interact with others in a manner that was suitable for a leader, but she also learned how to differentiate between right and wrong, as well as numerous other skills, thanks to all of the various viewpoints that her teachers provided.

While Freynora maintained her autonomy and personal interests outside of Alora, her commitment to the well-being of the kingdom, her belief in Princess Alora, and her potential remained strong. Her presence and guidance within the new hierarchy brought a different perspective and a touch of unconventional wisdom, ensuring that the kingdom's rebuilding efforts were grounded in both tradition and innovation.

Together, Freynora and Princess Alora forged a dynamic partnership, combining the wisdom of the past with the adaptability required for the future. Their collaboration symbolized the unity and cooperation necessary for the kingdom's resurgence. As they worked hand in hand, Freynora 's expertise and insights, along with Princess Alora's determination and growth, laid the foundation for a brighter and more prosperous future for Alora and its citizens. Their common goal and passion to progress drove them forward, motivating Alorians to embrace change and new ideas. The end effect was a culture that supported innovation while also honoring tradition, resulting in an everlasting blend of the two.

To protect Alora's heart, the inner sanctum, the Alorians went to great lengths to develop protections that would promise the preservation of their valuable knowledge and heritage. Recognizing the importance of this sacred area, they sought the assistance of talented arcanists whose knowledge of magic and enchantments proved essential in building an effective defense. The arcanists conjured complex wards and spells, imbuing the inner sanctum with an impenetrable barrier against any potential attacks. These enchantments not only protected the precious wisdom and history but also added to the overall aura of serenity and mysticism within the sanctum, further enchanting those who entered its consecrated corridors.

Under the guidance of Princess Alora and the leadership of Commander Relios, the arcanists labored diligently to craft a network of protective magical barriers that encircled the most inner sanctum. Through their intricate weaving of spells and incantations, a powerful shield manifested, rendering the most sacred area impenetrable to all but those deemed worthy by the Alorian elves. These elves would be called keepers, and they would maintain the sanctum and the preservation within.

These magical barriers were more than simply barriers of protection; they reflected the Alorians' perseverance and commitment to protect their ancestral wisdom. The boundaries around the sanctum released a faint ethereal glow that wrapped around the entire area in a beautiful, radiant illumination. The shimmering energy served as a constant reminder of the kingdom's strengthened willpower while also warding off any invading forces or trespassers.

The citizens of Alora regarded the magical barriers with a profound sense of admiration and wonder. They recognized the significance of this symbol of strength and unity, confirming their determination to rise above its past trials and defend its cherished traditions. The barriers became a focal point of admiration, drawing both locals and visitors alike to witness the tangible manifestation of Alora's resilience. The barriers stood tall, their shimmering energy captivating all who beheld them. It was as if the very essence of Alora's spirit was encapsulated within those ethereal walls, inspiring a sense of hope and security among its inhabitants. The kingdom's reputation as an impenetrable fortress grew, attracting scholars and historians eager to study the intricate enchantments that safeguarded Alora's future.

With the magical barriers in place, the Sanctum became a sanctuary of both knowledge and security. Scholars and historians continued their tireless work within its protective confines, writing into tomes and scrolls that contained the wisdom of generations past. The barriers not only safeguarded the accumulated knowledge but also instilled a renewed sense of purpose and dedication among the Alorians, who now felt a sacred duty to ensure the preservation of their heritage. The scholars and historians were not dwindled to losing most of their work from the rebellion; instead, they continued to recollect themselves to preserve their past and present.

The protective magical barriers, an embodiment of the kingdom's determination to shield its sacred knowledge and heritage, served as a testament to Alora's unwavering commitment to its elven kind. They stood as a powerful symbol of resilience, reminding all who beheld them that the kingdom would not falter in the face of adversity. Within the shimmering embrace of the magical barriers, the Alorians found calm and fresh hope, embracing the future with a collective sense of purpose and deep appreciation for their historical legacy.

As the dust settled and the elves of Alora began the difficult job of repairing their shattered lives, they learned to discover their inner strength and determination. The rebellion had originally broken the sense of community, but it gradually started to heal as elves united together in a shared purpose to restore their beloved kingdom. Citizens established work groups to clean debris, rebuild structures, and restore the once-thriving districts. The restoration process not only healed physical wounds but also acted as an encouragement for mental recovery. The residents of Alora discovered peace and harmony through their collective efforts, taking strength from one another as they took the first steps toward reclaiming their dignity and restoring their kingdom's glory.

Under the skilled leadership of Kleia and Aiden, the Arcanists underwent a significant transformation, shifting their focus toward both magic and defense, now known as the Arcanists Guild. Kleia, known for her unparalleled offensive prowess, guided the guild members in honing their skills in offensive magic. Her expertise in unleashing devastating spells and harnessing elemental forces inspired the arcanists to push their limits and unlock their true potential.

However, Aiden stepped up to a leadership role, becoming the master of defense for the guild thanks to his extensive knowledge of protection magic. He taught the arcanists the skills of defensive spells, enchantments, and barriers, enhancing their ability to protect themselves and their companions from harm. Aiden highlighted the importance of balance and discipline, ensuring that the guild's magic was not only offensive but also defensive, with the goal of protecting its objectives.

Kleia and Aiden collaborated to maintain a delicate balance inside the arcanist guild. They established an atmosphere of mutual respect and cooperation, encouraging arcanists to use both offensive and defensive magic. The members were taught how to combine their skills, seamlessly switching between releasing powerful attacks and creating strong defenses. This comprehensive approach to magic meant that the guild evolved into a strong force capable of not only unleashing fatal magic but also protecting themselves and each other from any threat that could arrive.

As the guild evolved under Kleia and Aiden's leadership, their teachings struck a deep chord among the arcanists. They believed that true strength is found not only in overwhelming force but also in the ability to defend and maintain oneself. The Arcanists Guild became well-known for their adaptability; their members were considered talented spellcasters who could adapt to any circumstance, whether it was in the thick of battle or in the care of precious artifacts and knowledge.

The Arcanist Guild accepted all Alorians, regardless of their talent or fortune. Kleia and Aiden believed in each individual's abilities and realized that exceptional magical skills could be developed with the right direction and training. They aggressively partnered with the Alorian Academy, an institution committed to developing fresh talents, to ensure graduates' smooth transition into the guild.

The collaboration between the Arcanists Guild and the Academy has proven to serve as an inspiration for the advancement of magical knowledge and skills among Alorian students. Promising students were discovered early on and given specialized training to help them improve their magical abilities. The guild's veteran members took those aspiring arcanist students under their guidance, assisting and directing them on the path to magical supremacy.

The guild's welcoming attitude produced an extensive community of spellcasters. Alorians from every aspect of life came together to contribute their knowledge and experiences. This encouraged collaboration and growth as members openly shared ideas and approaches that pushed the limits. The guild evolved as an organization based on discovery and creativity.

The Arcanists Guild aspired to promote fairness and unity among its members by breaking down wealth and social class barriers. No matter their origin, all elves were afforded the chance to develop, excel, and make contributions to the magical arts. This inclusive approach supported the guild's healthy growth. As a bonus, it helped the elven spellcasters bond with one another and work together toward a common goal. Spellcasters from various backgrounds may gather together, collaborate, and learn from one another in this atmosphere. The guild became a center of creativity as members were encouraged to experiment and explore unfamiliar territories together. This environment of unity and cooperation propelled the guild to unprecedented heights, earning its reputation as a significant organization in the realm of magic.

Aiden's expertise in the dark arts became a valuable asset to the newly established guild. With his guidance, he shared the intricacies of arcane magic, particularly the darker aspects, with Kleia and other arcanists. Aiden aimed to foster a deeper understanding of the dual nature of arcane magic, emphasizing the importance of comprehending both the light and shadow within the arcane, as well as the intricate connections with the elements and divinity.

The guild aimed to establish a setting where elven spellcasters could explore and master the vast spectrum of magic, drawing inspiration from Aiden's teachings. The goal was not only to empower individuals with knowledge but also to instill a sense of control and responsibility in wielding these powerful forces.

As the guild continued to flourish, its reputation as a hub of magical excellence spread throughout the kingdom of Alora and beyond. The collaboration with the academy became a shining example of how the pursuit of magical knowledge could transcend societal divisions and elevate the entire community. The guild stood as inspiration for all ages to embrace their magical potential and join the ranks of those who sought to unravel the mysteries of the arcane.

Together, the Arcanist Guild and the Academy worked hand in hand, nurturing the next generation of Alorian spellcasters. Their combined efforts not only enriched the magical traditions of Alora but also contributed to the collective growth and progress of the elven society. With open arms and a shared commitment to the pursuit of magical excellence, the guild and the academy welcomed all who dared to dream and aspire to master the art of magic.

The Genetic Pathway Organization changed drastically after the rebellion and during Alora's restoration. Recognizing the value of understanding an individual's own abilities and strengths, the organization moved its focus away from rigid testing and categorization to a more flexible and personalized approach. Magic became an important aspect of their examination process, helping scientists gain a thorough understanding of an individual's potential and genetic heritage through their unique individual characteristics.

With the integration of magic into the assessment procedures, the organization developed intricate plans and pathways for participants or parents, outlining the most suitable avenues for their future undertakings. Whether it was military service, mastery of magic, proficiency in archery, honing tradecrafts, or pursuing careers as skilled laborers, each person was directed towards a specific category that aligned with their unique abilities and attributes.

This restructuring aimed to empower the next generation by guiding them towards their own distinct paths based on their genetic evaluations. It recognized that not everyone's journey would be the same and that individuals possessed diverse aptitudes that should be nurtured and celebrated. By providing personalized pathways, the organization ensured that each person had the opportunity to excel in areas where they were naturally inclined, fostering a society enriched with diverse skills and talents.

The integration of magic in the evaluation process allowed for a more in-depth understanding of an individual's genetic potential, unlocking new possibilities and revealing hidden skills. The organization accepted the idea that genetics alone did not decide one's fate but rather provided a basis for individuals to craft their own unique paths. The combination of magical evaluation and personalized pathway planning enabled a more comprehensive and effective approach, allowing clients to find and pursue their actual passions and potentials.

As the organization adopted this new strategy, its primary goal switched from categorization to encouraging growth in individuals, self-discovery, and fulfillment. Participants and parents were given extensive direction and support, ensuring that everyone's path was met with understanding, encouragement, and the resources they needed to succeed.

By reorganizing themselves to better guide future generations, the Alorian citizens were able to improve their inherited characteristics by tapping into hidden talents and discovering unexplored paths of development through the use of magic.

The Genetic Pathway Organization, in collaboration with the kingdom's education systems, placed a significant emphasis on education and science. While engaged in various tasks and supporting educational initiatives, the organization found a particular fascination with enhancing the elven race. Unbeknownst to them, this interest in genetic enhancement set the organization on an intriguing and uncertain path.

As their passion for delving into genetics, magic, and the inner workings of mortals intensified, the organization became pioneers in a field that merged science and magic. Their research aimed to unravel the mysteries of enhancing individuals through magical means. The future for the Genetic Pathway Organization appeared uncertain, teetering on the brink of discoveries that could reshape the very essence of elven existence.

While Alora experienced a wave of positivity and progress, a new covenant emerged within the kingdom, seeking to explore the benefits and potential of forbidden magics. This group, comprised of spellcasters, scholars, and individuals with a deep fascination for the unknown, recognized that while forbidden magics had been shunned and feared in the past, there were untapped possibilities and hidden knowledge within these mystical arts.

The Covenant thought that forbidden magic contained secrets and powers that, when used responsibly, could result in tremendous breakthroughs in different realms of life. They attempted to solve the mysteries and misconceptions surrounding these magics in order to unlock their potential for the advancement of sapience. Their attention was not drawn to the chaos and destruction associated with prohibited magics but rather to the benefits they could provide when dealt with caution and understanding.

Devoted scholars within the covenant sifted through the remnants of the old books, examining practices and rituals that had long been regarded as forbidden or even harmful. They carried out experiments and investigations to discover the hidden potentials and applications of these magical powers. They reasoned that there had to be an explanation as to why Fumar and his cult stole most of the teachings. The task involved walking an impossible line between controlling the chaotic power and resisting the dark influence gained from using its immense power. However, the covenant's advocates held the belief that prohibited magics could potentially be safely and effectively adopted into

Alorian society through methodical examination, strict oversight, and moral conduct.

The creation of this covenant sparked debates and discussions within the kingdom, as opinions on the utilization of forbidden magic varied among Alorians. Some embraced the idea of exploring these magics, seeing it as a path towards greater knowledge and advancement. Others remained skeptical, fearing the potential consequences and dangers associated with such practices. The existence of the covenant stimulated a dialogue within the kingdom, prompting discussions on the boundaries of magic with its ethics and its impact on the future of the kingdom.

These discussions within the kingdom were not limited to the royal court or the elite but spread throughout the entire population. The streets of Alora buzzed with debates and arguments as citizens gathered in taverns, marketplaces, and even on the kingdom walls to voice their opinions. It appears everyone has an opinion on the utilization of forbidden magic and the implications it could have on their way of life. The division between those who embraced the idea and those who remained skeptical grew deeper with each passing day, creating a spreading tension within the kingdom.

An effort was made to demonstrate the positive elements of forbidden magic through the use of controlled tests and examinations that were carried out under the leadership of the covenant. They hoped to demonstrate how these powers may be used to heal, protect, and even enhance magical properties. The covenant also stressed the significance of responsible use, setting restricted regulations and protocols to ensure the safety and moral conduct of its members.

These restrictions included regular examinations and assessments of each member's abilities and intentions, as well as severe consequences for any misuse or abuse of forbidden magic. The covenant's efforts received mixed reactions from the kingdom's residents, with some calling out their work as groundbreaking and important for advancement, while others remained suspicious and terrified of the wickedness that such magic could unleash.

The covenant's commitment to studying and using forbidden powers for the greater good was unflinching, in regardless of criticism. They felt that with proper regulation and awareness, prohibited magic could potentially be utilized responsibly and lead to major advances in a variety of professions. However, suspicion and dread about these magics persisted, making it difficult for the covenant to gain popular acceptance and support. Nonetheless, they were keen to demonstrate the value and benefits of their work, seeking to ensure that any misuse or abuse of forbidden magic would result in devastating consequences.

The covenant's presence in Alora generated a wave of curiosity, questioning preconceived notions about forbidden magic. Rather than seeing these magics as naturally evil, the covenant attempted to highlight their potential as strong tools that could be used for beneficial purposes. Their method aimed to redefine the perception of prohibited magics, showing them as tools for growth rather than weapons of destruction.

The covenant's integration of their magic into the Genetic Pathway Organization marked a significant step forward. They demonstrated how these intricate magics could be used to unravel the unique identifying codes of sapient beings. This understanding, they argued, had the potential to enhance or even protect individuals. The magic they wielded was just a glimpse of the vast knowledge they had gleaned from ancient tomes and scrolls, once locked away in the Sanctum until Fumar's intrusion.

As Alora advanced, the covenant's exploration of forbidden magics added a layer of complexity and intrigue to the kingdom's magical landscape. It symbolized Alora's commitment to embracing knowledge, pushing boundaries, and unveiling new realms of possibility. Despite the challenges and uncertainties that accompanied their journey, the covenant remained focused on their pursuit. They believed that the secrets hidden within forbidden magics, when understood and controlled, could contribute to the growth and prosperity of mortal sapience.

········

After much time had passed since the rebuilding of the Alora kingdom. Within the Fumarian culture, a unique and distinctive belief system emerged, centered around the worship of Pyrothos, Aleron, and Fumar as their gods and divine leaders. The Fumarians revered these figures, considering them divine entities who had guided them through the trials and tribulations of their history. To honor their deities, detailed statues were erected throughout the Fumarian territories, depicting Pyrothos, Aleron and Fumar in all their glory and power. These statues served as symbols of admiration and devotion, reminding the Fumarians of their sacred bond with their godlike leaders.

The Fumarians, emerging from the mixed breeding of light and dark elves within the kingdom of Alora, embarked on a unique path, seeking to forge a distinct identity for themselves in the diverse world of Paranova. With no established history or cultural roots, they looked to the remnants of the dark ones for inspiration, adopting and adapting the traditions created by the dark elves.

As a new race born from a blend of light and dark elves, the Fumarians faced the challenge of defining their own culture and traditions. The legacy of the dark ones served as a foundation, offering a sense of belonging in the expansive world of Paranova. Whether pushed away, exiled, forgotten, or even met with disdain, the Fumarians clung to the hope of finding their place and purpose in the intricate tapestry of this fantastical universe.

The Fumarians also practiced forbidden magics and engaged in shadow arts that other elven races considered to be dangerous and taboo. They saw these forbidden magics to tap into hidden realms of power and understanding. Within their society, Fumarian spellcasters and witches practiced spells and rituals that allowed them to commune with the dead and spirits. They believed in the existence of a spiritual realm beyond the mortal plane and sought to establish connections with these ethereal entities. Through these practices, they gained insights, guidance, and even assistance from the spiritual entities they communed with.

The Fumarians, fueled by their loyal devotion to ethereal entities, surpassed even the achievements of the dark ones. Delving into uncharted realms of magic, they exhibited a mastery that extended beyond the boundaries of conventional understanding. Through their connection with these mystical forces, the Fumarians attained the ability to communicate with spectral avatars reminiscent of the ancient dark ones.

In their pursuit of knowledge and communion with the supernatural, the Fumarians pushed the boundaries of magical exploration. The echoes of the ancient dark ones resonated in their practices, but the Fumarians, driven by their own aspirations, forged a unique and potent connection with the ethereal entities that guided their journey in Paranova.

Curses held a unique fascination for the Fumarians, who developed a particular branch of magic known as the Wiccan arts. They embraced the power of curses, recognizing their potential for both harm and benefit. Fumarian witches, known as Wiccans, specialized in weaving curses, employing totems and witchcraft items to channel their magic. These totems, often intricately crafted and imbued with symbolic meaning, served as vessels of power, enabling the witches to focus and direct their curses towards desired targets. The Fumarians viewed curses not merely as instruments of chaos but as tools that could bring about transformative effects and shape the course of events.

Overall, the Fumarian culture stood as a distinctive and separate entity, distinct from the traditions and practices of the Alorians and Zelorians. Their worship of Pyrothos, Aleron, and Fumar, the utilization of forbidden magics, communion with the spiritual realm, integration of highborn women, and their embrace of curses and Wiccan practices all contributed to a rich tapestry of beliefs and customs that set them apart but kept them similar. The Fumarians were a diverse mix of elven races, forging their own path while venerating their godlike figures, preserving their heritage, and embracing the mystical arts that defined their unique identity.

Within the intricate tapestry of Fumarian society, the integration of highborn Alora women who had been captive during and after the rebellion became a pivotal chapter. Some of these resilient women chose to embrace Fumarian society, finding acceptance, respect, and esteemed positions within the community. Their skills, knowledge, and unique perspectives enriched the fabric of Fumarian life, fostering a sense of unity and shared purpose.

However, the paths chosen by these highborn women were not uniform. A divergence emerged as others, carrying the scars of captivity, opted to seek freedom beyond the confines of Fumaron. Escaping on a journey that took them to new lands within Paranova, where they aspired to forge fresh beginnings, liberated from the shadows of their past captivity.

The highborn women found themselves bound by expectations reminiscent of their roles in the kingdom of Alora. The weight of their responsibility echoed through the chambers of the Fumarian society, where the weight of the past seemed to linger. Their purpose, once dictated by the Alorian queen, has now shifted to serving the collective future of the Fumarians. Despite the undercurrents of resentment toward their old queen, the highborn women grappled with the realization that their unique gift of fertility held the key to the prosperity and continuity of the elven race.

In the absence of their leader, Fumar, the village continued to flourish and expand in size over the passing years. The Fumarians, deeply devoted to the ideals and legacy of their departed leader, sought guidance and leadership from the mysterious shadow council. That same council that had existed in the volcanic kingdom of Pyrothos and the time of dark ones. These council members honed their skills with the evaluations of Aleron and found ways to commune with the spiritual realms.

To honor and pay homage to their fallen leader, Aleron, a magnificent tomb was erected within the village. The tomb served as a sacred resting place for Aleron's remains, symbolizing his enduring presence and the impact he had on the elves. The tomb became a site of reverence and pilgrimage, where Fumarians would gather to offer their respects, seek inspiration, and connect with the spirit of their departed leader.

This hallowed site stood as a strong symbol of unity for elves who embraced the vision of Aleron and Fumar. Open to all who believed in the ideals of the dark ones, it became a pilgrimage destination. Elves from various backgrounds came together to honor their visionary leaders because they shared a common allegiance. The tomb echoed with collective memories, fostering a sense of shared heritage and reinforcing the cultural ties that united them within the village of Fumaron.

The ceremonies and traditions surrounding Aleron's tomb became deeply ingrained in Fumarian society. On the anniversary of his death, an extraordinary ceremony takes place annually, complete with music, dance, and passionate tributes. Elaborate floral arrangements covered the tomb's entrance, signifying Aleron's vivid and ever-present spirit. The village elders would lead the procession while carrying lit candles and singing traditional chants that echoed over the surrounding charred forest. As the sun set below the horizon, throwing a warm golden glow on the tomb, the Fumarians would form a circle in silence as the night sky ascended above.

The Shadow Council, comprising individuals of significant influence and knowledge, took on the responsibility of guiding the village in the absence of Fumar. They discussed matters of governance, devised plans for the village's growth and prosperity, and maintained a connection to the mystical forces that surrounded the Fumarian culture. While the council members held significant power and influence, they acknowledged that their role was temporary, awaiting the arrival of their true leader, who would one day come to guide them on their next steps.

In the meantime, the council members strived to uphold the traditions and values that Fumar had instilled in the Fumarians. They worked tirelessly to ensure that decisions were made collectively, considering the needs and aspirations of every villager. Their dedication to maintaining a harmonious and prosperous community was unwavering, and they eagerly awaited the day when their true leader would finally arrive and take charge.

The village of Fumaron thrived under the watchful guidance of the shadow council, balancing the preservation of their unique traditions with the need for growth and development. As the years passed, Fumaron expanded in size, with new structures and dwellings added to accommodate the growing population. The Fumarians found peace in their close-knit community, continuing to practice their ancient customs, commune with the spiritual realm, and honor their respected leader through the council's governance.

·······

Meanwhile, Fumar, consumed by his dark desires and thirst for power, subjected Queen Alora to unimaginable torment and humiliation. From the moment he forced her into an unwilling marriage, he reveled in his control over her, exploiting her vulnerability and breaking her spirit. Fumar took pleasure in exerting his dominance, leaving a lasting mark of suffering on the queen and Alora itself.

Throughout the years following the rebellion, Fumar and Queen Alora became entangled in a twisted relationship. Despite her forced submission, Queen Alora found moments of resilience and defiance, refusing to let Fumar's cruelty extinguish her inner strength. In the depths of her suffering, she secretly devised plans to preserve the knowledge and history of Alora, determined to safeguard her elven legacy.

The torment inflicted upon Queen Alora did not only manifest in physical pain and degradation. Fumar relished manipulating her mind and emotions, using psychological warfare to further break her spirit. He used her as a pawn in his quest for power, forcing her to bear his children and solidify his hold over the remnants of Alora. As Fumar continued to exploit Queen Alora's vulnerability, he also sought to erase any trace of resistance or rebellion from her heart. He subjected her to constant gaslighting and manipulation, distorting her perception of reality and instilling a deep sense of hopelessness. Despite these relentless tactics, Queen Alora's determination to protect her elven heritage only grew stronger, fueling her resilience in the face of unimaginable cruelty.

Despite the relentless cruelty she endured, Queen Alora's legacy endured. Her determination to protect the history and wisdom of the elves led her to hide scrolls, tomes, and historical documents that held the key to the kingdom's past. She had enough energy to cling on to hopes of revealing the existence of these hidden treasures, urging those who found her to preserve the kingdom's essence and ensure its resurrection.

During one of the rare moments when Queen Alora found herself alone and unguarded after giving birth, a glimmer of hope ignited within her. She knew she had to seize the opportunity to safeguard the precious scrolls and tomes stolen from Alora, which held the key to the kingdom's ancient knowledge and heritage. With a heart pounding with both fear and determination, she slipped outside on a daring escape. Queen Alora knew that the fate of her kingdom depended on the survival of these invaluable artifacts. She made a solemn vow to herself, promising to protect them at all costs and pass them down to future generations, ensuring the preservation of elven history and wisdom.

Quietly slipping away from Fumar's watchful eye, Queen Alora ventured into the depths of the enchanted woods surrounding their domain. She sought out a hollow tree, a secret haven she had discovered in her earlier explorations, following her intuition and her strong connection to the land.

As she approached the ancient tree, its weathered bark revealed the scars of countless seasons. It stood tall and proud, a silent witness to the secrets whispered among its branches. With trembling hands, Queen Alora carefully pried open the hidden compartment within the trunk, revealing a hollow space perfectly suited for her purpose.

One by one, she delicately placed the scrolls and tomes into the protective embrace of the tree's hollow. Each artifact represented a fragment of Elven's rich history and magical knowledge, and she entrusted their safekeeping to the guardian spirit of the ancient tree. As she closed the compartment, a sense of relief washed over Queen Alora. She knew that the guardian spirit would protect her cherished artifacts with its ancient wisdom and power, ensuring their preservation for generations to come.

With a final glance at the majestic tree, she whispered a heartfelt thank you before turning away, knowing that her legacy was in safe hands. Whispering a heartfelt prayer and a plea for preservation, Queen Alora bid a silent farewell to the treasured relics. She knew that hiding them away was a necessary sacrifice to ensure the survival of Alora's legacy, even if it meant relinquishing physical possession of their wisdom.

With the scrolls and tomes secured within the hollow tree, Queen Alora could finally breathe a sigh of relief. Though her escape remained a secret known only to her, she drew comfort from the knowledge that a part of Alora's essence was sheltered within the protective arms of nature itself. The weight of responsibility lifted from her shoulders as she imagined future generations stumbling upon the hidden treasures and unearthing the ancient knowledge that would guide them through their own trials and tribulations. Queen Alora's heart swelled with hope, knowing that even in her absence, her legacy would continue to thrive and inspire.

Fumar's rage burned like an inferno as he discovered Queen Alora's absence from the birthing hut. Due to his obsession with preserving the purity of the gray elves, his mind was racing with rage and thoughts of retribution. How dare she defy him by bringing an Alorian child into their world? Fumar set out on a relentless search to find the queen and exact his vengeance on her because of his perverted sense of dominance. The trail Queen Alora had left behind during her escape served as his guide, filling every step with rage and resolve.

Fumar's senses, which had been fine-tuned by a year of hunting and surviving in the harsh wilderness, sharpened as he ventured further into the woods. He followed the faint whispers of the forest, the traces of Queen Alora's presence leading him closer to his prey. His heart pounded with a mixture of anticipation and loathing. Fumar reveled in the thought of bringing Queen Alora to her knees, making her pay for the perceived betrayal against their shared vision of a pure and untainted elven race.

Finally, his relentless pursuit stopped in the distance as he stumbled upon a clearing bathed in a soft, ethereal light. And there, in the middle of it all, stood Queen Alora, the majestic backdrop of nature's embrace framing her delicate figure. Fumar's twisted smile curled upon his lips as he advanced towards her, his eyes gleaming with malice. He relished the power he held over her, knowing that he had the authority to condemn her for her perceived transgressions.

As Fumar grew closer to whom he loved, his twisted feelings began to rise within him, creating a terrible and distorted image of affection. Something deep within his core altered in that moment, and he felt a sudden burst of empathy. It was a strange sensation, new and unsettling, yet it compelled him to gaze at her with a certain comprehension. He realized his hunger for power had blinded him to the suffering he was causing her. The glimmer of empathy caused him to reconsider his behavior and explore the prospect of repentance, but he disregarded it immediately, fearful that sensitivity would weaken his grip on power.

In the years that followed, Fumar and Queen Alora bore witness to the birth of their four children together. Two sons and two daughters, each a testament to the union between light and darkness, two children bore the distinct gray skin of the Fumarians, while the other two possessed the delicate features of the Alorian and Fumarian mixed races. This unexpected blending of their lineages served as a haunting reminder of the past and a symbol of the tangled web that connected the realms of the elven lineage. The firstborn son shone as an Alorian through and through, and Fumar despised the Alorian-like children as they each grew throughout the years.

•••••••

In the shadows of concealment, Fumar, attempting to hide himself for countless years, unwittingly revealed his wickedness when he destroyed a farm nestled near his hidden home within the depths of the forest. Believing he had eradicated every trace of life on the farm, he remained oblivious to the presence of a hidden child who bore witness to the brutality inflicted upon his family and homestead.

The horrifying story spread out to the nearby Alorian village as news of the gruesome encounter between the local farm and a wicked spellcaster. A distinct wave of terror swept over the inhabitants, describing the harrowing details of Fumar's sadistic acts and the plight of his captive queen. This grim narrative ignited a volatile concoction of anger, fear, and justice among the villagers.

Amid this spreading dread throughout the territory, Commander Relios, a seasoned warrior and esteemed leader in the Alorian kingdom, found himself entwined in the tale. The unsettling echoes of chaos that emanated from Fumar's sinister actions had drawn him on a week-long search for his queen. He quickly set course for the kingdom to gather reinforcements to search the forest territories.

Recognizing the urgency and potential danger posed by Fumar, Commander Relios organized search teams to surround the forest where the horrifying events occurred. The vanguard, archers, and arcanists, armed with their skills and unwavering determination, ventured into the woodland with heightened senses and a resolute purpose. As they penetrated deeper into the woods, the search parties encountered a silence interrupted by the rustling of leaves and their own steady footfalls. The tension in the air was restless. Each member of the group keenly felt the lurking danger concealed within the shadows.

The search parties advanced further into the wilderness while keeping an eye out for any indications of Fumar's presence in light of the brave child's testimony that she had witnessed the horrifying scene unfold. The haunting image of the gray elf with a naked woman on a leash, as the story was told, remained etched in their minds, fueling their determination to rescue Queen Alora and bring Fumar to justice.

As they maneuvered through the dense foliage, the search parties encountered remnants of Fumar's malevolence, evidence of his reign of terror. Destroyed farms and shattered lives bore witness to the brutality that had unfolded in their midst. The search became a race against time, as they knew that every passing moment brought further torment and suffering to Queen Alora.

Commander Relios and his forces pressed on, navigating the challenging terrain with precision and alertness. Their dedication to protecting Queen Alora and reclaiming their kingdom remained steadfast. Every corner of the woods was meticulously explored, leaving no stone unturned in their quest for justice. As Relios eagerly awaited the reunion with his beloved, his heart raced with anticipation.

The recent events heightened the urgency, realizing that Queen Alora's well-being was on the line. They were resolute about finding her and putting an end to her torment. Their steadfast commitment to defending the queen and restoring peace to the kingdom fueled their determination, growing stronger with each step. No obstacle would deter them as they persistently searched through the dense woods, leaving no stone unexplored in their pursuit of justice.

As the search party combed through the woods in pursuit of Fumar, their eyes were drawn to a hidden shelter nestled amidst the dense foliage. Curiosity mingled with caution as they cautiously approached the structure. What they discovered inside sent shockwaves through their ranks. Within the shelter, they found a young elven boy whose resemblance to Queen Alora was unmistakable. The boy clutched tightly to his chest an infant girl, a fragile symbol of hope amidst the darkness.

The children cowered in the shelter, terror circulating from their shaking bodies as they realized their own father was in imminent danger. Their wide eyes reflected the pain they'd been through and the horrors they'd observed. It was a terrible sight, evidence of Fumar's twisted legacy. The evil of their father had shattered the children's innocence, and it would remain a mark on their lives for the rest of their lives. As they huddled close, their small bodies quivering, a flicker of resilience developed in their eyes—a will to survive and recover what had been torn apart.

The search group, their hearts filled with compassion, approached the children with kind gestures and soothing words. They gradually persuaded them out of their hiding place, their priority now being to protect and care for these innocent souls who appeared to have suffered significantly.

The small boy clutched the infant girl closely, his expression filled with fear and solution. He'd taken it upon himself to protect his sister from his father's rage, and his love and bravery shone through despite the circumstances. As the caregivers led the children to safety, they were taken aback by the boy's strength and courage. They recognized that it would take time and care to heal their wounds. It was their deepest desire to provide a safe haven where the siblings could grow up together and feel loved and supported.

Commander Relios, his heart heavy with the weight of their awful circumstances, offered a hand to the children, providing comfort and reassurance. He secured them in the protective hands of his fellow defenders, ensuring their safety and promising them a future free of Fumar's cruelty.

Recognizing the importance of providing the children with a safe and nurturing environment, the leaders of the kingdom planned to entrust their care to Freynora, the guardian of Queen Alora's first daughter. With her deep understanding of the kingdom's history and her newfound dedication to the wellbeing of Alora's offspring, Freynora was seen as the ideal guardian for these young souls who had suffered so much. Freynora 's compassionate nature and extensive knowledge of the kingdom's customs and traditions made her the perfect candidate to ensure the children's smooth integration into Alora's society. Under Freynora 's guidance, these resilient youngsters would have the opportunity to heal from their past traumas and build a brighter future within the loving embrace of their new home.

Finally, amidst a clearing surrounded by a patch of grass, they stumbled upon a seemingly inconspicuous shed. Their instincts told them there was more to this humble structure, and as they cautiously approached, their suspicions were confirmed. Inside, they found Queen Alora stripped of her clothing and broken, her limbs cruelly chained to posts.

Her life clung to her last breath as she revealed the hidden location of the stolen scrolls and tomes, a desperate attempt to safeguard the knowledge and history of elven civilization. She told Relios to take care of her eldest son; he was wise and pure. She uttered something under her breath, but it did not come out. As Relios tries to clarify, he could only hear "he's pure; I love you." Relios could not get all of what she said before she passed and was left trembling.

The healers rushed to her side; their hearts heavy with the weight of the atrocities she had endured. But it was too late. Queen Alora slipped away, finding peace in knowing that she had been found and that her legacy, despite the pain and suffering, would be preserved. Relios held her lifeless body, his grip tightening with a mixture of grief, determination, and a burning desire for retribution. He broke down in tears.

The words she spoke before taking her breath lingered in his thoughts, recalling a mix of confusion and disbelief. Relios found himself overwhelmed by grief at the loss of Queen Alora, and a whirlwind of emotions consumed him. Her final words echoed in his mind, leaving him both confused and skeptical. Trying to decipher the message she left behind became a struggle for him as he pondered its meaning and significance. Was it a clue to uncovering some truth? Were they merely the ramblings of a dying woman lost in delirium? As he grappled with his sorrow and attempted to unravel her utterances, he was enveloped by a sense of confusion and doubt. How could he possibly move forward without her? How could he untangle the mystery she left unresolved? These questions plagued his every thought.

The reality of Queen Alora's death had sent Commander Relios into an upheaval of emotions. Grief surged through him like a tidal wave, threatening to consume him. He clutched her dying corpse, desperately clinging to the last remnants of their mutual love and the life they were creating together.

As the search parties brought back the heartbreaking news of Queen Alora's demise, a chilling atmosphere enveloped the kingdom of Alora. What was meant to be a celebration transformed into mourning as the fate of their beloved queen became apparent. However, within the depths of grief, a newfound determination emerged among the kingdom's inhabitants.

The memory of Queen Alora became a driving force, igniting a collective resolve to rebuild their shattered kingdom, defeat Fumar, and restore peace to their lands. The hunt for Fumar intensified, with the vanguard warriors unbreakable in their commitment. They vowed to avenge their fallen queen, ensuring that her tormentor would face justice for his insidious acts. The quest for retribution had just begun and the elves of Alora were united in their pursuit of a brighter future.

. . . .

The Alorians staged an extravagant funeral service in her honor. The entire kingdom gathered to pay their respects and say goodbye to their beloved queen. The elves' sorrow over the death of their wise and compassionate leader infused the serene atmosphere. However, a fire had been ignited within the hearts of the Alorians amid their suffering. They were adamant about seeking justice for Queen Alora's tragic death and bringing death to Fumar.

In the coming months, Princess Alora will be named Queen, taking on the weighty responsibility of leading her grieving kingdom. As she respected and bid farewell to her beloved mother, she also carried with her the determination and resilience of the Alora citizens. With a fiery determination in their hearts, they embarked on a relentless pursuit of justice for Queen Alora's untimely demise and an end to Fumar's chaotic freedom. They were committed to avenging their fallen queen and restoring harmony and tranquility to their land. She would take on the mantle of Queen Alora II, the second.

In the aftermath of the War of Pyrothos and Alora's rebellion, stories of horror and resilience spread far and wide across Paranova.

Travelers, traders, and messengers carried these tales, illustrating the devastation and the fierce spirit of the dark ones. The atrocities committed during the war became cautionary tales, warning about the depths to which power and darkness could plunge the world.

These narratives inspired other races in Paranova to fortify their defenses and build strong armies. Witnessing the destructive potential of war, unknown energy, and the importance of unity, leaders across the world recognized the need to be prepared. Learning from the elves' mistakes and triumphs, they worked diligently to strengthen their civilization's military capabilities and establish defensive structures. The renewal of the Dark Ones as Zelorians emphasized the impact of societal directions, prompting caution and planning among the mortals of Paranova.

The events of the war and rebellion also prompted significant advancements and preparations within human, dwarven, ranuki, and gantum civilizations. Realizing the need for progress and adaptability, these races invested resources in research, magical studies, and technological innovations. Their goal was to develop new weaponry, enhance communication networks, and improve understanding of the magical arts. This period marked a turning point in their histories, with a renewed focus on progress and cooperation to safeguard their futures.

The slow progression of evolution among the other races experienced a breakthrough, catapulting them forward into a new era. The crucible of conflict and change forged them into societies with governance structures and military prowess, now on equal footing with the advanced civilizations of the elves. The echoes of war and rebellion became the catalyst for the metamorphosis of once-primitive cultures into formidable societies capable of navigating Paranova's evolving landscape.

While elemental chaos threatened mortal sapience on Paranova, a more significant danger lurked among the mortals themselves. The conflicts and struggles between them posed a greater threat than the mysterious elemental disturbances. Each race navigated their own path to success in creating a society, aspiring to emulate the great kingdoms of Alora and Zelor.

As the tales of the War of Pyrothos and Alora's rebellion echoed through the lands of Paranova, they served as a stark reminder of the fragile nature of peace and the potential for darkness to consume even the most prosperous kingdoms. The impact of these events extended beyond the borders of Alora, shaping the collective consciousness of other races and inspiring them to strive for greater strength, unity, and advancement. In a world forever changed by the scars of war and the consumable nature of chaos, it was a time of transformation as each civilization sought to forge their own path.

Chapter 13: Forging Paths

As stories of the Pyrothos battle and Alora's rebellion circulated among the races of Paranova, they became epic legends shrouded in mystery and filled with exaggeration. Once a clash between two kingdoms, the Pyrothos War evolved into an apocalyptic battle between gods and demons, with fire raining from the sky and mountains crumbling beneath the ground's rage. Heroes appeared with godlike powers, wielding swords capable of severing entire armies and sorcerers casting spells capable of reshaping reality itself.

Alora's rebellion evolved into a tale of defiance and revolution. The valiant Queen Alora evolved from a noble leader into a fabled character, with the beauty of a divine goddess and the skill of a master strategist. Her insurrection was portrayed as a disastrous struggle against unfathomable odds, with every step she took shaking the kingdom's very foundations. Fumar, the opposing force, grew into a hideous beast, a symbol of absolute evil with fangs as sharp as daggers and a heart as black as the abyss.

With each retelling, the stories grew more expansive, capturing the imaginations of those who listened. Alora's faithful subjects were claimed to have immense powers, capable of calling storms and healing the wounded with a single touch. It was said that the battles were spectacles of an impossible size, where the clash of swords rippled throughout the regions and the skies ignited with magical forces. The heroes rose to the status of demigods, with tales around their names reflecting awe and respect in all who heard them.

These fascinating stories helped to inspire and unite the races of Paranova. They became a source of hope for everyone, reminding them of their own resilience and the strength of solidarity. The stories instilled in each race a determination to stay firm, fortify their defenses, and strive for greatness. The echoes of the Pyrothos clash and Alora's uprising became guidance of bravery and fortitude, describing to all who heard them that even in the face of hardship, heroes could rise and triumph.

And so the stories lived on, captivating the imaginations of the young and filling the hearts of the elderly with nostalgic delight. They became a part of Paranova's fabric, crafting collective memory and inspiring many tales of bravery and heroism. The stories of Paranova's ancient beings instilled in the people a powerful mixture of wonder, fear, and curiosity. Whispers of these mysterious beings circulated among the races, capturing their imaginations and motivating their quest to solve the mysteries that lay concealed in the depths of the world.

The elemental forces were described as celestial beings of immense power who lived in spaces beyond mortal knowledge. They were depicted as towering creatures dressed in ethereal robes and crowns, glistening with otherworldly light. Every being was connected to a different aspect of existence, such as creation, destruction, knowledge, or the natural elements.

Pyrothos was presumed to be the god of fire and chaos; he was portrayed as a massive monster wreathed in unholy flames, shedding a burning glow that illuminated the world's darkest spaces. Pyrothos was said to emerge from the bowels of volcanoes, spilling molten lava and searing the earth only by being present. It was supposed to have unparalleled power, capable of unleashing destructive infernos and incinerating entire armies with a single breath.

Tales of Pyrothos' wrath have echoed throughout decades, detailing its ferocious reign of terror and the devastating events that followed. Legend has it that Pyrothos ruled over the destructive powers and used fire as a tool to mold the universe to his satisfaction. The mere spoken word of its name caused both admiration and terror, a reminder of the immense might that existed within the elemental realm.

According to legend, Pyrothos could call down fire from the sun, which he would then use to scorch the land and leave a path of desolation in his wake. The god's burning presence was believed to be so powerful that even the most fearless warriors trembled at the sight of his blistering form.

According to the stories, when mortal sapience crossed paths with otherworldly beings, they were either taught their immense wisdom or put through trials of an unfathomable form. Some claimed that elemental beings held the secret to unlocking magic's true potential and that ambitious spellcasters would sacrifice everything to gain its favor. Others warned of the risks of interfering with forces beyond mortal comprehension, warning that elemental fury could potentially have catastrophic effects for the world.

The myths also told of the select few who were able to strike a contract with an entity, earning vast power and wisdom in exchange for an amount of their own soul. These people became known as the chosen ones, and they were both admired and feared for their connection to the mystery entities. However, tales spread that such contracts came at a high cost, with the influence gradually corrupting the minds and bodies of their chosen vessels. The myths often referred to Aleron as the first chosen one, and his name either inspired or horrified many people.

The stories of the elemental entities stirred both interest and horror. Their existence prompted academic debate and inspired the creativity of artisans and poets. By incorporating the names of these mythical legends in traditions and prayers, individuals sought their guidance or protection when they were in danger. The mere mention of an elemental entity's name could bring shivers down a mortal's spine, a reminder of the unknown power that existed within the realm of elements.

However, for all the stories and legends, the true nature of the elemental entities and celestial beings remained hidden in mystery. They were entities of myth and speculation, existing at the fringes of mortal comprehension. Some claimed to have witnessed their presence in fleeting visions or in the whispering winds of ancient forests. But the truth, like the entities themselves, eluded their grasp while leaving room for endless wonder and speculation.

Thus, the tales of the elemental entities continued to captivate the minds of the people, weaving a tapestry of enchantment and uncertainty. Their stories fueled a hunger for knowledge and exploration, driving brave adventurers to seek out the forgotten corners of Paranova in search of answers. The tales' awe, fear, and curiosity had sparked an endless quest to find the truths that lay hidden in the realms beyond mortal reach. These brave adventurers were willing to risk their lives and sanity by delving deeper into the mysteries of Paranova. Each discovery only served to deepen the intrigue, as the elemental existence hinted at a world beyond comprehension, where reality and imagination intertwined in ways unimaginable.

Storytelling held profound significance in shaping the perception of the elves, leaving a memorable mark on the minds and aspirations of the other races in Paranova. The tales of the elves, with their ethereal beauty, ancient wisdom, and formidable powers, served as inspiration for all who heard them.

The other races found comfort and fascination in the tales recounted by the elves. As beings with longer lifespans, the elves held the unique position of witnessing the unfolding events over extended periods. Whether the stories were of triumph or tragedy, the wisdom and longevity of the elves lent an air of credibility to their narratives. The recounting of events by an elf became a cherished tradition among the diverse races, bringing joy and a sense of connection to the rich tapestry of history that unfolded across Paranova.

The elven races were portrayed in the legends as guardians of ancient wisdom, masters of magic, and examples of grace and beauty. The stories told of their peaceful living with nature, their deep connection to the realms of mysticism, and their ongoing commitment to justice and balance. The elves were represented as avatars of wisdom, with ageless faces expressing the weight of endless generations of existence.

As the other races looked upon the elves with admiration, they found themselves inspired to expand and reach new heights. The tales served as a catalyst for their own aspirations, spurring them to strive for greatness and emulate the virtues they perceived in the elven races. In an effort to equal the magnificence of the Elven kingdoms, the Human, Dwarven, Ranuki, and Gantum civilizations worked to expand their respective domains and utilize their unique strengths.

The Alorian elves' enemies also played a significant role in the tapestry of stories. The tales depicted formidable foes that tested the Alorian resilience, valor, and cunning. Whether it was the dark forces of Pyrothos or the rebellion in Alora, their enemies embodied the struggle between light and darkness, and their inclusion in the stories intensified the challenges faced by the elven races.

Through storytelling, the elves not only shaped their own perceptions but also influenced the perceptions of other races. They became heroes of virtue, knowledge, and power, inspiring others to launch their own journeys of self-discovery and expansion. The stories served as a bridge between races, fostering mutual understanding and respect as well as a desire to learn from the wisdom and experiences of the elves.

Through the art of storytelling, the elves skillfully shaped the perception of the Dark Ones. Despite the initial view of them as monsters, the narratives weaved by the elves helped paint a nuanced picture. The tales emphasized the influence of the shadow council and mysterious entities, portraying the dark ones as victims manipulated by external forces. Over time, this storytelling strategy succeeded in reshaping the image of the Zelorian elves, fostering a more understanding and sympathetic view among the broader population.

In this way, storytelling became a powerful tool for cultural exchange and growth, uniting the diverse races of Paranova under a shared appreciation for the elven races' achievements and ideals. It created a sense of interconnectedness and a collective pursuit of excellence, driving the other races to explore their own potentials and forge their own legacies.

Perceptions, imaginations, and acts of greatness were all shaped and sustained as the stories were handed down from one generation to the next. The storytelling tradition became an essential part of Paranova's foundation, combining the hopes, fears, and fates of its residents and maintaining their significant influence on the land they called home.

The tales and legends circulating among the races of Paranova brought with them a realization of the vulnerability of kingdoms and civilizations in the face of potential threats, particularly the return of elemental entities. These stories served as cautionary reminders that no civilization was resistant to the destructive forces that lurked within the world.

The narratives spoke of the cataclysmic events of the Pyrothos war and Alora's rebellion, which shook the very foundations of the elves and their adversaries. They highlighted the devastation and chaos that occurred when powerful entities clashed and unleashed their elemental might upon the world. Such stories instilled a sense of urgency and the recognition that contingencies must be established to protect against future calamities.

Aware of the need to be equipped to confront the unimaginable, the races of Paranova were affected by the stories. They realized that the reappearance of an elemental entity would cause catastrophic destruction and chaos, threatening the very existence of their civilizations. As a response, they worked to develop detailed contingency plans, strengthen their defenses, and expand their relationships.

Kingdoms and civilizations understood the importance of advanced magical defenses, strategic alliances, and well-trained soldiers. They put resources into the development and study of powerful enchantments and magical arts, hoping to use the elements themselves to guard against potential threats. The stories served as a precise cautionary tale that only through collaboration and preparation could they hope to survive the immense might of an elemental entity.

Furthermore, the tales emphasized the importance of cooperation and knowledge-sharing among the races. The realization that the vulnerability extended beyond individual societies led to a newfound willingness to set aside differences and work towards a common goal. The races engaged in diplomatic exchanges, forging alliances and treaties that would facilitate mutual aid and cooperation in times of crisis.

All races were encouraged to adopt a proactive stance in the face of potential dangers as a result of the stories, which functioned as a shared call to action. They inspired the races of Paranova to be attentive, to push for developments with magic, technology, and military tactics, and to establish a culture of preparedness and resilience.

In this way, fables not only raised awareness of the vulnerabilities of all kingdoms and civilizations but also motivated a collective commitment to ensure the survival and development of their individual societies. The narratives acted as a force for creativity, cooperation, and unity, allowing the races of Paranova to face the future with a lifelong resolution and a shared commitment to protecting their world against the return of an entity of elements.

The Alora rebellion, with its hardships in history and far-reaching consequences, served as an important piece of history that spread throughout Paranova, inspiring a newfound motivation for preparedness and effective governance among other civilizations.

The rebellion's narrative highlighted the dangers of unchecked power, internal strife, and the collapse of a once-great kingdom. It showcased the devastating impact of fragmented leadership and the vulnerability that ensued when a society failed to uphold the principles of justice, unity, and proper governance.

The tales of Alora's rebellion struck a chord with other civilizations, serving as a stark reminder of the importance of establishing robust governance structures. They realized that without sound leadership, clear laws, and effective systems of accountability, their own societies could face similar fates. These civilizations understood that a lack of strong leadership and proper governance could lead to chaos, division, and ultimately the downfall of their societies. They were inspired to take proactive measures to strengthen their own governance structures, ensuring justice, unity, and stability for their people.

Other civilizations set out on a journey of reflection and reform inspired by the stories of Alora. They recognized the need for stable governance that could withstand internal challenges and external threats. The tales served as a wake-up call, prompting them to reevaluate their own leadership structures, legal frameworks, and mechanisms for social cohesion.

Recognizing the need for order and stability, the primal civilizations understood the importance of formal governance and leadership structures. These institutions played a crucial role in maintaining societal harmony and ensuring that the diverse populations remained organized and united. The lessons drawn from the elven civilizations, particularly Alora and Zelor, inspired the primal races to establish their own systems of governance, paving the way for structured societies that could navigate the challenges of Paranova.

Drawing lessons from Alora's downfall these civilizations sought to cultivate transparency, equality, and responsiveness in their governance. They established governing bodies, court systems, and executive administrative branches, aiming to distribute power and decision-making processes in a manner that prevented the concentration of authority in a single individual or faction.

The rebellion's narrative also emphasized the significance of moral values and ethical principles in governance. The historic tales of the past had underscored the importance of leaders who acted in the best interest of their people, who upheld justice, and who were held accountable for their actions. Other civilizations strived to instill a sense of moral responsibility among their own leaders and they implemented mechanisms to ensure attachment to moral standards while protecting citizen rights.

Furthermore, the tales of Alora's rebellion served as an incentive for the establishment of effective mechanisms for conflict resolution and diplomacy. The civilizations recognized the need for peaceful means of addressing hardship, promoting dialogue, and preventing the escalation of tensions that could lead to internal strife or external conflicts. They invested in the development of diplomatic relations, mediation institutions, and treaties that brought peaceful resolutions to disputes.

In this way, the Alora rebellion served as an important tale and an important source of motivation for other civilizations to prioritize governance and preparedness. The stories resonated deeply, igniting a collective determination to build strong and resilient societies that would withstand the tests of time and hardship. As a result these civilizations commenced on transformative journeys striving to create governance structures that would promote stability, justice, and the overall well-being of their citizens.

Stories of the Pyrothos War and Alora's rebellion greatly influenced the other races of Paranova, especially with their attitudes toward defense and battle readiness. The other civilizations were motivated to fortify their walls and reinforce their armies by the tales of heroic conflicts, clever strategy, and bravery of the elven races.

Acknowledging the vulnerability of their own kingdoms and civilizations, they comprehended how important it was to strengthen their military forces and refine their societal organization for better productivity. The other mortal races had realized that in a world where entities and other threats existed, a strong and capable army was crucial for the protection of their territories and the safety of their people.

After learning about the Pyrothos conflict, where the elves bravely fought the elemental being, various civilizations began to invest in their armies. They built training academies, recruited skilled soldiers, and continued to improve their military strategies and tactics.

The stories also underlined the value of unity and cooperation in the face of hardship. Recognizing that individual strength might not be enough, civilizations organized alliances and military partnerships to form a united front against prospective dangers. They learned from the elven efforts to organize and coordinate their forces throughout history during the Pyrothos War and sought to imitate that unity within their own armies.

Moreover, the tales showcased the troubles of internal divisions and the consequences of weak defenses. These stories motivated the civilizations to fortify their cities, construct defensive structures, and invest in advanced weaponry and siege constructs. They took inspiration from the elven determination to protect their homeland during past hardships and sought to apply those lessons to their own societies.

As the civilizations focused on building defenses and strengthening their armies, they also recognized the need for capable leadership. They sought out skilled commanders and military strategists, establishing institutions dedicated to military education and training. These leaders studied the tactics employed by the elves during the Pyrothos war and Alora's rebellion, drawing valuable insights and adapting them to their own military doctrines.

The elves sought to share their stories with other races, aiming to convey the message that there were greater challenges to face than engaging in wars over minor conflicts. Their vision was beginning to materialize as they observed other races swiftly evolving into more formal and organized societies. While the elves understood that the pace of this evolution was rapid, their ultimate desire was for the other races to reach a mindset that equaled their own, fostering equality and understanding among the diverse civilizations of Paranova.

Over time, as the evolution unfolded and stories of the past were shared, the other races started to ascend while forming alliances and establishing their own kingdoms, cities, and townships.

•••••••

The rise and stories of Volantis and Galanor, two powerful kingdoms, captivated the imaginations of many. Other civilizations wished to form alliances and diplomatic ties with them in response to their stories of tenacity and strategic prowess. Recognizing the value of cooperation, Volantis and Galanor embraced these opportunities and formed powerful alliances that would strengthen their positions and ensure their mutual protection.

These alliances not only brought economic growth to both kingdoms but also fostered cultural exchange and innovation. Through shared knowledge and resources, Volantis and Galanor were able to expand their influence and establish themselves as key players in the world, setting the stage for a new era of peace and prosperity for humankind.

Bolder Peak, a small dwarven kingdom renowned for its formidable warriors, found inspiration in the stories of the disciplined Volantis army. Seeking to learn from their strategies, Bolder Peak initiated a military training program that emphasized discipline, teamwork, and advanced combat techniques. This new approach elevated their warriors to new heights of skill and efficiency, earning them a reputation as an elite fighting force. As word of Bolder Peak's success spread, neighboring kingdoms took notice and began to view them as a valuable ally in times of conflict. Recognizing the benefits of a strong alliance, Bolder Peak forged strategic partnerships with other kingdoms, forming a formidable coalition that deterred potential aggressors and ensured their mutual protection.

The alliance between Baldreth and the primal human colonies proved to be a mutually beneficial partnership. The primal humans gained access to advanced military tactics and fortified structures along main routes throughout the eastern landscape, enabling them to protect their territories from external threats. In return, Baldreth benefited from the primal humans' intimate knowledge of the rugged eastern lands, providing valuable insights into navigating treacherous terrain and uncovering hidden resources throughout the vast desert.

The tales of Alora and the Ranuk, two races known for their wisdom and magical prowess, inspired an exchange of knowledge and battle strategies. Recognizing the value of collaboration, scholars and veterans from both races came together to share their insights and develop new magical and battle techniques. This exchange not only strengthened their battle capabilities but also fostered a sense of camaraderie and understanding between Alora and the ranuk. As a result, the once-divided lands of Alora and the ranuk became united in their pursuit of knowledge and peace. The exchange of wisdom not only enhanced their magical abilities but also opened doors to previously untapped resources, leading to advancements in various fields such as agriculture, architecture, and medicine.

The kingdom of Zelor, scarred by the events surrounding Aleron and the forbidden magics, found an unlikely ally in Nightscar, a seclusive town growing into a sprawling city whose residents were skilled in observation and covert operations. Recognizing their shared interests in protecting their respective societies, Zelor and Nightscar formed an alliance, sharing intelligence and working together to uncover and neutralize potential threats surrounding their civilizations.

Nightscar's residents, consisting of a mix of various elves and humans, not only excelled in espionage and covert operations but also had a deep understanding of agriculture, construction, archery, and music. This unique combination of skills made Nightscar an invaluable asset to the kingdom of Zelor. Together, they were able to form a powerful alliance that protected both territories and ensured their success in the face of potential threats.

Gloomrot, a civilization with a deep connection to the dark and forbidden arts, discovered a surprising common ground with the city of Fumaron. The two had formed a troublesome alliance because of their twisted abilities and unconventional methods, exploring the depths of forbidden magic and using their combined forces against unsuspecting foes.

Between Nightscar and Gloomrot, the towns emerged as settlements born from the division within the human raider clan of the past. Those inclined towards morality found a home in Nightscar, while the aggressive and dangerous members settled in Gloomrot, the clan's original dwelling. Despite both towns evolving beyond the primal ways of their old traditions, a lingering rivalry and disdain persisted through the years of growth and evolution within Sapience.

Thornshade, a woodland and cavernous clan known for its guerrilla tactical prowess, saw an opportunity for collaboration with the Tranquil Tide clan, a peaceful clan society with a deep understanding of the sea and its mysteries. They joined forces to develop advanced naval technologies, creating a formidable fleet that would dominate the seas and ensure their dominance in maritime affairs. This would help the Thornshade expand their clan all over Paranova.

....

Human civilization experienced a significant transformation in the wake of the Pyrothos War and Alora's rebellion. Recognizing the need for protection and stability, human kingdoms and cities arose and fortified themselves against potential threats. Notable among these human kingdoms were Volantis, Galanor, Baldreth, and the Primal Human Colonies, each with its own distinct characteristics and contributions to the world.

Volantis, a kingdom that emerged from the ruins of the ancient elven Kingdom of Unity, stood as a testament to human resilience and adaptability. Built upon the remnants of elven civilization, Volantis blended the architectural glory of the past with human ingenuity. Its towering walls and well-trained armies became a symbol of strength and unity for the human population. The kingdom of Volantis also became known for its thriving trade routes, connecting various regions and fostering economic growth. Its strategic location and efficient governance attracted merchants from far and wide, making it a hub of commerce and cultural exchange on the continent.

Galanor, once a haven for elven survivors fleeing the Gantum onslaught in the past, has developed into a sizable citadel and a center of combat and magical knowledge. This kingdom, once known as the Eastern Kingdom, embraced its role as a center for education and honing the skills of aspiring warriors and spellcasters. Galanor became renowned for its combat and magical college, attracting ambitious individuals from all corners of Paranova.

The Citadel College in Galanor became renowned for its rigorous training programs and esteemed faculty, ensuring that graduates were highly skilled in both combat and magic. As a result, Galanor became a sought-after destination for those seeking to master their abilities and forge a successful career in the way of warfare and sorcery. The kingdom's reputation as a hub of knowledge and skill continued to grow, solidifying its status as a prominent center for both commerce and cultural exchange.

The Citadel College, situated on the opposite side of the continent from Alora, emerged as a formidable competitor. The citadel welcomed people of all races, fostering a diverse environment in contrast to the elves' exclusivity in offering education to their kind. This inclusive approach allowed humans and teachers within the college to gain insights into various magic uses and cultures from around the world, contributing to a more comprehensive and enriched educational experience.

The Galanor kingdom severed ties with Baldreth after years of utilizing their engineering knowledge. As Galanor began harnessing magical powers with the assistance of diverse racial groups, they deemed the alliance with a distant kingdom unnecessary. The leaders in the desert kingdom cultivated their own army through years of collaboration with Galanor. Despite differing views and opinions that sparked political opposition before the Elven War, the loss of the alliance proved mutually beneficial for both kingdoms, allowing them to pursue their paths independently.

The people of Baldreth developed the skills necessary for surviving in the harsh desert environment, building a self-sufficient kingdom using desert energy. Baldreth stood as a large oasis in the middle of the desert. Their ingenuity in harnessing natural resources, constructing underground tunnels, and utilizing advanced irrigation systems made

Baldreth a marvel of human engineering. The kingdom became a sanctuary for those seeking refuge and a bastion of resilience against external threats.

Baldreth's reputation as a hub for trade and cultural exchange grew rapidly, attracting merchants and travelers from distant lands. The diverse population brought with them a wealth of knowledge, traditions, and languages, fostering a vibrant atmosphere of cross-cultural learning and understanding. This exchange of ideas further enriched the kingdom's already-thriving arts, literature, and cuisine, making Baldreth a truly cosmopolitan center in the heart of the desert.

Baldreth, despite being located in the desert, established outposts throughout the territory, constructing small villages atop ancient ruins uncovered from past elemental disturbances. While these ruins remained unexplored, the villages served as outposts, providing refuge across the vast desert. The people of Baldreth didn't suffer significantly from the severed alliance with Galanor. Instead, they sought treaties with the emerging primal human colonies unified under one banner. However, dealing with the Rook primal clan on the outskirts of the desert proved to be a persistent challenge.

Gloomrot and Nightscar, although not human kingdoms, were evolving into thriving cities. Gloomrot, situated under Fumarian territory, held significance for the gray elves. Meanwhile, Nightscar, under Zelorian jurisdiction, played a crucial role in Zelorian expansion. The growing city became instrumental in absorbing elven refugees from the rebellion. The influx of human growth had brought new character and liveliness to the dark elves' way of life, fostering a sense of diversity and cooperation in Nightscar.

Gloomrot emerged as a city based on forbidden knowledge and necromantic practices, shrouded in mystery and darkness. Even though some people questioned the morality of their actions, the people of Gloomrot found strength in accepting curses and using undead powers. Their unique understanding of necromancy and dark magic brought forth both fear and curiosity from neighboring civilizations. Gloomrot had a sickly fascination with alchemy and the mystical arcane magic that seemed to gather their energy from another realm. Their unorthodox methods always intrigued the Fumarians. Gloomrot's populace saw all races of Paranova reside in this eerie city full of eerie peace, but with a twist of chaos amidst the atmosphere.

Nightscar emerged as a harmonious blend of elves and humans, embodying the Zelorian rule while incorporating unique traditions and customs from both races. The humans, reminiscent of the dark ones within the Sinister Shadows caste of the past, brought a sense of secrecy and observation to the kingdom. Nightscar's atmosphere shifted throughout the day, maintaining a quiet and private demeanor during daylight hours. However, as night fell, the cityscape came alive with vibrant entertainment and secretive gatherings that lasted until the first light of dawn. Nightscar became a destination for people to visit to unwind from their daily tasks and enjoy the community that thrived at night.

The primal human colonies, scattered throughout various regions, including forests, mountains, plains, islands, and desolate lands, thrived on their connection to nature and their primal instincts. These colonies, consisting of tribes with their own distinct traditions and ways of life, maintained a harmonious relationship with their environments. Their knowledge of survival in diverse landscapes and their fierce loyalty to their tribes made them formidable allies and a force to be reckoned with.

The tribes, for the most part, maintained mutual respect, and in times of quarrel, leaders from the individual colonies would negotiate agreements or hand out punishments. Participants associated with the quarrel often engaged in battles as punishment, which typically resulted in death or an assumed peace. While some colonies initially acted as clans, they gradually became more open to the evolving world around them. Despite this evolution, they clung to old traditions and customs formed by their ancient clans. Each colony had its own leader, but they all united under one banner as the primal human colonies, with a commander who assumed the role of King or Queen. Operating similarly to modern human kingdoms, the primal colonies mimicked their systems but remained stubbornly rooted in primitive traditions, resisting intellectual and innovative progress. Content to be left alone in their version of the world, away from the commotion created by other races, the primal human colonies existed in a self-imposed stasis.

In times of instability or the absence of a commander, the leaders from each primal human colony convene to select a new leader. If objections arise or someone challenges the current commander, a crucible is held, a tournament of survival where the leader vies for command and up to two challengers from each colony enter. The tournament is a fight to the death, and the last survivor becomes the new commander of the colonies.

This brutal tradition is only requested in times of significant unrest or the absence of leadership. While participation is not mandatory for each colony, abstaining could be perceived as a sign of weakness.

Leaders entering the crucible fight for their lives, and anyone daring to challenge leadership is encouraged to participate.

To lead a colony requires strength, a commitment to uphold traditions, and the respect of the people. Without admiration, a leader may face challenges from within as others vie for the role of leadership. In this timeline, the colonies work together to preserve their sacred traditions, keeping them within their boundaries as modern civilizations encroach upon their territories. A Gorn commander is currently in charge of the united human colonies.

Together, these human kingdoms, cities, townships, and colonies showcased the resilience, adaptability, and diverse capabilities of former clans. From the rebuilt ruins of ancient elven kingdoms to the self-sustaining desert kingdom and the primal connection to nature, human civilization expanded as they carved their path throughout Paranova, contributing to the ever-evolving tapestry of the world. Their capacity to thrive in such a wide range of environments displayed their adaptability and determination. Whether it was climbing hazardous mountain ranges or harnessing the energy of the sea and desert, humanity proved time and again that they could overcome any challenge that came their way.

Exploration and trade served as connecting factors between the kingdoms of Paranova as human civilization expanded. Trade routes widened, connecting distant lands and promoting growth in business. Volantis gained popularity as a trade government thanks to its beneficial position and well-developed infrastructure. Merchants and traders from various races traveled to Volantis, sharing goods, knowledge, and ideas, enhancing the region's cultural structure.

Volantis, the mighty kingdom born from the ashes of the once-destroyed elven kingdom of unity, emerged as the central authority governing human affairs in the realm of Paranova. Situated at a strategic crossroads in the center, Volantis wielded its influence with strength and wisdom, fostering unity among the scattered human settlements and kingdoms.

Volantis established laws, regulations, and a court system that protected its people's rights and welfare. Volantis ruled by monarchs were supported by a council of knowledgeable advisors and experienced ambassadors, maintained diplomatic contacts with other races and played an important role in settling disputes and creating alliances. As the seat of human power, the kingdom personified the well-being of hopes, dreams, and desires, ensuring their interests were represented and their voices heard in the vast variety of Paranova's governing system.

While Volantis excelled in trade and governance, Baldreth rose to fame in the arts and sciences. The cultural revolution in the kingdom was greatly enhanced by the numerous artists that performed there, including painters, sculptors, musicians, and entertainers. The pursuit of knowledge and creativity blossomed in Baldreth as philosophers and scientists pushed the boundaries of understanding in fields such as alchemy, astronomy, and engineering.

Gloomrot, with its dark reputation, found a unique purpose in the world. It became a place for housing prisons and administering justice. The kingdom's understanding of necromantic practices and curses allowed them to develop effective systems of confinement and punishment for the most dangerous criminals. Gloomrot's rigorous enforcement of justice sent a clear message to human civilization that transgressions would be met with severe consequences.

The city's expertise in the arcane, dark arts, and illusion magic also played a crucial role in the development of their prison systems. By combining their knowledge of these fields, Gloomrot was able to create highly secure and fortified prisons that were nearly impossible to escape from. This further solidified the city's reputation as a place where criminals would face the full force of the law.

Gloomrot had a diverse population of people of various races, with humans making up most of the population. Although they maintained a certain distance from the human governance centered in Volantis, they agreed to construct a prison for the human kingdom. In exchange for their cooperation, Gloomrot received essential supplies and enjoyed the benefits of being considered an ally of the kingdom.

On the other hand, Nightscar took a different approach, deliberately keeping its distance from other human settlements. Instead, they forged strong ties with their Zelorian allies, the dark elves. Grateful for the substantial support received during challenging times, Nightscar remained loyal to the elven kingdom, emphasizing their commitment to their neighbors in Zelor.

Galanor, with its prestigious Citadel College and vast library, became a beacon of knowledge and intellectual pursuit. The college attracted aspiring warriors and spellcasters from far and wide, providing comprehensive training and education in combat techniques, magical arts, and arcane studies. The massive library in Galanor housed countless volumes of ancient texts, grimoires, and scholarly works, drawing scholars and researchers seeking to expand their understanding of the world and its history.

The college's reputation rose as those who graduated continuously demonstrated themselves to be fierce combatants and powerful spellcasters. Over hundreds of years, the Citadel grew into an elite college that outperformed every other institutions throughout Paranova, providing exceptionally sought-after lessons in all types of warfare and magic. The library's collection was not only wide-ranging, but meticulously handled, ensuring that students and academics had access to the most accurate and dependable sources of knowledge.

Galanor's library became a significant counterpart to Alora's own sanctum, the library had boasted an impressive collection of knowledge and ancient texts. During the rebellion many years ago, not all literature and tomes were safeguarded. The Fumarians, resourceful in their own right, copied these invaluable pieces and dispersed them among scavengers or traders. Over time, these artifacts found their way to trading hubs like Volantis or Baldreth.

The scholars of Galanor proved adept at swiftly acquiring these circulated materials—literature, tomes, scrolls, and artifacts—that possibly traced back to elven lineage or even pre-sapient civilizations. The library became a hub for the pursuit of ancient knowledge, further enriching the cultural and historical tapestry of Galanor.

This era of expansion and exploration marked a pinnacle in human civilization, witnessing remarkable advancements in culture, science, and economics. The exchange of ideas, the relentless pursuit of knowledge, and the thriving trade networks created a profound sense of interconnectedness among the diverse races of Paranova. The accomplishments of Volantis, Baldreth, Gloomrot, Nightscar, and Galanor served as shining examples of human ingenuity and creativity, contributing significantly to the collective progress and prosperity of the civilization.

Even the primal human colonies, without adopting the advancements of their counterparts, demonstrated their own unique achievements in growth. Holding onto traditional primitive structures, they showcased resilience and the effectiveness of their time-tested ways within the ever-evolving landscape of Paranova.

•••••••

The Dwarven people dedicated themselves to fortifying their mountain strongholds, ensuring the safety and preservation of their rich cultural heritage. One of the notable kingdoms, Loden, which lay hidden deep beneath the surface, evidence to the remarkable craftsmanship and engineering prowess of the dwarves. Its vast network of interconnected tunnels and chambers housed bustling markets, magnificent halls, and impressive forges.

Loden's strong stone walls and gates formed an impenetrable barrier, protecting its people from outside dangers and supporting the active trade and interaction among cultures that were unique within the kingdom. The dwarves of Loden were renowned for their skill in mining and metalworking; they made intricate jewelry, armor, and weaponry that were treasured all throughout the land. Its strategic location, situated among rich mineral bounty and trading routes along the mountains, which attracted merchants and traders from all over the world, was another factor that contributed to the success of the kingdom from a strategic standpoint.

Loden, evolving into a kingdom as organized as the humans, established structured governance, trade routes spanning the northern continent, and alliances with fellow dwarven settlements in the north. Unlike kingdoms centered around military might, Loden was nestled in a strategic location offering natural defenses and focused its pride on craftsmanship, construction, and providing support for allies in times of potential conflict.

In the southern border region of the northern continent, the peaks stood as natural guardians of the dwarven lands. Bolder Peak, a magnificent mountain stronghold, rose proudly amidst the jagged peaks, its colossal stone walls adorned with intricate carvings. Protected by these fortifications, Bolder Peak stood as a symbol of dwarven resilience and strength.

It guarded a crucial mountain pass, the primary gateway through the treacherous mountain range. Sentinels stood watch day and night, vigilant against any potential intruders, as the dwarves maintained their vigilance to secure their northern territory. The multiple strongholds they forged on top of its peaks gave great insight into the border and beyond.

Bolder Peak assumed the vital role of a scouting party for the dwarves, playing a crucial part in observing the movements of travelers entering and exiting the northern territories. While the north was often treated as a lawless wilderness, Bolder Peak took on the responsibility of relaying valuable information to weary travelers and traders. At times, they even offered guardianship, ensuring safe passage in exchange for valuable resources.

In the rugged expanse of the northeastern mountains, the Lagdohr dwarves faced relentless battles against the formidable Ranuk Ironspine clan. Undeterred by the challenges, Lagdohr dwarves showcased their ingenuity by developing advanced machinery and tapping into Paranova's abundant natural resources. These earth-powered contraptions not only provided a strategic advantage in their ongoing conflict but also facilitated efficient mining and extraction of valuable minerals from the mountains. The newfound wealth bolstered Lagdohr's resistance against the Ironspine clan, enabling them to fortify their defenses and sustain their growing population.

The Lagdohr dwarves, renowned for their innovation among the northern settlements, didn't merely rely on their contraptions for survival in the harsh wilderness. They actively looked up to the kingdom of Loden, expressing unwavering loyalty. Additionally, Lagdohr played a crucial role in supporting the ancient wilderness clan, situated at the heart of the northern wildlands. Through their inventive constructions and contraptions, Lagdohr contributed to the survival of the wilderness dwarves, aiding them through rough winters and protecting against the myriad dangers within the untamed wilderness.

Deep within the heart of the Wildlands, amidst the withered trees and frozen lakes, Hearth Loch stood as a testament to the dwarven ability to adapt and thrive in even the harshest environments. The sprawling villages specialized in survival fishing, utilizing the frozen lakes to provide sustenance for their inhabitants and trade goods with other settlements. The resourcefulness of the dwarves of Hearth Loch was on full display as they navigated the unforgiving cold and transformed the challenging landscape into a flourishing hub of activity.

The dwarves of Hearth Loch had developed ingenious methods to break through the thick ice and catch fish, ensuring a steady food supply throughout the year. Additionally, they had constructed intricate underground tunnels and heated chambers, providing shelter from the biting cold and allowing for year-round productivity in their bustling villages.

While the wilderness dwarves maintained a steadfast neutrality towards human politics and the kingdom of Loden, they adopted a more open stance towards other races traversing through their wild domain. Recognizing the unpredictable weather patterns and the inherent dangers of the wilderness as greater threats than the presence of various races, the wild dwarves chose to prioritize survival and cooperation over involvement in the political affairs of neighboring kingdoms. This neutral outlook allowed them to peacefully coexist with diverse travelers and navigate the challenges presented by the untamed wilderness.

The dwarves, who took great pleasure in their various mountain strongholds, displayed a ferocious spirit and relentless persistence as they committed to build in their garrisons throughout the northern continent's borders. They etched forth a legacy of strength and community through their shared efforts of innovation, craftsmanship, and endurance. This lineage not only insured the survival of their rich culture, but also demonstrated their dedication to preserving the mountainous environments that contained the spirit of their ancient homeland.

The dwarven civilization welcomed technical advances, leveraging their knowledge of mining, crafting, and construction to move their culture forward. The kingdom of Loden's distinct approach to mining and craft resulted in an arsenal of outstanding weapons, armor, and trinkets. The dwarves of Loden developed their skills in collecting valuable metals and jewels from the world's depths, pouring their knowledge into their creation of sophisticated and long-lasting objects.

Their complex network of tunnels and ventilation allowed their subterranean settlements to effectively circulate air, a clear indication of their capacity to adapt to their challenging surroundings. Furthermore, their knowledge of mining and metalworking enabled them to forge lethal weapons and armor, reinforcing their reputation as masterful craftsmen.

Bolder Peak and Lagdohr, on the other hand, integrated their architectural prowess into the very mountains they inhabited. Bolder Peak, nestled amidst the rugged peaks of the southern border, showcased the dwarven talent for blending construction with the natural landscape. The mighty stone walls and impressive structures seamlessly harmonized with the rugged terrain, creating a stronghold that stood as a tribute to the dwarven craftsmanship.

Bolder Peak's dwarves found joy in their brewing prowess, balancing their military focus with a desire for entertainment atop their lofty mountains. Victorious celebrations echoed through the peaks, with hearty chants and laughter reaching even the ears of those below. These gatherings became vibrant expressions of their triumphs, a blend of martial might and communal celebration that resonated throughout the rugged heights.

Lagdohr, known for its ongoing conflict with the Ironspine clan, employed its remarkable machines to expedite the construction of strongholds. These advanced contraptions, fueled by the earth's energy and the dwarves' ingenuity, enabled them to build fortified structures quickly and efficiently. The utilization of these machines not only fortified their defenses but also facilitated their involvement in trade with human civilizations.

Through their technological advancements, the dwarves of Lagdohr amassed wealth and influence, establishing themselves as prominent figures in the way of commerce. Their strongholds became renowned for their impenetrable defenses, attracting merchants and traders from far and wide. As a result, the dwarves became the primary suppliers of rare minerals and precious gemstones, further enhancing their wealth and influence in the realm of commerce.

Fleeing the persistent conflict with the Ranuk Ironspine clan, numerous dwarves from the Lagdohr stronghold migrated south. Carrying their wealth, mining expertise, and tools, they established formidable strongholds in the southeastern mountains of the continent. The exodus brought a wealth of knowledge and resilience to the new settlements as the dwarves sought to forge a secure future away from the relentless challenges of the northeastern mountains.

Hearth Loch, located in the unforgiving Wildlands, relied on machines to endure the harsh and cold landscapes. The dwarves of Hearth Loch employed these devices to navigate the frozen lakes and extract resources necessary for sustenance and trade. These machines were crucial in overcoming the challenges posed by the extreme cold while enabling the dwarves to flourish in an environment that would otherwise be impossible.

The machines used by Hearth Loch were not only essential for their survival but they also played a significant role in expanding their wealth and influence. With the ability to extract valuable resources from the frozen lakes and surrounding area, the dwarves were able to establish prosperous trade relationships with neighboring communities, further enhancing their economic standing. Additionally, these machines gave them a competitive edge over other settlements in the Wildlands, solidifying their position as a dominant force in the region.

With their technological advancements in mining, craftsmanship, architecture, and machinery, the dwarven civilization forged a path of progress and prosperity. Their mastery in these fields not only bolstered their own society but also fostered valuable trade relations with other civilizations. Dwarven ingenuity and resourcefulness were instrumental in shaping their identity as a people renowned for their technological prowess and the wealth it brought them.

The dwarves of the northern continent uncovered the secrets of their mountainous territories, enriched by the elemental entity Valash. This otherworldly being bestowed the land with precious crystal gems, stones, and minerals. The dwarves, quick to recognize the value of these unique materials, began extracting them from the depths of the earth. Through careful study and observation, they sought to understand the mysterious energies emanating from these extraordinary resources.

The elemental disturbance that shook the world opened new pathways within the depths of the kingdom of Loden. Beyond extracting rare minerals, the dwarves uncovered ancient secrets hidden below the surface. The tremors revealed hidden chambers and passages that held untold stories and mysteries, adding an additional layer of intrigue to the dwarven kingdoms.

Following the elemental disturbance and during the elven events of the past, the dwarves discovered old runes and tablets deep within the kingdom of Loden. These relics contained illogical wisdom and arcane knowledge, laying the groundwork for the dwarven mastery of construction and deep understanding of natural magic. The dwarves went on an expedition to understand the complicated relationship between the ground, stone, crystals, and the magical energies that coursed throughout their subterranean kingdom by studying and implementing these ancient texts. The insights from these old artifacts propelled the dwarves of Loden into a new period of technology and mastery over their craft.

The wisdom provided by the runes and tablets regarding construction and engineering extended beyond simply physical workmanship. The dwarves acquired the ability to weave the natural elements of the world into their creations, thereby providing them with a sense of enchantment, stability, and toughness. They used the power of the runes to improve the durability and functionality of their structures, guaranteeing that each structure would last.

In addition, the tablets included wisdom regarding natural magic and an in-depth comprehension of the world's fundamental elements. The dwarves perfected their talents at controlling these natural energies, channeling them to aid in their construction efforts. Through harnessing the natural enchantment of the world, they were able to reinforce foundations, precisely carve stone, and conjure up protection of the environment.

These precious relics were passed down from generation to generation, ensuring the preservation of their architectural expertise. The dwarves thought that their command of natural magic not only made their structures enduring but also gave them a sense of harmony and balance among their surroundings.

The ability to read runes and tablets became an important aspect of their culture and identity. The sacred texts were carefully preserved and passed down through several generations, ensuring that ancient knowledge did not perish with the passage of time. Skilled dwarven architects and artisans studied through these texts, hoping to learn more about the magical qualities of the materials they utilized and how to improve their profession.

Their mastery of artifacts and their connection to natural magic allowed Loden to construct both engineering and architectural wonders, which became renowned around the world. Their buildings stood as living proof of their ancient wisdom and skilled craftsmanship. Whether it was a grand citadel, a towering fortress, or a beautifully adorned hall, each structure bore the mark of the dwarven mastery of runes and the fusion of art, science, and magic.

The dwarves of Loden advanced their civilization with unprecedented speed thanks to the newfound knowledge they learned from the ancient runes and tablets. They extended their influence, aiding strongholds, settlements, and surrounding villages in the north, ushering each society into the modern era. The once-dominant dwarven clans have given way to a network of connected societies, each of which is able to survive in a rapidly multiculturalizing world with a variety of races, cultures, and traditions. The dwarves' commitment to progress and cooperation became a beacon in the ever-changing tapestry of Paranova.

•••••••

The Ranuk civilization underwent significant developments in various aspects, propelling them forward as a formidable force. Their focus on martial prowess and combat techniques led to the advancement of their martial arts and the creation of innovative combat styles. Warriors dedicated themselves to rigorous training, honing their skills, and mastering intricate techniques that pushed the boundaries of their physical and mental capabilities. These warriors were not only skilled in combat but also deeply connected to the spiritual realm.

The Ranuk believed that their mastery of martial arts was a way to channel and harness the mystical energies of the universe. Through their disciplined training, they were able to tap into these energies, enhancing their physical abilities and unlocking extraordinary powers. This unique combination of physical prowess and spiritual connection made the ranuk warriors an unstoppable force on the battlefield.

To support their martial efforts, the ranuk strengthened their martial guilds, establishing a network of organizations that fostered kinship, shared knowledge, and provided platforms for friendly competition. These guilds became centers of excellence where warriors from different clans and regions could gather, exchange techniques, and participate in tournaments and challenges to prove their prowess. The warrior arenas became iconic symbols of the Ranuk civilization, bustling with intense battles and showcasing the incredible skills of the combatants.

While not all Ranuk clans embraced the martial prowess that became a widespread tradition, the warrior arenas were a cultural fixture in every clan. These arenas served as a showcase of strength and honor, where warriors, monks, and shamans engaged in battles, highlighting the unique power and traditions of their respective cultures. The arenas became a communal gathering point, fostering a sense of unity and pride among the ranuk clans as they celebrated their diverse martial heritage.

With growing confidence and prowess, the ranuk expanded their influence, venturing into new territories across the central and southern regions of Paranova. Through diplomatic negotiations and displays of martial might, they secured alliances and partnerships, gradually establishing a formidable presence in these lands. By establishing trade channels and accessing previously unreachable resources, their expansion strengthened their standing as a potent influence.

The Ranuk's constant dedication to martial arts, the formation of their martial guilds, and their adventurous exploration of new regions all contributed to their rise into status as a civilization. The disciplined warriors, coupled with their unique combat techniques, became subjects of admiration and intrigue among other races in Paranova. The transformation from primitive clans engaged in conflict with outsiders to building sophisticated societies rivaling kingdoms marked a significant turning point in ranuk history, opening doors to new opportunities and securing their reputation as skilled warriors and shrewd diplomats.

The Ranuk clans steadfastly clung to their cultural roots throughout the ebb and flow of evolution. While their skin tones had been a source of conflict in the past, in the present day, a tolerable coexistence has emerged. Despite this newfound tolerance, the ranuk clans retained a crucial aspect of their culture: the belief that the tone of their skin tied them to a specific clan, a spiritual connection that had persisted through generations. This theory, although arguable between clans held sway among them, as each believed it was best to separate based on their skin tones to avoid disturbing the delicate balance of elements, divinity, or nature, depending on the clan's belief system. The Mirefang clan, the largest among the ranuk, predominantly exhibited brown hues in their skin tone, leading many ranuki to believe that Mirefang was the chosen clan destined to guide the civilization into the future generations to come.

In the heart of Paranova's mysterious marshlands, the resilient and resourceful Mirefang clan carved out their kingdom. Embracing the mystical forces of nature, they delved deep into shamanism, forming a deep-rooted connection with the elemental energies that resided within the world. Amidst the verdant depths of their swampy domain, the Mirefang clan conducted intricate rituals and ceremonies, paying homage to powerful entities and elements that shaped existence. This honor manifested in their daily lives as they sought guidance and inspiration from the forces of nature, harnessing their power to protect and nurture their kingdom.

With a deep understanding of the delicate balance between life and death, chaos and order, the Mirefang clan navigated the intricate web of elemental energies with wisdom and respect. Their swampland kingdom stood as a testament to their unwavering faith in the mystical forces guiding their path and the deep connection they shared with the natural world. Constructing their kingdom within the marshlands north of the scars left by the elemental entity Pyrothos, the Mirefang clan employed the earth itself as their architecture and utilized the rich soil and stones.

Evolving from primitive ways, they embraced modern civilization, adapting a governance structure while living harmoniously with nature. While learning the common language, they also communicated with other races, known to them as outsiders. Among the ranuk clans, the Mirefang evolved rapidly, earning the distinction of being the largest clan, yet they retained their ancient traditions, upholding the roles of warlord and chieftain as rulers through the course of evolution.

As time progressed, shamanism evolved into a prominent force, retaining the foundations of martial arts but incorporating the bending of elements. Referred to as an Elementalist by the elves of Alora, the ranuk embraced the elements differently, infusing their martial arts knowledge to create a unique blend distinct from elven practices. This fusion of elements and martial arts showcased the ranuk's innovative approach to harnessing the powers of nature, weaving a narrative of strength and harmony that echoed through their clans and territories.

Remaining steadfast in their loyalty to ancient traditions, the Mirefang clan persistently engaged in the art of taming and raising the diverse creatures inhabiting the mysterious swamp. These creatures became invaluable to the ranuki, serving multifaceted roles in their daily lives. From aiding in mundane tasks to fortifying their defense, these creatures played a vital part in the intricate web of the Mirefang kingdom. The individuals who mastered this unique bond between ranuk and creature became revered as the first beastmasters in Paranova. Their skills extended beyond mere control, evolving into an intimate connection that allowed them to become one with the creatures they tamed.

The kingdom of Mirefang, shrouded in solitude, reflected the ranuk's innate desire to be left undisturbed by outsiders and the accompanying tribulations. This sacred bond between the Mirefang and the creatures of the swamp endured through time, creating a harmonious coexistence that intricately defined their way of life. This ancient practice set the Mirefang apart, establishing them as pioneers in the intricate dance between ranuk, nature, and the creatures that inhabited their kingdom.

Within the Mirefang clan, leadership responsibilities were distinctly divided between the chieftain and the warlord. The chieftain shouldered the daily tasks essential for maintaining the unity of the clan, especially with the increase in population and the various elements necessary for sustaining a large kingdom. On the other hand, the warlord assumed a crucial role in the defense of the sprawling Mirefang kingdom. Acting as a commander and leader, the Warlord oversaw the Mirefang warriors, shamans, and beastmasters, ensuring the protection and coordination of the clan's military forces. This division of leadership allowed for a harmonious balance between the internal affairs of the kingdom and the external defense required to safeguard Mirefang's territory.

The Tranquil Tide clan, dedicated to the serene life of seafaring, continued to traverse the vast oceans, sharing their expertise in maritime exploration with the Alorian and Human civilizations. The azure hues on their skin, believed to be a divine blessing, marked them as stewards of the seas, entrusted with caring for their waters. There was disagreement within the clan as to whether their distinctive characteristics were a result of long-term isolation on their islands or a gift from divine spirits. Regardless of the belief, the clan found peace and joy in the tranquil environments of the seas.

In the ebb and flow of time, the Tranquil Tide clan experienced a distinctive evolution in leadership. The once formidable council of elders transformed into a serene monastery nestled within the tranquil islands. No longer seeking direct governance, the elders became revered for their profound wisdom. Departing from ancient traditions that sought the council's guidance for the clan as a whole, the Tranquil Tide's spiritual leaders now guided the path of spirituality and enlightenment, offering a beacon of wisdom to those who sought it.

The tradition of boatsmiths evolved over time, adapting to construct larger ships for continent-spanning journeys and smaller boats for navigating winding rivers. The clan assisted outsiders in travel, trade, settlement, and learning the art of boatsmithing. They claimed two territories—an island north of Alora, where they built vessels, and Tide

Cove, a renowned dock port that initially thrived as a hub for travelers but eventually transformed into a pirates' haven.

The division between the Warlord and Chieftain, reflecting conflicting visions—one of aggression, the other of tranquility—persisted through the ages, causing civil discord within the clan. This rift shaped the clan's governance and leadership, echoing into the modern day.

On the serene Tranquil Island, the clan delved into meditation practices, gradually embracing martial arts infused with divinity magic. This fusion birthed the Monk form of art, a unique style that eschewed conventional weapons in favor of techniques and, when needed, the use of staffs or moral magic. This art form became a distinct hallmark of the clan's warrior tradition, emphasizing harmony, technique, and spirituality.

A schism emerged within the Tranquil Tide clan as divergent ideologies clashed over the path to be trodden. The warlord, a staunch advocate of traditional combat methods, championed the use of swords, armor, and ingeniously engineered cannon machines. Faced with the perceived threat of pirates in Tide Cove, the warlord stressed the importance of military preparation and the need for a formidable defense. On the opposing side stood the Chieftain, a proponent of passive resolutions, deeming the use of force unnecessary.

This ideological rift became an enduring struggle, etching its mark on the clan's identity and influencing its approach in times of conflict. Despite the warlord's insistence on preparing the Tideguard for combat against pirates and potential invaders, the Chieftain held firm in resisting such militarization. The Tideguard, rooted in tradition, found itself repurposed for defensive purposes in Tide Cove, a compromise born out of the constant clash of viewpoints within the clan.

Respecting the Alorian elves, the Tranquil Tide clan had aided in rebuilding their kingdom after the great rebellion. This act of kindness forged a lasting alliance and support from the elves, influencing the clan's evolution. Another alliance was formed with the Thornshade clan, contributing to the expansion of both clans across Paranova. Together, they established safe trade routes, connected distant lands, and fostered cultural exchange and prosperity among the diverse races of the world.

The Thornshade, renowned for their warrior spirit and deep woodland connection, traversed a path of reconciliation with their old rival, the primal human colony in desolate lands. Seeking unity and understanding, they opened their territories to the primal humans, offering a chance for peace and a new home within their lush domains.

With hues of green skin, the Thornshade clan believed themselves to be the protectors of nature, custodians of wildlife, and plant life. They built a large village nestled between the kingdoms of Volantis and Alora, sharing their woodlands with the primal human colony. Though the Thornshade permitted the primal humans to live in their territories, they asserted their ownership, establishing a system to resolve disputes through the Thornshade Arena and settling clashes with honor and discipline.

Widespread throughout many woodlands, the Thornshade maintained the chieftain and warlord roles, assigning tribal chieftains known as huntsmen or huntswomen. These leaders held governance over smaller Thornshade villages, conducting grand hunts a few times a year for communication and information exchange. The Thornshade were seen everywhere woodlands existed, with some tribes being hostile and others welcoming. Each Thornshade member strove for peace within the forests, meeting aggressive trespassers with their skilled hunters and warriors.

Priding themselves on hunting and fighting, the Thornshade utilized martial arts infused with nature and elemental prowess. They were capable hunters who used elemental arrows, causing chaos when attacking intruders. The clan practiced divinity and shamanism in battle, blending various ranuk practices into their own. However, the Thornshade clan despised the fire element; the use of fire could potentially destroy their woodlands. This became the sole reason the clan had hatred for the Zelorian and Fumarian elves due to their praise for the fire element. Stealth and navigation in the woodlands set them apart, making them formidable when provoked yet generally peaceful. The Thornshade, the first clan to make contact with other racial civilizations, learned the common tongue from the Mirefang, but their territorial assertiveness stirred conflicts in modern times as other races sought resources for expansion.

In the vast expanse of Paranova, a unique clan emerged through the evolution of the ranuk. The mighty Dwarven of Loden's underground way of life served as inspiration for the creation of the Wormroot clan, which came from the union of the Thornshade and Mirefang clans. This daring clan delved deep into the earth within the lesser-known mountain regions of the southeast, seeking to carve out a hidden sanctuary where they could thrive.

Hues of mostly purple, black, and dark colorful shades adorned the skin of the Wormroot ranuki. Despite their unique appearances, they believed that their purpose lay not in their skin color but in their harmonious coexistence. Preferring the natural defense of caves and caverns, the mixed clan was considered wild and primitive compared to more structured ranuk clans.

Within their subterranean abode, the Wormroot clan combined their knowledge of shamanistic practices and martial arts, incorporating wisdom from the Thornshade and Mirefang lineages as well as the teachings of the dwarves. The mastery of runes and tablets, passed down from the dwarves, enhanced their construction and arcane magic. While not master crafters, they developed unique architectural styles within their domains.

Navigating a complex network of tunnels and chambers, the Wormroot clan uncovered precious resources and formed alliances with subterranean creatures. Similar to the Mirefang, they befriended and tamed these creatures. However, unlike their more civilized counterparts, the Wormroot clan remained distant and primitive. Resorting to cannibalism and adorning themselves with the bones of their victims, they clashed with migrating dwarves, resulting in a division of territories in modern times.

Straying away from divine magic, the Wormroot clan embraced dark magic, focusing on totems, curses, and blood magic. Viewed by other ranuk clans as chaos balancing the order within their civilization, the Wormroot clan maintained a unique and wicked presence.

Deep within the heart of the mountainous regions, the Ironspine clan, renowned for their ingenuity and resourcefulness, thrived amidst a continuous conflict with their formidable enemies. Developing cunning strategies and tactics that outwitted the dwarven machines, the Ironspine clan became renowned for their mastery of guerrilla warfare and their purpose to defend their ancestral lands.

The Ironspine, distinguished by hues of white or pale-colored skin, viewed their destiny through a different lens than the other ranuk clans. Nestled in the winter weather of the northern continent, they believed their pale complexion was a manifestation of their will to blend seamlessly with their frosty surroundings. Unlike other clans, the Ironspine did not attribute their purpose to a divine calling based on skin color; instead, they embraced a unique mission.

Rejecting the conventional beliefs tied to skin hues, the Ironspine clan saw their purpose in combating the Gantum race. Despite the gantum undergoing an evolution that reduced their size compared to their ancestors, the Ironspine remained steadfast in their conviction that their sole purpose was to confront and overcome these giant-like beings. This stubborn determination set the Ironspine apart, marking them as the last clan to uphold the ancient duty of opposing the gantum.

Nestled upon a colossal ancient Gantum spire, resembling a formidable spine stretching towards the heavens, the Ironspine clan established their mighty stronghold. Rising up and down the towering structure, their kingdom stood as proof of their resilience and their unyielding spirit. Ingeniously carved dwellings and fortified structures adorned the spire's craggy surface, intertwining with the natural contours of the ancient structure. The Ironspine stronghold was not only a symbol of their strength but also a strategic advantage in defending their lands.

From their vantage point atop the spire, they could immediately identify any approaching dangers and prepare their defenses. The clan's skill in adapting to their surroundings enabled them to survive despite the most dire circumstances, driving their passion towards protecting what was rightfully theirs. The Ironspine clan's strategic location gave them an overview across the vast northern territories, allowing them to study their enemies' movements and strike with efficient and fatal force. They created elaborate networks of tunnels and hidden passages beneath the spire, allowing them to traverse the hazardous terrain undetected and unleash surprise attacks on their opponents. These hidden passages also functioned as a means of escape in times of danger, giving the Ironspine clan an essential edge to evade their opponents. Additionally, the strategic position of the spire allowed them to control key trade routes and resources, further solidifying their dominance in the region.

The constant battles with the Gantum and Lagdohr dwarves pushed the Ironspine clan to refine their defensive techniques and leverage their intimate knowledge of the terrain to their advantage. They constructed intricate networks of traps and pitfalls, cleverly concealed within the rugged terrain, to ensnare and confound their enemies. The Ironspine's ability to adapt swiftly to changing circumstances and exploit their enemies' weaknesses became the cornerstone of their defense.

The Ironspine clan, steadfast in their dedication to their ancestral traditions, carried on a unique practice that set them apart from other clans in Paranova. With their unmatched craftsmanship and their significant purpose, they embraced the art of replacing lost limbs with intricate iron prosthetics with their Ironforgers. This ancient tradition held deep significance for the Ironspine, symbolizing both honor and a striking visual display of their resilience and strength.

For the Ironspine, replacing a lost limb with an iron prosthetic was more than just a physical restoration; it was a declaration of their unbreakable spirit. Each iron limb was precisely constructed, demonstrating the expertise and workmanship passed down through generations. As a rite of passage, warriors eagerly dealt with the augmentation process, overcoming physical and spiritual hardships to become symbols of their clan's unyielding tenacity.

The sight of an Ironspine warrior, with their shimmering iron limbs and seething gaze, terrified their foes. It served as an affecting symbol of the clan's unrelenting will to stand up for their home and protect their kin. The sound of the iron limbs clanking against the ground carried echoes of battles fought and victories achieved, sending a message of defiance and everlasting determination. Beyond the physical benefits, the iron limbs gave the Ironspine warriors a sense of pride and identity. They wore their artificial limbs as emblems of honor, representing their strength and willingness to conquer adversity. The metallic limbs became extensions of their own bodies, allowing them to wield weapons with unparalleled precision and instilling fear in anyone who made an attempt to challenge them.

As the Ironspine warriors marched into combat, their iron limbs gleaming from the sun, they symbolized their clan's unstoppable resolve. With each step, they carried the weight of their history and customs, channeling the power and determination of their ancestors. Their iron limbs became a representation of the Ironspine clan's unrelenting might to safeguard their territory and way of life.

All those who attempted to challenge the Ironspine warriors were either killed or severely injured by their legendary fighting proficiency. Their reputation as vicious fighters had echoed throughout Paranova, establishing them as an intimidating force to come across. As the Ironspine warriors marched towards conflict, their battle cries would ring through the air, instilling fear and horror in their enemies and boosting unrelenting confidence amongst their clan.

In the strict and organized society of the Ironspine, primitive tendencies coexisted with a sense of eerie presence. The kingdom perpetually resonated with the atmosphere of war, fostering an environment where each member felt the ongoing call to arms. Within this kingdom, the chieftain assumed a role that held little regard for the intricacies of daily life. Instead, their focus lay on tending to the wounded and overseeing efforts to fortify the kingdom.

In contrast, the Warlord emerged as the authoritative figure who dictated the course of almost everything within the Ironspine clan. Tasked with handling the most pressing matters, the warlord became the driving force behind decisions that shaped the destiny of the kingdom. When confronted with the weight of challenging choices, the warlord would turn to the chieftain as a valuable resource or source of guidance, seeking insight to navigate the complexities of leadership in times of conflict. This dynamic between the chieftain and warlord formed the backbone of governance in the structured yet war-driven society of the Ironspine.

In the vibrant realm of Paranova, the Ranuk clans add distinct colors to the tapestry of the land. From the resilient Mirefang clan, deeply connected to the marshlands, to the fierce Thornshade warriors guarding the woodlands, each clan weaves its own unique narrative. The seafaring Tranquil Tide clan shares its maritime expertise, while the mixed-hued Wormroot clan carves a subterranean sanctuary. Lastly, the war-driven Ironspine clan, with its pale skin, stands ready for conflict. Together, these clans paint a diverse and captivating picture, contributing to the rich history and cultural blend of Paranova.

In the annals of ancient history, the leaders of bygone eras bestowed the mantle of authority upon their descendants, carrying forward the storied legacies of the Bloodthorn, Shroudfang, Ironbark, and Ragnof bloodlines. For generations, these noble lineages held sway over their respective clans, shaping the destinies of the Ranuk clans. However, as the sands of time continued to flow, a new lineage emerged, weaving itself into the tapestry of Ranuk history. The Tranquil Tide, in harmony with the Wormroot clan, witnessed the rise of Jortorr as the warlord of Tranquil Tide and Kezzenmire as the brilliant chieftain of Wormroot. For hundreds of years, these leaders stood strong, steering their clans through the currents of evolution and guiding them to an enduring legacy.

········

The Gantum civilization, with its roots tracing back to the ancient gantums, stood as a witness to the enduring legacy of their colossal ancestors. The gantum, once towering giants of immense stature, were now the proud descendants who carried forward their formidable lineage. While they had inherited the unmistakable physical traits of their predecessors, their size had diminished over the ages, yet their spirit remained adamant.

As the descendants of ancient gigantic beings, the Gantum civilization upheld a deep admiration for their ancestors and the rich history that shaped their identity. They cherished the tales of the colossal giants, their fabled feats, and their indomitable strength. These stories served as a reminder of their heritage and inspired a sense of pride in the hearts of the gantums.

Though their physical stature had diminished, the gantums retained a deep connection to their ancestral roots. They possessed an inherent affinity for the dark arts, a lingering gift from their giant forebears. This connection to the dark energies of Paranova fueled their relentless pursuit of magical knowledge and their mastery of elemental forces.

They tried to honor the legacy of the ancient gantum by dedicating themselves to the mystical arts. Their quest for magical knowledge led them into forbidden domains, where they studied necromancy, shadow, and conjuration manipulation. The gantum were infamous for performing rituals that tapped into Paranova's arcane essence, taking power from its darkest corners to feed their spells and enchantments.

The Gantum civilization, became known for their innate connection to the dark arts and mastery of elemental magic, embarked on a path of relentless magical research and experimentation. With a deep understanding of the dark forces that spread throughout Paranova, the gantum delved into the mysteries of the mystical arts, seeking to push the boundaries of their knowledge and harness the untapped power that lay dormant within.

As the gantum's research progressed, they made great advances in elemental magic. They perfected their skills in manipulating fire, water, earth, and air, developing a deep connection with the very fabric of nature. By exercising remarkable concentration and unfaltering commitment, they successfully unleashed additional spells and enchantments, thereby attaining a previously unattainable degree of precision and mastery over the elements.

To cultivate their magical skills and secure the transmission of old wisdom, the gantum founded renowned magical institutions within the hallowed Eternal Pillars. These academies evolved into places of instruction and training for aspiring gantum spellcasters, offering a caring atmosphere for the development and refinement of their magical powers. Learners polished their talents in the complexities of spellcasting and combat under the supervision of veteran gantum spellcasters, preparing them for the trials that lay ahead.

In the way of combat, the gantum crafted unique techniques that seamlessly integrated their mastery of magic with physical prowess. Their warriors became formidable opponents on the battlefield, wielding spells and weapons with deadly precision. The gantums embraced a harmonious approach, blending martial discipline with arcane finesse to create a truly formidable fighting force.

With their larger physical features compared to the other races, they faced challenges wielding smaller weapons crafted by other races. With the gantum not being masterful forgers, they instead used their magical expertise and found ways within the arcane magic to be able to conjure up weapons and armor through magical essence, which they called conjuring and enchanting magic. This magical fusion empowered their weapons and armor, allowing them to wield formidable tools of war. Their unique approach to craftsmanship, blending magical essence and practicality, had set them apart on the battlefield of Paranova.

Throughout their civilization, the gantum became known for their deep connection to the dark arts, channeling the shadowy forces that existed alongside the elemental energies. They explored the vast magics of necromancy, illusion, and the dark arts, delving into realms that were shrouded in mystery and trepidation. While some viewed their practices with caution, others recognized the gantums' unique perspective as an essential aspect of Paranova's magical tapestry.

The advancements made by the Gantum civilization not only elevated their own magical prowess but also had an impact on the magical landscape of Paranova. Their research and experimentation sparked new ideas and inspired other civilizations to delve deeper into their own magical traditions, leading to an era of unprecedented magical growth and understanding.

The gantum living in the Eternal Spires defied expectations despite being considered mere muscle by other civilizations. They evolved into masterful spellcasters, rivaling the magical expertise of other races on Paranova. The majority of gantum spellcasters focused on practical magic, showcasing a unique blend of strength and intellect that challenged preconceived notions about their capabilities. The Eternal Spires became a beacon of magical prowess among the gantum, demonstrating that their civilization involved not only physical might but also formidable mystical knowledge.

Within the Gantum society, amidst the richness of their civilization, a dark and hostile kingdom emerged known as Molgan. Unlike the other gantum settlements, Molgan stood as a stark contrast, devoid of the laws, justice, and order that defined their society. It was a primitive kingdom that Molgantusk, a dictating leader with a burning desire to imitate the shady practices of his ascendants, ruled over.

The ruler of Molgan harbored a twisted fascination with the ancient gantums' shadowy reputation, seeking to embody their darkness and ferocity. In his relentless pursuit of power, he discarded the principles of justice and fairness that were deeply ingrained within Gantum society. Instead, he reveled in chaos, lawlessness, and the unrestrained exercise of authority.

Under the ruler's iron fist, Molgan became a place of fear and oppression. Its inhabitants lived in a constant state of unrest, subject to the ruler's whims and cruel decrees. Arbitrary decisions that only served to strengthen the ruler's power stood in for justice. The kingdom became a breeding ground for darkness as its ruler reveled in the primal and savage nature that he believed mirrored the ancient Gantums' legacy.

Remnants of the Molgan faction lived in the shadows of the Eternal Pillars, driven by a relentless desire to reclaim the enormous power and stature of their ancient Gantum ancestors. These small factions, fueled by ambition and a thirst for forbidden knowledge, delved deep into the realm of dark magic and experimentation.

These Molgan remnants sought to discover the truth about their ancestry and recreate the enormous forms that once inhabited the area under the guidance of their twisted obsession with the past. They delved into ancient tomes and scrolls, studying forgotten rituals and incantations that promised a glimpse into the realm of giants. As their experiments progressed, the Molgan remnants began to harness the power of forbidden artifacts, sacrificing their own sapience in exchange for the potential to wield immense strength and size. With each successful ritual, they grew closer to achieving their goal of resurrecting the ancient gantum beings and unleashing chaos upon the world once again.

Through their relentless pursuit, the Molgan factions managed to achieve partial success in their struggles. They discovered ways to temporarily enhance their physical forms, gaining an imposing stature reminiscent of the ancient gantum. These dark-empowered Molgans' towered over their counterparts, with their size and strength serving as chilling validation of the depths they were willing to explore in their quest for power.

However, their achievements came at a great cost. The dark magic that coursed through their veins corrupted their minds and bodies, leaving them forever altered and detached from the noble heritage of the Gantum civilization. Their physical transformations were twisted and monstrous, bearing little resemblance to the majestic giants of old. Their once regal features were contorted into grotesque forms, with elongated limbs and gnarled, claw-like hands. The darkness within them consumed any trace of compassion or empathy, turning them into ruthless beings driven solely by their insatiable thirst for power.

The enhanced and unsettling faction among the gantum, known as the Shadow Gantum, underwent dark rituals that increased their size, strength, and savagery. These formidable beings exhibited a disturbing trait—they consumed flesh and grew in power when fed. However, the success rate of the dark rituals was not high, resulting in a limited amount of shadow gantum. As of today, they pose a threat, but their scarcity prevents them from becoming a widespread menace.

In the twin towering spires of the Eternal Pillars, the gantums chose a different path, one that melded their primal nature with a disciplined approach to magical studies. They recognized the power and allure of dark magic, as well as the potential for chaos and destruction it held. Instead of succumbing to its temptations, they sought to understand it through controlled experimentation, study, and observation.

The Gantum of the Eternal Pillars delved into the mysteries of the elements and the dark arts with a sense of responsibility and moral guidance. They recognized the importance of harnessing their powers for the greater good and the preservation of their society. Their studies covered the manipulation of the elements, the channeling of raw energies, and the mastery of dark magic in a controlled and measured manner.

Within their twin spires, the gantums established academies dedicated to the pursuit of knowledge and magical expertise. These academies functioned as sites of research and creativity, as gantum experts dug into ancient texts, carried out elaborate experiments, and sharpened their understanding of the dark forces that molded their world. The gantum thought that through intense study and focused practice, they might unveil the mysteries of the universe and wield incredible power. They aspired to push beyond the limits of what was known, constantly looking for new methods to manipulate the elements and tap into the vast reservoirs of raw energy that surrounded them.

Unlike the Molgan factions, the gantum of the Eternal Pillars valued structure and discipline in their pursuit of magical mastery. They followed to a rigid rules of conduct that guided their experiments and research, ensuring that their studies were carried out in a way that respected the delicate balance between the magical and natural realms. This code of conduct further stressed the significance of sharing knowledge and working together with other gantum practitioners to develop a strong sense of community. The gantums hoped to use their magical abilities in a responsible and secure manner by following to these principles.

The Gantum society, while primitive at their heart, recognized the value of structure and organization. They formed hierarchies within their places of learning, with accomplished researchers and experienced practitioners advising future generations by teaching magical studies. Mentorship and apprenticeship enabled an exchange of knowledge, methods, and moral principles from one generation to the next.

Their research and observations of arcane magic and the elements enabled the gantum achieve a greater understanding of the world around them. Their quest to understand and use the power of the four elements—fire, earth, water, and air—led them to learn more about the complexity of these energies.

The Gantums' disciplined approach to magical studies not only elevated their understanding of the dark arts but also fostered a sense of responsibility and moral compass within their society. They recognized the potential dangers of unchecked experimentation and the dire consequences that could arise from the misuse of dark magic.

The Gantum civilization, while establishing the grand kingdoms of the Eternal Spires and Molgan, also scattered smaller settlements across the northern continent. These outposts varied in size and influence, with some engaging in conflicts with neighboring forces like the Ironspine, the Wildlands, or the Snowdrop primal human colony. Despite the dominance of the larger kingdoms, these smaller settlements played a vital role in shaping the gantum civilization's presence and interactions on Paranova.

In the rough relationship between the gantum society and the dwarven kind, conflicts and quarrels were not uncommon. The gantum, known for their primal instincts and dark inclinations, had a disturbing tradition that involved the consumption of dwarf meat. However, it is important to note that not all gantum participated in such practices, and it was not a widespread or endorsed custom within their society.

The Gantums, with their immense size and strength, viewed the dwarves as formidable enemies, both in battle and in their elusive nature. While there were instances where gantums targeted dwarves for their grim feasts, it was not a regular occurrence. The dwarven kind, known for their cunning and resilience, proved challenging to capture, making them an elusive prey for the gantum.

Trade was not a significant part of Gantum society. They preferred to embark on quests and expeditions, seeking out treasures, artifacts, and relics for their personal pleasure. The allure of unearthing ancient secrets and amassing rare items fascinated them, driving their explorations and adventures. They were more inclined to hoard their discoveries, cherishing them as prized possessions rather than engaging in traditional trade with other races.

It is crucial to realize that not all gantum adopted these practices and behaviors. Just as with any society, individuals held varying beliefs and engaged in different activities. While some gantum may have maintained the traditions of cannibalism and isolationist tendencies, others pursued alternative paths and sought to establish connections with other races on different terms.

Overall, there were tensions and sporadic clashes between gantum society and the dwarven kind. The primal nature of the gantum clashed with the industrious and resilient spirit of the dwarves, resulting in conflicts that echoed through the ages. However, it is important to recognize that individuals within both societies held the potential for change, growth, and the forging of new paths towards understanding and cooperation.

These conflicts often stemmed from misunderstandings and miscommunications, as both societies had different values and ways of life. Despite these challenges, there were instances where gantum and dwarves found common ground and worked together towards mutual benefit. These moments of collaboration serve as a reminder that even in the face of differences, there is always potential for harmony and progress.

••••••••

As the races of Paranova embarked on their respective journeys and forging their own paths within the world, they were met with numerous challenges and difficulties. However, it was through these trials that they discovered the true potential of their civilizations. Challenge became the catalyst for innovation and growth, pushing them to explore new territories, develop advanced technologies, and master formidable arts and sciences.

Through the wars, rebellions, and alliances, the diverse races realized that unity and cooperation were essential for survival and progress. They learned to set aside their differences for the most part and embrace the collective strength of their diverse cultures. The exchange of knowledge and ideas between the races fueled a wave of inspiration, inspiring them to push the boundaries of their civilizations even further.

With each passing day, the anticipation for the future grew as the races of Paranova witnessed the continued advancement of their societies. They looked ahead with optimism, eager to see the fruits of their labor and the success of their alliances. New possibilities unfolded before them and the collective determination to forge a better future spurred them onward.

They recognized that by accepting variety and working together, they could achieve greatness beyond their greatest expectations. The sharing of knowledge and culture between races became an accelerator, propelling them toward a future in which unity and progress were the foundations of their civilizations.

By looking back on their forged paths, the races of Paranova realized how interconnected their fates were. Everything from the hardships they experienced to the victories they encountered, became linked events that shaped their reality. They stood ready to confront whatever obstacles lay ahead, knowing that hardship would allow them to evolve, grow, and eventually achieve success.

The events surrounding Alora, from the Pyrothos war to the rebellion and the fall of the queen, had an evolutionary impact on the other races of Paranova. The tales and legends that circulated about these events instilled a mixture of awe, fear, and curiosity among the races, shaping their perceptions and influencing their trajectories.

The stories of the Pyrothos war, with its epic battles and the existence of a formidable entity, left the other races in awe and with a deep sense of respect for the power that resided within their world. It served as a reminder of the immense forces that could shape their destinies and the need for preparedness.

The Alora rebellion, with its defiance against a structured ruler, became a cautionary tale for the other races. It highlighted the importance of governance and the consequences of unchecked power. The rebellion served as a motivation for the other civilizations to establish their own systems of governance, ensuring that their rulers were accountable and that the rights and well-being of their people were protected.

The fall of the queen and the following aftermath had a ripple effect on the trajectory of the other races. It inspired them to build defenses, strengthen their armies, and advance their civilizations. They recognized the vulnerability of their kingdoms and civilizations and understood the need to be prepared for any future threats that might arise.

The impact of the events went beyond military preparations. It sparked advancements in various fields, including the arts, sciences, trade, and governance. The other races looked up to the elven race and found inspiration in their resilience and determination. They sought to expand their own territories, develop new technologies, and establish alliances to ensure the survival and growth of their civilizations.

As the various races of Paranova emerged from the shadows of past conflicts and embraced the lessons learned, a promising future began to take shape. The hardships they faced had ignited a spirit of resilience, innovation, and collaboration, setting the stage for a new era of growth and benefit.

With their newfound unity, the races of Paranova were able to pool their resources and knowledge, leading to groundbreaking advancements in technology, medicine, and sustainable practices. This collective effort not only improved the quality of life for all inhabitants but also fostered a sense of shared responsibility for the planet they called home.

Trade routes expanded, connecting distant lands and fostering economic prosperity. The exchange of goods, ideas, and knowledge fueled the advancement of the arts, sciences, and technology across Paranova. Cities and kingdoms flourished, becoming centers of culture, commerce, and governance.

In this promising future, the races of Paranova found common ground and formed alliances. Volantis emerged as a central governance hub, uniting human civilizations and providing stability and guidance. Galanor, with its renowned Citadel College, became a beacon of knowledge and training, attracting aspiring warriors and magic users from all corners of Paranova.

The Dwarven strongholds stood as formidable fortresses, fortified through advancements in mining, craftsmanship, and architectural ingenuity. Their mastery of runes and tablets allowed them to tap into ancient knowledge and wield natural magic, enhancing their construction prowess and deepening their understanding of the world.

The Ranuk, known for their advanced martial arts and combat techniques, saw their warrior guilds and arenas thrive. Their exploration and expansion in the central and southern territories, particularly the kingdom of Mirefang, brought new influences and cultural exchange, enriching their society.

The Tranquil Tide continued their legacy as peaceful seafarers, sharing their maritime expertise with Alorian and human civilizations. Through their alliance with the Thornshade, they facilitated travel and expansion across Paranova, fostering cooperation and harmony.

The Thornshade, who were devoted to their way of life and discipline, sought to increase their influence throughout Paranova's woodlands. Their desire for coexistence and harmony with the natural world inspired other races to embrace a more balanced and sustainable way of life.

Even the Gantum civilization, with their focus on magical research and experimentation, found a more controlled and moral path in the Eternal Pillars. Through their development of combat and conjured magic, they contributed to the collective understanding and advancement of the magical arts.

All the diverse races were excited about the future as they forged their own paths toward greatness, since they all believed that hardship had led to innovation and growth. Their common goal of a prosperous and peaceful world, in which previous lessons directed them toward a future full of opportunity, cooperation, and a deeper understanding of the wonders that Paranova held which brought them together.

Chapter 14: Everlasting Legacy

Those celestial beings called Shapers, possessing the power to manipulate and alter reality itself, were the ones responsible for shaping Paranova. Their perspective on the world was unique because they were experienced in its founding principles and could control its course of events. The Shapers were gifted architects who, with their extensive knowledge, created awe-inspiring kingdoms, landscapes, and structures that appeared to defy the rules of the surrounding environment. Every Shaper collaborated tirelessly to make sure that Paranova fulfilled their vision of an ideal system where every individual could function effectively and live in peace with the natural world.

The Shapers gained knowledge of the dynamic between structure and disorder, creation and destruction, through their challenges and experiences. They were aware of the effects caused by their actions as well as the responsibility that followed their outstanding talents. They understood that even minor changes to natural laws may have far-reaching consequences, and they were determined to use their abilities effectively. The Shapers believed it was their responsibility to maintain the natural order and conserve the delicate ecosystems that supported life on Paranova.

The Order and Chaos sectors gleaned valuable lessons from the creation of a mortal sapient world. They witnessed the intricate cause-and-effect relationship that accompanied any changes made to this realm, realizing that every action carried consequences, shaping the legacy of the mortal inhabitants. Seeing how civilizations have changed through the years has given both sectors a new perspective on life and helped them better comprehend all aspects of being sapient.

As the Shapers processed the Oracle's passing, they were filled with both sadness and appreciation for her vital contribution to Paranova's birth. Her impact was so significant that they felt it was right to celebrate her life with a solemn and sacred ceremony.

This ceremony involved gathering all the Shapers of each sector, and they would offer prayers and blessings, sharing stories of her teachings and how she had shaped their celestial lives. Through this ceremony, they hoped to not only pay tribute to the Oracle but also inspire future generations to carry on her legacy of wisdom and responsibility.

Gathering in her sanctuary, the Shapers prepared for the descent of the Oracle's remaining celestial energy, a symbolic act that would bless her remains with their collective energies. They adorned the chamber with intricate patterns and symbols, representing the interconnectedness of all things and the eternal cycle of life and death.

The Forger, using his unparalleled skill, crafted a vessel as unique as the Oracle herself. This extraordinary creation was designed to hold the harnessed energies and essence of the Oracle, serving as a special homage to the world of Paranova. Once the funeral rites were completed, the vessel planned to take its place in orbit above the world, a celestial presence that would forever weave the Oracle's legacy into the very fabric of the universe surrounding Paranova.

With reverence and solemnity, the Shapers carefully placed the Oracle's celestial energies in a specially crafted vessel, adorned with precious gems and inscribed with ancient incantations. They surrounded the vessel with glowing crystals, each representing an aspect of the world they had shaped together.

The Provisioner, with a voice loaded down with the weight of countless ages, shared sentimental tales of shared experiences with the Oracle. As he spoke, his voice trembled, and a radiant aura enveloped the celestial space. Observing the Oracle's celestial energy gently dimming, the Provisioner, filled with his own admiration, began channeling his own celestial energy by bestowing blessings upon the vessel that had housed the Oracle's energies of wisdom and guidance.

In a somber but respectful ritual, the other Shapers were given the opportunity to pay their respects individually. Each approached with a mix of gratitude and sorrow, acknowledging the profound influence the Oracle had on their existence. The celestial realm resonated with a bittersweet ambiance, capturing the essence of a moment where cosmic energies intertwined with the passage of an eternal celestial being.

As the Shapers channeled their energies, they conjured the powers of order and chaos, blending their essence with the sacred vessel. They poured their sorrow, gratitude, and love into the ritual, infusing the Oracle's remaining energy with the transformative energies of the Shapers and Paranova itself.

The Archon, overwhelmed by remorse, channeled her energy onto the vessel, tears streaming down her ethereal form. As she poured her essence into the vessel, a flood of memories surfaced, haunting her with the recollection of the envy she once felt towards the Oracle. The regret pierced through her, especially the memory of the moment she deprived the Oracle of her sight—an act that once brought the Archon pleasure but now filled her with self-disgust.

In this moving moment, the Archon's gaze shifted to the Provisioner, who bore the weight of profound loss. Though a deep desire to be by his side tugged at her, the Archon hesitated, convinced that her past actions had forever distanced her from the comfort he desperately sought. The celestial realm echoed with the complexity of emotions, encapsulating a shared history among the Shapers that seemingly demanded reflection and redemption.

As the funeral rites concluded, the Shapers entered moments of respectful silence. Gazing down at the world below, they witnessed the evolution of all races, finding a newfound sense of peace and harmony after the sorrow that had dwelled. The celestial energies of the Shapers resonated with a serene feeling, and both the Order and Chaos sectors exchanged smiles. In this moment, they recognized that the vision of the Oracle and the Shapers was finally taking hold, bringing a sense of fulfillment and tranquility to the celestial realms.

In a moment of deep sorrow, the Anarchist approached the Provisioner, offering a heartfelt embrace that conveyed the comfort the grieving Shaper desperately needed. Expressing his condolences, the Anarchist sought to ensure there were no lingering ill feelings toward his chaotic sector. The Provisioner, despite his significant loss, he managed a smile, assuring the Anarchist that their joint efforts had achieved far more than the chaotic causes that once plagued their sector and world.

The Provisioner emphasized the overarching purpose of their collaborative project—to find common ground between the Order and Chaos sectors. He reminded the Anarchist that the lessons learned were essential, and the project was a means to show him the importance of harmony instead of imprisonment in the death realm alongside other Chaos sector members. The Anarchist, taken aback, discovered that the Provisioner had a grand plan dating back to the incidents in the Life and Death realms. The Provisioner revealed his awareness that the Anarchist wasn't solely responsible for past events; rather, it was his brother, the former leader of the Chaos sector, manipulating events and placing blame on the Anarchist.

As the other Shapers left the chamber, the Archon remained behind to offer her final condolences to the grieving Provisioner. Initially filled with hesitation and awkwardness, the room soon embraced a painful silence. However, the Provisioner, holding his head high, fixed his gaze upon the Archon. She approached slowly, and in a moment of shared grief, they embraced.

During this tender exchange, the Archon offered sincere apologies for everything, but the Provisioner gently shushed her, finding comfort in the embrace he desperately needed. She expressed her commitment to uncovering the truth about Havoc, seeking redemption for his actions. Grateful for her presence, the Provisioner acknowledged her efforts.

Curious, the Archon questioned why he had been so forgiving toward her despite the irreparable actions she had committed. The Provisioner, with a long and heartfelt gaze, explained that he saw the good within her—the impactful leader, the loving and caring side, the goodness amid the chaos that consumed her mind. He conveyed that, all along, she had a choice, and her energies revealed that she chose loyalty to him, not to the world or the cause. The Archon was impressed with his perception and realized why he is the Shapers' leading figure, as she was awed at his profound understanding of the celestial realms.

•••••••

In the year following the Oracle's fall, the Shapers resumed their solitary existence, patiently observing the evolution of mortal civilizations. However, with the shift in celestial events and the Provisioner's words about exploring other realms, a renewed sense of accomplishment enveloped the sector. The idea of creating more mortal realms ignited a spark of interest in each Shaper. They delved into planning, dreaming, and channeling effort into the mundane of their daily tasks and discoveries, collectively embracing the potential for new cosmic creations.

During this period, the Keeper and the Forger formed a close bond, spending considerable time together. They engaged in lively discussions, often showcasing their ideas to each other and engaging in friendly arguments about whose concept was superior. When presenting their ideas to the Provisioner, he acknowledged the uniqueness of both perspectives, appreciating the marvelous ideas each Shaper brought to the table.

The Forger, immersed in blueprints and landscapes, meticulously crafted worlds and delved into the intricate elemental cycles that would define them. While this was going on, the Keeper, who was passionately exploring the possibilities of creating Avatars, was fascinated with their function as custodians and the invaluable role of serving as the Shapers' eyes on the mortal planes.

Their discussions, though at times passionately agreeable, often turned into a competition as they sought to impress the Provisioner and leave their fellow Shapers in awe with the creative energies they brought to the celestial realm.

With a renewed determination, the Anarchist collaborated with the members of the Chaos sector, actively engaging in the observation of the evolution of each race on Paranova. His perspective had shifted, and he now sought to be more involved in understanding the profound lesson that the Provisioner had revealed to him. Recognizing that he had distanced himself from the process of creation in the past, often delegating responsibilities to the Archon and Havoc, the Anarchist was now eager to be closer to action. He aimed to keenly observe the signs of understanding that mortals exhibited, acknowledging that there was much yet to be learned from their evolution.

Over time, within the celestial realm, the Archon immersed herself in her chambers, diligently decoding and deciphering the notes recovered from Havoc's domain. The intricate details within the notes unveiled a broader and more elaborate scheme than she had initially comprehended during their past collaboration. With a determined mindset, the Archon saw herself as a detective, tirelessly working to piece together the scattered information. Her goal was to uncover the full extent of Havoc's plans, not only to regain the Provisioner's trust but also to assist him in coping with the profound loss of the Oracle. She persisted in trying to figure out the mysterious schemes that loomed menacingly before her out of a sense of justice for the Provisioner.

During the period of mourning for the Oracle, the Provisioner withdrew into solitude, distancing himself from the seemingly positive atmosphere of the celestial realm. Seeking peace in the sanctuary that once echoed with the Oracle's presence, the Provisioner concealed himself in the shadows, surrounded by remnants of the plans they had crafted together. Although he initially processed the Oracle's passing well, the loneliness and the weight of their shared memories drove him into a descent of madness and anger at his perceived failures. His anguish was directed inward, and the Archon, who frequently checked on him, witnessed his outbursts.

One eventful night, the Archon heard the Provisioner yelling at himself and rushed to his side. He, however, rejected her efforts to console him and expressed his displeasure at her for attempting to fill the void the Oracle had left. The Archon, hurt by his words, understood the depth of his pain and embraced him until the storm of his emotions subsided. As he calmed down, the Archon gently reminded him to look outside the window, urging him to appreciate the beauty of the world he had created and the vision he and the Oracle had shared.

In the following days, the Provisioner experienced a rollercoaster of emotions, from good to bad and terrible. During the terrible days, it was the Archon who provided support, reminiscent of the Oracle's role in comforting him in the past. The Archon, aware of the boundaries she couldn't cross, acknowledged that she could never replace the Oracle, recognizing the irreplaceable role she played in the celestial realms.

Meanwhile, in the shadows of the celestial realms, Havoc, the traitorous Shaper from the Chaos sector, vanished through a mysterious portal after committing the forbidden act of killing the Oracle. Unbeknownst to the other Shapers, he emerged in the Death realm, a realm created by the first Shapers, including the Provisioner. This realm, alongside the Life realm, housed celestial worlds where energies combined to give rise to the Shapers themselves.

The intricate process crafted by the Shapers involved harnessing energies from multiple realms and worlds. These energies traveled through the cosmos and were collected at the Nexus, a system that sifted through the gathered energies and dispersed them to their respective realms and worlds, fostering growth. However, Havoc's sudden appearance in the death realm triggered devastating consequences. His actions rendered the realm unlivable for the energies that resided there, disrupting the delicate balance that had been maintained for a celestial age. The repercussions echoed across the celestial realms, leaving an ominous shadow over the harmonious order that had prevailed.

Havoc, having ascended to the sector high above the death realm, shattered the chains that bound the remaining Chaos sector members. The leader of the Chaos sector greeted Havoc with a wicked smile, embracing him as they welcomed the formation of the newly established Death sector. Unbeknownst to the other Shapers still residing within the mortal realm, Havoc had successfully freed the imprisoned Shapers responsible for overseeing the death realm. This liberation foreshadowed inevitable conflict for the future of the celestial realms.

While Havoc reveled in his achievement, his mission was far from complete. He issued a command for the Death sector to construct a colossal world, intending to harness the energies lost in the destruction he had caused. The nature of his plans remained mysterious and shrouded in questions, with the Shapers in the mortal realm unaware of the impending conflict. It fell upon the Archon to unravel the intricacies of Havoc's plans and decipher the potential threats that lay ahead.

. . . .

The Archon, beginning to discern the chaotic patterns indicative of Havoc's schemes, recalled the intricate ways they used to communicate to conceal their intentions from other Shapers. Her past collaboration with Havoc in the Chaos sector provided her with insight into his strategic thinking. As she deciphered the cryptic messages, she realized that Havoc's plan aligned closely with their original intention of freeing the Chaos Sector rebels. However, she also uncovered a darker aspect of his scheme, involving the creation of an evil force within the death realm.

Despite this revelation, her primary focus shifted to the immediate threat Havoc posed. One of his plans included a Shaper traveling through a portal to a distant realm, triggering the obliteration of worlds within that realm. The effects of such an action might upset the delicate balance that the Shapers keep in place throughout the celestial realms. Especially if that plan aligned with the original intention of seeking the remaining Chaos sector imprisoned in the death realm. Determined to unveil the mystery of Havoc's layered plans, the Archon understood the urgency of informing the Provisioner, as the unfolding consequences may already be in motion.

Hastening to the Provisioner's sanctuary, she bore a burden heavier than sorrow. Her eyes betrayed an intense sense of urgency and concern. In the sanctum, she unveiled a dire revelation that echoed through the room: Havoc, the rogue Shaper responsible for the Oracle's demise, had been unearthed in the death realm—filled with ancient worlds crafted by the Shapers.

The Archon's voice trembled as she conveyed the unsettling truth. Havoc, driven by his insatiable thirst for chaos and rebellion, had hatched a nefarious plan to connect the original realms to Paranova, thereby unleashing a cataclysmic wave of chaos upon the world they had labored to shape. The Archon's words hung heavy in the air as the severity of Havoc's plan sank in. She realized that their own creation was now under imminent threat, and they were faced with the daunting task of stopping Havoc before it was too late.

It became evident that the Archon's previous devious intentions had undergone a significant transformation. She now stood as an ally, a staunch defender of the world she had once sought to undermine. Determined to prevent Havoc's malevolent designs from coming to fruition, she sought the aid and support of her fellow Shapers.

In the midst of his own celestial turmoil, the Provisioner maintained a stoic demeanor. Recognizing the Archon's dedication to the cause and recalling her support during his lowest moments, he swiftly convened an emergency meeting with the other Shapers. The Archon, acting as the informant, provided a thorough debriefing on the plans that she had successfully decoded, withholding only the details she was still deciphering. The Provisioner, now refocused and driven by a newfound purpose, turned his attention to the imminent threat that could potentially alter the course of existence. The Shapers, united in purpose, prepared to confront the unfolding chaos within the celestial realms.

The Shapers recognized the seriousness of the situation because they shared a common goal. They realized that their sacred duty to preserve the delicate balance of order and chaos was under imminent threat. With resolute determination, they pledged to stand against Havoc and protect Paranova from the impending chaos that loomed on the horizon.

As the news reverberated among the Shapers, the once somber atmosphere of mourning and celebration shifted into a tense urgency. The Provisioner, still grappling with his grief, found newfound strength within him. He was determined to honor the Oracle's memory by ensuring that her tragic demise would not be in vain.

The Provisioner, recognizing the need for clarity and preparation, took the initiative to explain the intricate details and history of the Life and Death realms to the Shapers, who had not experienced these realms since their creation. He felt it was essential for the entire sector to understand the worlds on which they were born and what to anticipate in dealing with the liberated Chaos sector prisoners. These rebels, notorious for their pleasure-seeking creation and destruction, were known to be unpredictable and dangerous, having taken celestial lives in the past. Embarking on a journey to these realms meant leaving the mortal realm behind and confronting uncertain outcomes in the celestial realms. Moreover, it entailed the possibility that thousands of years might elapse during their absence, and Paranova, as they knew it, could undergo immense changes in their absence.

In the face of adversity, the Shapers embraced their destiny as the guardians of Paranova, their resolve unending. With the memory of The Oracle guiding them, they prepared to set forth on a difficult journey to confront Havoc in the death realm, fully aware that the fate of their world hung in the balance that they had created.

As they prepared to embark on this harrowing quest, the Shapers understood that their lives would forever be intertwined with the eternal struggle between order and chaos. With each step they took, they carried the weight of their shared purpose and the legacy of the Oracle, determined to protect the world they had come to cherish.

The Provisioner and the Anarchist, understanding the urgency of the situation, rallied their respective sectors for battle and made the decision to set aside mortal realm projects. The Shapers had taken every measure to prepare Paranova for evolution and to safeguard it during the thousand years they would be absent. Despite the somber realization that they would miss many significant moments in the development of mortal sapience, the

Shapers found comfort in the anticipation of the world's evolution upon their return. As the leaders shouted, "For a legacy has been shaped, and the legacy will remain," the Shapers rallied in excitement, ready to face the challenges ahead.

The battle against Havoc in the death realm would be a difficult one, fraught with danger and uncertainty. But the Shapers, fueled by their conviction and fortified by their unity, would stop at nothing to safeguard Paranova from the coming chaos that threatened to engulf it. Taking the battle to the death realm would stop the threat before the opposition brought it to the mortal realm.

In the depths of their sadness, the Shapers found reassurance in their collective mission and united power, forging an unbreakable bond. Despite being aware of the looming threat and unfathomable difficulties, they persisted. They were fully aware that Paranova, the world they had nurtured and shaped, had just begun having its destiny settled.

....

With one final glance at the sacred vessel that housed the remains of the Oracle, the Shapers pledged to honor her memory by carrying on her legacy. They vowed to protect their world from the impending chaos and to safeguard the delicate equilibrium that held Paranova together.

As they prepared themselves to face the unknown, the chapter concluded, shrouded in suspense and promising an epic showdown that could decide Paranova's fate. The scene was set, each side had assembled, and the outcome was unknown. With a shared mission and the Oracle's memory and symbol as their guides, the Shapers set out eager to face their greatest challenge yet.

The Shapers, standing at the edge of departure, felt a profound mix of urgency and anticipation. Their celestial journey was unlike any undertaken before, transcending the familiar confines of Paranova. No mere portal would whisk them away this time; instead, they prepared for a voyage across the cosmic expanse, venturing towards distant stars untouched by Shapers for millennia. The unknown beckoned, and with determined spirits, they readied themselves for an odyssey through the vast tapestry of celestial wonders.

With absolute care and profound reverence, the Shapers unveiled the vessel cradling the Oracle's remains. A sentimental symbol of sacrifices made and wisdom gained, the vessel carried immense significance. At the edge of departure, the Provisioner stood, guiding the release of the Oracle's ethereal essence into Paranova's atmosphere. It was a final tribute to the world she had co-shaped—a passionate offering of her essence to the world she had helped nurture.

As the ethereal glow settled onto Paranova's fertile soil, interweaving with the very essence of the land, the Provisioner couldn't help but shed a tear. "Thank you for the celestenial time of memories you had given me," he whispered, acknowledging the profound impact the Oracle had on his existence. Preparing the Order and Chaos sector ships for their cosmic journey, the Shapers watched the radiant glow on the horizon, a silent farewell to the world they had shaped and the memories that would endure through the ages.

The Shapers were mesmerized by the slow dispersal of the essence, which cast a dazzling light throughout the atmosphere. It appeared as though the Oracle's spirit had merged with the life force that infused every blade of grass and tall tree. There was a sense of sadness and hope in the atmosphere, a bittersweet reminder that everything, no matter how exceptional or gifted, will eventually come to an end. The final traces of essence began to disappear, but the Shapers' resolve was renewed. They understood their journey was still not finished.

Though she was no longer around, the Oracle's words of wisdom and teaching would survive. The process became their mission to shape and lead the world towards greater potential, and now it was their turn to carry the flame of hope. The glow in the atmosphere represented the challenges and obstacles that remained ahead, but it also served as a reminder of the great power and potential that they possessed. They would honor the legacy of the Shapers and the impact that the Oracle had on their history.

Aware that their journey would be lengthy and fraught with uncertainties, the Shapers cast their gaze upon the familiar landscapes one final time. They bid farewell to the kingdoms and civilizations they had guided and safeguarded, trusting the Avatars to manage dire situations and the capable leaders and resilient people to thrive in their absence. The Shapers' departure marked the closing of a chapter—a farewell to the realm they had known for ages, ushering in a new quest that would lead them into uncharted territories.

Chapter 15: Journey Concluded

As the final chapter of Paranova's tale unfolds, we reach the closing pages of this epic journey. The complicated structure of vital kingdoms, races, and stories had been completed, revealing a world full of wonders and dangers, triumphs and tragedies. The time has come to draw the curtain, bid farewell to the characters and stories that have captured the imagination, and reflect on the lessons discovered throughout this journey.

With each page turned, the threads of destiny have been carefully woven, leading the races of Paranova towards their destinies. From the wars of Pyrothos to the rebellion of Alora, sapient evolution has occurred throughout the world, and the struggles and triumphs of each race have shaped the course of their civilizations. Through hardship, they found strength, innovation, and growth. The echoes of their experiences reverberated across the realms, inspiring awe, fear, and curiosity in the minds of all who heard the tales.

The Shapers, those celestial beings who stood as architects of Paranova, bore witness to the world they had crafted. They understood the delicate balance between Order and Chaos, the ever-present forces shaping existence. Their journey will take them to the far reaches of Paranova, unveiling hidden truths, facing a looming threat, and making sacrifices along the way. The loss of the Oracle, who was a beacon of wisdom, left a void in their celestial cores, but her legacy remained etched in their memories.

Now, as the Shapers prepare for a new chapter, they embark on a significant quest, far beyond the realms they have come to know. They seek the mysterious Death realm, a realm untethered to Paranova, where they hope to confront Havoc, a rogue Shaper who threatens to disrupt the delicate balance of existence. The journey ahead is dangerous and filled with uncertainties, requiring the Shapers to leave behind the world they helped shape.

As they depart, the Shapers release the remains of the Oracle's essence onto Paranova, a sentimental and symbolic gesture. Her essence becomes a gift, a final offering to the world she guided and cherished. The fate of Paranova now rests in the hands of its inhabitants, who must shape their own paths, embrace their own destinies, and navigate the intricate dance between Order and Chaos.

As the essence of the Oracle is released onto Paranova, a world ripe with magic and untapped potential, one cannot help but wonder what mysteries may emanate from this profound gift. Within that celestial essence resides the wisdom accumulated over thousands of years and boundless energy waiting to be discovered. The essence itself holds the potential to inspire the hearts of poets, stimulate the minds of scholars, and lead the hands of artisans. New regions of knowledge may emerge from its ethereal embrace, revealing insight into life's mysteries and exposing previously untapped possibilities. It is a motivation for transformation, an incentive that may bring extraordinary discoveries, shape the destinies of civilizations, and forever alter the course of Paranova's captivating tale.

As the chapters of our tale draws to a close, the horizon of Paranova stretches beyond the known, harboring secrets and whispers of untold adventures. Among these mysteries, there are rumors of beasts born from the very essence that the Shapers bestowed upon the mortal world. Yet, these tales are like veiled shadows that await their moment to step into the light—a story for another time, another chapter in the grand tapestry of Paranova.

The closing of this book marks not an end but a transition—a moment of anticipation for the future. Paranova will continue to evolve, with its civilizations advancing, its civilizations growing stronger, and their stories taking on new forms. The universe includes the promise of untold adventures, untamed magic, and an unwavering pursuit of knowledge.

As we turn the final page, we bid farewell to the enchanting world of Paranova, a world full of imagination and boundless possibilities. Its echoes will carry with them the everlasting allure of discovery, the life-changing potential of our decisions, and the immense influence of stories.

May the Legacy of the Shapers continue to inspire us as we venture on our own journeys and weave our stories into the tapestry of life.

To be continued...

Follow for all things Paranova! At www.parachrono.com

You can help promote awareness about this book by leaving an online review. I would appreciate input from readers like you.

Thank you for reading!

Love,
Joel D. Lundberg